LEAH'S WAY

A NOVEL BY RICHARD BOTELHO

ISBN: 0-9643926-8-2 (Hardcover)
ISBN: 0-9643926-9-0 (Softcover)

Library of Congress Catalog Number: 2003110249

Published by Windstream Publishing Company
303 Windstream Place, Danville, CA 94526

Manufactured in the United States of America

First Edition: 2004
0 9 8 7 6 5 4 3 2 1

Publisher's Cataloging-in-Publication
(Provided by Quality Books, Inc.)

Botelho, Richard.
Leah's way : a novel / by Richard Botelho. -- 1st ed.
p. cm.
LCCN 2003110249
ISBN 0-9643926-8-2 (hardcover)
ISBN 0-9643926-9-0 (softcover)

1. Spirituality--Fiction. 2. Religious fiction.
I. Title.

PS3602.O848L43 2004 813'.6
QBI33-1554

For Mom and Dad

Acknowledgments

I wish to thank the following people for their contribution to the creation of *Leah's Way*, from those who made suggestions affecting style and structure, to those who inspired from the living of their lives. First and foremost, to my sweet, precious Sue Annie, the most gentle of hearts, the kindest of souls. You are and always will be the embodiment of human goodness. Next, to the wonderful friends who have filled my life, too numerous to mention, but all appreciated for the joy and happiness they bring. For my mother, who raised me to believe in the goodness of the Lord; and the loving memory of my father, who gave me so much during the example that was his life. I miss you so much still. As always, to Dr. Richard Hughes, Dr. George Tokmakoff, Dr. Charles Houghton, and Dr. Clyde Enroth, all of California State University, Sacramento, thank you for providing the intellectual ideal that results from pursuing the dream that is your passion. To Lisa Rojany Buccieri, Les Stobbe, and the good people of Scribendi, thanks for the advice, the edits, and most of all, for your time. To Sarah Hinman of Stornetta Publications for the layout work. Lastly, rather oblivious to the rigors of writing and the notion of scheduling, to my constant lap companion, the silver and white tabby known simply as Mitten.

Disclaimer

Leah's Way is a work of fiction; as such, its characters are fictional as well. No direct resemblance to persons living or deceased is intended. Moreover, in those instances where a reference is given to God, in both His action and His voice, it must be remembered that this is also a fictional account. The Bible is a perfect work, and requires no addition or deletion from the author, nor from any other person, for that is the way the Lord intended it, and that is the way it should be.

"With my whole heart I have sought you;
Oh, let me not wander..."

Psalms 119:10

Chapter 1

THERE WERE ALWAYS TWO of Leah, and both of them breathed in the frigid air that day.

She tried bundling up, cinching up the pull knots in her soiled and tattered sweatshirt tightly to her throat, but the cold darted in anyway, penetrating deeper into her body. Leah shivered as she looked upward. Dark clouds swirled overhead as snow flurried off in the distance. Somewhere out over the river the winds were gathering again. Those winds had been relentless since dawn. So Leah clutched her Bible, the old King James her mother had given her on her eighth birthday, tightly against her shivering chest. Her mind, torn against itself, separated from the moment and went back to the past. As she trudged forward, Leah remembered the sound of her mother's voice piercing her ears like it was yesterday.

"Cover up, child. The cold air will kill you. Do you want to die or something?"

Leah saw that gray January day, so many years ago, when she had been standing ankle deep in the snow. The barren trees were bending in the biting wind behind her, as her mother rushed angrily forward, a scolding finger pointed directly into Leah's frightened face.

"Where's your boots, child? I paid good money for them boots, and you done ran off and left them on the front porch again. How many times have I got to tell you: Snow kills younguns. You want to die next? Well, do you?"

Leah glanced up past her mother and into the grayness, afraid to look her mother in the eyes. "No, ma'am."

"Well, it sure seems like it to me. Sometimes, girl, I swear you want to die. And the smallest die first, remember that. Where's my switch? Oh, if I only had me my switch."

Her mother had sure been right about smallest. Leah was ever so slight as a child. Her wrists and arms were tiny and narrow and she was as delicate as a fawn, but she was also pretty and full of life. Her big eyes, chestnut brown and radiant, had an irrepressible vivacity about them that every friend remembered. The neighbor ladies spoke of her often, saying she was as sweet as frosting on a cinnamon bun, sweeter still when she had to be. The neighbor ladies all said that when Leah wanted something from you, her fragile face tugging at your heart, just the slightest of sniffles could make you reach down and give it to her. Then she'd smile and skip away. You'd laugh, thinking you'd been taken, but then Leah would turn 'round and mouth a kindly "thank you" from afar. She meant it, too. Mostly though, she believed in friendly faces and joyous laughter, and it showed to everyone who knew her, everyone, that is, except for Margaret, her mother, who beat her that day anyway, switch or not.

But time had sure changed Leah now. Still frail, but now older, like a sick and shaken deer, starving and forgotten, her once beautiful hair matted together in greasy clumps and the road-dirt caked on her skin like centuries of forest rot over a fallen tree. She looked so much older than fifty. She coughed painfully, her head pounding and shaking from the thunder in her chest, and her breath was hard to come by.

Leah trudged on for another city block, pondering how it might be fitting to die this time, the icy winds needling her face, freezing her bones, as one clear message repeated itself over and over again: *It's better to leave this place.*

Somehow, as sick as she felt, Leah managed to tramp on that afternoon and one wish grew ever stronger: She wanted to lie in some fresh grass somewhere, to gaze up at the nighttime sky, to think about her life and what it had all meant, so that finally, she could understand her life completely. She sought someplace peaceful, away from people and away from shame, and where, if the Lord was willing, the sky might clear enough for a momentous contemplation, for Leah sought a feeling of wholeness as if it were her destiny.

She knew of a nice, quiet little park, protected from the wind, where nobody would notice her. She had been by once before, and had noticed then that it seemed especially serene. She girded herself to try and find it against the stabbing wind, but the storm was a hammer that knocked her backward and Leah took refuge in an alleyway.

After a long pause of much needed rest, Leah trudged on for six more city blocks. She faintly recalled seeing a brick building near that quiet little park that day she had passed by. Squinting, she thought she saw it again. Leah opened her sticky eyes as wide as she could and kept on trudging. She was glad she wasn't toting much. Most of her belongings she had hidden behind an old storehouse, not far from the Willamette Valley Ale House, and as the weak sun descended beyond the horizon, Leah made out what looked like a few of the brick buildings situated near the tiny park.

"Please God, let it be," she prayed into another chilling gust.

The purple that hugged the last of the sky had nearly faded, when just ahead Leah thought she saw some trees. She took a few more longing steps, her eyes straining for every last ember of daylight, stumbling as she spit blood again, her head ringing like a church bell at noon, her will failing and her spirit sagging with each new freezing gale.

"I'm so tired," Leah prayed frantically into the darkness above her head. "I don't know if I can go on anymore. Please God, help me. I need you now."

Where before the patch had seemed dark, a light from one of the buildings suddenly shone down on it like a tiny spotlight. All of the other windows in the building were black. There were no pedestrians or cars passing by, no planes overhead, and no moon. The glow in the office provided just enough light for Leah to see what lay in front of her.

She peered across the street at the obscure patch of ground.

The little park sat there like a lost key.

"Oh God, my sweet and loving God," Leah prayed thankfully into the night, her hands shaking at her face, as she wiped more gunk away from her eyes. "You haven't forgotten about me."

The grass in the park had grown winter wild. Leah made her way back to the far corner of the park where a long line of shrubs and low trees protected the area against the harshness of the wind. The dripping black wetness had moved further to the east. The winds at once seemed much less colder. Once in the middle of the trees, Leah could see high into the sky as the last of the clouds were blown away, the faraway stars glittering brightly against the blackness of the night. Leah flopped down onto the ground, her wet bag unfurling as she did, and she laid back on it, resting her weary head.

Everything in her body ached. The search for the little park had taken a lot out of her. She sighed a long, deep sigh, the kind that quakes your body out after a good cry, and cradled her Bible to her side. She would start her remembering with her childhood, in the Nashville neighborhood she had once treasured so dearly, and as the night deepened Leah closed her eyes and thought of her home, her family's home, where her life had begun.

Chapter 2

SPRINGTIME IS A WONDERFUL time in Nashville, the clouds puffy and light, the wind never more than a gentle breeze and the sky a pretty marble blue. In such a sky there are only suggestions of sundry seasons, of winter passing and the mugginess of July. The air itself feels impartial, as life begins its awakening dance. It is the sky of a twelve-year-old girl, a sky of innocence, a sky of a time to wonder and contemplate the meaning of the world.

"Hey, Mama, I heard the dinner bell ring and ran home as fast as I could," Leah said, panting, crashing in through the front porch door.

"Well, you barely made it in time, child. I dinged that dinner bell three times, the last time so loud I thought I'd lose my hearing. You deaf or something? I about gave up on you. The pot roast is on the table, and Marian is buttering up a big bowl of mashed potatoes. And I made two skillets of cornbread for y'all."

Disappointment fell over Leah's tender face. She moved her dangling blond curls away from her eyes. "I thought tonight was biscuits and jam, Mama."

Margaret stopped in her tracks. She dropped her arms at her sides and scowled at her daughter. "It is, just like I promised it'd be. But for smart talking me, you'll eat cornbread and like it. No biscuits for you. Maybe one day you'll learn to appreciate me around here."

"I appreciate you."

"Sure you do," Margaret said sarcastically. "Like a mouse appreciates a cat. Now wash yourself up before supper to take the Lowell's yard off your face, and when you're done, grab us some place settings and call your daddy from out back. William, you coming to dinner? I didn't slave three hours over this boiling stove for nothing."

William, Leah's only brother, a junior on academic scholarship at Vanderbilt University, endowed with the pompousness that comes from a career of unrivaled academic excellence, tossed uneasily in his chair. He wanted to finish the physics problem he was working on. "Be right out," he shouted indignantly. "Start without me if you want to, I don't mind none."

"Not a snowflake's chance," Margaret yelled back to him. "You know everything in them books anyway; now get your tail out here."

"Okay, okay, I'm coming," he added impatiently. "Man, what's the big rush, anyway?"

"Come on before it gets cold. And don't give me any of your lip."

William's head was buried in a stack of books and the thickness of the stack muffled his next response. "But Schrodinger was a genius, Mama; I'll tell you that much. A real genius. Just another minute, and I'll have the differential operator calculated and be right out."

"The what?" Margaret squawked.

"Don't trouble yourself, Mama," Marian chimed in from the kitchen. Her cheery face of fair-skinned sparkle and gleaming grin wore a look of sympathy. "You wouldn't understand him anyway. None of us would. I'm sad to inform you that your son is an egghead."

Margaret seemed displeased to think so. "Oh, he's not. You think?"

Marian smirked at her mother. "Come on, Mama, face it. He's as big an egghead as the Lord ever made."

"Mama, is Kay around?" Leah asked her mother.

"I'm right here," a voice said, coming 'round the corner. Kay's platinum blond hair, goddess green eyes, cheap perfume, and full red lips filled the room with a sense of profligate prodigality. The only thing missing was a spotlight for her arrival. Dressed in a revealing pink outfit, she looked exactly like the cotton candy person she was: fluffy and showy, the kind of person who never filled you up, while too much of her made you sick to your stomach.

"He's not a full egghead," Kay offered. "Christy Huntington has a crush on him and so does that Milford girl, Casey."

"See, Marian. Christy's a doll," Margaret threw in.

"Well, Casey sure ain't," added Leah.

"Leah, was anybody talking to you?" Margaret blared at her youngest.

"Sorry, Mama."

Marian, bringing out a large bowl of buttered mashed potatoes from the kitchen, set the dish down on the chestnut wood dining table that was the centerpiece of Leah's childhood home. It was a handsome table passed down from Margaret's farmhouse days in Madisonville. That farm had been a pauper's penitence, and Margaret never let a soul forget about it. A white lace tablecloth covered the old table, surrounded by seven mismatched chairs and a tall wooden hutch that hugged the wall in full tradition. "Mama, is that a new platter from church I'm seeing?" Marian asked sweetly.

"Why, yes it is, Marian. So kind of you to notice."

On top of the hutch sat three etched silver platters the church had bestowed on Margaret for her good works. She had perched them there not for any material sensibility or recognition, but because they were examples for her children to follow and good ones at that. The latest was the biggest and the most fully engraved. "And if you do God's bidding, child, you'll have platters of your own one day," Margaret said, loudly enough for all her children to hear.

Leah, after wiping herself with the kitchen rag to clear the dirt smudges from her face, had hustled the place settings from a hutch drawer, spreading them out on the table, proper and smooth, and she called to her daddy out back to come in to supper. Walton limped in from the garage, his lower back hurting him again; he was covered in little white splatters and smelling like paint thinner and cleaning solvent.

"What's for dinner?" he asked hungrily.

"Roast," Margaret answered snappishly. "And when dinner is done, you've got a lawn to mow."

"William will cut it, won't you, son?"

"Can't today," William said, taking a seat at the table. His curly, light-brown hair waved in the late afternoon sun while his robin's-egg blue eyes spotted his personal drinking glass. He sat down and waited to be served. "Got a final tomorrow in physics."

"I'll help you, Daddy," Leah volunteered.

It was as if Margaret had been suddenly slapped in the face. "The two of you?" she asked in amazement. "Why, that weed of a lawn has a better chance of being trimmed by lightning than by either of you. Every growing thing on the block tries to crawl its way over here. There's safety in this yard. You two doing yardwork? Shoot, they'd have to bury me from the shock. Leah, your daddy is as lazy as a sloth, and you're as scatter-brained as a chipmunk."

"You're too young anyway, baby girl," Walton said, smiling at Leah. He leaned forward as he took his seat, his needle fine gray hair falling haphazardly into his eyes.

"Daddy, you need a haircut," Leah said fondly.

Walton's eyes always softened when he spoke to his youngest daughter. He smiled at her. "I know I do," he said with love. "I'll get a haircut next week. I promise I will. But twelve isn't old enough to push that old mower around. I need to grease the blades, but there won't be enough daylight tonight for a good greasing, so they're gonna catch in the weeds. You can help me with the bush clippings out back when you're finished eating, if you're factual about pitching in."

"My Lord, Kay, what have you got on?" Marian blurted out.

Kay straightened herself. She scrutinized her apparel. "What's wrong with it?" she asked. The outfit was especially low cut over Kay's large bosom and extra tight in the hips. She looked quite the tramp.

"What's wrong with it?" Marian echoed incredulously. "Why there's nothing covering you. All I'm seeing is skin. Good Lord, Kay, I wear more clothing than that when I take a bath. Mama, you can't let Kay go out like that. You just can't. What will the neighbors say?"

Margaret had a rag in her mouth, her hands full of dishes and large trays of food, so she couldn't speak just then. Her eyes, though, cast a scolding glance at Marian as the girls began to take their seats and join William and Walton at the dinner table.

"Murph is gonna like what he sees tonight," Leah said, trying to be funny.

Margaret yanked the rag from her mouth after setting the dishes down on the table. "Shut up, Leah," she screamed at her youngest. "You just best shush up before I get me a switch."

"Why don't you yell at Marian, Mama? She's the one who brought it up."

"Leah, I'm not going to tell you again."

"I'm sorry, Mama," Marian interjected. "It's my fault." She turned to Kay. "But really, Kay, when you wear get-ups like that it makes you seem no deeper than a puddle. Dressing up like that makes us all look bad. It really does. A rotten pecan can ruin the entire pie, you know."

"You wish you had my body," Kay countered.

"That's enough from everybody," Margaret commanded.

Dishes clanged as everyone dug into their food. There was two and three of everything to eat, the spread seeming more like a feast for a council of southern bluebloods than for a family that watched every single penny. There was no spare table room and half the hutch ledge was filled with water pitchers and kettles of teas and coffees.

"Mama, you outdid yourself," Marian said. "Everything is so delicious. But, Kay, I still think you should change your clothes for tonight."

"I said that's enough," Margaret admonished.

"Marian, you should mind your own business," William said, ignoring Margaret. He never did listen to his mother. Aware of his own genius and status in the household as the only son, he was supremely confident. "Let Kay be what she is. Do we get after you because you're an insufferable prude? Good is as boring as bad is deplorable. Remember that. Kay dates around and she deserves credit for it. There's a certain power in her vamping, in not needing a boyfriend for her self-possession and care. Heck, what would you know about personal fortitude anyway, Marian? You've had a steady since you were an embryo."

"Son," Walton said, rebuking William in a deep voice.

"Thanks, Daddy," Marian said. She cast an evil glare at her brother, who smiled to himself in amusement. "That scholarship was the worst thing that ever happened around this house," Marian concluded.

"Worse for you, good for me," William told her. "But I guess there's always one success in a family."

"Mama, if you don't mind I'll take some plates over later to the Craft's house for dinner tonight," Leah said. "Mrs. Craft has been sick and can't cook for her boys, Manny and Sean. That flu bug is sure going around Nashville. Everyone at school has it. I guess Sean puked in class yesterday all over Anita Broadstone's back and then puked all the way home from school. I've never seen so much food here, and we could spare a little for neighbors in need."

"Don't say puke," Marian said firmly to her sister.

"William, hold yourself up straight," Margaret said, chiding her eldest. She ignored Leah as usual. "Twenty is too young to be stooping over like your fool daddy. And pass the biscuits to me."

"Oh, now I'm a fool," Walton said laughingly. His bluish gray eyes glimmered in the fading light of the room as he leaned his head back against his chair and rested his jaws.

"No, you've always been a fool," Margaret said brusquely. "The sidewalk out front is lumpier than an old cake mix and the porch is missing half its planks. I nearly tripped and killed myself this morning. I swear I see more rusty nails on that porch every day. The swing creaks like an old haunted house, and the neighbors never yell over the fence anymore because it's about two boards from collapsing. I miss the neighbors yelling over the fence. In fact, I used to look forward to it. But would you ever think to nail a few measly boards together?" She stared displeasingly at her husband, who didn't answer. "Why, nope, you'd rather laze around and fiddle with your stupid tackle box. And time, lest you forget, is never a friend and always a foe. That old fence ain't gonna fix itself. While I'm on it, you ever going to trim those old hickory bushes?"

"Thought I might."

Margaret stared at her husband in disbelief. Walton's long spindly arms rested on the table, his hands looking like two giant rakes. His big floppy ears and pronounced jawbones seemed to stretch down to his shoulders. It was hard to stay mad at such a sight for any length of time. "No, you won't," she finally sighed, all too familiar with his life of dissuasion and procrastination.

"Yeah, I just might."

"Nope, the next time I check on them bushes you'll be sprawled out on a hammock behind Walter's, reliving fish stories or hunting grouse at that old, abandoned field near Pressman Road. I hope the sheriff catches you one day and arrests you. No sense in killing them birds. No sense at all. I'll have to check for ticks on you and the blessed dog, like I always do."

"I like to fish and hunt. What's wrong with that?"

Margaret's curly raven hair shone an auburn streak in the last rays of the afternoon sun. Her face in the light was full, stern and surmising. Her dark eyes, tight together like two beads on a string, glared even when she was happy, but thankfully she had a fair complexion and large grandmother breasts that softened her some. Still, it was hard to tell when she was about to go on a rampage.

"Why did I marry you again?" she asked rhetorically.

"Because you would have rather had a house painter than that chicken farmer before me," Walton threw in.

The sun began to set and the room grew two shades darker. Margaret rose from her chair, casting a shadow double the girth of her body, flicking on the globule hanging lamp and then making her way over to the end tables in the living room, past the curved mahogany arms of the plum colored velvet couch, where she turned on the King Louis style lamps, tassels hanging down to the wood. Margaret loved those old lamps. She had bought them with her first married job taking care of rich, old folks in the Peabody District. Bibles and the world's great novels rested on the end tables. There was no television set.

"He wasn't a chicken farmer," she said, returning to the table. "Sammy raised goats."

"Goats?" Walton sneered. "It was chickens and you know it."

Margaret did her best to suppress a smile, but Walton saw it and grinned his biggest grin at her. They both looked at each other and their eyes softened in the low light of the fading afternoon.

"Leah, would you like a biscuit?" Margaret asked kindly.

"Thank you, Mama," Leah said, taking the plate of biscuits from her mother's hands.

Forks and knives clanged noisily against the dishes. Steam still rose from the gravy boat. For a time, no one said a word, too busy in their hurry to satiate their appetites while the food was at its warmest.

Finally, Marian talked a piece of news. "Mama, I have a teacher who said Tennessee needs to start teaching evolution in the public schools. Can you believe they might teach evolution instead of God's creation?"

Margaret was quickly back at it. "Well, Honey, that's East High for you. Downtown District Seven will be the first to go. I've said that for years. I wanted to send you to private school, but your daddy don't work enough hours for us to afford a real education."

"What's wrong with teaching evolution in schools?" William asked. "If any of you are going to amount to anything, especially you, Leah, since you're still in your formative years, you need to learn what science says about how the world works. Science isn't some type of fiction; it's real, proven through the scientific method. Started with Aristotle thousands of years ago in Ancient Greece and found its permanency in the Age of Enlightenment. It's still around today in case any of you haven't noticed. That proves its validity. Knowing the ways of science can put you ahead in life."

"See, girls, what did I tell you," Margaret said scathingly. "Your brother, genius that he is, still isn't smart enough to understand that God made evolution, too. Sure enough he did. Why, God made everything we see, including the books your ingrate of a brother reads from. I'm telling you, girls, there will always be those who try to lead your soul astray from the Lord. Even your own blessed brother."

"Not this again," Kay muttered.

"Boy, you got that right," Leah threw in.

"Leah, you're one more smart talk away from a switch," Margaret threatened. "This is my last warning, child."

"Sorry, Mama."

"What do you think, Daddy?" Marian asked, cutting into a skillet of cornbread. "I mean about evolution and all."

"Now why ask your daddy something like that?" Margaret interrupted. "Your daddy never heard of Charles Darwin or his theory of evolution. Never had a deep thought in his life, for that matter. Stubbornness is what it is. Can't get him to go to church with me, can't get him to think about nothing but those dad-blessed fish. Got the sense of succotash. William and Kay got the stubbornness from him. That's why they won't go to church with me, either. Ain't that right, you two?"

William and Kay continued to feed their faces in silence.

"Well, am I right or not?"

Kay stood up in a huff and made her way to the front door after first taking a shoulder wrap from the closet. Springtime nights in Nashville could still turn plenty cold. "Seeing as how I'm a sinner and all, I don't know what time I'll be home," she said over her shoulder. "Maybe I won't come home at all. Goodnight everyone."

Panic struck Margaret's face. She looked like the roof had caved in. "Oh, Sugar, now stop it. I was just teasing you. Besides, I was mainly after your brother. He's the one throwing science up to us all the time. You know I don't mean what I say, and I'm sorry if I upset you. What time you really be home?"

"I don't know, Mother," Kay answered curtly. "I'm seeing a movie with Murphy. Then we're going out for a drive. I'll be home sometime before midnight, I suppose."

"Well, now, that's fine with me. Midnight is a good hour. I'll leave the backdoor unlocked for you like I always do. Remember, I love you."

Leah and Marian looked at each other after checking to make sure Margaret couldn't see them. They shook their heads in shared disgust. Had it been them being insubordinate to the point of walking out on their mother, it would have been a switch for sure.

Margaret kept an eagle eye on Kay as the girl crossed the street and walked past the far corner where Murphy lived with his drunkard father, Everett. Mrs. Murphy had died years ago, when Murphy was only ten. Elms swayed in the twilight breezes. The sky reddened forlornly on the horizon. When Kay disappeared from view, it seemed Margaret's shoulders fell all the way to the floor. Leah felt so sorry for her mother as she watched her watch Kay.

"Well, Mama, my plan is to keep my heart right with the Lord until the day I die," Leah said enthusiastically. "Just like you've always taught me to do."

"I think the Lord is right proud of you, little Lee," Marian said in camaraderie. "And Mama, I want you to know I'm going to keep doing what the Lord wants me to do, too, for as long as it takes. I figure on doing it until I die, just like Leah."

"Good meal," William said, rising to take his dishes to the kitchen. "I've got some studying to do. But Leah, someday you'll wonder if I wasn't right about evolution and knowing the ways of science. Science will eventually explain all that needs explaining. Someday, you'll figure it out for yourself. Just remember the time I could have saved you if you'd have listened to me. See you all tomorrow."

"Oh, go on, before I lose my patience with you," Margaret said, threatening her son. Her face was a woeful glower. "Just go on now, and leave us be."

"Son, go study," Walton said.

After William returned to his room and closed the door, Leah leaned in as Margaret and Walton grabbed seconds of potatoes and collard greens. "Mama, I'm sure worried about Kay. Seems the older she gets, the worse it is on you. I love you, Mama, and I don't like it that she makes you so upset as she does."

"Me too, Mama," Marian added.

"Thank you, girls," Margaret managed. "I'd get after Kay more around here myself, but if I do she might run off and never come back. Then, where'd we all be? If I'm hard on you sometimes, it's because I never want you to end up like your sister. It's like I've told you time and again: Life is a gamble. I don't have the foggiest notion how Kay will end up someday. Lord knows I pray on it. Marian, you I don't worry about so much, but Leah, I see some of Kay in you, and I don't like it none at all. Not enough respect and plenty independent. Apt to just get up one day and go live on your own, forgetting all about your family. So I'm going to keep with the switch until I see you through to a good girl."

"Yes, Mama," Leah said.

Walton got up and left the table, uncomfortable with his wife's threatening but naturally seeking to keep the peace, and he returned to the old wooden garage that stood off by itself in the corner of the backyard.

"Can I be excused, Mama?" Leah asked.

"Sure, I suppose you ate enough for one supper. Go help your father with them bush clippings. And read your Bible when you're done in the yard."

"I will, Mama."

The back porch door was loose in its hinges and nearly fell off when Leah stepped from the stoop into the backyard. Leah had always been clumsy, especially in her coltish legs, and she had brushed the door hard as she stepped past. Walton stuck his head out of the old garage, smiling when he saw it was Leah who'd come outside.

"Door coming loose, isn't it?" he asked her.

"Yessir, it sure is. Mama is going to be after you to fix it, she hears it again."

"What do you think I ought to do?"

"Fix it."

Walton grinned at his daughter. "Well, now, baby girl, I just might. I just might after all." He bent over to clear the blades of the old mower from some dry grass cuttings. His movements were deliberate and slow, his back aching from a paint job that had begun that day in the early morning darkness.

Leah came over to her daddy, her movements much like her spirit, unhesitating and happy, but always with a mind for what's proper. Living with Margaret had forever imbued in her a sense of rigid conformity. She thought hard on what she might say and how to word it.

"You know what, Daddy?"

"No, what?"

"Kay sure looked a sight tonight. And William couldn't wait to get up from the table and go back to them books of his. Mama is upset about Kay, Marian is upset about Mama, and sometimes it seems like you'd rather be anyplace but around the bunch of us. Daddy, am I the only one who likes it here?"

Walton stepped over the gravel driveway, which had lost most of its marl, around some splotchy oil drippings that had managed to kill any stray grass, and came over to his youngest daughter. His massive hands held her shoulders in place. "Baby girl, William is a college boy, Kay is seventeen, and

Marian is fifteen going on thirty. I always knew that being younger was tough on you, but I'd like to think that when they was your age they were as happy as you are. They're just growing up, making their own way."

"But Daddy, I look forward to the nighttime around here. How come they don't? Shoot, we used to play games and sing songs. I hope I don't grow up and turn into one of them."

"You want me to bring it up?"

Leah eyed the ground. She kicked at a rock. "No, Mama will just yell at you and whip me for stirring up a mess," she said. A thought came to her. She looked up at her daddy. "Say, will you play a game with me tonight after you cut the lawn? Marian might play if I ask her nicely, or maybe we could lay out front on a blanket and look at the stars together. We used to look at the stars whenever the sky cleared up. Remember those nights, Daddy? That sure was fun in them days. The three of us could have a right nice time."

"Sure, I'll be glad to play a game or two with you. Star gazing might be fun for us again. We haven't done that in awhile. But don't be too hard on your brother and sisters. You've always wanted to catch up to them, and I think that's why it bothers you to see them go their separate ways. I'm just saying it's not that wrong a thing to do. It's like you wanting to see the ocean. None of us want to see the sea as much as you, but we don't mind it any. Heck, we're happy for you. Be happy for them. And if it means anything to you, you're still my baby girl. Always will be. Now I best be cutting the lawn while I still got a little light left in the day."

"Thank you, Daddy."

"Oh, don't mention it," Walton said. "It'll be fun to do something tonight." He reached down again to clear another blade, then pushed the mower forward. In two steps, the mower caught on a high patch of weeds and the blades stopped. He stooped over to clear the blades once more. "But you mark my words: One day, you'll be wanting to be on your own like your brother and sisters, going off, working or married, making a life for yourself. Happens to everybody. And that will be the saddest day of my life."

Leah watched her daddy yank the mower clear and cut a ways. "Well, if and when I do go off, I'd sure like to know why God put me here in the first place," she said pensively. "Especially with all the trouble in this house. It's tougher than Job to be a Christian living with Mama sometimes. Just once, I'd like to figure out how I can like it here so much one day and then Mama and Kay drive me so crazy the next. William isn't much better, and Marian is more of a mama than Mama. It's like I got two mothers, a brother so smart he don't hear a word I say, and one sister who's the town floozy. So where does that leave me, Daddy? It all seems so confusing, I can't make any sense of it. You ever been torn, Daddy?"

Walton shook the mower free of another weed patch. He removed a knife from his back pocket and dug out the largest weed, wiping the blade clean again on his coveralls. "Baby girl, we're all torn and we all want to know why we're here. Shoot, I've been asking that question for more years than I care to remember, and I still don't have an answer to it yet. Don't know if I ever will. Life seems to work against you on finding answers. There's too much to do just getting by."

"Well, I sure hope I find out before I die. I sure hope I do."

"I hope for your sake you do, too," Walton said, smiling. "But I sure as shooting wouldn't count on it. Better than us have tried to find out the meaning of life, and as far as I know ain't nobody found the answer yet. Stars be out soon, though. You've always loved them stars, Leah, sure enough you always have. Seems like it'll be a pretty night tonight for some star watching."

Walton sniffed the air. It smelled springtime clean. Whenever the magnolia leaves turned their dark, shiny green and the bees buzzed around the first marigolds, it was sporting time. He thought of fish jumping and birds scurrying into the brush. "Now, I got to get to some serious cutting, baby girl, if I'm going to make my fishing hole this weekend. I still got to get to them hickory bushes and trim the low oak next to the garage. Find us a good viewing glass for them stars, will ya? But first, how about finding me that lawn bag for all them bush clippings?"

Chapter 3

IT WAS IN HER senior year of high school that Leah began to break away from her family and from all things Nashville. There was a reason for what happened.

His name was Blake.

If you read any of the Nashville papers during the mid- to late-1950s or you talked to anybody in town, you couldn't help but have heard of Blake Palmer. Blake was a college senior at Georgia Tech University in Atlanta, an athlete of much acclaim from the Belle Meade district of Nashville, the city's richest neighborhood, graced with landed estates, gated driveways, and enough regal elegance to satisfy a king. He showed more promise than anyone who had come through the public school system in a long, long time, as his family forbade his attendance at private schools so that the record would clearly demonstrate his affinity for the common man, thinking far in advance for the moment when he would enter politics and carry forward the torch of civic responsibility. The Palmers were that kind of people, and their goal for their son was no less than the Presidency of the United States.

Marian, whose boyfriend at the time was also a star athlete, a tall, blond quarterback named Dennis O'Casey, from East High School where Marian had been a yell girl, introduced Leah to Blake at halftime during a Vanderbilt basketball game that winter of 1955. Dennis and Blake were good friends and chummed around Nashville together when Blake was home from college.

"Blake, this is my baby sister, Leah," Marian said briskly. Blake turned to Leah and presented his hand for a cordial handshake. His black hair was thick and stylish and his eyes were the color of an early evening sky. He had an air without airs and the grace of a diplomat.

"It's nice to meet you, Leah," he said amiably.

Leah was mesmerized. The sum total of everything she had ever desired in a man stood less than an arm's length away. She noticed Blake's ingratiating smile and that his style combined proper manners with boyish enthusiasm. He seemed so at ease. He was also one of those young men who possess a finely detailed presence about them, as if to affirm their distinction, the human form in a symbiotic dance with light, like the characters in Rembrandt's *Nightwatch*.

"Well, say something Lee," Marian said to her sister. "He won't bite you."

"Leave her alone, will you?" Dennis said jokingly to Marian, having seen first-hand a million girls behave the same way around his good buddy. Marian shot Dennis a look that let him know he was lucky to be out with her. "It's halftime," she said to him, obviously perturbed. "Go get me a coke before I die of thirst in here."

Dennis slid into the back of the concession stand line, heeling like a whipped dog.

"It really is nice to meet you," Blake said again to Leah. "And I mean that."

"It's nice to meet you, too," Leah said shyly. She smelled Blake's manly cologne, supplanting wonderfully the musty wood and sweaty odors of the gymnasium. "I was thinking on something before when you first said hey, and I didn't mean to seem uppity. Marian says you play ball at Tech."

"Played. I graduate in a few months and then I'm going on to law school. My family, the progressives that they are, want me to go North, away from the legacy of the South. Seems they think an Ivy League education will increase my political standing with the more forward thinking of us Southerners. But I'd rather practice law. How about you? Are you a student here at Vandy?"

"Heavens, no," Marian interrupted. "Lee here is still in high school. She's the baby in our family, and I look after her."

"Thanks a lot," Leah said.

Two guys passed by and nodded to Blake. He smiled back at them.

"Blake, don't you think my sister is a doll?" Marian asked.

Blake returned to the conversation at hand and gave a slight nod. He studied Leah for a moment. "Yes, but it's more than her beauty, Marian. She also has a possessing innocence about her. Yes, that's it, a possessing innocence." His eyes fixated on Leah as he said the words, holding her in their gaze. Leah felt herself swoon.

"Where are you planning to attend college next fall?" he asked Leah.

Leah felt the flush leave her face. "Christian College, I suspect. My Mama has always wanted me to go to Christian College here in Nashville."

Blake seemed pleased with the choice. "Then make your mother happy," he said. "A Christian education is a good education, and the football team isn't as awfully bad as the *Record* makes them out to be. Next season they'll win a few games and the year after they'll play Bethany, which is ranked in the division. Cleo Dawkins plays at Bethany and he'd start for us and probably make All Conference. I'll tell you what: If your sister will let me, I'll take you to a game next fall on a break home from law school."

"Why wait until next fall?" Marian chimed in. "Lee isn't dating anyone, are you, Lee?"

Leah shot her sister a look full of daggers.

"Good, I'll get the number from Dennis," Blake said to Marian reassuringly. Blake's friends, just ahead of Dennis at the concession stand line, were summoning him over to their clique, a swarm of preppily dressed guys wearing tan and maroon cardigans and gray slacks over penny loafers. Blake signaled that he'd be over to them shortly.

"I'll call you then, Leah?" he asked, his words technically a question, but his manner one of coolness and confirmation.

"Sure, do that," Leah responded immediately. An unnatural pause followed, and before she could help herself she blurted out, "Call me anytime." Blake was moving away from her, but he turned 'round at the sound of her voice and smiled a victory smile before stepping into his throng of friends. The last

Leah saw of him that night was his finely tailored khaki slacks and the manly exactness of his pressed shirt and tie.

"You lucky dog," Marian said, her blue eyes swimming in delight. "He's the living end."

Leah rolled her eyes at the understatement of a lifetime. "Are you nuts? He's so far beyond that," she said condescendingly. "He's got it all, and I mean all. Lord Almighty, Marian, did you see him?"

"Yes, I saw him. He was standing right in front of me. And don't take the Lord's name in vain."

"Why, he's more handsome than Tyson," Leah went on, oblivious to her sister. "William's friend who graduated from that little private college up in Massachusetts, the guy who worked as an assistant for Adlai Stevenson in '52. Remember Tyson? You remember him. Amherst. Tyson went to Amherst. Anyway, I didn't think anyone could be as gorgeous as Tyson, not from Nashville least how, but Blake sure is."

"I'll see to it Mama understands and lets you date him," Marian said.

Leah frowned. "Shoot, he won't call. He could have anyone, what's he want with me?"

Marian smiled knowingly. She wrapped her arm around her sister. "Something, Sis. He saw something special in you, that's for sure."

***

Blake finally called five weeks later. He was back in Nashville for a short stay on spring break before heading down to Fort Lauderdale with some fraternity brothers for a beach bash thrown by the son of Jordan Elliot, the famous congressman from Charlotte, North Carolina. A confidant of Henry Cabot Lodge who had graduated at the top of his Yale Law School class, Elliot was a man with powerful connections and ambitions, who was not only an alumnus of Yale, but also an avid financial contributor and dealmaker as well. Leah had read about him in a civics class. A daybreak sail was set for the weekend hence, with the congressman and two of his staff manning the helm. Jordan Elliot had big plans for Blake.

Leah was dutifully impressed with the affiliation, which only added another layer to Blake's mystique, and with each subsequent revelation of his greatness Leah grew further infatuated with him. Other guys became practically invisible, and she refused two dates with nice boys from church and one from the senior class president at her high school. Simply put, other guys didn't compare with such a handsome college man.

One date became three and then Blake went off sailing the political seas of Florida before completing his undergraduate work in Atlanta and graduating summa cum laude in June. For Leah, the wait for his graduation was an especially nervewracking time: anticipating his replies to her twice a week letters; several phone calls here and there whenever Blake managed to find the time; a butterfly stomach at the mere suggestion of him; talks with Marian about everything that pertained to him; and endless thinking about their closest moments together. Leah read and kissed each of his return letters, living for the phone to ring at night, and she swooned each time the local radio station played her favorite lyrics from her favorite song:

> "They told me be sensible with your new love,
> Don't be fooled into thinking this is the last you'll find.
> But they've never stood in the dark with you, love,
> When you take me in your arms and drive me slowly out of my mind."

When Blake returned to Nashville the last week in June, their dating became an almost daily affair, and by the end of July Leah was hopelessly in love. Her chores stacked up and she said her prayers rather quickly, preferring to think of Blake instead of the Lord as she fell asleep at night. She ignored her friends and read her Bible only sparingly, spending an inordinate amount of time on her looks and dress, and minutes seemed like hours before he came to call on her.

Summers in Nashville are hot and muggy and Blake's favorite pastime was to stroll through Vanderbilt and lie in the shade of the draping elms, stretched out on a blanket, a tall glass of lemonade in one hand and a freshly lit cigar in the other. During this latest stroll, the two of them walked hand in hand, the trees clustered full of emerald colored leaves and darting sunlight, and below the shaded woody sprawl a number of squirrels scampered about the grounds while bluejays squawked loudly and chased each other through the trees.

"You like it here, don't you?" Leah asked Blake lovingly.

Blake reached over, playing with Leah's rolling curls, and he kissed her once softly on the mouth. "I can taste the lemon on your lips," he said contentedly.

Leah tried again. "Tell me why you like it here so much?"

Blake backed away, sensing Leah didn't want to be kissed again, not just then anyway. His transition to seriousness came with grace and without irritation. "I suppose it's because a university is the finest place I know of," he said categorically. "Knowledge happens here, and what we know of the world is invented in these halls. Moreover, the college experience is the best opportunity to learn about oneself, and nothing people do is more important. The best of life comes together at a college—the academics, the introspection—and we're wondrously challenged by it."

"I thought the best of life was love," Leah replied.

"It is," Blake answered her assuredly. "I *love* it here. I want to teach law at this university someday, after I practice and try my hand at politics. I feel I owe my family that much first."

Leah's look soured. "Will I ever get to meet your family?" she asked.

"Sure, someday perhaps. I've met yours, and I suppose that would only be fair."

"I thought you'd want me to meet them."

In an instant Blake's face lost all pleasantness. It seemed as though an old wound had been reopened. "My family is different than yours, Leah. They're serious people, and meeting a girl I date is serious business. They interview, they don't acquaint; they're not very good at making nice or welcoming girls into their home, and I'd rather not put you through that unless it's absolutely necessary."

"When will it be necessary?" Leah's look was that of an abandoned kitten at the back porch door. She nearly cried from want.

Blake rubbed his chin and feigned a serious contemplation. He noticed Leah's furled brow and hungry gaze. "Necessary. Let's see now. If we got serious, I suppose."

"Aren't we serious?"

That was a tough question to duck, but Blake didn't respond to Leah's probe. He tightened up and rotated his head for relief instead, and then his eyes closed in a long pause that was broken only by the insistence of Leah's next words.

"Well, I sure am," she said emphatically. Her look had changed and her eyes interrogated as much as they cajoled.

"I don't know, are we serious?" Blake asked her listlessly. He seemed unsure and detached and something was clearly weighing on him, his eyes glazed over and far away, seeing past the campus grounds to another image in his mind.

"Blake, I love you," Leah said imploringly. "You're everything I've ever wanted and everything I've ever dreamed of. I'm so full with you, as happy as can be, and I want it to stay this way forever."

Blake's eyes narrowed. His rugged jaw and sleek nose became rigid, yet he was still extremely well poised. He sought with great care for the words to come as planned. "I'm glad, Leah, and I do care about you. But love takes time. If we keep seeing each other, who knows what might happen for us."

Leah's face fell. She felt a twinge in her heart. "What can I do to make you love me sooner?" she pleaded with him, inching closer, resting her head gently on his shoulder. "I'll do anything, anything at all."

Blake gently upraised his shoulder as a message for Leah to lift her head from him. Her face was filled with a needy inadequacy, as girls in love so often reveal. "You wouldn't do *anything*, would you?" he said, baiting her. "I mean, you wouldn't let us go all the way?"

Leah yanked her head backward. She thought of God. "No, I wouldn't. Not until we were married. You wouldn't want me to, would you?"

Even the greatest of actors have a hard time hiding disappointment. "I guess not," Blake said rather flatly, secretly desirous of a different answer. He stared off into the distance. Leah was so tempting, her lips so sweet, and the daisy patterned summer dress she wore that day caught her curves and then some. Her silky white skin called out to be made love to, and it seemed rather odd when so many girls from superior backgrounds had said yes to him that a girl like her would say no. He looked at her again. Leah was so gorgeous sitting there.

"You sure are handsome," Leah said. "And I wish you loved me as much as I love you." She smiled longingly. But when she leaned her head back on his shoulder again, Blake had stiffened.

"Just know that I have to do what I have to do, for both my parents and myself," he said inexorably. "I'm in no hurry to be married. I have to establish myself in law and pave the way for a political career, and in my life there is no opting out of those two responsibilities. Not with my family. Especially since my brother died."

Leah lifted her head from Blake's shoulder, looking at him with empathy. Her perfectly oval face was so trusting and so pretty at the same time. "I'm sorry there's so much pressure on you," she said. "I'll be there if you need me. I may be young, but I know what I feel. I love you, Blake, and I think I always will."

***

Blake didn't call for the next couple of days and on Thursday afternoon Leah bumped into Kathy Wyatt at The Soda Fountain after running some errands for Margaret. The bus ride had been hot and Leah felt the perspiration under her arms and on her stomach. She was already in a bad mood.

Kathy was a nice girl, as outgoing and warmhearted as they came, and she knew Leah from high school, although they had never been close friends. Kathy's only fault was that she was a bit of a gossip, but her credibility ran high since she only repeated what she knew to be true and no one had ever caught her in a lie.

The Soda Fountain was a classic 1950s diner: vinyl cushion booths, a checkered tile floor, and a parking lot crammed full of hot rods, cruisers, and leathers revving motorcycles. Carhops on roller skates hustled trays of burgers and fries. Fights were frequent. But Leah loved the chocolate shakes. Kathy sat one booth over with a girl named Tammy Blue, whom Leah didn't know very well. When Tammy left, Kathy leaned over the padded, boysenberry colored booth as she swallowed her last bite of banana split.

"Say, Leah, how you doing?" Kathy asked easily.

"I'm fine, Kathy, how are you? I haven't seen you since graduation. Good split, huh?"

"It sure was," Kathy said. "I wish I could eat another one, but I'd gain twenty pounds. Yeah, Leah, I haven't been around that much. I've been working at a sewing shop, Lisa's, next to Town Square Fabrics and Drapes, and I don't think my manager knows that some time ago this country abolished slavery. I was thinking about reporting him, except I don't know who to complain to."

Leah laughed a good laugh. "Kathy, you've always been such a riot."

"Say," Kathy said, changing directions like a cheetah, "are you still going out with that hotshot from Tech? His name is Blake, right?"

"Why, yes it is. How do you know Blake?"

Kathy had the same look on her face as someone does watching a television game show when the contestant can't answer the simplest question. "Golly, Leah, who doesn't?" she exclaimed. "He's always in the papers for something: scoring touchdowns or making baskets or throwing a javelin. Geez, he's a legend in Nashville."

Leah looked worried, but at the same time resigned to her fate. "Gosh, don't tell him that. That's all I need," she said, shaking her head and frowning. "Him knowing how wonderful he is."

"Hey, don't let him have the upper hand," Kathy said supportively. "You're so darn cute yourself. Half the guys in our class were in love with you, and they would have asked you out except they were scared to death of your Mama."

Leah and Kathy both broke up on that one. When Leah quit chuckling, she dipped her napkin into her glass of water and wiped her face with it. "She's that bad, isn't she?" she asked, shaking her head back and forth, the grin on her face making a comeback. Kathy lost it again and Leah couldn't stop herself either, and together they laughed for a full five minutes.

When they finally stopped laughing, Kathy shifted in the booth and faced Leah more directly. "Leah, can I come over there and talk to you about something?" she asked, respect in her voice.

"Sure."

Kathy left two bucks on top of her check and spun around into Leah's booth, leaning forward and speaking in a quiet way. Her eyes, however, were perky. "When some of my girlfriends and I heard you were seeing Blake we didn't know what to think. I probably shouldn't say anything, but we all heard he has a girlfriend. Some rich chick from Belle Meade, but word is they break up a lot and get back together again."

"What else did you hear?" Leah managed bravely.

"Only that he uses the breaks to date other girls for a while until his family pressures him to get back with the rich chick. It seems they think she'd be the perfect wife, and I'd hate to see you be the sucker in that game. I know we weren't the best of friends in high school, but I've always liked you and my sister knew Marian real well and liked her as much as anybody she ever met. Anyway, I just thought you'd like to know."

"Thank you. I'll ask him about it," Leah said, doing a poor job of hiding her fright. Her eyes wandered down to the shiny black-and-white checkered tile floor where a spilled chocolate shake lay foaming in the center aisle. Leah hadn't heard the shake drop to the ground. She had no idea how it had gotten there. She looked at her tabletop. It was her shake on the floor. Gobs of chocolate lather spread out across the checkered aisle, each gob filled with a swarm of bursting bubbles as a waitress hustled to the back room for a bucket of water and a mop.

"You okay?" Kathy asked.

Leah needed to climb out of the booth and run away. She felt a surge of panic in her chest. "Sure, I'm fine," she croaked, clearing her throat. "Thanks for the word, Kathy, I know you mean well."

"Hey, you know what?" Kathy said. "Why don't we get together some time? You know where I work; call me. We'll check out that new burger place across from Parker's."

Leah lifted her troubled head and the words she uttered were hollow. "I will. I'll call you." Kathy had to strain hard to hear her.

"Please do, Leah. I'd love to hang out with you. Say hi to Marian for my sister."

***

The time to find out where she stood with Blake came the following Friday evening. After dinner and a picture show, their first date in a good long while, Blake stopped his car half a block from Leah's house for their customary goodnight kiss.

"Come on up to the house," Leah said. "My mother is overnight in Shelbyville, welcoming my cousin's new baby to the world. We can sit outside on the front porch and talk for a spell. My daddy is sure to be asleep."

"You sure?"

"It'll be fine. Pull on up."

It was a warm summer's night that evening, a damp heaviness in the air as swarms of fireflies sparked in and out of the mulberry bushes. A hound dog yelped in the distance. Leah and Blake tiptoed to the front of the house and listened for noises, but the house was silent.

"Let's sit here on the swing for a minute because I want to talk to you about a worry I have," Leah began, her body language inimical and her face without its usual softness.

Blake was as silent as arctic ice at dawn.

"The summer will be over before we know it, and you've got law school in the fall. We haven't spent much time talking about us; it's almost like you've been avoiding the subject, but you know how much I love you," Leah said.

"I know you do," Blake replied, his leg jiggling.

Leah stared straight at him. Her entire world was riding on her next comment and she felt her stomach tense up into a nervous ball. She gulped hard before speaking. "But you've never told me that you love *me*. I want to know why. I have my heart on the line, here, and I think I have a right to know what's in our future."

It was impossible to escape the issue this time. Blake swept his hair back with his hands. "Well, I guess it's because you're still so young, Leah, with college starting soon," he began unwaveringly. "I don't want you to be tied down while I'm gone to law school. I see how many guys look at you when we're out, and I can't blame them. You should date as many guys as possible to see if another guy is better suited for you. That's what dating is for. Courtship is half the fun in life. I know we'll see each other in the summertime months and during vacations when I'm home from school."

Leah frowned. "What about the other times, which is most of the year?"

"Well, I suppose we'll call or write to each other," he added nonchalantly. "I don't see why we wouldn't."

"Are you going to date other girls while you're off at law school?" Leah asked him bluntly.

"I haven't thought about it that much."

"So, you haven't fallen for me because the time isn't right, is that it?"

Blake stretched out his arms, hands clasped together, and cracked his royal knuckles. He saw for the first time another side to Leah, an accusatory and caustic side, and he didn't like it. "Something like that. If we make it through these years, then we'll know for sure if we're meant to be together."

They had both been standing the entire time. "You want to sit down?" Blake asked.

Leah sat down on the swing first and Blake soon followed her. The swing creaked severely under their weight. They listened to make sure the house remained quiet.

"Is there anything you haven't told me?" Leah asked him quietly, her face revealing that she knew far more than she was letting on.

Blake drew in a deep breath and exhaled. Leah knew about the other girl. Her look was unmistakable. "Well, I probably should have told you sooner," he began. "There's another girl I've seen off and on for years. My family wants me to marry her. She's gone to mass with us since we were in the first grade, and her father is Thomas Clausen, of Clausen, McGrady & Monroe, the firm that represents the governor. She's in law school, up at Yale, in New Haven, just finished her first year there. She did her undergraduate work in three years, that's how smart she is, so she's my age but already way ahead of me, and my family wants me to go Yale and join her."

Leah stood up from the swing. "You lied to me, Blake. I asked you if there was someone else, anyone, back on our first or second date, and you said no. Don't you remember? I love you, and I thought we were going to be married someday. She's a tramp, whoever she is, and you need to get rid of her."

"I can't Leah. I can't do that. And she's not a tramp."

His defense of the other girl stung Leah. She lashed out at him. "She is too a tramp if she takes you back every time you go out with other girls," Leah said sharply. "You have to be a slut to do that. You deserve better than her, someone moral and fine, someone who loves you like I do."

Blake sighed. This scene had repeated itself too many times, more than he cared to remember. He motioned for Leah to sit by him again, which she obliged. "It wasn't going to work, Leah, not when you look at it objectively, not with everything that's against us," he said, confessing more than persuading. "We have to be realistic. I'm still young myself. I'm not through dating around, and it seems so unfair to give up other women so soon. Besides, my family would never support me in this."

Leah's face filled with horror and disbelief, her expression the same as if she'd been slapped. She began to tremble. "You're not going back on what you said. You're not. You can't do that to us. I won't let you. I love you, don't you understand that? I won't let you end us on account of some slut."

"I have to, Leah. And she's not a slut. I want you to quit saying that about her. I'm so sorry about not being up front with you. I'm just so sorry for what I've done."

The blood drained from Leah's face, and she looked sickened to her stomach. She cried a woeful cry, uttering no sound, her eyes dry, like a baby cries when it doesn't know how to cry yet, a godawful silence filling up what should have been an unbearably loud wailing. She had not a thought for her embarrassment nor her desperation. She only cared to cry.

Blake sat patiently, waiting for Leah to find her composure again. When Leah looked at him, his was the most withdrawn expression she had ever seen on another human being, like the face of an ancient statue buried at the bottom of the sea, so unreachable and lost, and she finally understood that she had loved alone.

Blake got up from the swing and drove away without saying another word. Leah stumbled into her room, drowning in disbelief. It didn't seem possible to have lost him. She saw the callousness of Blake's gaze again and again, his face stony where there should have been tenderness, his eyes empty where there should have been love. Leah cradled blankets and pillows and anything else within her grasp, pulling them into her body. She sobbed into her pillow. Nothing seemed real. She felt like she needed to run, to run forever, away from Nashville and away from that horrible pain in her room. Then, she heard her door creak open and her daddy came 'round to the edge of her bed.

"You okay, baby girl?"

"No, Daddy, I'm hurting real bad. I'm hurting as bad as I ever hurt before."

Walton sat down on the bed. He took Leah's hand and held it. "You want to tell me what's wrong?"

"Oh, Daddy, Blake doesn't love me, he doesn't love me at all. He's been with another girl this entire summer. I can't believe we had all those times together, and he had those times with somebody else. I thought we were special, but I guess I was blind. But I love him anyway. I can't help myself."

Walton pulled the sheet up to Leah's chin. He felt the tears on the bedding and saw the swelling in Leah's eyes. He wiped a tear from her cheek.

Leah stared nothingness in the face. "Part of what I was is gone and now I have to be me," she said despairingly. "Just me, and I don't know how to be just me. Before I didn't know any better. Oh, Daddy, I was so naïve. But now, how can I ever trust again? It hurts so bad to be betrayed. I feel so alone, like I wasn't good enough for him, like I'll never be good enough for anyone."

Walton took in a deep breath. He knew how traumatic a moment like that could be for a young woman. "Sometimes life is hard, baby girl," he said comfortingly. "The world can be cold and people hurt each other. But you have to remember that it don't reflect none on you. You're as good as you ever been. Blake is under pressure, probably more pressure than you'll ever know. His family doesn't much approve of folks from where we're from, not enough to marry their only son anyway. You can blame this one on your Daddy, sweetheart, I'm afraid I don't make enough money for families like the Palmers."

Leah sat up in bed. "Daddy, it's not your fault. Don't ever think it is. People ought to be good enough for love no matter where they're from. God teaches us that in the Bible. Jesus comforted prostitutes and beggars, the sick and the afflicted, just plain wrecks of folks. You're the finest man I know. I just love Blake so much I don't know how I'll ever get past him."

Walton reminisced. He hesitated before speaking, patting his lips with his fingers, mulling something over in his mind. Finally, he spoke words he had vowed to keep secret his entire lifetime. "In times like these, you get past it by going with what matters most to you. I doubt Blake is more important than what you value most in this world."

"What do you mean, Daddy?"

"Well, don't tell your mother, but I'll tell you a secret of mine," he went on, speaking even softer than before. "When I was young, I loved a girl before Margaret. She was a smart young thing, pretty as pie, came from a nice family, certainly richer than mine, and she had her pick of the litter. She knew it, too. She left me for a college boy. Told me I wasn't good enough for her, that the college boy would make a better husband someday. Hurt like the dickens at that time. But I got past it."

"How?"

Walton sighed a sigh of remembered pain. "Believing that there'd be somebody else for me. There was, too. Your mother came along, and I haven't looked back. But it was more than that, baby girl. I like being out in the country, fishing and such, being in the wild feels like home, and I wasn't going to let that girl take that away from me. I wasn't going to let her ruin my life by being so sad that I forgot what I loved about living. Being outdoors is what I valued most. There is something in all of us that we love more than anything else in the world, and that will be true for you until the very end."

"What do you think it is for me, Daddy?"

"I don't know. It may be something you've learned from how you're raised, or maybe something to come. More than likely, it's in you already. Only you'll know what it is for sure. I can't give it to you or tell you when you'll know it. It may have something to do with the stars. You've always loved looking into the sky at night. Looking at stars means more to you than it does for most folks. It's like you're a part of the stars, and they're a part of you. But whatever it is, you'll find it. Trust your daddy on that one."

Chapter 4

LEAH NEARLY FELL APART in the weeks that followed. Her cheerfulness disappeared and she no longer cared for her clothes or looked after her room. Rare was her nightly stroll to appreciate the wonder of the nighttime sky. Her radio went unplayed, and she didn't call her friends or make any appointments to come visit them. She also stopped dropping in on the neighbor families. Concentrating on her reading or the words folks said around her was exceedingly difficult, and most nights she sobbed herself to sleep. The senselessness of living filled her every thought and she thought often of dying and of hell.

One night, when she didn't think she'd make it through until the light of dawn, she prayed for God to save her. It had become difficult to breathe, and she hadn't eaten in many days. Each day had brought only increasing misery and the endlessness of her pain wrought panic and despair. That night, the night of her prayer, Leah fell asleep with the pages of her Bible pressed underneath her face, the crinkled paper of God's word her only hope in life. She remembered her last entreaty before the room went completely black: "God save me. I can't take it anymore."

That next morning, Leah awoke to a bright sunshine that filled her room in a golden swath of confidence. Although a summer sun, the sun's rays felt cool on her blankets and a gentle breeze accompanied the light into her room through her half-open window. Except for the soft breeze, her room seemed remarkably still. The steadfast sun was especially bright, but unlike the bright sunshine of other mornings she neither squinted against it nor shielded her face. Instead, the sun seemed to soothe her. She couldn't remember her dreams or if she had dreamt that night at all, but she felt a peacefulness in her mind like never before, and she smiled her first smile in nearly a month.

Although Leah never stopped loving or wanting Blake, the pain of losing him finally dulled as the days turned into a collection of diminishing tears and gradual acceptance. Nightly, she prayed for God to give her additional strength, and slowly, like the accumulation of silt in a lazy alluvial river, Leah regained some of her vigor, and soon she noticed the stars again.

***

At church, where Leah felt she deserved loving Christian support and rarely received any, there presided over the First Avenue Congregation, unofficially of course, a group of snooty old women that Leah had dubbed "the accusers." The accusers lived to pass judgement and cast aspersions on any of their brethren as they saw fit, mostly none of it for cause and all of it with malice. Their words were the sound of branches snapping. All sixty years of age or older, these were women who were virgins when they married, not necessarily out of choice, and also the kind of women who were bitter about their station in life, women whose husbands were nothing spectacular and whose families were the envy of no one. Leah was convinced their lack of stature ate at them like the swooping stabs of Prometheus' vulture, returning again and again, unmercifully pecking and gnawing at their pride, and by claiming the moral high ground, these women believed they could somehow transcend their standing and thereby change the will of God.

One day, after church services, Marian came to Leah and told her of some of the rumors she'd been hearing from sources in the know.

"Hey, Lee, have a seat here with me on the sofa. I want to talk to you."

Leah took a seat on the plum velvet couch in the front room. "About what?" she asked, sitting down.

"Well, the last couple of weeks at church, I've heard some nasty things being said by Maude and her circle. Carol Lee Robinson and Maxine Webster are in the outhouse with her, as usual, and Millie Curtis told me the rumors are spreading like wildfires. That's why we're getting the looks down the nose from Carol Lee and Maxine and their girls. Old Lady Thomason is sure a witch, I know that much."

"What kind of things?"

"Heck, Lee, it's no secret they've harbored a resentment toward us for a long time. I'm not telling you anything you don't already know. You know all about covetousness and pride. And Maude's is a witches' coven. I think it has to do with the fact their kids aren't too fetching and they're none too bright, neither. Maude is a bitter woman. Plain and simple."

"What kind of things?" Leah asked, growing impatient.

Marian sighed. She looked away quickly before returning her gaze to her sister. "They say you slept with Blake," she said hesitatingly.

"Well, I didn't. What else did they say?"

Marian looked around to make sure they were alone, then went on. "That there's no way you couldn't have, him being such a prize and all, and that you're Kay's sister and whoring's in the blood. Those old bats have sure had it out for Kay over the years. They hate she don't come to church with us. Millie told me Maude never recovered when Kay refused her eldest boy Bradley for his junior prom. Remember back when? Kay was a freshman and went to the prom instead with that scoundrel Meekins boy that got Jenny Tomlinson pregnant. Plus, Blake being older and having a man's needs, and, well, you know Maude."

"What else?" Leah was beginning to turn red.

Marian saw the first smoke rising from her sister. "Now, just calm down, little Lee. I'm not telling you another word until you take a deep breath."

Leah breathed in a good breath and sat up straighter, but she was still stewing inside. "What else, Marian?" she asked.

Marian fretted for moment before continuing. She knew what followed would set Leah off a good one. "And that it all makes sense because Daddy don't come to church, and that painting houses gives him plenty of time for the mistress he has on the side."

"They said what?"

"That Daddy has a mistress."

"Daddy? Our daddy? With a mistress? Why that old bitch. That jealous old cow. Those are the last words that crusty old bitch is ever going to say about my daddy."

"Leah, dad bless it, don't you go do something stupid. Don't you dare. And stop swearing. Mama will kill us if she hears you. Listen to me, now, Mama will whip us like never before."

Leah rose from the couch. She stared hard at her sister. "I don't care, Marian. Maude has said her last lie about Daddy. That old witch's time has come. She's spoken bad about me for years because I don't bow to her, and I didn't join her visitation committee for this fall. First time I ever declined her. I told her I don't have time with college coming up. Fat old witch. Who does she think she is?"

"It isn't just Maude."

"I know that. Carol Lee and Maxine are nothing but snoops and blabbermouths and both hate Mama because Mama has won more plaques than the two of them combined. Besides, both those old broads are dumber than rocks. The three of them are everything that's wrong with this place. Ignorant and jealous, for no good cause. It's because of people like them that I want so desperately to leave Tennessee. I've had enough of those old bags to last me a lifetime."

"Look, don't do something you'll regret forever, Lee. Mama is a good woman, and she'll pay, too. Mama has been going to First Avenue since before you and I were born. If you blow up at Maude, Mama is sure to be shamed in the scandal. We're her girls, and Mama will pay, sure as sunup."

Leah didn't hear a word her sister said. It was doubtful she would have felt an earthquake at that moment. "A mistress? Why Daddy wouldn't have a mistress if Mama said it was fine by her. They got no right to say anything bad about Daddy, Marian. I don't care what Mama thinks, they ain't saying another insult about my daddy, so help me God."

***

The vast majority of churches in Nashville are extremely well-funded and are thus well-equipped with large facilities to host special events and conferences and the ubiquitous monthly potluck; in fact it is a distinguishing feature of faith in the South to appear grandiose, as if grandiosity connotes a superior faith in the Lord. Potlucks are as much for show as they are for fellowship. As such, that following Sunday the accusers presided over an emperor's table of comestibles at the back of the auditorium, strategically positioned to monitor and respond to the events of the day.

Fans whizzed in the corners next to large buckets of ice. It had been a hot morning. The first flies buzzed around the accusers and the giant table spread with food. Maude, Carol Lee, and Maxine sat in a row, the three of them, smug and coy, with the occasional "good afternoon" or "good to see you" patter, their airs loftier than a mountain kingdom, and Leah grew angrier and angrier as she watched their phony politeness after all they had insinuated about her and her family.

When she couldn't stand it a moment longer, Leah marched up to the accusers like Patton at Palermo. She stood waiting, trembling with anger. Maude looked up at her first.

"Afternoon, Leah."

"I've heard what you've said about me and my family," Leah fired, her face turning a brighter shade of red, "and none of it is true. So get off your high horse."

Carol Lee and Maxine took notice of the harsh tone. All three sat bewildered, sensing more was on the way, Leah's first salvo stunning them, while the conversations in the room hushed to an anxious silence. Instinctively, those in attendance encircled the bitter language, the accusers shifting their bodies to close ranks, girding themselves for what appeared to be an impending battle.

"Trash like you has no reason to say anything about anybody," Leah fumed, the veins in her forehead popping up like worms through soft dirt. "You have no right to accuse me or my family of any wrongdoing, and you have no right to judge any of us. God is the only judge, and my conscience is clean."

Maude, an overblown woman with chubby cheeks and shifty crow eyes, her nose long and pointy, a master of the outwardly genteel but inwardly spiteful, started to speak in her defense, but Leah quickly cut her off.

"Don't say a word, you heathen. Instead of ridiculing me and telling lies, you should worry about what God will do to you as punishment for disparaging a sister in the faith. Sinning against brethren is a despicable sin. I'm one of your own. Instead of putting my daddy down, you should be working with me to save him. Kay, too. All of you know how hard my Mama has tried with my oldest sister. Ask yourself how God looks at us sinning against each other."

Maude Thomason blinked hard. Her eyes scanned the room for signs of support.

Soon, some of the men got up and came forward. Finally, one of the men, an elder named Cecil Smith, approached Leah and calmly asked her, "Why don't we get your mother, Leah. Maybe she can help calm you down." Cecil turned to the crowd. "Has anyone seen Margaret since services ended?"

Leah wasn't through. She felt inspired by God in her mission to straighten the house of the Lord. "It's a little late for intercession, you hypocrite," Leah said to Cecil in reprimand. "You've heard what these women said about me and you did nothing. You're an elder, God's keeper in His house, and you let the wickedness continue on your watch. An *elder*, how shameful that is, to be so weak in front of the eyes of the Lord. Get away from me, Cecil, you should have done something over a week ago."

Cecil looked like the last guy standing in his gang when the opposing thugs come to finish off a rumble. None of the accusers moved or said a word. Not even the flies buzzed anymore.

The faces in the room seemed like those in a painting, depictions of life incapable of speaking. Then, after what seemed like a century of silence, Chester Flower, a man Leah liked for his jovial disposition, yelled out from near the side doorway, "Has everyone got something to eat?" Another man chimed in quickly, "Get it while it's hot," and that started the bravest people to moving forward and forming a line in front of the spread of food.

Leah stormed out of First Avenue Congregation without ever looking back. Never had the church felt like it ought to, full of support and Christian love. Marian drove Leah home before coming back later to get Margaret, who had some explaining to do to the elders and the deacons. When Marian and Margaret returned to the house, Leah was waiting for them in the front room.

Surprisingly, Margaret didn't whip her with a switch. Maybe it was because Marian took a seat at Leah's side or maybe it was because Margaret had never much liked Maude herself. It wasn't because of Leah's age. Leah was still a child in Margaret's mind, and Margaret would whip a sixty year old for the wrong offense. Leah thought she had been spared a whupping because she had defended Kay as well as her daddy, and Margaret had always been plenty partial to Kay.

"Leah, I'm ashamed of you today," Margaret began. "I've raised you better than to make such a scene. I'm not sure we can stay at First Avenue any longer. Next Sunday we'll go to the Morse Street Congregation and declare our membership there. Morse is a fine church. I know Elder Sanders from Save a Soul work at the infirmary and the river baptisms of Sewanee. What upsets me most is how you can high and mighty Maude and her clan when it was your fault for dating Blake in the first place; and Marian, I'm ashamed of you for introducing Leah to such a villain. I've told you both: Date in your own faith. Now both of you get out of my sight."

***

That afternoon Leah lay ruminating on her bed, watching as a tired sun drooped below the last of the withering curtain shade. Her daddy hadn't replaced the old shade and one day it was sure to drop off from neglect, but he was the single finest man she knew and the accusers had no right to say anything bad about him. He was worth changing churches for, and the accompanying ridicule that goes along with such a notorious move was well justified, as the old bats at First Avenue surely had it coming.

The first exhausted leaves of late summertime fell outside the window, one by one, drifting down in gentle swirling circles to form competing clusters that would soon need to be raked into one large pile; Margaret was sure to rail about the leaves, too, when the time came. The sky that day was a dirty brown haze, making Leah's world seem especially musty and gray. The dog days of summer in Nashville can be an especially trying time, the heaviness of the air imbued with a suffocating drudgery and an unending immutability, and Southern humidity is peculiar in that way: It can often appear that the world is no larger than what you can see beyond your nose, and sadly it is often true.

Leah glanced over at her dresser. It was cluttered with empty bottles of perfume, handed down from Marian and Kay, and Leah had often smelled the traces of their sweet fragrances sitting on the edge of her bed. But she'd never dabbed a drop on her neck or her wrist, for there were no droplets left, as Margaret had emptied each bottle to the last, forbidding her youngest from wearing sachet since it was sure to attract the wrong kind of man. Instead, Leah had smelled of soap and shampoo and hygienic powders. Her jewelry box was empty, save for the string of pearls Margaret let her wear that past Easter to church, and Leah had never worn a set of earrings in her lifetime, nor a ring on her hand.

Laying beside the empty bottles of perfume were letters of recommendation for college, next to them Bible workbooks and texts from the church bookstore. Every skirt and dress Leah owned went down to her ankles and Margaret had forbidden her from the cheerleading squad since the outfits showed the calf and the knee, and the splits the girls performed were vulgar and obscene in the eyes of the Lord. Yet Margaret had made an exception for Marian, who had been allowed on the squad, on the understanding that her purse and closet were subject to random inspections, and once a month there would be an exhaustive search of her room. The house was in many ways more like a prison than it was a home. Leah was tired of living with a mother who never heard a single word she said and who so often seemed as if she didn't care whether Leah lived or died.

Leah thought on Margaret's diatribe in the front room, laying on her bed for a good long while, and then it came to her, an indisputable fact, one she had avoided for far too long, a golden nugget plucked from a cracked open rock of quartz, one that had been with her in that house since her first memories of living with her mother: *Margaret was, and had always been, an accuser.* From that moment on, Leah knew she'd eventually have to leave her home and that thought saddened her and made her cry herself to sleep.

Chapter 5

THE TUMULTUOUS SUMMER GAVE way to a steady autumn. No storms signaled the change of the season that year, only a gradual easing of the heat and an appreciated break from the oppressive humidity. It took a long while for the crisp fall mornings to arrive, well into the last week of September, but as the daylight hours shortened and the sun lowered in the sky came the season of learning and of leaves.

Christian College was best that time of year. The school was small, with fewer than a thousand students, but its grassy grounds were filled with blazing trees and inviting wood benches. Despite its small size, the College felt like a much larger university, the buildings traditional brick and creamy gray mortar, with paned glass windows and stone archway entrances, all covered with sprawling ivy and interlaced with pretty tiled courtyards. Each hallway had been named after a campus founder or wealthy alumnus and each also had its own customized insignia over a large cathedral door. A golden chapel bell dinged sweetly on the hour. Leah thought the campus looked absolutely beautiful, as she had always loved the firebrand colors of autumn, especially the flaming month of October, and although she loved the green of spring and gold of summertime, she was most happy when the ground turned brown and the branches came alive with a rustic vibrancy.

Leah's was a heavy load for a freshman: Chemistry, Biology, Algebra, American History, and a Bible class on the Old Testament. The latter was her favorite course of study, and she shone in it like a freshly minted penny twirling brightly in the sun. Often, as Leah walked from class to class, in an autumn air so cool and crystalline, she imagined herself a flower blooming in a lovely country garden, and in those days she felt happily optimistic about her future.

But all was not rosy at Christian College.

One day not long after classes began, as Leah strolled through the campus, a sudden breeze jostled some papers from her folder, where they landed at the foot of a nearby bench. Two students sat on the bench arguing over who enters heaven and the method of admission. They didn't notice Leah's papers rustling about, and in order to cram her papers back into her folder Leah took a seat on another wooden bench near the boys. One student, wearing glasses and with straggly hair, had gaps in his teeth that provided an unnatural flow of air through his mouth. He seemed to hiss as he spoke. The other, clean-cut with fair skin and delicate features, lacked the resolve of a staunch Christian, slumping timidly before the sibilant words of the other, and Leah pretended to read her biology book while remaining seated quietly at her bench, eavesdropping.

"See, if God should show himself to you in your heart and you secure Jesus as your savior, then why be baptized?" the apologist asked, his words interlaced with seduction.

"Then why was Christ baptized in the first place?" the timid student replied.

"Simple. As an example. Should the saving aspect in salvation prove to be the acceptance of Jesus into your heart, baptism is then a sheer formality, is it not?" the apologist asked.

Leah stirred uneasily while seated on her bench, but she listened intently. "That's not the way I was taught," the clean-cut student responded. "But I understand your point that acceptance is the key or otherwise you'd never get to the point of baptism."

"So true, and so well said," the apologist asserted. "And if it satisfies you any, I still think people should be baptized out of respect for the example Our Savior set."

Leah was flabbergasted. She couldn't believe what she was hearing, not on a Christian campus anyway, the apologist's defamation of God's consecrated word appalling to her, and she couldn't control what came out of her mouth next either, but it rose from the heart of her beliefs and came out fiery.

"Who are you to question the example that Jesus set for man to follow?" Leah demanded of the apologist, slamming her biology book shut on the bench while rising to face him. "Who are you to say baptism may not be necessary? The scripture is perfectly clear on it: 'Repent, and be baptized.' Baptism is not up for interpretation by you or anybody else, and it is most certainly required for souls to enter heaven. The Bible says so, it's plain and simple, in black and white."

The apologist, realizing he'd been overheard, recoiled. "I'm sorry," he said. "I hope I didn't offend you." His eyes, small for his face, seemed especially beady behind his glasses.

Leah's face was a roaring fire. "Forget offending me, you've offended God. I'm not important, God is. It's that kind of thinking, interpreting the Bible in your own way, that can lead man astray, lead man to create his own Bible, to slander God's words until their redeeming power is nullified. God's word is perfect; it needs no revision from you or anyone else. You'll never be smarter than God, no matter how much your pride might want you to be."

Leah faced the clean-cut student next, her eyes still ablaze. "And you. You should know better than to cower before such an affront to God. I could tell from how you spoke you know the truth of God's word. So defend it. Satan comes in many guises and many forms, even in so-called friends, so stick up for what you know to be true, and don't be sorry about it for one single second."

The apologist pulled at the sweater of the clean-cut student and motioned for him to get up and walk away. They made off together behind the school chapel without looking back, walking briskly straightaway, and Leah watched them disappear behind the chapel yard before she calmed herself down.

Leah took a long look around and sat back down on the bench. Slender trees curved casually in the early fall breezes. She scanned the campus. Something caught her eye. Across the way, she saw a distinctive gait, a man walking hunched over with short shuffling steps and long looping arms, with snow white hair that was balding on top, and then she recognized his face: It was a kindly old gentleman, Calendar Jones, whom Leah had known as a teacher from Vacation Bible School. She hadn't seen him in years. She waved to him and the old man saw her and came over.

"Leah? Leah Caffrey?" he asked.

Leah smiled at him. His face had aged much since she last saw him, his skin sagging, the right side of his face drawn and discolored. She thought he must have had a stroke. Age spots filled his face, but his eyes still sparkled as before. "Yes, it's me," Leah said excitedly. "How are you? I haven't seen you since I started high school."

"That's right, you haven't, have you? I left First Avenue about five years ago. My daughter and her family worship at Countrybrook near Houghton Flat. I figured in my last few years I ought to be around my children and their children as much as I can. I'm eighty-three years old now and Countrybrook is a smaller church and they still need teachers."

"You still teach Bible School?"

"Sure do."

Leah looked at him. She thought she might have offended him, and she tried to cover for herself. "What I mean to say is that I'm both impressed and glad you do," she said, hoping he'd buy it. "You were a great teacher."

The old man smiled a toothy smile. "Nonsense. You're surprised I can still teach at my age. Leah, little Leah Caffrey, all grown up and still putting her foot in her mouth. You used to do the same thing in my class. Such a darling little girl you were. Speaking of those days, how's Margaret?"

"Doing fine. And I'm sorry if I offended you. Calendar Jones, you never cut me any slack."

The old man smiled again, the kind of smile filled with good memories and remembered love. "Nashville is still a small town," he said. "I heard you told off Maude and her cohorts. Good for you. Chester Flower and I talk on the phone once a week. I still see him sometimes. I also heard Margaret declared her membership at Morse. I knew Maude would get it one day. But never hate, Leah, life is too short for hate. You were a loving, sweet child, and I'd never want you to lose that."

Calendar Jones extended his hand and Leah held it. His hand was soft, yet olden and dry. It quivered slightly from a palsy. She felt the frailty of an old man's body in the touch of his hand.

"Can I ask you something?" Leah inquired politely.

"Sure you can."

"I just overheard two students here talking and one of them tried to tell the other that baptism isn't necessary to enter heaven. I jumped into it, and they left hating me. But I don't think I was wrong for defending the truth."

Calendar Jones had a twinkle in his eye. "You weren't, Leah. You were always a stickler for the truth. And never stop supporting the word of God. Remember, the Scopes trial was here in Tennessee and evolution is still worming its way into the schools. There's no security from the wicked rebel, not even in a college of the Lord. I'm not just an old man paranoid of the modern world; corruption within the faith is very real, and I see it all around me. You've seen it, and it's ugly. I'm here to do a talk today for a professor friend of mine, and I'm going to tell his class what I've told my students for years: Be watchful. God will love you for sticking to His word."

"I guess I'm just disappointed, that's all," Leah said sadly. "I had such high hopes for college. I figured if there was one place where I was most likely to find my purpose in life, it'd be here. I've always believed the meaning of life must be somehow connected with my soul, and that a Christian education afforded me the best chance to both find myself and safeguard my beliefs. Now, I'm not so sure."

Calendar Jones patted Leah's hand. "Leah Caffrey, college won't give you the purpose of your life. You'll have to find that out on your own. It can help you eliminate possibilities, give you direction perhaps, but the purpose of your life is up to you. The same applies to its meaning."

Calendar Jones looked at her. His face was heavily wrinkled, red and purple capillaries bursting through the natural color of his skin, high on his cheeks and sunken temples. There were scars where moles had been removed. Tissues sagged. His kind eyes said goodbye. Leah watched him shuffle across campus, hunched over as before, the leaves crinkling at his feet. His shuffle was so labored that Leah wondered why he didn't use a cane. He had to stop often and rest. Other leaves soon fell to the ground, their life exhausted, and Leah watched sadly as Calendar Jones made his way past the chapel and disappeared from view.

***

It snowed early that year, just after the first morning briskness had frosted the windows, and it was a big storm that came down from the north, mighty and icy and swirling about, with a powerful bluster behind it, blanketing Nashville in two feet of clumpy white snow. Leah didn't mind though; when she peeked out through the front room window that next clear sunny sky morning, a brilliant white blanket of snow put her in a jolly mood for the holidays.

But Leah also had her worries.

Walton was slowing; he had recently turned fifty-three, and he coughed more than he had in previous years. After a hard shoveling of snow, he came inside and coughed a bad turn until his eyes reddened and his face discolored. For the first time, her daddy seemed old to her. Leah brought him a glass of ice water for his throat.

"Daddy, you all right?" she asked.

Walton sipped the water slowly. He coughed a couple more mushy coughs and then nodded a yes.

"You scared me half to death," Leah said.

Walton cleared his throat. "I'll be fine now. Just let me sit here a spell."

He took a seat in his chair and Leah sat on the sofa near him. On the floor was a torn-open padded brown pouch of tobacco, the tea-colored leaves spilling onto a newspaper that Walton had placed underneath to catch the precious spillage. Leah saw the postmark on the pouch was from Connecticut.

"Daddy, that pouch come all the way from Connecticut?"

"Sure did. One last week came from the Carolinas. Strongest tobacco I can afford."

"Well, you sure enough ought to stop smoking the strongest stuff. I think that's why you cough so much. Mama says it will kill you someday."

Walton began to roll a cigarette without filters. He had always smoked unfiltered cigarettes. "That's one sorry choice I've got then: cigarettes or your Mama. One of them is bound to kill me."

"Daddy, I'm being serious. I don't like you smoking as much as you do. Dr. Branden says your lungs are filling with fluid. Mama says you don't take your blaster out hunting anymore on account of it's too heavy to haul around. She says you take the twenty gauge out instead. You hate the twenty gauge. I bet if you quit smoking you could carry the blaster again."

Walton stretched from the stiffness in his joints and tired bones. "Don't forget, I'm also fifty-three years old. And these pouches are my gold. I'm not giving up one of life's greatest pleasures without the biggest stink you can imagine. Dr. Branden is always warning me about something or other. He could find an ailment on Hercules."

Leah shook off a grin. "Mama says you never leave before five-thirty in the morning for fishing, either. You used to leave at three or three-thirty at the latest. She says you take donuts with you now instead of frying up your sausages. I think you're smoking has something to do with your laziness, too."

Walton's laughter made him cough again. He took another sip of water. "I'll try and cut back on my smoking after Christmas," he said, a rasp in his voice. "But I'm not promising a thing."

"Well, I'm going to be after you to quit altogether. Don't you think I won't be. I love you too much to just sit here and watch you kill yourself."

That year Leah's home was the gathering place for the holidays, and Christmas Eve of 1956 was nothing short of postcard perfect. It was the largest gathering of family and friends anyone had ever remembered seeing, the neighbors stopping by in droves and the cars honking from the street and such. The front door opened and closed so many times Leah thought it'd fall off its hinges. At about eight forty-five, as Leah stood near the front door retrieving a ball thrown by one of the neighbor babies, she looked into the family room and past it into the kitchen and she counted twenty-four people in all, excluding herself, the faces all stuffing their mouths full of Margaret's homemade apple pie topped with her specialty of strawberry whipped cream. Leah saw the layered lay of blankets on the sofa and the softness of pillows and cushions under elbows. She smiled as if she had a secret to keep. William dropped a cup of coffee on the floor and Margaret quickly soaked a rag in the sink and wiped the floor clean without making so much as a peep. Folks were walking in and out of rooms like politicians at a convention, arms around backs, friendly clutches on the shoulders followed by hearty laughs and cautious ducks under the low-hanging mistletoe.

Then the front doorbell rang. Leah reached over and opened the door to sounds of joyous laughter. It was the O'Donovans and their kids, all eight of them, including two sets of twins, six boys in all, Miss Childress following closely behind, with a large platter of sugar fudge chocolates stacked up to her nose.

"Careful on the slick sidewalk, Miss Childress," Leah said. "I wouldn't want you to fall and hurt yourself."

"And spill my chocolates?" Miss Childress asked. "Why, your sister Marian would kill me. You know how much your sister loves my chocolates."

"We all do, ma'am. Your chocolates are the best in all of Nashville."

"Well, thank you, Leah. I don't mind saying so myself."

Miss Childress had never married, talk around town implied she was a lesbian, but Margaret brought her to church every Sunday despite the gossip and read the Bible with her two nights a week in the front room. Miss Childress had been baptized only three weeks prior, and Margaret said some women just never married but that God loved them just the same and that the girls should forget all the foolish talk in town and mind their own business besides. Margaret bawled her head off that day of her baptism, so happy for Miss Childress when she rose from the waters, her soul cleansed pure and sinless, and she ran to the entryway when she saw Miss Childress' face at the door.

"Hey there, Miss Childress," Margaret said beaming. "I'm so glad you could come. Merry Christmas to you. Leah, go get Miss Childress a cup of coffee, will you?"

"Sure, Mama."

"Thanks for having us," Mr. O'Donovan said to Margaret. "What a fine group you have assembled here. We can't stay for long, but we wanted to stop by and bring the kids because they love your apple pie and me and the wife love seeing you."

"Nothing else?" Margaret asked him slyly.

"Well, I suppose you might twist my arm into a bite of that apple pie of yours. Tell me you made that strawberry whipped cream."

"Sure did," Margaret said proudly, and with that she gave them all a big hug.

"I see Marian and William," Mrs. O'Donovan said. She waved to them. "Let me go give them all a kiss."

Leah brought back the cup of coffee for Miss Childress and closed the door. The fire popped loudly as Leah's cousin Rayford threw in another log to a commotion of sizzles and sparks. William hugged Mrs. O'Donovan and then held court at the kitchen table for anybody who cared to listen to him. Walton had himself scrunched up on the couch, wearing a wearisome look, his body bent over to one side, uncomfortably surrounded by screaming kids and neighbors he hadn't known were coming over, his red flannel shirt sagging on him like a wet sheet draped over a tall pole. He was straining to hear Leah's Uncle Cleveland mutter something about the work being done on the street near his woodworking store. Leah wanted to go over to her daddy's other side and lean on him, just for a moment, but she thought it might embarrass him too much. As she watched him though, her heart filled with love for the lanky old man with the balding head and the massive ears who lived to smoke, fish, and hunt game. Small thumps patted the roof, soon to turn to snow, but inside the house it was warm and glowing, and Walton caught Leah looking at him with that adoring stare of hers.

"Hey, come on over and grab a seat on the couch while you still can," he said, summoning her over with a wave of his hand.

Leah came over to the couch and set down beside her daddy. "What y'all talking about?" she asked.

"Your Uncle Cleveland here is telling me about how the city keeps screwing up his street," Walton said. "He says customers can't come in because of the barricades and the huge hole the city dug in the ground. Isn't that so, Cleveland?"

Leah's Aunt Martha had come from behind Cleveland and brought him a second helping of pie. Cleveland didn't hear Walton's question as he carved up a bite for himself.

"Well, that ought to keep your uncle quiet for a spell," Walton whispered to Leah.

"Daddy, it can't be all that bad."

"Just wait till he finishes that pie. You'll see."

Sure enough, when Cleveland finished the last of his dessert, he started in again on the imbeciles in charge of the city, and, together, with a few yawns from the both of them, Leah and her daddy endured the rest of Uncle Cleveland's saga.

Something in Leah, something prescient and deeply knowing, descended into her living room that evening, something full of maturity, inevitability, and wisdom, and it told her things would never be quite the same way again. The thought caused her to cherish the sight. She had always wanted her family to be as that evening, getting along, Kay not being any trouble, William happy to spend time with those who loved him. That night, that wonderful Christmas Eve night of Leah's freshman year in college, the warmth of her family and her friends radiated like a halo glow above an angel, and that night life was as it always should be.

***

Two days before the new year arrived, Leah's college grades came in the mail. Margaret opened the grades to find a C in Chemistry, stewing for an hour before Leah came prancing through the front door like a show horse in a circus, happy in the season of snow and in the easy life between semesters. Needless to say, she was caught off guard.

"You think I'm going to work like I do to watch you fail?" Margaret fumed, her thick neck boiling over her shoulders like water bubbling in a cauldron. "Well, do you?"

"What are you talking about?" Leah said trembling.

"You're better than a C in Chemistry, aren't you? I've left you alone again, believed and trusted in you, and again you've let me down. William never got anything lower than an A and Marian got one B because the teacher hated good girls. I'm not living in this hell of a home with your ignorant fool daddy gone fishing all the time for you to get C's in school. Do you hear me, you little tramp?"

Leah fought back without thinking, her defense coming from a place of accumulated resentment and pain, in a form of brinkmanship designed to finally set the record straight. "What about Kay, Mother?" she screamed back. "What about comparing me to Kay once in a while? She's never done anything right, never in her whole miserable life."

Margaret turned a horrid shade of red. It seemed as though she might explode. Leah had no idea what her mother might do, but Margaret's look was so deplorable, so contemptuously incensed in fact, that Leah ran to her room before she could see more.

But before Leah could close the door behind her she felt two fast lashes rip her arm and another whistle by her head. A further whistle split the air before Leah could react, the switch lashing the back of her neck and wrapping itself around the front of her throat like a boa constrictor hanging from the lowest branch of a Java tree.

Margaret jerked the switch back forcefully, the length retracting and untangling, peeling skin from Leah's neck as it unwound. Again and again Margaret attacked, the switch gouging Leah's legs viciously, her mother's eyes crazed and eerily satisfied, delightedly so, her wrath escalating in lunacy with each additional lash forward. One after another the whistles came, and Leah, with a presence of mind borne only of survival, grabbed a wooden hanger from her dresser and swung it at Margaret in self defense. She lost grip of it, the hanger flying into Margaret's forehead, cleaving for a time, before loosening and falling to the floor. The beating had turned into a brawl. Margaret fell back a step into the doorway, bleeding from the slice in her head, but she recovered quickly and brought the switch back up again, a vile vengeance boiling in her eyes.

"Stop it, Mother, or I'll call the police," a voice from the hallway yelled.

In the hallway stood Marian, her face aghast, in a fury of her own, and she grabbed her mother's arm and held it high in the air, the switch eventually dropping to the floor. She had stopped by to drop off a skirt for Leah to try on. Margaret staggered off into the kitchen, dabbing her forehead with a dampened dishrag until the dishrag filled with the distinctly shiny redness of blood.

Marian had never shouted much in her lifetime, but then seemed the perfect time. "What the heck is going on?" she asked her sister.

Leah's face was in her hands. Shakily, like a skier fallen down a mountain slope, she gathered herself and looked up forlornly at her sister. Her eyes had lost their usual luster and she trembled as if laying in a bed of ice.

"I got a C in Chemistry," she mumbled through her fingers.

Marian couldn't believe her ears. "That's it? All this for an average grade? Good Lord, that's it?"

Leah's voice still quivered from the shock. "It's probably much more than that," she groaned to her sister. "I think she's still mad about Maude and us having to leave First Avenue. She never forgave me for that." Marian saw the painful lashes across her sister's face and neck, red and glowing, like suture lines after a recent surgery. The beating had been a hard one. "But this was the worst it's ever been," Leah said despairingly. "If you hadn't shown up, I don't know what would have happened. It was awful. I couldn't stop her. I thought she was going to kill me."

Marian bolted into the kitchen, coming up to Margaret squarely. "Mother, you're not to hit Leah again. If I hear of it, I'm telling William. He's told me for years that if you went past a certain point to tell him about it, and he'd take care of it. I'm not going to say anything this time, but you don't want him coming home for that reason. He's been hungering for years to get at you, but he hasn't out of respect for Daddy."

Margaret stared off into the distance in full disdain.

"Do you hear me, Mother?"

Margaret ignored her.

"I'm leaving now," Marian said, a stern message to her words. "And I mean it, Mother."

Marian hurried into Leah's room on her way out of the house to look in on her. Her baby sister was doing as well as could be expected, applying emollient to her welts, sitting upright on her bed in the strange confounded silence of the disbelieving, still wobbly, a bottle of body lotion wedged firmly between her legs.

"You all right?" Marian asked her sister sweetly.

"Sure, I'll be fine."

"I love you."

"I love you, too. Is that the skirt?" Leah pointed to a checkered wool skirt hanging from a cabinet handle in the hallway.

"Sure is. Do you like it?"

"It's beautiful. Thank the Lord for stockings, huh?" Leah stuck her leg out to demonstrate her welts.

Marian's face filled with concern. "Are you sure you're all right? I can phone in sick to work. I don't mind. I've got three sick days to take, and now is as good a time as any."

Leah didn't want to be a bother, although inside she was hungering for a hug. "No, go on," she said. "You need the money for school. Daddy told me Peabody raised tuition again. I'll be fine.

Hey, next year you graduate. That'll be something, huh? Go on and go to work. It's not like it hasn't happened before."

"You sure?"

"Yeah, I'm sure. Go on."

In her room nursing her wounds, Leah wanted to stay angry. She wanted to hate her mother for what she'd done to her. Margaret was capable of being decent; she had often treated William and Kay like grown ups, discussing matters with them and working through their troubles when the situation demanded it, and she hadn't hit Marian once since the eighth grade. But for some reason the beatings had continued for Leah, and that was the hardest part for her to understand.

Leah looked around her room, fighting back tears. The welts on her arms and legs stung through the lotion, and the welts on her neck felt like she was being strangled to death. One of the lashes had caught the corner of her eye and at the edge of her sight the world was twitching and blurry. Eighteen years old and still being beaten. In her own room, no less. After all those years, she was still a pariah to her mother and she was still an outcast in her own home.

Shivering, Leah found her Bible on a chair. She picked it up and read quietly to herself, mouthing tender words from the book of John, the book of love, her favorite book of the New Testament. She read from the scriptures with a mind made easy from the familiarity of its pages, and it seemed to her as if her room poured solace from its walls.

"For this is the message you have heard from the beginning, that we should love one another. Beloved, let us love one another, because love is of God. If we love one another, God remains in us."

Leah placed her King James down softly on her bed. The pain of her welts had lessened, the severity of their stinging gone in her reading. The loving words of John soothed her soul and shortly thereafter a lone thought wandered into her mind, one she never expected at a time of such deplorable insult and inconsolable hurt: *Mama does work hard, and she wants the best for me.*

Leah rose from her bed, cracked her door open for a peek, and then treaded lightly into the kitchen where her mother stood staring absentmindedly into space, stirring a pot of gravy on top of the stove, so defensively closed and unapproachable as to be a human fortress. Leah stood next to her mother in an appeasing way, her eyes soft and her face willowy, her shoulders relaxed as she came up to her mother for a hug.

"I'll try harder next semester, Mama," Leah said, her slender arms coming up to her mother's neck. "I know how hard you work for me. I do know that."

Margaret continued stirring the gravy, as silent as a canyon in the desert. Her posture was rigid and unforgiving, and she wanted nothing to do with a gesture of love.

Spurned, Leah released her hug and made her way out to the front room, where she picked up a scarf and a jacket from the closet and headed out for an afternoon walk. Her legs still stung, but she needed to get out of the house. She thought walking might do her legs some good. As she closed the door behind her, she heard her mother reach for another pot and run the water for boiled potatoes she would eventually squish into mashed potatoes. After that, she'd make a country gravy with drippings and peppered flour that Leah loved to pour over her potatoes and bread. Margaret was a good mother in so many ways and Leah was sorry the incident had happened as it had; it could have just as easily been prevented.

Leah wrapped the scarf tightly around her neck and buttoned up her coat. She walked slowly for half a block, thinking of God and of absolution, and she prayed for the Lord to forgive her of her trespass against her mother. She looked upward into the sky. The sky had a softness that Leah had never quite seen before, a pastel beauty and airy tranquillity about its ethereal blue that gave her a sense of comfort and ease, and Leah resolved to treat her mother with ancillary kindness whenever the opportunity arose again.

It wasn't that hard for her to contemplate showing her mother love in the future. The words of John were still fresh in her mind, God's words, the words of love, *that we should love one another,* and as Leah approached the far corner of her block the sky grew much more beautiful, and she felt much warmer than she had only a moment before.

Chapter 6

THE START OF THE next semester came on a dazzling winter day. Snow had fallen during the previous night, and it scrunched beneath Leah's feet as she sauntered through campus. Ribbon clouds like long arching party streamers stretched high above her head, and it seemed as though the sky itself might fly away. Taking the sky in, Leah felt as though she were a cloud of her own, free and floating, the whims of the winds carrying her to destinations only the breezes knew for sure, as she drifted into her first class that morning.

Leah took a seat in the front row. Next to her sat a girl from the countryside named Elizabeth.

Elizabeth went by Beth, and if you called her Elizabeth you were sure to catch a glare. Leah took to Beth like a squirrel to a tree. Beth was a defender of God's truth, fresh from a farmland church on the outskirts of Nashville, Sojourn Creek Congregation, Leah had heard of it but never worshipped there, and theirs was a reputation for the doctrinaire. Typical of country churches, it had a fiery minister, passionate in his double-edged delivery of God's word, for he preached condemnation as much as salvation, and he had made a lasting impression on Beth. Problem was, Beth's impression was purely one-sided, focused conveniently on the Lord's forgiveness but without any of the reprehension or judgment. Beth never wasted a precious moment dwelling on God's potential for requital, and to her a Christian gal could have a rip-roaring good time as long as she defended God's basic truths and sought His forgiveness with a truly repentant heart.

Beth was also one of those girls most folks can't figure out; not quite an enigma, she wasn't sufficiently mysterious enough for that much speculation, and although she was country, no amount of country can account for that much simplicity and singular focus on being married. Beth wanted a family more than a dog wants a bone. Feeling practically ancient at eighteen, every primitive instinct in Beth coalesced into one elementary drive to get her a man before life passed her by.

Beth had always settled for guys below her station just to have somebody to call her own, and that was the incongruous part of her because nobody could understand why all her boyfriends had been so blessed ugly when she was so darn cute. A darling blond, buxom and curvy, Beth was as tempting as a hundred-dollar bill laying on a sidewalk at two in the morning, her face a collage of cheerleader dimples, strawberry cheeks, and laying-in-front-of-the-fire blue eyes. She smelled as fresh as the springtime air, her heart caring and honest, and her spirit a morning star rising over a homeland valley. She had the bravado of a heavyweight champion and the same determination to get her title, but worst of all was that you couldn't help but like her for it. Leah soon realized the moral compromises she made for Beth were a small price to pay for the rewards of their friendship.

Beth quickly became Leah's best friend, and for awhile they were inseparable. The first few weeks of the spring semester went by much faster than fall semester because Beth kept the action going like a night at the fights, being what a southerner calls a "hoot," always talking and giggling or laughing at some such thing, and she flirted with whatever jaunty boy passed by and with half the men twice her age.

Beth never did understand why Leah's style wasn't the same as hers, and one day she confronted Leah about it.

"Hey, we've been pals for weeks now, well onto a month, and you aren't the slightest bit boy crazy," Beth said disapprovingly. "That's never happened to me before. I rub off on everyone. You aren't old maidin' on me, are you?"

"What do you mean?" Leah asked.

"Like some sixty-year-old never been had, living alone down by a creek, with another old bag stopping by now and then, that's what."

Leah's eyes grew to planet size. "Beth, are you joshing me?" she said flustered, turning a bright neon red. She had never heard such talk before. "Why heavens no."

"And you better not like squares. I don't cotton to no squares."

Leah felt the flush go off her face. She should have been mad, but she suppressed a laugh instead. "You shouldn't worry none about that. I don't like squares," she said. "I have never gone for that type of guy. I'm attracted to athletes."

Beth clapped her hands together and they made an earsplitting, popping sound. "Now you're talking, girl," Beth said emphatically. "Baseball season starts soon, and we're gonna snag us some ballplayers. It's about time you came around."

"My gosh, you scared me half to death," Leah said, fanning her face. "Don't ever clap that loudly again. The deans will throw us out of here. How's our team here at school anyway? They any good?"

Beth rolled her eyes, then stared piercingly at her friend. "School? I'm not talking about these one-whisker boys walking around here," she said to Leah. "I'm talking about men, girl, real men: hairy and strong, with mounds of muscle and loads of cash. That's what I'm talking about. Nashville's got a pro team, one stop from the big leagues, and the majors pay big money. My friend Josie roped a stallion of a fella last year, only you and I don't look as good as Josie, and probably never will." Beth smiled a regret. "Heck, who am I kidding, we'll never be that pretty, but that's Josie and she's gone now, so good riddance to her." She paused for a minute and then came to it. "Anyhow, Josie had her pick of the litter, but you and me, well, we'll have to come up with a plan."

"What makes you think we can get us men?" Leah asked her. "We're only freshmen in college, eighteen years old, with no experience at this kind of thing. I've only had one boyfriend my whole life, for heaven's sake."

Beth stuck out her breasts like weapons. "Because we're cute, young, and almost willing," she said seductively. "Ballplayers want to hit home runs, and I'm betting a couple of them will marry us just to trot around the bases."

Leah's eyes were galaxies this time. "Marry us? Now what kind of talk is that for a good Christian girl?" Leah asked in dismay. "Man alive, Beth. You know, sometimes I wonder about you."

Beth rolled her eyes back into her head. "Oh brother, will you please relax? I'll be a virgin when I marry, just not by much. That's all God requires."

Leah was so flabbergasted she didn't know what to say.

"Well, you in or what?" Beth asked her friend impatiently. "They start ball practice in a month. We can't wait for the real games because by then it'll be too late."

Leah looked confused. Practice didn't sound nearly as enticing as a real game. "How come?" she asked.

A look of resignation came to Beth's face, and her words slid into the voice of experience. "The competition gets too brutal," she said despairingly. "The bleachers behind home plate turn into a blessed beauty pageant, girls strutting their stuff in two sizes too small, the hot nights giving 'em an excuse to show off their tits in all manner of raunchy get-ups, and each gal wearing more make-up than a whore working Millersville Flat. Most of them put out and some are bona fide sluts."

"Beth? No?"

"Heck yeah, girl. By summer, snatching a guy would be impossible. We gotta make an impression early or we'll never get seen, and hanging around after practice is the best way I know of to increase our odds."

Leah grew worried. "I don't know. If my mama finds out, it's a whipping for certain."

"Hey, if you leave it up to your mama you'll marry one of these goobers," Beth said, pointing to a slim guy wearing coke bottles for glasses, volcanic pimples sprouting up all over his face. The guy was reading a differential calculus book and sipping milk through a bent straw from a red and white milk carton, as homely as a peasant in first light. Beth whirled around and spotted another guy walking behind them near the library. She pointed him out to Leah. "Or like that clown there, carting around a stack of folders higher than Mount Everest and a note from his mother. I'm talking men here, girl. That guy you fell for, he was older, right?"

"Yeah, and what did that get me?" Leah asked, her face drooping.

Beth, however, could rally a sick pup to fetch a ball on a hot summertime afternoon. It was an especially endearing trait of hers. "One beau lost ain't the end of the world," she said encouragingly. "By July, you'll be so in love with another guy you won't remember that last loser. You told me once that day at Peabody Square, but I forgot his name. What was it anyway, Snake?"

"Blake."

"Same difference. Now get ready for a ballplayer, girl. I'm already thinking on something to tell your mama."

***

The first practice came on a rainy day that muddied up Winningham Park and whipped paper trash along the bottom of the outfield fence like a tornado in a garbage dump. Lightning flashed in the distance. A Laura Lou's Dairy sign had faded into the pale outfield wall, the rest of the wall blank of writing and in desperate need of some sponsors, and probably a third of the wall's planks were missing or lying flat on the ground next to what remained of the fence. Out past the stadium, the wind had bent the flagpole in half and was tearing up Tennessee's state flag into a tattered rag.

"Laura Lou's still there?" Leah asked, shivering. "I haven't heard about them since grade school."

"Must be," Beth answered.

Leah waxed nostalgic, and Beth was brought back, too. "They used to do routes near my folk's farm," Beth said, remembering the time. "My mother said the milk tasted like it had metal shavings in it. Laura Lou's got no business from my family, that I can tell you."

The two girls sat close together for extra warmth against the bite of the wind. The lightning flashed closer.

Leah smiled a sly smile as something dawned on her. "Hey, wait a minute. Y'all were country folk. You told me you grew up on a farm. Didn't you have a cow or two for milking?"

Beth bumped up against Leah in a joking way. "I call it a farm, but it really wasn't," she said apologetically. "About the only thing my daddy grew was turnips and squash. He made his living as a parcel driver. The chickens we had were more like house pets, and I can't remember a one of them ever getting killed for supper. They all died of old age. One old rooster outlived half my relatives. Some farm we had, huh?" Even on a cloudy day Beth's blue eyes sparkled and her dimples deepened the wider she grinned.

"Pitiful. That's what I'd say," Leah said teasing her.

"Yeah, pitiful sounds about right. Forgive me?"

"Sure. Your secret is safe with me."

The team came out and did stretching exercises, their uniforms flapping wildly in the gusty winds. After ten minutes passed, the players broke into different squads, one squad hitting to ten guys standing along the outfield grass, another running wind sprints near the wall, and the last group throwing effortlessly behind first base. Leah and Beth watched them. Bats smacking and gloves popping filled the air with the sounds of baseball. Coaches barked out orders, the rain falling intermittently on their heads, light as granules in the wind, then heavy as sheets in the pauses, the lightning drawing nearer while thunder rattled the bleachers and shook the backstop.

Leah noticed someone in the last bunch of players, a pitcher, left-handed with a powerfully built upper body, fairly tall, throwing the ball so hard his catcher had to periodically remove his mitt to shake out his stinging fingers. The pitcher's profile revealed a prominent nose that contributed to his good looks, his skin dark and his face handsome, his eyes flashing through the distance and smiling on their own. He had full lips and perfect white teeth, his hair wavy and black, and watching him, Leah allowed herself to wonder what it would be like to kiss him.

"What you looking at?" Beth asked her friend.

"Golly, that guy is gorgeous," Leah said. "You see him standing over there?" Leah pointed the pitcher out for her.

Beth squinted and then nodded. "Sure do," she said eagerly, happy her friend was finally coming around. "He's one of the best looking ones on the field."

"One of?"

"You like him, don't you?"

Leah frowned at such a suggestion. "Why, I don't even know him."

"Yeah, but I bet you'd like to."

Leah turned to her friend, a mischievous look on her face. "Well now, you know what? Maybe I might. I just might after all."

Beth wasn't about to give Leah any credit for an attitude she should have had all along, and she snorted a snicker. "I think it's high time, that's what I think. But we don't have us dates yet, so get off your high horse, Princess. We're a long way from being married."

After another hour or so, the manager gathered the team around and called for a three-inning practice game. The rain and thunder had let up, but the lightning still flashed without drawing any closer. The winds died down and that seemed to keep the lightning at bay. The coaches motioned the pitchers off to the side, the guy Leah noticed standing furthest away, off by himself, special like. He soon zipped up his windbreaker all the way to his neck, fiddling with his cap and adjusting his socks. The scrimmage began, but it seemed that he was finished for the day.

"Beth, why isn't that cutie allowed to play?"

"I'm not sure," Beth replied. "But I can tell you like him."

Leah sighed. "There you go again. I don't even know him, but he sure is handsome. What a smile."

Beth couldn't have cared less about the pitcher. "I got my eyes on that little fella running out to left field," she said, her sapphire eyes following a small guy with sandy hair and skinny legs. The guy was frail looking, his gait that of a newborn colt.

"Him?" Leah said in amazement. The guy was plain sorry, even from that distance. "Well, who else around here might know something?"

A man seated one row behind the two girls, wearing a wrinkled tweed sport coat, loose tie and crinkled white shirt stained brown around the collar, was busily scribbling notes on a yellow pad. A potbelly hung out over his trousers. He seemed indifferent and devoid of life, definitely withdrawn. When he glanced up, Leah saw that his face was a maze of gin blossoms and that his eyes were tired and spiritless.

"Say, do you know why that one pitcher has a coat on? It doesn't look like he's gonna get to pitch today," Leah asked the man.

"Sure do," the man replied insipidly. "The manager wants the ball in play today to evaluate some of the new talent. If Boletti pitches, it's a game of catch because nobody can hit the guy. He throws the ball too stinkin' hard."

"That's the fella's name, Bocetti?" Leah asked politely.

"No, Boletti. Vic Boletti," the man said. He was slurring his words. "He won't be around here long. The big club will call him up before August. Count on it."

Beth chimed in. "Are you with the team, Mister? Sure seems like you know a lot about the players. Mind telling us your name?"

"Does it matter?" the man replied hollowly. "I'm not with the team. I'm just a sportswriter." The man spoke directly to Beth, but his eyes were far off and lazy. Leah felt instantly sorry for him; she wondered what could have caused him to surrender to a life of alcohol.

The man mustered a reserve of enthusiasm. "Interesting your friend here should ask about Boletti, though," he went on, still looking at Beth. "I'm here to do a story on him. If he doesn't get hurt or get into trouble with gals, he'll be an All-Star someday, maybe make the Hall of Fame. Never seen a guy throw smoke like this guy. Curveball, slider, plus a wicked change. Come out and watch him; he's worth the price of the ticket."

"Is he a Nashville boy?" Leah asked.

The man's eyes found Leah's face. Leah could tell he was plenty drunk. "You're joking, right?" he said to her, finally locating her face. "Does he look like anybody you've ever seen from Nashville?"

"Guess not, huh?" Leah said, as Beth shot her a glance.

"Boletti, he's from California," the sportswriter continued. "Played out west two years ago, was the league MVP in class A ball, in Modesto or Visalia, I can't recall which town, and that's something when you're a pitcher. First guy in some time to do that. Cincy should have called him up then, they could have used another lefty in the pen, but that's Cincy, always afraid to rush a young arm after that Grigsby kid tore up his shoulder a few years back."

Leah turned 'round to face the playing field again and the writer went back to jotting things down on the notepad behind her. Beth huddled over to Leah before whispering to her. "Did you hear that?" she said excitedly. "From California. You still want to look at college boys?"

Leah turned back around toward the man and ignored her friend sitting beside her. "Mister, can I ask you just one more question?"

The man looked up from his notepad. His pause told Leah it was fine to ask him whatever was on her mind.

Leah swallowed hard. She knew Beth might not understand what followed, as she spoke to the man in a sweet, melodious voice. "You seem so nice, I was wondering if you attend church services anywhere? It was especially kind of you to answer our questions today, and I just thought it would be nice to have you attend services with us sometime. We're students at Christian College here in town and there's an on-campus service every Sunday at ten in the morning. We'd love to have you join us for the worship hour."

The man seemed touched by Leah's invitation. He set his pad and pencil down on the bleacher, as his wayward eyes found their focus. "No," he replied forthrightly, "I haven't attended church services in many years, not at least since the divorce. You see, my wife left me back in 1950, said she couldn't take me anymore, and I guess I, well, I guess I kind of lost my faith after I lost her."

Leah reached into her coat pocket. She pulled a bulletin from chapel service and gave it to him. "Well, Beth and I would love to have you attend church service with us. The address and phone number are on the bulletin there. Afterward, we could take you to lunch as a thank you for your kindness today. It'd be our treat. There's a fish place near campus that has the best catfish and cornbread you ever tasted in your life. And if you wouldn't mind, we could pick your brain about baseball over lunch, since it's obvious you know a lot about the game."

The man took the bulletin in his hands. "Thank you," he said with a smile. He looked the bulletin over. "Now I best get back to writing my story."

Out of view, Beth took Leah's hand a gave it a gentle squeeze. "That was beautiful," she whispered to Leah. "You did the Lord proud. Now get back to baseball because that pitcher you like is starting to make his way over here."

***

Vic Boletti made his way over to the stands where Leah and Beth were seated. He took his sweet time getting there, scuffling dirt, kicking a dirt clod, adjusting his cap to his liking, and once bending over to pick up a discarded bat before casually tossing it back toward the dugout. He looked like a stray dog contemplating a handout: unsure, wary, circling, but hungry enough to take a chance, and he finally approached the two girls with a broad smile and disarming yawn.

"Hi, girls," he said in a deep voice, "are you here because you know one of the players?" His face was even handsomer up close. Leah couldn't take her eyes off him.

"No, but we'd like to," Beth said impulsively.

An awkward silence followed, and after what seemed like an eternity Leah mustered an explanation. "What my friend here means is that we don't understand the game, but we'd like to learn more about America's favorite pastime. We're college girls. We want to understand some of these popular sports, to round ourselves out, not just study sixteen hours every day. We're thinking baseball might become a hobby of ours. If we knew a player or two, we might get good seats and learn about the game."

"I can get you great seats if you want them," the pitcher said, gaining ground with every word. He looked pleased with himself and more at ease. "But first you ought to come to our get-together we're having next week. All the players will be there, some with their girlfriends or friends or members of their family and whatnot, and the local Boosters Club is sending a group of people they tell me is a lot of fun. I'll introduce you around to the guys I know. Think you can you make it?"

"Are you crazy?" Beth shot out, faster than light travels. "Of course we'll be there. Who could turn down an invitation like that?"

Vic gazed at Leah. "You want to come, too, don't you?" he asked her courteously. "I promise you'll have a good time. Skip and the coaches will be there so there won't be any trouble, if that's what you're worried about."

"Who's Skip?" Beth asked.

"Skip, he's the manager," Vic replied. Vic's hair was razor cut on the sides and his baseball cap had slid down to his ears. Although manly, he looked like a puppy boy. "You'll like Skip; everybody does."

"Well, I guess we can come," Leah said indecisively. Beth glared at her so intensely it almost drove a hole through her, and Leah knew it was now or never. There was no choice but to agree to attend. "Sure, I'd love to come," she said agreeably. "But I can't stay out too late; I've got to study. I'll be glad to go for a soda or two."

"Study?" Beth said, stupefied. Her laser was still burning Leah's face as she slowly returned her eyes to Vic, letting the last of her glaring ray singe Leah for effect. "Please ignore my friend here; she's delirious. And I may kill her before the day's over."

"Here," Vic said, removing a piece of paper from the pocket of his warm-up jacket. "These are the directions to the restaurant. I'll get another copy from one of the guys. Next Friday night, seven-thirty, and dress casually. It's nothing fancy. The name of the joint is Johnny's and they say the food is delicious. Bring a few friends if you like."

Beth was so excited she actually glowed.

"By the way," Vic said, "I'm Vic. Vic Boletti. I pitch for this team. It's my first year here in Nashville, and I don't know any places in town to hang out yet. I'm hoping you can help me in that." Vic had a gentleness to his words, and they made Leah feel at ease. It seemed odd for someone so handsome to be so nice and thoughtful.

"Where are you from?" Leah asked, playing dumb, surprised she beat out Beth with a question of her own.

"Oh, I'm from California," Vic said proudly. "The Bay Area to be exact. I played in Florida for a few weeks at the beginning of last season, near the resorts of Captiva and Sanibel, and I spent a month in the Carolinas two years ago. One time I even got down to Louisiana for some fishing in the bayou country. Now there's a place."

"Well, none of them amount to a hill of beans compared to Nashville," Leah said, showing some pride for her hometown she didn't know she had. "You'll like it here. I'm Leah, and this here is Beth. Next week, we'd love to hear all about California, if you wouldn't mind filling us in."

The thunder had stopped. A stocky player with a barrel chest and two continents for shoulders, older and darker than Vic, hat twisted carelessly sideways, shouted out to Vic in a booming voice from behind the third-base line. It echoed through the stadium like a yell through a mountain ravine. "Hey Boletti, you want to play some catch or bore those two girls to death? Skip wasn't talking about you when he said be nice to the fans."

Another player hollered from atop the dugout in a resounding voice. "You tell him, Vince. You gotta catch him, baby, so he's your property. Get him out to the bullpen where he can't do any harm."

A third player, also massive, his jacket off and his jersey wet with rain, smiled a cocky smile and then yelled out from across the third base side. "There's no beach here, Boletti. Those are southern belles; they don't fall for that sand crap."

Vince roared in laughter, then pivoted to face the last guy who had shouted out. "Hey, Gunocho, there's another one we can call him: 'sand crap.' Like a sand crab, only sand crap." Vince wheeled around to face Vic's direction again. He yelled loudly for all to hear. "Hey sand crap, leave the girls alone, will you?"

That did it. An hilarious chorus of 'sand crap' rang out from the dugout and most of the players in the field fell over in laughter. The little guy Beth had noticed was on the ground rolling around like a playful dog. He couldn't stop laughing, the tears streaming down his ruddy face as he pounded the outfield grass with his fist to call off the laughing gods, and that made the other players chuckle even louder. Any semblance of baseball practice vanished like a runaway car off a cliff, so one of the coaches, a portly guy with an enormous bald head, suddenly put an end to all the hooting and hollering. "All right, let's play some ball," the coach bellowed. "We're a ball club, not a comedy routine."

Vic had to leave. "See you both on Friday. I've got to go now," he said, backpedaling, grinning as he retreated. Despite the ribbing from his teammates, he looked pleased. "I'm looking forward to it."

Beth was a jumping bean, ecstatically waving her arms, laughing the laugh of newly crowned champions, the joy on her face so sweet and so happy that Leah would remember it forever. "I told you we'd get us dates," Beth said, squirming with delight. "Oh Leah, we're in now, just like I said we'd be. What did I tell you, girl? Did I not tell you this would happen? Why, we're gonna have the best summer of our lives."

"Lord Almighty, Beth. All that happened is we got invited to a party," Leah said, downplaying it.

"I'm gonna get me that little one," Beth said scheming, ignoring her. "He's mine. I liked the way he laughed."

Chapter 7

FRIDAY NIGHT CAME AFTER two days of uninterrupted downpours. It rained so hard Friday afternoon that Leah fretted Margaret wouldn't let her go out that evening because the roads were too slick to drive. Then the clouds blew past and the weather turned clear and cold as the sky welcomed a bright full moon; fortunately, the roads didn't ice over and the wind died down to a mild swaying of the treetops.

When Leah and Beth arrived at Johnny's forty-five minutes late, the place was jammed full of people. Photographs of local country and jazz singers hung on the walls. The floor, made of wood planks, was rotted from years of spillage and wear. Ceiling fans did little to cut through a pall of cigarette smoke that hung out over the main lobby like a low thundercloud over a plain, but through the haze Leah made out a large group of people wearing red baseball caps gathered around two large picnic-style tables overflowing with buckets of fried chicken and bowls of mashed potatoes and gravy.

"You want to go back there?" Beth asked Leah excitedly, pointing toward the tables.

"No, let's wait a bit and see if we see Vic. I'm sure he'll be here," Leah said.

Just then, Leah felt a firm hand under her left elbow. It was Vic, who had been watching for the pair, and he tapped Beth on the shoulder with his other hand as a friendly hello.

"Let me take you back," he said smiling. Even in the low light, his teeth flashed a pearly glimmer. Vic shouldered a path, and the two girls followed him through the maze of people toward the back of the restaurant.

Vic led the girls to the two large picnic tables. Breezy chatter died down to a subdued murmuring as the three of them arrived in a seeming showcase. Everyone looked them over. Leah and Beth's hair both had the waxy sheen of a new and pampered washing and both were beautiful in their cardigan skirts and pink wool sweaters. Vic introduced the girls around proudly, but before he could finish the introductions one small fella squirted through the throng like a pumpkin seed through oily fingers. A diminutive guy, he had hopeful anticipation written all over his mottled face, his features small for a man, his nose pug and tiny, and Leah recognized him as the scanty guy who had laughed so uncontrollably at the practice that day, the same one Beth had set her sights on. His name was Tommy, and he was immediately taken with Beth. Tommy wasn't handsome or cute, rather plain looking, with thin oily hair, trashy even, like he was from the poor side of town, and his teeth were set crooked in his mouth and stained from chewing tobacco.

But after five minutes Leah felt ashamed for judging him so poorly, for he was as nice as they came and a gentleman besides. Tommy, like Vic, had a genuineness about him, generous and thoughtful, offering to get Leah a plate before anyone else had the chance to wait on her, including Vic, and he refilled Leah's soda three times without being asked, waiting on Beth like a servant as well, and taking his eyes off the blond country beauty only when it was obvious he'd been staring too long.

After a few more minutes of standing around, Leah had to find out more about California, so she went to stand next to Vic as he was talking to one of the other ballplayers. The crowd in Johnny's had thickened past capacity, and with all the shifting bodies Leah lost track of who was who and whether they were with the ball club or unaffiliated. The Booster Club had brought along a bevy of bimbos, all wearing tight fitting sweaters and bright shiny lipstick, determined to grab a ballplayer for a husband before one of the other girls did the same. They were easy to spot and pissing Beth off something terrible, who was glaring at them like a boxer at a weigh-in.

Vic bent over courteously to hear Leah's question as soon as the other player quit his rambling about a double play ball that he booted for an error that afternoon.

"You're from California, right?" Leah shouted over the noise.

Before Vic could answer some of the ballplayers standing nearby started whistling and shaking their hands up and down, making an "oooh" sound, bowing at the same time, like they were in front of a great king or something. Their actions seemed almost rehearsed. Soon, they were all doing it, even some of the coaches.

"California Boy," one of them yelled out, screaming so loudly that everyone in Johnny's stopped their conversations and turned toward Vic in unison. Most wore the gleeful looks of a momentous occasion in the making. Even the pall of smoke seemed to waft over to where Vic stood.

"West Coast Flash," said another ballplayer, equally as earsplitting and in mock respect. Soon, more guys joined in, the bimbos circling around Vic like hookers at a bordello, all smiling and posing themselves for a chance at him. Some were flat out gorgeous, and a few were the kind of women who rarely woke up in their own bed the following morning and who weren't afraid to show it the night before.

"Pacific Vic," still another guy chimed in, seizing the opportunity. The guy was laughing so hard Leah thought he'd crack his face wide open. He looked so funny Leah began to laugh along with him.

Through Vic's olive skin, he began to blush a beautiful burgundy color and his eyes flashed twice their usual gleam. Though he stood straight, inside he was wincing with anticipation of still more jesting to come.

"Palm trees, girls on his arms, riding the waves at Santa Cruz," another ballplayer thundered. "Ooh, la la, ooh, la la."

Vince couldn't resist one final shot. "Hey sand crap," he called out loudly, the crowd awaiting his every word. "You still putting those two girls to sleep with glory stories from the beach?"

Johnny's roared.

Vic, now a brighter shade of red than before, turned his back on the crowd and spoke quietly to Leah and Beth. He seemed used to being ribbed by the guys. "Sorry about that," he said, getting more subdued with every word. "They can't hit my fastball, so they look for every chance they can to get even. To answer your question, I'm from Oakland, near San Francisco, in northern California."

The crowd returned to their conversations. Someone nudged Leah into Vic as they pushed past, then two more people followed on their way back to the restrooms, laughing as they grazed by Vic, one guy patting him sympathetically on the back. To keep Leah from being jostled or drifting away, Vic held Leah's shoulders firmly in one spot with his strong hands. Leah later remembered feeling safe and protected, and she remembered liking the feeling as well as being amazed at the power of Vic's muscularity.

That much captivation meant Beth needed to move on. She meandered over to Tommy and they talked together for the next thirty minutes while the crowd swelled and the air thickened into a brownish, hazy soup. To stay together through the undulations of the crowd, Beth took Tommy's hand and held onto it for support. Squished together, Tommy was eventually forced to rest his arms on Beth's shoulders, just to have someplace to put them, and pressed together as they were Beth wrapped her arms around his waist while her breasts massaged Tommy's chest in the suffusion of Johnny's.

Leah and Vic stood together and braced themselves against the surges of the crowd. Their eyes met in a quiet moment. Leah had to say something to end the awkwardness. "By the way, I'm very impressed you're from California," she said. "I think California must be the grandest place in the world."

"Why is that?" Vic asked.

Leah seemed taken aback. "Well, from everything I've ever heard, California is the land of opportunity," she said. "It's Hollywood, the movies, the land of Steinbeck and Jack London, y'all have artists and poets and wide open spaces, it's free and untamed and more beautiful than anyplace else on Earth. I've seen pictures of it. I've also heard that living is easy on the coast, that being an individual with your own ideas isn't necessarily a bad thing to be."

"Being an individual is wrong here?"

"You bet it is. Tennessee is the capitol of conformity. That's why I hate it here so much. Too many judgmental people and charlatans. You talk about your hypocrites?" Leah shook her head and closed her eyes. Vic saw that she remembered something painful. Then she went on. "Why, the culture here will spit oaths before God Almighty to convince you sugar is poison and poison is a delicacy. I know, I've seen these frauds in action myself. You don't stand a chance with these naysayers."

Vic looked skeptical. Leah noticed his look. "You think I'm lying?" she asked him. "The backwardness of this place can kill you if you let it. The South is a smothering blanket. Folks like it that way. They do everything in their power to preserve the old ways and keep you in line. Makes you feel that nothing you do is important. I've often wondered if anything I do counts in the end. Well, try finding yourself while you're struggling for air. I'm telling you, living here is like being buried alive. I rather liked it as a child, but as I grew older I learned all about Nashville's true colors. My spirit cries to be someplace else, part of me has since I can first remember, but exactly where I don't know. I figure the coast is so pretty it's as good as any."

Vic seemed astounded. Then he spoke to Leah in a manner of straightforward affinity. "Sounds like you may need to get to California someday. But don't be fooled. The living isn't that easy anywhere. There's hypocrites everywhere you turn. California just has a big reputation for freedom and equality. I've learned that big reputations are not always well deserved. Rarely do I feel regret, but the few times I have, it involved people who were two-faced and pretended to be something they're not, and California has plenty of those types, too, don't kid yourself."

***

At a few minutes past ten the group began to break up. Empty pitchers, dirty napkins, and discarded red-mesh chicken baskets littered the ground, the tables sopping sticky wet with beer foam and dribble.

"We have curfew," Vic said to Leah, "and we have to stick to it. There's a practice game tomorrow, and the coaches want us out of here. But let me walk you out to your car. This neighborhood didn't look so hot when we drove in."

"Oh, you don't have to do that," Leah insisted. "Beth and I can manage. We're big girls."

Beth and Tommy had come within earshot during the last surge of the crowd. Beth's makeup was smudged on Tommy's team jacket like a cake mix, the two had been pressed together during the closeness of the night, each of them loving every minute of it, and both their faces were the definition of glee. "Tommy, let's walk the girls out," Vic yelled over to his buddy, ignoring Leah's answer and waving his hand in a come over gesture.

Beth and Tommy came over together, holding hands and leaning on one another like two buildings after an earthquake. "That's right, we got curfew," Vic reiterated to his pal, as Tommy stood disappointed before him, a plea for indulgence in his eyes. Vic gently grabbed his buddy's shoulder for reassurance. "We'll see them again, little man. Count on it."

"We'd better," Tommy said.

"Now be a gentleman and help me walk these ladies out."

As Beth drove down the street in her daddy's pickup truck, Leah looked out at the sidewalk in front of Johnny's and watched as Vic put Tommy in a playful headlock and half twisted him to the ground. Both guys were laughing so hard neither had any strength left for a good tussle. The moon shone down on the street in a silvery aura, Vic and Tommy's bodies silhouetted against the row of street buildings like shadow dancers on a stage, and Leah saw the two ballplayers exhale forcefully into the night, their breathy puffs trailing off into the air high above their heads. The two jocks shared a handshake, and Leah watched them head back into the throng standing in front of Johnny's to join the rest of their team.

Chapter 8

ON MONDAY AT SCHOOL all Beth wanted to do was talk about Tommy.

"No guy, especially a ballplayer, is going to ask for more of your time unless he wants to get serious with you," Beth began happily. "I can tell you that much. And he wants me to go to all his games."

"Why is that so serious?" Leah asked skeptically.

"Because, silly, if I go to all his games, he won't have a chance to be with any other girls, now will he?"

"I guess not," Leah said dubiously. "At least none around Nashville. What about when the team is on the road?"

Beth's happy bubble had expanded like the early universe, and no one was going to burst her dream. "I'll trust him. I know he wants to go steady soon," she said confidently. Her sugar cute face was full of joy and her nose twitched with satisfied excitement.

Leah was amazed. "Steady? Geez, I was hoping we'd have more time together, not less. I want us to be friends forever, and I'd sure hate to see a couple of guys get in the way. You sure about going steady? Are you ready for that? I mean, so seriously involved so soon?"

"Are you joshing me? That's what I want more than anything else in the world," Beth replied. "What's the point of getting a guy if you don't get him to go steady with you?"

"What about having some fun, that's what," Leah said, reprimanding her friend.

Beth grew sarcastically Southern. She sounded like one of those spoiled debutantes on the porch at Tara. "Why, is that all you want with Vic, sweet princess, some little ol' fun? Why, I bet you haven't stopped thinking about him, now have you?"

"Beth."

"What, Princess?"

"Beth."

Beth returned to her usual talk. "Oh, all right. But give me a break, will ya. I saw you two the other night, leaning and bumping on each other like two frogs on a mud bank, you batting your eyelashes at him like a vixen and him flexing like a muscle man. I was there, you know, I saw it myself. I might be from the sticks, but I ain't stupid."

"I thought about him some," Leah said nonchalantly.

Beth frowned derisively at her friend. "Yeah, I buy that. You're going to get as serious as me, starting as soon as he calls you."

Leah sunk her head into her hands.

"That's right, I gave him your number," Beth said unconditionally. "Make up whatever excuse you have to for your mother, but you promised me way back when that you were in on this."

Leah looked up at her friend in surrender. "I know I did. But what am I going to tell my mother?"

Beth smiled a country wide smile. "Oh, I don't know. Something devious as all heck. Now listen, girl, what are we going to wear?"

***

On Saturday morning a freshness was in the air. Walton had gone fishing early and Margaret was up with the sun, building a booth for a bake sale over at Elder Price's house to benefit the orphans at Forest Green Home.

Leah read the sports section of the newspaper for the first time in her life. On the front page was a huge article about the Vols, with a picture of Vic atop the column. Nothing was mentioned about Tommy. According to the writer, Vic Boletti was the best prospect Cincinnati had and the finest pitcher in the minor leagues. Teams from all over the country were trying to trade for him. The article said he had a strong arm and a muscular build with a good bat for a pitcher, but that he could benefit from one more year in the minors to work on his breaking pitch. The next year, the writer was certain, Vic would be a full-time major league pitcher, possibly even an All Star. Vic was twenty-three years old, born and raised in California, in Oakland, and his was a fine family, a mom, a dad, and two younger sisters, and he played the guitar and sang in a band back home called the Four Moons. Talk was the group might someday cut a record. His only flaw was that he grew frustrated when things didn't seem to go as planned. He liked to travel and his dream trip was to the islands of Hawaii. He wanted to be married and have a family someday, and he liked to hunt and fish and play cards with the guys after games.

Leah took the article and hid it under a pile of spare blankets in the corner of the closet. Margaret never removed more than the first few comforters of the stack, in even the coldest of winters, so Leah figured her secret was safe as long as her mother didn't get a burr to launder the entire heap or straighten the entire closet.

***

On Sunday after church, Vic called shortly after four in the afternoon. Walton was just back from a trip to Sam's Bend, his favorite fishing hole on the Tennessee River, catching up on his sleep on the couch, his feet perched up on the armrest. Margaret was busy in the kitchen humming a church hymn while she made out a list of sick children for the women's group to visit come next Thursday evening.

That day, Vic had pitched a shutout, whiffing fourteen Barons from Birmingham, plus he had two doubles to knock in three runs to help his own cause, and the Vols won the game 4–0. He was in a great mood. Margaret picked up the phone on the first ring, surprised at the deep male voice on the other end of the line, but she summoned Leah immediately and slipped out of the kitchen quietly to sit in the family room within earshot of whatever was said.

After a few minutes, Leah gently hung up the phone and began to walk gingerly toward her room without once looking over in Margaret's direction or saying a word.

"Who was that, Honey?" Margaret asked her daughter sweetly, too sweetly for any good to come of it.

Leah did her best to keep walking. "Oh, just a guy named Vic, that's all."

"Vic? Do I know a Vic? He doesn't sound very familiar. No, I'm sure I don't know any Vic."

Walton woke up from his nap. "What's all the ruckus?" he asked groggily.

"Go on back to sleep," Margaret commanded him. "And get your smelly feet off my couch." Walton lowered his feet to the floor and blinked his eyes like a machine gun in an effort to wake himself up, but he dozed off again with a nasally snore.

"Who is this Vic, child?" Margaret insisted.

Leah had stopped in her tracks. "He's a friend of the Christian guy Beth and I know through Corrine, Mama. The nice guy on the team. Remember, I told you about Corrine," Leah said reassuringly.

"What's this Vic calling for?"

"Just to talk and ask me out, I think. But he sounds more interested in being my friend than in dating me. Shyest guy I ever met."

Margaret was an inquisitor general summoning an army of investigators. She was about to begin a full interrogation when Leah preempted it with one of her sweetest glances; it was the same look the neighbor ladies used to talk about in their homes at night when guests brought up the subject of Margaret's girls, that vulnerably innocent look a young girl has when she asks the vet if her sick puppy will live.

"He's a nice guy and a perfect gentleman," Leah said delicately. "He's a star on the team, and it seems very kind of him to call me. I told him you and I hadn't been feeling well, what with the flu bug we had a week ago, he was particularly concerned about you, Mama, and he asked me if you were feeling any better."

Margaret relaxed a bit. She remembered Leah saying something on the phone about her mama feeling fine. "Did he really ask about me?" Margaret inquired.

"Yes, Mother, he did. That's the kind of guy he is."

"I don't know, Sugar, a ballplayer? Is he a Christian?"

"Why, he most certainly is. I wouldn't talk to him if he wasn't. And he has the most wonderful qualities about him: He loves to make other people laugh, and he thinks of others before he thinks of himself. You talk about your Christian examples? Oh, Mama, there's nothing to worry about. I don't even like him very much. There's a tall blond guy at school I have the worst crush on. You might have heard me speak of him: Stephen Rule. His mama is Missy Rule from the *Etiquette Minute* on television, but he's got a steady and she's a real pill. I don't know what he sees in that gadabout, but with any luck they'll break up soon and he'll be free of her. Until then, I need someone to go out with. The school has some socials coming up and this Vic is positively harmless. All we'd ever be is friends."

"Well, as long as he's a good Christian, you can go out with him. But that's all. And I'd like to meet him. I insist on meeting any boy who wants to take you out on car dates. But you've done such a good job with your chores and your schoolwork lately, I guess I don't see the harm in it none. And leave the tall blond fella and his girlfriend alone; don't get mixed up in the middle of that. A good Christian woman doesn't covet another girl's fella."

"I won't, Mama. I promise."

***

The next weekend Leah went on her first date with Vic without Beth and Tommy at her side. They met again at Johnny's. Leah drove herself because she had to drop Margaret off at a church banquet on account of Margaret spraining her foot falling off a ladder in the yard; some deacon's wife was to take Margaret home from there, and it just made more sense to meet Vic at the restaurant. Walton was in Kentucky on another fishing trip so Vic couldn't meet Leah's folks that night anyway, and Margaret thought it best for Leah and her date to meet in public rather than at home alone where the neighbors might suspect the worst.

Johnny's was next to empty except for a few older couples having dinner and smoking at the end of their meals. It was steak night. The kitchen sizzled with the sound of choice sirloin on the grill, while a jukebox played the maudlin horns of Glenn Miller, the Dorsey Brothers, Harry James, and some bluesy sax player Leah had never heard before, but that Vic knew well. At the night of the Booster Club dinner, the music in Johnny's had been rock 'n' roll and country, but now it was big band and wartime melodies. Vic explained that he knew the songs because his mother had often listened to the radio during the war while his father worked nights at the naval air station in Alameda.

Vic wore a black pullover sweater over a silky gray shirt and his black hair was up high and dreamy. He looked like some producer's next movie star. But he stood back a ways, uncomfortable and distant, which was clearly not his style or his manner. Something was clearly on his mind and troubling him.

"I can't believe this is the same place," Leah said, trying to ease into a conversation.

Vic disregarded her comment. "I'm not agreeing to this ever again," he said. "A gentleman arrives at a girl's house, meets her parents, spends a little time with her and her family, and together they drive off in his car on their date for the evening."

Leah was relieved that was all that was troubling him. "Oh that," she said nonchalantly. "We would have, but my daddy's gone fishing, and my mama is at a church banquet. Besides, you may not want to see me again after I tell you how horrible my mama is about me dating a guy. But I hope you do."

Leah was suddenly struck with the memory of their last conversation when Vic had mentioned he wanted to discuss something with her when they were next alone. "I'm so sorry," she said apologetically. "You have something you want to talk to me about. Let's hear what you have to say first, shall we?"

Vic stiffened and felt an anxious perspiration dampen his body. He hadn't thought his time would come so soon. "I guess I should just come out and tell you," he said shyly, with a fretful grimace.

"My sister Marian says that's the best way to speak your mind," Leah said, encouraging him. She tucked her hair back behind her ears. "Just come out and say it. You'll feel much better when you do."

Vic squirmed like a worm on a hook in a pond full of hungry bass. The entire time the two of them had been standing, but the hostess soon came over and took them to a quiet booth near a side window that looked out over a lonely sidewalk. That bought Vic some time.

"Here's you a menu," the hostess said with a smile. "Enjoy your dinner."

The hostess walked back to the front of the restaurant without turning around.

"Well?" Leah asked, unfolding her napkin. She smelled the appetizing aroma of grilled onions and sizzling steak, and her stomach gurgled in anticipation.

"I've been doing some thinking," Vic started, "And I'd like to run a thought by you."

"Fine by me."

"You, uh, you ever know when you haven't been feeling right?"

"Yes," Leah said, trying to encourage him. "Many times."

Outside the window, cars passed by; the movement of the lights caused Leah to look up at the street. A flashing sign across the way, minus a few light bulbs, almost spelled out Travis Place Bar. A drunk fell into the street, lying face down on the concrete until a bartender came out and propped him up against a lamppost. After that, the guy took to yelling obscenities. The bartender must have called the police because a squad car came in no time and two cops folded the guy into the back seat and took him away without handcuffs or a scuffle. A light rain fell outside as Leah and Vic watched two pedestrians pass by where the drunk had been, both laughing heartily and shaking their heads. Soon, they ducked into another restaurant across the street and disappeared. The commotion over, Leah and Vic's eyes met again, Leah thinking how wonderful it was to be out with a guy like Vic and not with someone like the vulgar drunk in the street. Vic inhaled the deepest breath of his life and began.

"I have a girl at home that I don't want to see anymore, back in California," he rattled off quickly, snapping Leah back into the present. His words sounded more like a recitation than an impromptu conversation. "She's a sweet girl, my parents like her a lot, but it's never felt quite right for me. At one time I thought I might marry her, but once I started traveling, playing pro ball, I knew I couldn't be her husband. She still thinks we might end up together, but after being on the road these last few years, there's no way, no way, I could ever marry her. Especially now."

Vic sat there, groping for the right words to say. He hadn't done badly already. Leah leaned across the table to make it easier for him. Surprising to herself, she did not feel hurt or insulted that he had a girl at home, more curious than anything else.

Vic paused a moment to gather his thoughts.

"What I mean to say," Vic suddenly blurted out, "is that when you travel, and you're a ballplayer, you meet a lot of people. The South, just about all of it, has more beautiful women than anyplace I've ever been in my life, and some of them aren't bashful, if you catch my drift. So I've dated plenty. I haven't been cheating on my girl at home, since I told her I was going to see other girls while I was playing ball, and for as long as nothing ever happened with anybody else, like me falling for somebody, I felt it was okay to continue on that way. But maybe it's not fair to her or to me. I mean, what's the point, right?"

"I suppose so," Leah answered, confused.

"Anyway," Vic explained, "being a ballplayer has kept me from liking someone because I'm always going from town to town. Having a relationship with a guy like me is difficult to say the least. I was content with that, too, until—"

The waitress brought some ice water.

"Until what?" Leah asked as soon as the waitress left.

Vic was one step from the end of the plank. He closed his eyes and sighed a sigh for the ages. "Okay," he said, with a hint of apology in his voice. "I haven't been able to stop thinking about you. From the beginning, from the very first time I saw you in the stands, that's how it's been for me. You're so young, but I know what I know, and I've been around long enough to know more. I've always been confident in anything I do, except for this, and my insecurity here tells me it's the real deal. So I guess we might as well discuss what we're going to do about it because it won't go away. I've tried to make it stop."

Leah's jaw dropped. She blinked hard. *Is this happening? Is he talking about me?* A light rain fell outside and the street went another shade deeper of gray. *Is he kidding me? My gosh, he's got to be kidding me.*

"Why me?" was all she finally managed to say.

"I have no idea," Vic said honestly. Leah's eyes finally joined his, but her face was as emotionless as a concrete slab. "I can't figure it out," he went on. "But I want you to know I can be faithful on the road, and in a few years, if we're still seeing each other, then we could talk about maybe having some kind of a life together. You do want a future with someone, don't you?"

"Yes, I do," Leah said automatically, unsure if she wanted it with Vic. She hadn't known what else to say at that moment.

"Well then, it's settled," Vic said, relieved. "From now on, let's consider ourselves dating. I'd like to meet your family, get to know them, and show them I'm a straight-up guy. I'm sure your family will be worried about you seeing a ballplayer, but I'll show them I can be trusted with their daughter. They must love you a lot."

"They do," Leah responded dizzily.

"Then I won't let them down. By the way, you're not seeing anybody else, are you?"

Leah's confusion dropped to an instant sadness. The transformation was incredible. She looked like a woman in one of those existential paintings, with melancholy eyes, her shoulders slumping and her hands held low in anguish, revealing a past and inner trauma. "No, but there was a guy not too long ago," she said in a low voice. "But he's gone now."

"Gone forever, I hope."

"Yes, he's gone."

Vic saw how much Leah had cared for the guy, whoever he was, and he waited a while to speak again. "You seem to have come through it fine enough," he finally said hopefully.

"I had to," Leah said. "God wanted me to, and He saw to it that I could."

Vic put his hand out on the table, palm up, a gesture of empathy and understanding. It didn't seem possible to Leah that such a powerfully built and worldly man could show such a deep caring for her. That much virility ought to belong in the body of one of the world's great womanizers. But not Vic. His eyes, so gentle, more like a poet's than a sportsman's, held Leah's in their gaze, and he took her hand and put it into his own. Vic rolled up her fingers and held them in his hand like a young girl holds a kitten.

"I'm sorry it didn't work out for you. Perhaps there was a reason," he said. "I hope that reason is me."

"Do you know how handsome you are?" Leah asked him, her eyes recovering from her sorrow. "It can stop me from crying, just to look at you."

Vic took Leah's frail wrists in his hands and gently rubbed her arms across the table. He talked long of California: of its surf and sand, of its rolling hills, of its many valleys that lay between the mountains and the shore. Leah rallied from her gloom, her face resuming its natural color, as she listened to his descriptions of the coast, the small seaside villages and quaint little ports of call, the sailboats anchored in the pretty shallow coves. She sat enthralled by his stories, and the more he talked of seaside villas and lazy inns the more Leah dreamed of seeing them, and by the end of the evening she had made up her mind that someday, in fact, she would.

Chapter 9

IN TIME, VIC CAME around the house and met Margaret and Walton, who both liked him a lot, but only after Leah confessed to her mother about having told a lie regarding the Christian player on the Vols. Weakly, she blamed most of the happenstance on Beth. Surprisingly, Margaret didn't throw a conniption or otherwise punish Leah, her mind too preoccupied with Kay's latest problem, a loser from Gainesboro named Dalton, whose track record included a conviction for robbery and time spent in the Davidson County Jail. Dalton was unemployed, had no desire for a job, smoked like a chimney, and drank shots of Kentucky Grain Whiskey and bootlegged firewater to fill the senselessness of his hours. Margaret despised him, and only for the incomprehensibility of Kay's poor judgement had Kay convinced herself she was in love with him.

A month of the baseball season passed and then Beth called late on a Sunday afternoon, a lazy day it was, Leah remembering the dripping humidity and eerie stillness hanging in the air, an hour before the evening church services were scheduled to begin, Beth saying she had to come over and talk at once. With services nearing, Leah knew there wouldn't be much time for a long conversation and she wondered what the heck could be so all-fired important that it couldn't wait until Monday at school. Beth arrived with her usual hard knock on the front door, startling Walton, who was down on the couch for an afternoon nap on account of a good crappie run that morning at Sam's Bend. Beth was so excited she didn't bother coming inside to greet anyone, instead yanking Leah out to the porch by the sleeve of her blouse, before leading her for a walk down the tree-lined sidewalks of Groveland Street, arm in arm with her best friend.

"Tommy has been sent down to a lower league where they can work on his swing," Beth said, gasping for air.

"Oh no, what's going on with you two?" Leah asked, fearing the worst.

"Tommy wants me to go with him. I told him I wouldn't go unless we were married," Beth said, proud of her stance.

Leah knew what was coming next.

"And he wants to marry me. Can you believe it? Oh, Leah, I'm going to be married." Beth's blue eyes sparkled and her skin glowed with excitement.

There was no reason for Leah to say anything. It wouldn't have carried any weight anyway. She managed a grin and gave her friend a warm congratulatory hug.

"There's no time to plan a wedding," Beth said regretfully, pulling back from the hug. "But you would have been my maid of honor. I wanted you to know that."

"No wedding. What do you mean no wedding?" Leah said in disbelief.

Beth looked insulted, fumbling for an explanation. "Why, why there's no time, that's why. We're leaving tomorrow. We're just going to have a justice of the peace marry us and be gone."

"What about the church, and school next year?"

"Hey, I'm getting married, you know. *Married.*"

To say anything more would have been both inconsiderate and inappropriate. Leah's eyes wandered down Groveland Street and the road seemed so much longer than it had only yesterday. "I am happy for you," she finally said. "I'll just miss you, that's all. You're the best friend I've always dreamed of having. Compared to you, everyone else has been an acquaintance." She hugged Beth again, and Beth grinned two big dimples.

Just then, a young girl came flying out of a house a few doors down from where they stood, a new neighbor who had moved in the Tuesday before. She flung herself toward the street, and without stopping threw her rump over her bicycle seat, one leg dragging and scraping behind her, leaning over the handlebars, before pushing off in a series of kicks, each one coming faster, as the bike slowly gained speed and steadied itself around the farthest corner. Leah felt old for the first time in her life.

"I've got to go," Beth said, as pumped up as a kid at a carnival. Her face glowed again, the sulking over, her cheeks like two holiday plums at Christmas time. "I'll write to you as soon as I can and fill you in. Isn't this something? Isn't this something, Leah?"

Leah put up a good front for her friend. "I'm so happy for you. I really am," she said, her eyes embracing her friend. "But I'll miss you something terrible."

One last hug, then Beth scrambled into her car, smiling broadly, waving her hand wildly in a frantic goodbye to her best friend from college, racing off to her dream, the dream she had wanted since the first day she thought of love and how nice it would be to have someone to share it with. The sprawling elms and the hickory bushes seemed to lean from her getaway as Leah watched Beth screech around the far corner and disappear.

***

Three days after Beth's hurried getaway, Vic left Nashville with the team for an extended road trip through the deep South: Georgia, the Carolinas, Florida, and into the delta region of Louisiana. Leah was home alone after she hung up from his latest phone call, sitting happily in her room, when someone came quietly into the house. The front door didn't close all the way behind whomever had come in and for a time there wasn't any noise made in either the foyer or the hallway.

Then she heard the slow, familiar shuffling of her mother's feet on the wooden floor followed by what sounded like sobs of sorrow that trailed off in the distance, Margaret drifting past the hallway and by Leah's room. Leah got up off her bed quietly and listened.

The crying soon stopped. Out in the kitchen, Leah heard the coffee pot percolating, but then she swung her door wide open and raced out of her room when the sobbing turned to a frightful wailing. As she came into the kitchen her mother was barely standing up, her face looking ten years older, wrinkled and worn like an old parchment, her eyes sagging down to her jaws and her chest slumped forward toward the countertop. Margaret's black leather purse had toppled onto the kitchen table, spilling its contents: a plastic bottle of sleeping pills, nerve medicine from Dr. Culpepper's office, plus a bottle of aspirin and some antacids for her stomach. Whatever was troubling her was bad, as Margaret rarely took any medicines unless she absolutely had to.

Margaret rested her head on Leah's shoulder, bawling like a baby. Leah felt the wetness of her mother's tears soaking through her own nightgown. Margaret's usual firm and feisty mannerisms had been reduced to a tottering whimper. After a good cry, Margaret moaned and straightened herself up a bit, looking disheveled and weak, but Leah waited and let her mother speak first.

"I've got some bad news, Honey," Margaret said, her eyes a stormy sky.

"What is it, Mother?" Leah asked impatiently.

"It's Kay, child. She's done it this time. Your sister is pregnant."

Margaret began to slump further. She leaned on the counter for support. "There's nothing we can do. Dalton is going to marry her, and they're moving to Atlanta. My whole life, I tried to do right by Kay, to keep her from destroying herself, but my business of it has been a failure."

Leah's first thought was for the baby. "Mama, oh Mama, what about the poor child? It can never amount to anything coming from Kay and that thing. It can't be, it just can't be. A baby? Are you sure? Are you sure, Mama? How in the world will Kay ever raise a baby by herself?"

"It'll only be something if I take care of it," Margaret said despondently. "God is going to judge me on that, and I'm gonna have to do his will. That baby will be mine someday. I can't let that blessed little baby be lost and end up in hell because it's got the wrong mother and a scoundrel for a father."

"Oh Mama, what ever will they do?" Leah said in desperation. "How will they make it? It's not your fault, you can't believe it is. You've done everything a mother could do. You've loved Kay more than a mother can love a child, done more for her than any parent ever could. It isn't fair, Mama. We all know that."

Margaret looked at Leah without looking at her. "Just be a good girl, Sugar, and don't ever do me as Kay has done me. One child like that is enough. I need to sit a spell and be alone with my thoughts. I pray God will help me on what to do next."

"Oh Mama, I can't believe it myself, that Kay would do this to you, to herself for that matter. Lord Almighty, what has she done? Does she ever think about what trouble she causes you? I can't believe she'd do this to you. I just can't believe it."

Margaret stumbled to the front room couch and collapsed into a heap. She stared at the ceiling, her mind in a daze. She thought of her choices in life. Never one for the trivial, since Kay's birth she had focused almost exclusively on the raising of her eldest daughter, often preoccupied to the point of exclusion, to the neglect of her other children, as Kay was born sickly and then her carefree nature quickly revealed itself. Margaret's mission had been that of a lioness to the protection of her cub, straight and direct, as early on Kay had been mischievous and found in a sexual situation in her room with the neighbor boy, Doyle. Kay was only ten years old that time in her room. Other times followed. Kay stole from stores and smoked and drank beer, and she ran with a crowd at school that had the morals of hyenas. For whatever neglect Leah had endured, it was equally as true that Margaret had suffered as well, and laying there on the sofa she suffered more still.

Kay married Dalton a week later, without a formal wedding or a reception, only a judge and a hasty exit in an old beat-up truck. Dalton took a job in Atlanta doing construction work, and Kay found a job in a beauty parlor, sweeping hair cuttings off the floor and setting appointments for the other girls. It all happened so fast there was no time to wish anybody well, just a legal signing and then on the road to the peach state of Georgia.

***

Leah felt the texture of her life changing in bold and dramatic ways. She was sick and tired of Nashville. She was sick and tired of common sense. She felt impulsive. There was a pressure to rise quickly, as one feels when one sits in an old rickety chair that can't bear the weight. Everyone was moving on. So for her next date with Vic, Leah picked a fine restaurant, May's Country Kitchen, out of Nashville about fifteen miles on the road to Taylorville, tucked away and plenty private. She wanted to hear more about California. She wanted to hear more of places besides Tennessee.

May's was originally built as an elevated lodge in a parkland hollow, the lodge surrounded by blooming magnolias and flowering dogwood trees, overlooking a rippling creek that flowed through the center of the hollow. The owners, May and her husband Harold, had a few years prior abandoned the lodge concept and converted the building into a homestyle restaurant. Down below, next to the creek, they had added a number of elegant white latticed gazebos, each gazebo wrapped in sweet smelling honeysuckle and harmony iris, the flowers filling the senses like a splash of candied perfume. Leah thought the view downstream into the glassy pools of water from the balcony of May's was about as romantic as Nashville got, and she was confident Vic would enjoy it.

When Leah and Vic finished eating, the sun was setting behind the trees and the sky had turned into a silky pink taffy. The clouds were way up high and wispy. The forecast had called for light showers that evening but Leah didn't see how that could happen, not on such an agreeable afternoon anyway, and Vic wanted to follow the stream up to its source, but the thickets were buzzing with biting bugs, so the two of them crossed a little wooden bridge and took a path that meandered up the far side and enough away from the creek to avoid the irritation.

They walked for a time before Leah began.

"I'd like to see California someday. I mentioned that to you before, that first night at Johnny's."

"Oh, you'll love it," Vic said, excited at Leah's suggestion of being someplace other than Nashville. "You should plan a trip and go and see it."

"No, I mean I'd like to see it soon, with you," Leah said directly. "I've been having dreams about California ever since we first met. Actually, I have all my life. I've always wanted to see the ocean."

"Will your folks let you go?"

"Probably not, but I can't let that stop me," Leah said adamantly. "I'm tired of it here. I need something new. There has to be a state or a country where things are different, where you can be free and act like your real self. I'm so sick of the people here. I don't believe I can find myself in Nashville, to find the meaning of my life in such an ignorant town."

Vic stopped on the path. He swatted at two nagging bugs. Leah paused with him. The gurgling of the creek below was nature's music, beautiful and serene, the water slurping over the large protruding boulders before bubbling gently into the vitreous pools below the rocks. The water was as crystal clear as a glass of drinking water. Rounded amber pebbles covered the creek bed like good-wish coins and near the creek were spread beautiful flourishings of purple cyclamen and Lenten rose.

"California is different," Vic said instructively. "That's one of the things I like about it. It's so unlike anyplace else. But in other ways it's the same. Every place is a little bit different than some other place, the terrain and the customs and whatnot, but for the most part, people are the same everywhere. California offers more because it's still so new out west, so people can be new themselves, at least for a few years. But over time, they end up like everybody else."

"How do you mean?" Leah asked.

"They end up with what's real, with what's important to them. All places are like that; it's up to the person to decide what counts, and no place can give you that. Only you can. The advantage of California is that it gives you more choices. But it will always come down to what matters the most."

"What matters most to you?" Leah asked, a sweet curiosity in her voice.

"To make the major leagues. That would mean the most to my mom and dad. They worked like dogs to give me and my sisters an opportunity. And I don't want to do it alone. Being a ballplayer, which is what I want to do, can be a lonely business. It's not all glamour and fun and people yelling your name all the time. I want someone to see it with me. But I didn't want to settle, I wanted to wait until I felt it with someone. And I want to be married to the woman I love for a lifetime."

"What if you don't make the major leagues?" Leah asked.

Vic paused. His eyes searched and he was most pensive, taking Leah's question very seriously, almost with foreboding. He surveyed the scene before him and scratched his chin. "I have to make it," he said candidly. "My mom and dad deserve that. It's my one constant demand. I've never really thought about not making it, not until you just asked me, so I guess I don't know what else I'd do." Vic drifted off again for a second. "But, if I had the right gal for me, then I'd have something, now wouldn't I? Know anybody who might want to sign up?"

"I might. Let me think on it."

Leah took Vic's arm and together they walked up the high bank of the creek and into the night. Soon, a million stars came out and a lazy moon crept its way slowly up the sky. Leah saw the dark outline of some near-bursting clouds draped precariously above their heads, separated from where they were by a cool layer of air and a prayer it wouldn't rain. She thought of marriage and felt the first sprinkle land on her face, resting her head on Vic's strong shoulder, feeling safe and secure, his strong arms wrapped around her sides in protection.

Chapter 10

MARIAN ALWAYS SAID IF you play coy and let the man do the talking, revealing very little about yourself and even less about your feelings for him, a girl can control the relationship and where it ends up.

The night of the walk up the creek at May's, Leah hadn't wondered whether it was suitable to marry Vic; it simply felt pleasing to know she could. But in the following days no answer came to Leah about whether she *ought* to marry him. When Leah held his hand or kissed him, it felt good, certainly more than pleasant, and his touch produced more than a few casual stirrings, but it felt nothing like her moments had with Blake. That, Leah reminded herself, had been love, and that, as hard as she might try to convince herself otherwise, was the undeniable truth.

Vic did, however, have a lot going for him. He was incredibly manly and handsome, a professional ballplayer, destined for stardom and glory, extremely kind and considerate and always respectful of her, mature for his age, ready to settle down and raise a family, and wonderful with her folks. Best of all, he was from California. Leah had long fantasized about seeing the rocky coast of California, with its towering plumes of briny spray rising high above the shoreline, since she first saw pictures of it as a young girl in a travel book her aunt Victoria gave her brother William for Christmas. To someday see it, to actually walk beneath the jagged cliffs and feel the drizzle of the sea on her face, *possibly to live there*, well, that had been much more than a dream; it had, in fact, been her fantasy, a destination of almost mythic proportions; her own personal Oz.

There was one more facet of that time in her life that fed well into Leah's plans. Where once her life had been lived for the simple joyous act of living, to take each day as it came and then to make the most of it, since the loss of Blake Leah had begun to strategize at winning and manipulating events toward that very end. Life had in many ways become a game to her, a game that Leah reasoned could no longer be won in its entirety, but that might at least be salvageable if she masterminded it to match her desires.

Leah hatched her plan for her future in California on her next date with Vic.

Since the night at May's, Vic had been pushing for more time when the two of them could be alone, and each of his most recent phone calls had ended with a plea for more nights like that one, times when the two of them could be together in private. Vic wasn't one to neck in cars, never cheap or trashy or lewd, and he had upbraided Leah the one time she suggested they park at The Row, Nashville's favorite necking spot where Grant Road dead-ended near Erinsbridge Bar, but he liked to be alone with her and he was oftentimes romantic, and Leah liked that in him. Great settings relaxed this ballplayer come a courtin', and Leah thought about where such a fine place might be to unleash her devious plan.

After thinking about it for an entire week, she had finally come upon it.

About an hour out of Nashville on the way to Clarksville lay a small lake named Lauren Lake, after some state senator's daughter, who had founded a prestigious school for deaf children back in the 1850s. Lauren Lake was surrounded by rustic summer cottages built to accommodate the students. The school had long since rotted out, but the cottages lay tucked behind an old stone wall that had miraculously held itself together through the passage of time. Legend had it the wall was built during the Civil War to protect the school in case the Yankees ever attacked, although legend also said the Yankees never did seem to mount a charge, and Leah figured that was why the wall was still standing in the good shape it was.

One of the simple homes behind the first section of the wall was Leah's Aunt Rita's summer getaway. The bungalow had been in the family for eons, and Leah's cousins used to take her there every summer the last week of August before school started, but she hadn't been for a number of summers and she'd all but forgotten about the place. No one from Leah's immediate family had been to the cottage in years. Walton was the last to use it, but he hadn't caught any bass in the muddy water that day and nearly got bit by a cottonmouth, so he never went back and never recommended it to any of his fishing buddies. Leah reckoned she and Vic could drive to the lake, eat a late afternoon picnic lunch, and walk the long trail that meandered into the nearby woods. Aunt Rita never locked the place, there was no reason to, and Leah's cousins had all moved to other towns so it didn't figure any of them would be around to spoil things.

Vic picked Leah up on the one remaining Saturday of the schedule without a baseball game and they drove the hour up to the lake. When they arrived, most of the cottages looked vacant; no cars were parked in the narrow lanes that led up to the little homes and none were in in the driveways themselves. The road in was deserted. The lake was as olive brown and muddy as Leah remembered it and didn't look as deep as in years before. Leafless trees twisted into the water beside creeping bank brush that had grown well into the first ring of wavelets, but all in all the lake was still pretty in the sun and the weather that day plenty more than fair. On the far shore, a kid, accompanied by a brown and white speckled spaniel, heaved a large fetching stick that splashed just past a thinning patch of reeds, but the dog ignored the throw, taking off instead into a field of waist-tall grass after a stray cat. The boy didn't return. The sun was still a ways from setting, the air that day as still as a held breath, and nearly twice as quiet.

Leah and Vic walked for awhile without speaking. Around a bend in the lake, Vic stopped and turned to her.

"Why are we here?" he asked her curiously.

"I thought you'd like this place," Leah said defensively. "I know you like being outdoors, and when we're tired of walking the lake we can go into my aunt's cottage and be alone."

Vic wasn't convinced. "Something's up," he said. "What is it?"

"This." Leah put her arms around Vic's shoulders and pulled herself to his face. She stretched upward to get at his full lips, and he dipped down just low enough to kiss her. They kissed deeply to make up for all the weeks of saying no.

After a few breathless minutes, Leah stopped herself. "We need to cool off. If we don't, we'll be in the cottage next, and you won't get to see the whole lake."

"What a shame that'd be," Vic said, thinking the cottage sounded like a marvelous idea.

Leah smiled an easy smile at him. "Let's walk a bit more, and then we can have our picnic," she said. She was somewhat aroused, but not completely, kind of how one might enjoy a day at the fair without wanting to go back again, while Vic was near to bursting with desire.

The stone wall that hid the cottages was far behind them now and the trees that lined their path had all but disappeared. A field of waist-high grass lay off to their right, and behind the clearing stood some straggly softwoods and two barren knolls. A thistle-filled hollow stretched between the hillocks. A cobblestone road carved a path up the furthest hill at the back of the hollow and ended at an abandoned farmhouse sitting alone on top of the ridge. Together, Leah and Vic stood capturing the view, soaking in the warmth of the sun's rays, the heat on their backs like a good rubbing oil.

"Anybody living in that old farmhouse?" Vic asked.

"I don't reckon so," Leah said. "I can't imagine there still would be."

Now was the time to implement the plan. Leah stared down at the ground and then up at Vic with those delicious brown eyes of hers. "I want to be a virgin when I marry, and I want a guy who wants me to be," she said resolutely.

Vic's kind eyes conveyed agreement, an expression of understanding to her words. "I want my wife to know only me," he said. "That's the way it should be."

All men know what follows next. Vic tried to look away, but Leah's eyes were gravity.

"Vic, have you been with any other girls, I mean, all the way?" she asked him.

Vic paused, shifted his gaze to the old farmhouse on the hill, and then nodded a subdued confirmation. Some time passed. "Yes, I have," he finally said apologetically. "I never want to discuss it again after today. Ballplayers do that sometimes, we make mistakes, sometimes you're just so lonely on the road and it leads to that, but it never meant anything with anyone. I know I used them in a way, and I should be sorrier than I am. But I never promised them anything or lied to them. I was up front, and each girl knew what she was getting into. I hope you believe me."

Idealism met reality that day by the lake, but Vic's confession didn't hurt Leah like it would have if it had been Blake owning up to it, and in a strange way it even felt promising for a guy to be so honest with her. "I guess I can live with it," she said. "It's not the way God intended, but I kind of figured that's how it'd be."

"What about him, the guy you were with?" Vic asked her. "Anything there?"

"No. He never cared about me. He turned out to be a disappointment," Leah said, with as much certitude as she could muster. "It was time to move on. But I never let him, if that's what you mean."

"Then I'll be what he wasn't. And I won't be with another girl again. You can always count on that. Life has given me this chance with you, and I want to make the most of it."

At that precise moment, the sun shone through a gap in the softwoods and lit up Leah's face in an afternoon glow of sheer radiant beauty. She looked like a starlet in the lights of a thousand cameras, and there is something magnetically seductive about the way a Southern woman looks at a man when she is manipulating him, a suggestive naughtiness that comes with a lazy blink of her eyes and a prolonged lick of her lips. The late afternoon sun cast Leah at her most ravishing, and if men were truly as wise as they so often claim to be, they would flee for their lives instead of succumbing. Worse, Leah's look also evinced a sufficient amount of desperation. Her eyes pleaded with him to rid her of Nashville. Alas, for Vic it was entirely too late for any evasive action, as Leah's beauty was immobilizing. He simply stood before her and awaited her every command. Leah knew she had him. She stretched up and kissed Vic softly on the neck with a purposeful glide of her tongue.

"When?" she asked him tantalizingly.

"Whenever you're ready," Vic said. His rich voice was full of enthusiasm. "My feelings for you are that strong."

Leah backed away. "No, that's not the way it should be," she said to him firmly. "You tell me when we should be married. It's up to the man to ask the woman for her hand. You'll just have to take your chances that I'll say yes."

They kissed again deeply, their mouths open wide, and in no time Vic began touching Leah in places where she had never been touched. Leah put her arms out to stop him. "We can't, Vic. I promised God."

"I know, I know. But I can't help myself," he said, huffing. "You feel so good."

Leah pulled away from him. It wasn't that hard for her to do. A bead of sweat ran down her forehead from the heat of the sun. "We have to stop," she implored. "I want to, just like you do, but we can't. Please don't hate me for what I honor. I want to be a virgin when I marry."

Vic stared at her in disbelief. For an instant, Leah thought of going through with it, just to hook him for sure, but good men come through when they have to. They overcome their natures. Vic's love for her superseded his own drive for immediate pleasure, and he turned and sprinted down the path by the lake like an Olympian in full stride. He ran for as long as he could, past the lake and through the grassy field and beyond the little knolls. He quit at the cobbled road. He hadn't known what else to do except to run, and as he wiped sweat from his forehead he glanced back at the lake and thought of the girl that he loved, trying with all her heart to be so good for her God, and he vowed to honor her and her wishes no matter how long it took to satisfy his own.

When Vic returned, the two of them ate a picnic lunch by the lake and walked a goodly distance without kissing again. They talked of many things: the lay of the land, southern ways, baseball, college and the merits of an education, family and siblings and the rules of a home, the type of conversation that is nothing too risky and nothing too close to the heart. Revealingly, they did not discuss each other or common interests shared between them, Vic much too enthralled to worry about something as trivial as basic compatibility and Leah much too preoccupied with a vision of California. The sun eventually slipped behind some low clouds and it grew darker on the trail, and night fell without so much as a held hand or a gentle hug.

In the car ride back to Nashville neither spoke very much. When the car joined Route 57 again, Leah caught the tired, old downtown of Nashville far off in the distance, a feeling of dread coming over her like a smothering veil of death, realizing that not far past the downtown lay Groveland Street and the same boring life she had lived for nineteen years, and Leah didn't know how many more days of it she could stand.

Leah rested her head on Vic's shoulder while he drove into the quiet of the night. "Today was a great day," she said softly to him. "We need to visit the country more often. Those flowers were so pretty, all purple and gold like that. Those dainty, little lavender ones were my favorite. I don't like it when you take me out for dinner all the time. I like going places and doing things."

"You don't like going out to eat?" Vic asked her, disappointment in his voice.

"No, I do, it's just that we're good together in the great outdoors."

"Yeah," Vic said sarcastically. "Indoors might get us into trouble. We never did get to see your aunt's cabin."

Leah gave him a carefree smile. "We'll always have indoors, Vic," she said, lifting her head. "You know I loved today. I just mean, well, I mean that we both like being in the countryside and near the water and feeling the sun on our faces. It's like when you told me about California, how pretty it is, with the wide open spaces and the wilderness. I like to see you in places where you feel most comfortable. It makes me happy."

Vic drove on, thinking. He was choosing his words carefully, rehearsing for the right thing to say, and he decided to be bold.

"When we move to California, the best living is in the East Bay hills, looking out over the tallest buildings of Oakland, across the estuary and over to the skyline of San Francisco. You can see the cities from the hills, but it's kind of like being in the country. Wide open spaces of trees and meadows. You'll see what I mean."

Leah nibbled on Vic's ear. "Are you proposing to me?"

"I might soon, you never know," he said coolly, relieved he had gotten as far as he had. "But you have to guarantee me that you know what you're doing because I only want to be married one time."

Leah felt the pride of victory fill her breast. "Well, if you do propose, you'll have to go through my daddy, traditional-like, like they do in the movies. I'm his little girl, and he wants the best for me. But first, you'll have to win over my mother. She's the tough one." Leah nibbled some more on Vic's ear. "Think you can do that?"

"Do you want me to?"

Leah rubbed Vic's chest with her hand for assurance and she sighed a long and yearning sigh. "Yes, I do," she answered. "I want to live in California with you and be happy. I want us to see all that can be seen and do all that can be done." She rested her head again on him and closed her eyes. "But like I said, you've got to win over my mother first."

"Could be difficult after Dalton," Vic said, glancing down at Leah on his shoulder, one eye diligently on the road. Leah gazed up at him for a second and then rested her head on his shoulder again.

One of Vic's best lines went without a laugh; Leah was too busy reveling in her own success. She kissed his neck as softly as she could and stroked his thick black hair with her long princess fingers for the rest of the boring ride home. When her eyes returned to the road, the road led all the way to California, and before her on the highway leading back to Nashville she actually saw the waves breaking beautifully in the sand.

Chapter 11

THE PROPOSAL CAME THE following Tuesday evening. Leah knew about the events only later, when Margaret told her what had happened, and the story became one of Leah's favorite memories of her mother and father in her childhood home. Vic called on Monday when he knew Leah would be out and spoke with Margaret directly, arranging for an evening visit for the following night after ball practice had ended. He arrived on the front porch at a few minutes after seven, rubbing his anxious palms against the side of his khakis to keep them dry. A clump of nerves tightened at the bottom of his throat as he rang the front doorbell.

Margaret met him at the door.

Walton was sitting nervously on the couch in the front room, as Margaret took a seat on the chair next to the sofa beside her husband, perplexed and somewhat withdrawn. Vic sat down like a boy fresh from a whipping, deliberate and contrite, on another chair closest to the entryway, an apology already filling his otherwise most apprehensive of faces, fearing the worst. When he finally settled in to his liking, he took a deep breath and clasped his hands together, barely an inch from the tip of his nose. He looked like an attorney readying himself for the final argument.

"I wish I knew you both better," Vic started sincerely. "It would make what I'm about to say a whole lot easier for us all."

Strangely, it didn't appear that either had any idea of what he might say. "We're both curious as to what's wrong, so just go ahead and say your mind," Margaret said reassuringly. "If Leah has offended you in any way, I'll handle it. Sometimes, she don't respect people enough. I know you called for her the other day, and when I asked her about the call at supper, it reminded her that she hadn't phoned you back. I thought that was pretty inconsiderate myself. And if my daughter lied to you or hurt your feelings in any way, I'll whip her sure as we're sitting here."

Vic shuffled in his seat like a poker player with a bad hand. "No, nothing like that, Ma'am," he said amenably. "Leah has always been respectful of me, and she's always been a good girl. When I first saw her at one of my practices, something hit me hard, and I didn't know what it was. Then we started talking and it grew stronger, and when we dated it finally got so bad I started having headaches and itching from the uneasiness of what I've been feeling. My coaches thought I was allergic to the rosin bag. I've tried to run from my feelings, and I broke down only when it got so unbearable not to hear her voice that I had to call and talk to her. With every day that goes by I haven't been able to stop thinking about her. She's in my head more than any other thoughts I have. And there's nothing wrong, she's a lady at all times, that's one of the reasons I like her so much, so I don't want either of you to worry about her being in trouble."

Margaret and Walton sat still as stones.

Vic inhaled and blew out hard. He was so nervous his stomach was in a spasm and pulling at his shirt. "Your daughter is a wonderful girl," he said anxiously. "I guess you could say that I'm in love with her. And I want us to be married one day."

Margaret jumped up from her chair, a sudden horror on her face. "But she's only nineteen," she exclaimed. "Just turned it. My God, Vic, no, she's still a child. She can't be married. She's got so much more schooling to go."

"I want her to finish school, too, and I'll be able to pay for it," Vic replied quickly. He had anticipated that objection and the suddenness of his answer stifled Margaret's objections for a moment.

Walton merely scratched his itchy nose and waited for more to be said.

Margaret, however, was like a prisoner before a firing squad, rifles raised to the shoulder. If this child went, none were left at home. "But she's only had one boyfriend her whole life, and she didn't date much before that," Margaret protested. "I didn't allow her to go out with boys until she was sixteen years old. My God, I can't lose my baby, I just can't lose her. She's the only one I got left."

Walton wanted to hear more before he put in his piece. Margaret sat down again, the incredulity still on her face, looking at her husband for support, desperation in her every expression and every glance, but at least she wasn't yelling anymore. She stayed quiet and waited for someone else to speak their mind.

Vic sensed it was his turn to talk again. "We don't have to be married right away," he appealed to them both. "To plan the wedding, to get my family involved, it could take months or maybe even a year. She'd be twenty by then. That's old enough to marry me, isn't it?"

"Your family will come to Nashville to plan a wedding?" Margaret snapped in frustration. "Don't people work in California?" She began to rise again but she thought better of it after Walton looked askance at her and she stayed seated. After what seemed like an eternity, she glanced over at her husband who remained hushed and pensive, spinning an unlit cigarette between his thumb and his fingers, his initial nervousness ended, replaced instead by a calm contemplation.

"If the wedding is in Nashville, they'll come," Vic said defensively, a soldier hearing the shells exploding all around him, knowing the battle is on with nowhere to hide. "My mother doesn't work, so she could help out immediately. If the wedding is in California, all of you could stay with my family. They'd love it."

Margaret jumped up this time. "No daughter of mine is going to be married in California," she ranted. "Nashville is where we're from. It's Leah's home. All the people Leah knows are from here. None of them would go all the way to California for a wedding, not when it could be done here in town."

Margaret turned toward Walton. "You haven't said a word," she chided her husband. "She's your child, too, or don't you care none about her?"

Something in Vic told him that what followed would be momentous.

The lanky old man sat upright and leaned forward. His eyes had within them the perfect firmness of a deeply-held conviction. "I could tell it straight off," Walton began, in a calming voice to help quell the tempest, "that there was something serious with you. I don't say much around here, seems I don't get much chance to. I keep things to myself, but I see what I need to see. I didn't feel I needed to say anything about my Leah, not yet anyway, so I kept my mouth shut. But I saw it in you, son, I really did. What troubles me is that I don't see it in Leah the same way. She's plenty proud of you, that's as plain as that lampshade over there, but she looks like she could live without you. With the rich fella, she had the look, and it pretty near killed her when he left her. I like you, Vic, not just because you fish and play ball, but I can read people, and you're a fine young man. Somebody done raised you right. I see that in you, or I would have stepped in some time ago and stopped it. The other kids around here, they all belonged to their mother, but Leah is mine. If you're convinced she loves you enough for a lifetime, I'll go along with it, but I'm just afraid she wants out of here more than what she feels for you."

"What do you mean, *more*?" Vic asked him.

"Well, it's no secret she ain't happy around here," Walton said. "The others have all left the nest, and she's always wanted to be like the older ones, grown up and going on to what comes next. Grown ups get married, it's what they do, so marriage is a way to prove she's grown up and become a woman now. It's also her ticket out of here."

Vic hadn't thought about any of that. He sat in his chair motionless, listening to Walton's every word, like Socrates before the Oracle.

Margaret sat stupefied and speechless. She couldn't believe it was her husband doing the talking, and that he was making some sense.

"You won't have to worry at first," Walton went on. "Leah will try to be a good wife because God wants her to be. But she can be like them other two: hell bent on getting what she wants when she wants it. I've seen it in her, and women, especially women in this family, do whatever it takes to get them a man. Say sweet things and promise you the moon." Walton leaned forward even more. His eyes were fatherly and wise. "You understand my meaning, now don't you, son?" A wily grin came to his face, and Vic understood exactly what he meant. Vic had seen that sexy, manipulative look on Leah's face many times already. The two men smiled at each other while Margaret sat in amazement. "But someday," Walton continued on, "when they got what they want from you, they change. And boy, you gotta make peace with that, because it's a coming. Even Leah, my sweetest child, the one who loves me most of all, has that much woman in her."

Margaret shot up again. "And what are you, some kind of prize?" she said, her arms outstretched, bent at the elbows, with her arms and palms wide open, as if to hold up a trophy. "Some victory cup you turned out to be."

"You see what I mean, Vic?" Walton said snickering, thankful for the on-cue response. "If they can live without you, that's what they turn into. But each man makes his own life, so if you think you'll be happy, then you can marry my daughter. Leave her mother to me."

"Oh, so now you're the man around here," Margaret screamed at her husband like a gorgon. "After all this time, now you think you can decide our child's future? Why, I ought—"

"Shut up, woman, will you?" Walton shouted, cutting off his wife before she could continue. "Do you know how dad gum tired I am of listening to you scream and moan all the time? One time, just shut your mouth and listen to somebody else for a change."

Walton had never exerted himself like this in thirty years of marriage. Margaret was too flabbergasted to speak, and she sat back down on the chair in a stupor of shock and dismay.

"With William," Walton went on, speaking directly to his wife and slowing to his usual drawl, "I didn't have to decide a single thing. He's smarter than you and me put together, smarter than all them professors he learned from at college and then some, and for some fool reason you still thought you could argue with him. Kay you made a mess of. Marian was gonna do what she wanted to do regardless of what you said, but thank God she's got good sense and she's a plenty fine girl.

Leah tried to make you happy by giving in to you, but she's finally run out of patience; Vic's proposal here is proof of that. Now let her live her own life with a fine young man who wants to make her happy."

Margaret sat motionless, unable to move or speak.

Vic had his blessing. It was time to leave. As he started to get up, Walton looked at him straight on, so there would be no mistake as to his meaning, pointing to the chair in which Vic had sat for his proposal, a signal for Vic to sit a while longer. Vic got off his haunches and set back down and waited for the words that Walton held most dear to him.

"I only want two things from you," Walton said sternly. "First, provide for her. Second, be true. Don't ever play on her. If you can do those two things, you and I will get along just fine."

"I will, sir, and don't worry about Leah using me to leave this house. I love her so much I'll give her a home she'll never want to leave."

"Then we'll always be here for you," Walton said. "And I mean that. This family has more problems than you can shake a stick at, but it sticks together through thick and thin and then sticks together some more. Consider yourself one of us now."

"I will, sir, and thank you."

A look of long-in-coming resignation crossed Margaret's face. Her lifelong calling to be a mother and to cling to her youngest daughter was outweighed by the transformation she saw in her husband. Walton's word on Leah was the first law he had ever laid down in their home. He was a man after all. Margaret felt her first feelings of respect for him. She also felt relieved. She had fought for all her children and the war had been a long and arduous one. She was tired now, but from his words Margaret also knew her husband had been faithful to her and had never cheated on their wedding vows. He respected fidelity, respected their marriage, and despite her bitching, certainly enough through the years to drive him away and into another woman's arms, Walton had remained true to her. He wasn't only a man, he was a fine man, and she had worried all those years for nothing. That knowledge gave her peace of mind and she went over and placed her right hand softly on her husband's shoulder and massaged it, the tears welling in her eyes.

Vic rose, shook Walton's bony hand, and went over to Margaret. She opened her arms wide and hugged him with an abounding embrace, a loving welcome to her family, a family that was now to be his family as well.

"Take care of her, Vic," Margaret said sniffling, her eyes pink and her cheeks puffy. "Listen to Leah about God and the Bible. It's the one thing she's an expert on. God gave her a gift of understanding and she loves the Lord with all her heart. She's clung to God against the science of her brother and the chidings of sinners at church and that takes a mighty faith in Him. Shoot, come to think of it, she's stood against me for the Lord and took a switch for it more times than I care to admit. Sure enough, I was wrong. Leah can lead you to where the Lord will save your soul, and nothing in this world counts for more than a saved soul."

"Thank you," Vic said appreciatively. "I'll take good care of her because I love her so much. Leah and I have talked about God, and we decided to let God have His say through our conversations. Leah is sure she can convert me, and I'm going to listen to her. I won't promise you anything, but I'll keep an open mind on it, I swear I will. I knew she was the one for me the first time I saw her at Winningham Park."

***

That night, Vic called late, well after ten, and well after he had celebrated with some of his teammates over a broiled steak dinner at Johnny's. When the phone rang Leah ran to answer it.

"I was by your house today," Vic said, "and I have something I want—"

"I know, I know," Leah said, interrupting him. "I know all about it, and my answer is yes. We're moving to California. So, help me, we are. Finally, finally, finally. California, here we come. Oh Vic, I can't wait to see the beauty of California."

"You'll do more than see it; you'll live there. I just hope the Bay Area is ready for you. I just hope—"

"It better be," Leah said, interrupting him again. "I'll bring a little class to the place. Southern charm and hospitality. I betcha California won't believe the girl from Tennessee."

This was the most excitement Vic had ever heard from Leah during all the time he'd known her; it was like it was a different person on the line. "I've never seen you so happy about anything," he said in amazement. "Is this all it took for you to open up, a little marriage proposal?"

"Why, yes, as a matter of fact, and I'll make you very happy," she said confidently. "You'll see. You should have asked me to marry you sooner, that's what you should have done. You're lucky I'm still available. Have you told your mother and father about the wedding yet?"

"Yeah, I told them. They're all shocked. They didn't know what to say. My sisters were in the background screaming and yelling so loudly I could hardly hear a word anyone said. I had forgotten how young my sisters are."

"Oh, Vic, can we live in the hills like you talked about? Please? With a view of the water? You described the hills so well to me, they sounded absolutely beautiful, and I just love the hills. I want hills. Hills or bust. Please, Vic, say we can live in the hills. Oh, please, I want to live in the hills."

"The hills? What about just being happy married to me?"

"I'll be happy to be married to you, but you shouldn't have told me about the hills unless you were sincere about us living there. The hills or nothing. Can we please?"

"If Cincinnati signs me, yeah, we can," Vic said. "We could live almost anywhere, I suppose."

"How about the ceremony?" Leah asked, still thrilled. "Can your folks make it out to see us get married?"

"My dad doesn't think they can come to Nashville. My mother hasn't been feeling well. The doctors are doing some tests on her blood. But they want to have a reception for us, and I thought we could honeymoon in California, most likely in Carmel."

"Where?"

"Oh, you'll love it," Vic said assuredly. "It's on the coast. It's a quaint little seaside town on the most beautiful stretch of ocean you've ever seen. Real high-rent district. Magnificent beaches, great restaurants, lots to see and do. Stars go there to vacation."

Leah hadn't thought of where in California to see first and even less about where to honeymoon. To her, California was

California. "I'll trust you, Vic. I'm sure Caramel will be just fine."

Vic chuckled. "Carmel," he said, correcting her. "It's Carmel. Someday we might be able to live there, if I have a long career with about ten no-hitters."

"You will," Leah said supportively. "You're the best player on the team. And I'm going to want a big house and a fancy car and three days of uninterrupted shopping for brand new clothes. And a big diamond ring. My family has been poor long enough, and a girl can only take so much poverty. Now I've got to go. I've got so much to think about and do. Planning a wedding and telling everybody about it won't be easy, you know."

"You need any help?"

"Nope, not a bit. You just pitch well, and I'll take care of the rest." Leah closed with the coup de grâce. "And you know what else? It won't be long before what we started at Lauren Lake can be finished. My man isn't gonna miss a one of those tramps you had before me. Just you wait and see."

Vic nearly fell over. "Teaser," he said in delighted anticipation. "You're a nasty girl, did you know that? How the heck can you be so saintly one minute and then so smutty the next? Wait until I tell your mother."

"I thought you'd like that," Leah said with aplomb. "So call me tomorrow, and we'll talk on it some more."

"All right, I'll talk to you then."

Vic started to hang up on his end of the line, but before he could Leah suddenly remembered something and yelled madly into the phone. "Oh, Vic, wait, don't hang up," she cried. "I forgot to tell you. I got a postcard from Beth today. From the little mountain resort of Grandfather Mountain in the backwoods of North Carolina."

"North Carolina?"

"Yes, Beth and Tommy spent a few days' honeymoon there, in a log cabin surrounded by pretty pines and purple mountain flowers. The place looked lovely in the postcard."

"What else did Beth say? How's Tommy doing?"

"Tommy still isn't hitting the ball very well. He's striking out as much as when he played on the Vols. Finances are tight, and Beth is looking for a job as a waitress. She said Tommy misses you an awful lot. They took an apartment in the Wilmington area, and Beth promised to call again when they get more settled in."

"Wilmington. That's Class A. If Tommy isn't hitting the ball there, he's as good as done. Poor little guy. He needs to gain weight, get bigger and stronger in his upper body."

"Well, Beth can cook up a storm. That ought to help him gain some weight."

"Can you?"

"Can I what?"

"Can you cook?"

"Cook? Me? Why, just you wait."

Vic laughed. "Well, when you write Beth back, be sure and tell them both hello for me. I miss Tommy, and tell Beth to tell Tommy the clubhouse hasn't been the same since the team sent him down. Tommy was the kind of player who is good for the team's morale. All the guys miss him."

"I will, I'll tell her. Now, listen, I have to go. Call me tomorrow."

And that was it. A son from Oakland and a daughter from Nashville were to be married to each other. One was a long way from home and the other wanted to be. Neither thought much of the consequences of their decision and neither bothered with circumspection or contemplated what lay in the days ahead. Each had their reasons for marriage and assumed the reasons of the other to be the same as their own, and both were rather oblivious to the dangers of assumption, choosing instead to believe their motivations were motivation enough to see them through the pitfalls of life. The only holdup to such thoughtlessness was the baseball season, and in only a few months' time that season would be over like so many other seasons before it.

Chapter 12

THAT SUMMER, THE SUMMER of 1957, was a scorcher in Nashville. The days turned muggy, the nights turned sweaty, and the only tolerable time was the first balmy light of the morn. Thunderstorms lumbered in late at night, rolling thunder and cracking lightning, not more than twenty feet above the shingled rooftops of Leah's neighborhood, cooling things down for a time, but as soon as the sun came up again the storms moved on and the breezes stopped. By mid-morning it grew so hot the air took to shimmying. Good folks prayed for the coolness of sundown, but around dusk droves of pestering mosquitoes flew in low from the creeks, sneaking inside the window screens and crawling their way under the covers, and the more the bugs bit her that sweltering summer the more Leah dreamed of California and its cooling, oceanfront clime.

In the hustle and bustle of making arrangements, no one noticed Vic's last few pitching starts of the season. He was shelled like a Pacific island, removed from his last two games earlier than at anytime in his career, yanked by the third inning in both, and in one of the games he gave up nine runs. The coaches blamed it on lost velocity from the long season, the southern heat and humidity taking its usual toll, as it had on just about everyone by then, and Vic still led the team in innings pitched, earned run average, and he led the entire league in strikeouts and wins.

But Vic knew better than to blame his last few starts on the heat. Something in his shoulder felt like a blazing fire, invariably followed by a warm, seeping sensation in the joint area and a sharp pain that extended up and into his neck. The mornings after he pitched he couldn't lift his arm much above his head, not without throbs of excruciating pain anyway, but he hid his misery from the team and from Leah and he tried not to think of the agony, packing his shoulder in ice when alone and gorging on aspirin tablets when the pain became insufferable.

Nashville was a dance of leaves and a peeping sun on the Saturday of Leah's fall wedding. Autumn is a transitional time everywhere, but especially in the South, when the hot, lazy days of summer vanish like a first kiss, over before you know it, but never quite forgotten. Leah had decorated the Morse Street Congregation in sashes of burgundy and gold, her two favorite colors, each pew adorned with its own golden ribbon and red summer rose, and as she put on her wedding dress in the antechamber Leah thought back on that summer fondly, the lure of California fresh in her mind, the beaches sparkling out before her like stardust sprinkled down from the bough of heaven and the ocean rolling softly to the sand.

The wedding, though, was like the third glass of water when the second glass has thoroughly quenched your thirst. It didn't help that only half the guests arrived on time, as Leah had provided the wrong starting hour on the invitation, one in the afternoon instead of twelve. Nobody caught the error and Leah cried when she realized her mistake and smeared her makeup with her tears. Vic had William and Walton help him hustle people in from the parking lot, and by the time the bride and groom said their vows, the church was nearly full and the error long forgotten.

That night, the newlyweds stayed with Leah's family in the old home on Groveland Street, the air thick with smoke from the burning of leaves and the hearth warm and glowing. Leah insisted on having one final night with her family, Marian and William agreeing to spend the night in the old home for the sake of their sister, but by ten, after such a long and tiresome day, everyone was plainly exhausted.

"I think I've had about all the excitement I can stand for one day," Margaret said yawning. "I'm going to bed."

"Mama, Marian and I are sleeping with you tonight," Leah said. "Daddy, you'll have to sleep on the couch, and Vic, you're on a cot in my room with my brother."

Vic looked like the blood had been suddenly drained from his body. "Come on, Vic," William said to him encouragingly. "What's one more night when you've waited this long?"

Vic smiled. "Well, when you put in that way."

"At least you get a bed," Walton groaned. "Uncle Cleveland has Marian's room for the night, and William's old room is now a sewing shop."

"That's gonna stay that way, too," Cleveland said, laughing. "Y'all invited me and the wife to stay over, and I'm not about to sleep on the floor."

"Go get that bed while you can, Cleveland," Margaret said. "It may not be empty much longer."

Uncle Cleveland and Aunt Martha made off down the hallway and into Marian's room, retiring for the night. William and Vic went into Leah's bedroom and closed the door, William laughing his head off, Vic trying hard to keep a positive attitude while his new bride slept in another room. Walton stretched out on the couch with a pillow and a blanket in front of the fire.

After Leah and Marian commandeered the master bedroom, Margaret finally broke down from the stress of the day. "I can't believe Kay and Dalton couldn't stay the night," she said despairingly, her daughters helping her underneath the covers. "Driving back to Atlanta in the dark, Kay showing and all. Lord Almighty, what am I going to do about that blessed baby?"

"Mama, don't cry," Marian said. "It'll all work out."

Margaret shook her head in disgust. "No, it won't. It just won't, that's all. That poor, precious baby, with that awful creature for a father and Kay for its mother? So help me, tell me how that baby can turn out fine? I tried so hard with your sister, and she never listened to me a day in her life. That poor baby. What am I going to do to help that child?"

"Mama, how about some nice hot cocoa?" Leah said. "How about we make you a nice cup? It'll sure cheer you up. It always does. I'll get Daddy to help us."

Margaret kept crying. She didn't even look up at Leah. Marian stayed with her mother and rubbed her shoulders while Leah summoned her daddy into the kitchen.

After making a big pot of hot cocoa, Leah and Walton brought the pot into the bedroom and Margaret drank three cups, sloshing as she moved about under the covers and gradually cheering up. Walton settled back on the couch and the girls stroked their mother's hair and hummed church songs in her ears until she fell soundly asleep.

After the house had quieted down, and after making sure William had gone to sleep, Vic headed out for the kitchen for another bite of wedding cake and a cold glass of milk. As he came around the corner of the hallway, he noticed embers still burning low in the fireplace. Their soft glow provided just enough light for Vic to see Walton stirring on the couch.

"Vic, that you?" Walton asked.

"Yes, sir, it sure is. Thought I'd get me one last bite of that cake. What are you still doing up?"

"Oh, just doing a little thinking back on my Leah. She was mine, you know. Now she'll be moving all the way to California, halfway across the world. Oh, Vic, you should have seen her as a little girl."

Vic took a seat on the chair nearest the sofa. "Tell me about her," he whispered. "I'd like to hear what she was like when she was younger."

Walton sat up on the couch. "Well, all right, I will." The slender old man tossed Vic a spare blanket because the room had taken on a chill with the fire low. "She used to stumble by me when she'd get up like you just done," Walton started. "She'd want a drink of water. I'd be reading the paper or tying on lures, and her little night dress would be tugged around to the side, caught on her thumbnail. Bare-legged, little white legs, a strawberry on one knee, mumbling to herself and rubbing her eyes against the light. Cutest thing you ever saw. She never thought to take a glass back with her, just gulped down as much water as she could stomach in the kitchen. And I mean to tell you gulp. Had her own glass in the hall bath and wouldn't think to use it. She'd only drink out of the kitchen faucet."

"What else?"

"She never wore slippers. This floor gets colder than an ice box in wintertime, and she'd come out in her bare feet, every single time. She refused to wear socks. On the way back to her room, she'd give me a hug, as tired as she was."

Walton choked up. Vic waited patiently for him to continue.

"Oh, Vic, I love her so," Walton said. "It's hard to see your baby grow up and leave the nest. You'll see what I'm talking about when you have your own daughters one day. It seems like only yesterday she was a child. Sometimes, she wouldn't be so cold and in such a hurry to get back to bed, and she'd curl up on the couch next to me and fall asleep. I loved those nights the most. I'd carry her in to her room later, when I was done reading my paper."

"She sounds like she loved you a lot."

"She did, Vic. And she knew I loved her. But I'll tell you another thing about her, though. A strange thing. I never told nobody about this."

Vic leaned in closer. He felt chill bumps on his arms. He wrapped the blanket around himself tighter for warmth and waited for Walton's words.

"Sometimes," Walton continued, "I just knew she was special. Look over yonder." Walton pointed to a space outside, between two tall elm trees growing over the fence in the side yard. "When the sky is clear and there's no moon, you can look out the window from here on the couch and see the stars through them trees. Stars sparkle so close to the house it seemed you could grab 'em. Many nights, I'd look down at my Leah and her eyes would be wide open, taking in the sky like she was mesmerized, even though I knew she was sleepy tired. It was like she couldn't take her eyes off them stars."

"Really?"

"Yes, I'm telling it to you straight. It was like she was drawn to them. When she was younger, she'd go out into the front yard and stare at the sky for hours at a time, like she was looking past the sky to someplace beyond it. Margaret would have to threaten a switch to get her back inside."

"I know she likes to walk at night."

"Yes, she liked to walk all her life. In the summer, she'd sit out front and watch the stars, laying on the grass, after her walking was done. Many nights, I'd lay on the ground with her, just watching the sky. But what struck me most was the way she looked on the couch, late at night, the stars in her eyes, like they were calling for her. It seemed to me that she wanted to be one with them, her eyes so far off, so taken in with them stars. Like I said, she seemed mesmerized. There was something special about her look, something special, I tell you, like how an angel might look at the gates of heaven."

A long silence followed that let Vic know Walton was through talking. "Well, I better get me some cake," Vic said, rising from the chair. "Thanks again for taking care of so much of today and for raising such a wonderful daughter."

Walton looked deeply into the last of the fire. "Good night, Vic. Take care of my baby girl."

***

The next morning, following an early rising, Leah and Vic flew west toward the coast and toward the golden state of California. Leah took a window seat near the back of the plane, the sun glinting off the silver wings like the finale lights in a grand Broadway spectacle, as the plane rose slowly into the sky. Vic sat next to her and held her hand, but Leah kept her head turned out the window as she bid farewell to Nashville and to all that she had known for nineteen years. She said good riddance to the accusers, to boredom and backwardness, and she said it also to Blake, to the green countryside now trailing behind her, the rolling hills and flat farmlands and the tired old downtown, to his land, for Nashville was always much more his city than hers and she left the South to him as well. The pain in her heart hurt too much to wish him well, and when the plane climbed into the first layer of thickening clouds Leah closed her eyes and thought of California and the beauty that lay ahead.

The landing in Monterey was a pageant of pure sunshine, but it was already late afternoon by the time the plane landed and drizzly gray clouds were forming out at sea, ready to encase the shore in one long enveloping bank of fog, as Vic drove from the small Monterey airport down to Carmel before the sunset.

"Keep your eyes closed from here on out," Vic said, two miles north of Ocean Avenue on the coast route of California's

Highway 1. "I don't want you to see a thing until we get there. Remember, you promised me."

Leah, her eyes dutifully closed, felt the rental car climb a last good grade before she heard the blinker click on and Vic pull off the main highway, braking the car to a stop. Then the car moved forward again, braking down another good grade, before flattening into a smooth long roll.

Vic rolled the windows down, and immediately Leah felt a crispness of moisture on her face. Shopping bags crunched on the sidewalks beside her. She heard people talking in groups, pedestrians strolling by her side of the car, and storefront doors opening and closing with a jangle bell sound, and she wanted to peek, but Vic covered her face with his free hand while he drove on, laughing softly, his manner smooth and self-possessed, a confident anticipation in his cackle. At one of the last stops down the boulevard, Leah caught a whiff of dark chocolate and what smelled like a freshly roasted cup of coffee, only richer and more exotic, coming from the corner off to her right and she nearly drooled on herself.

"Can we eat soon?" she asked impatiently. Being on land again had brought back her appetite.

"After you see the ocean. Hang in there."

An amber sun was dripping on a tranquil sea when Vic finally stopped the car. He walked briskly around the trunk and over to the passenger side where Leah sat with her eyes still closed. Vic opened her door for her and took her hands. They were cold from sweaty excitement. As he pulled his new bride up, Leah heard the sound of gentle waves tumbling onto a beach somewhere down below where she stood. They surged in the sand when they broke, and then fizzed like seltzer water as they flattened out, the little bubbles tingling like a fine champagne. Leah giggled as she listened to the waves. Suddenly, a big breaker thundered in front of her, its prickling spray rushing up to her face and splashing her with a cold ocean mist. It spilled her backward and she pulled on Vic's arm to right herself, but her eyes were still closed as some kind of tree filled her nose with a scent that wasn't quite pine.

"What's that tree I'm smelling?" Leah asked curiously.

"Cypress trees. They're everywhere down here. You'll see."

More waves massaged the beach, the furthest on the right roaring every third or fourth breaker, and to Leah's left she heard seagulls screeching and dogs splashing into a retreating tide. A brackish odor began to fill Leah's nose, but was swept away by the next cold whoosh of fresh ocean air.

"You can open your eyes now," Vic said. "We're in Carmel."

Leah slowly opened her eyes. She had waited for this moment for as long as she could remember. In front of her, white-tipped turquoise waves tumbled in a long line one after another onto a sudsy white beach; when a wave crept back out to sea, a shallow mirror formed where the breaker had spread, cracked only by another roller that pushed past the line of the first, re-wetting the sand and scattering the small sea birds that frolicked in front of it. The waves played their game between the swirls, the birds hovering and diving between the combers, picking at morsels and then flittering up again, before the next surge of Pacific Ocean came and swept the shore. Salmon streaks were etched low in the sky. Breakers boomed into half-submerged rocks out on the furthest rocky point, the crashes launching giant water plumes high into the air in wide graceful arcs, the splashes peaking with each fourth roller, followed by a lull, and Leah watched as broad billows of great watery girth swamped the rocks again. The sun was now a giant orange ball on the farthest edge of the earth, surrounded by low guardian clouds of peach and wine, and the first glow of a moon was breaking through from behind a veil of seaside mist.

Leah trembled from the majestic beauty before her, speechless.

"Look behind you," Vic said, turning Leah's body with his hands.

Lounging cypress trees and a row of manicured flower bushes lined an oceanfront drive lockstepping with the shore. On the lane were situated charming sea mansions, atavistic houses of glass with Hadrian stone walls at their fronts and sides, some with wood picket fences and paths that coursed to the courtyards of their home. Smoke rose from tall stone chimneys. Other homes were more like English cottages, with wrought iron gates in their driveways and meandering, cobblestone walkways, and one even had a fountain that trickled into an Italian tiled pool and made a delightful slurping sound.

Leah turned to face the beach again. Kelp beds muddied the water. To the far right, the line of the bay extended away, the mist thickening at those points closest to the shore. Famous Pebble Beach sat high above the ocean's climbing spray like a reigning emperor, its highlands lush in emerald cypress groves, its meadows decorated with moorland swaths of pretty colored flowers and fields of golden poppies. Sweaters of ice plant clothed the land. Leah breathed in the deepest and most satisfying breath of her lifetime. The glory about her was endless.

Leah's hands came up to her open mouth and she shook her head without speaking. After another minute she still couldn't speak a word.

"You okay?" Vic asked her.

"Can this be?" she finally said in amazement. "Everything and everyone is so beautiful here. There's nothing like this anywhere else on Earth, is there, Vic?"

"Do you like it? I knew you would," Vic said proudly.

Leah paused without acknowledging her husband. She absorbed herself in the view, still amazed, caught up in the grandeur of California and in the most magnificent ocean view found anywhere on the planet.

"This is why people come here, isn't it?" she asked rhetorically. She was speaking so softly Vic could barely hear her. "This is why. I can't believe what God has made here. It's a perfect paradise. A paradise on Earth." In an instant, Leah turned giddy. "Do you smell the air? Oh, can you smell it, Vic? It's like the best dream you ever had, a dream that finally came true."

Whatever gold was in the clouds had disappeared, and the scattered pink blushes had given way to a full cabernet. A gray bank of fog hovered out on the horizon, obscuring the last sparkle of sunlight. A strong breeze swept up from the ocean bay, and Vic put his arm around Leah to protect her from the cold. Leah hugged him back, but her gaze was still transfixed on the wonder before her.

"We should check in at the hotel," Vic said. "Get situated, get changed, then go have some dinner."

Leah continued to take in the sea, her face riveted on the now darkening waves. Tears of happiness dribbled off her cheeks.

After another minute, Vic turned toward Leah's door to suggest their leaving. When he did, Leah moved like a prisoner to the gallows, stopping for one last look, just long enough to immerse herself one final time in the glory of California.

"It is real, isn't it? We're really here. I made it after all."

"What do you mean?" Vic asked.

"I made it to California," Leah said, still looking out on the ocean, her fine features outlined by the glow of the moon. "God let me see it. All those times in my room, alone and crying, hurting so much, when no one seemed to care about me, I had to have something to look forward to. And now I'm here."

"You want to tell me about it?" Vic asked.

Leah shook her head, speaking to her husband as if he wasn't there. "Someday maybe. Not now, though. I just want to be here, with nothing bad in my mind, only me here in this place."

Another minute passed, the waves spilling endlessly onto the beach, and Leah finally climbed into the car with her new husband and bid farewell to the shore. She looked back over her shoulder several times as if saying goodbye to a long lost-friend, unaware that she'd see the shore again tomorrow. After checking in at the hotel, freshening up a bit, and spending some awkward moments in the room wondering whether to jump into bed before going out to eat, Vic took Leah for a splendid steak dinner at a local favorite called The Rail Post.

The restaurant was a large single room with an exceptionally high wood beam ceiling and wooden bridge trestle siding, dark and cavernous, and Leah had to strain to see Vic across the table. The aroma of French onion soup and parmesan cheese filled the air, and the bread was a mouthwatering sourdough with ice cold butter.

Not much was said over dinner. The food was too delicious, and there was too much anticipation of what was to come. With the last bite of chocolate torte, a silence descended on the two of them like the start of a funeral.

"We should probably go back to the hotel," Leah said fretfully. "You've been so patient and good with me. I'm so nervous. I guess you could tell I've been on edge since we saw the ocean at the beach. I want it to be so good between us." Leah quivered as she said the words, her face a portrait of insecurity.

"If it doesn't happen tonight, it's fine with me," Vic said, taking Leah's hand across the table. "It will sometime."

Back at the room, Leah couldn't get comfortable. Until two in the morning Vic tried to relax her, but when Leah finally locked herself in the bathroom out of embarrassment she was still a virgin. She came out an hour later and found Vic sound asleep. In front of the bathroom door Vic had placed a box of chocolates and a card of love with the note *Thanks for Marrying Me* written by hand; Leah never did learn when or how he managed to purchase them that day, but he had, and Leah breathed a sigh of relief. He had never once gotten mad or frustrated with her, content to be with the woman he loved, happy to have the one girl who truly made him happy in this life.

These were the best days of Vic's life so far, walking on the beach and holding her hand, seeing the rocky coast of Big Sur together, retaking the coast route back up to Carmel again, watching her sleep in the first light of morning. For whatever could be said of him, and there was much to say about so fine a man, it was most fitting to say that he loved her so, and in those days he loved her most of all.

The next few days were also some of the best in Leah's life, but for totally different reasons. She walked until her feet ached, taking in each new view, breathing in the invigorating air of the sea, wading in shallow tide pools, sifting the pure white sand through her hands and building nighttime bonfires of driftwood on the beach. Vic bought her things, frivolous things her mother would have never allowed her to buy: purses and scarves, silly shoes, party jewelry, fattening candy, and three or four "Carmel-by-the-Sea" shirts in myriad colors and logos. Leah was free to let go and the freedom felt as wonderful as Nashville had been stifling.

The nights, however, were the worst of times. The slight arousal of the time at the cottage at Lauren Lake was long gone, and what Leah saw in Vic, for all those many months of clinging black sweaters, Hollywood hair, and bulging muscles, was somehow transformed into obligation and chore and a sense of finality. Disappointingly, Vic was nowhere near as attractive as he had been before their marriage. The fact that Leah didn't love him made all the difference in the world. There was so much pressure: pressure to be good for him, pressure to look her best, pressure to feel something erotic whenever he touched her, and pressure to make her husband feel better than he had with the women before her. Leah figured she had something similar to what happens to actors who suddenly can't speak their lines, nicknaming it "bed fright." It started earlier every night, and when it was over she often lay silently and thought of Blake and how natural sex would have been with him because she loved him.

Vic knew something was missing, the key ingredient to making their nights as good as their days. On the last night of their honeymoon in Carmel, he had to find out the cause of such a remote sadness in her eyes.

"Is there anything else I can try?" he asked lovingly. "I love you so much, and I want you to feel as good as I do."

"I will," Leah snapped at him irritably. "Just don't worry about it. It's feeling better every time. And I'm glad you're finally getting to enjoy it."

Vic was undeterred. Sex was a big issue for him as he planned on being married forever, and sex was also a way for a man to be close to his wife. "It just seems like you hold back on me, like you don't want to let yourself go all the way," he said, trying not to get frustrated with Leah's patronizing. "It's like you're worrying too much about the sensation instead of just being with me. Maybe if you think about how much you love me, it will happen for you."

Love. What an awful word to hear when you've married the wrong man. Blake quickly filled Leah's mind and her face sank like an anvil in quicksand, as she lay rigidly on the bed while Vic waited patiently beside her.

"Hey, you still here?" Vic asked her, his words bringing Leah back to their hotel room and to their bed.

Leah refocused because she had to. "That will come, Vic," she replied. "Someday it will. I'll loosen up, and you'll see I love you. Be patient with me. Love like that takes time."

"But I've always felt it for you," Vic said sadly. "Don't you feel any love for me? Sometimes, it seems like it's almost there for you, that if you let your heart out your body will respond."

"Just be patient with me," Leah said, beginning to get angry, her eyelids closing and her teeth clenching together. "I'll be a good wife. I know I can. Just give me some time."

Chapter 13

LEAH NEVER FORGOT THE day, just a few months after her honeymoon in Carmel and three days after finding out she was pregnant, when Vic had to tell his family that baseball was finished. Two doctors and a shoulder specialist had given him the same prognosis: There was little that could be done for a torn rotator cuff. It was the end of his baseball career.

Leah accompanied him as Vic drove over to the same mint-green stucco home with the clover filled front yard and the sparkly concrete front porch where the baseball dreams had all begun, not more than a few blocks from their new apartment together as husband and wife. As he drove up, Vic saw the azalea bushes thick beneath the family room window, remembering years of missed catches and baseballs spinning away from him, the balls rolling past the lowest prickly branches and then underneath the shade of the house. With a flashlight, Vic and his father could still make out their outlines, the silhouetted roundness between two darkened boards, bunches of balls in places, and all lying just a good stretch of the arm away.

Ilene, Vic's mother, a stocky woman with lily white skin and apple red cheeks, came out to greet her only son, followed by her daughters, Noreen and Lorraine, both stout teenagers with broad, happy smiles, while Anthony, Vic's father, remained inside and read his newspaper. Anthony was never in any hurry to meet anyone, content to stay seated until the others stepped into his domain, wearing his fraying straw hat and the same wine-stained white T-shirt that he always wore on the weekends. He loved baseball, and he had pushed his son hard to make it to the major leagues, instilling in him the same toiling work ethic that had characterized his own immigrant success, so proud of Vic for his accomplishments in America's favorite pastime, the big leagues his one all-consuming hope for his boy.

Leah had spent much time already with Vic's family and she liked them. She smiled when she saw Ilene. Ilene led Vic and Leah in and brought a gigantic piece of lemon chiffon pie and a cold glass of milk into the front room for her son, Leah declining a piece for herself, much too nervous to eat given the circumstances, as the family sat down to hear why Vic had called them together.

Ilene noticed that her son wasn't eating much of his favorite dessert. "You not feeling good, Vic? I've never seen you poke at my pie without digging in. What's the matter with you, you getting sick?"

"No, I'm not sick, just worn out," he said, fooling nobody.

"Nervous about being a dad here soon?" Ilene asked, her flawless white skin a soft, pearly satin and her face full of love. "Don't worry, the girls and I will take care of the baby. You and Leah can go out on dates like you was dating again. Have dinner at Francesco's, go to the movies, buy Leah some new clothes."

"I'd like that," Leah added smiling. Nobody smiled along with her, the nerves too high for any laughter or casual ease, but at least from Leah's quip they could all tell it wasn't a divorce or marital trouble.

"I've got something I need to tell all of you," Vic started, his voice beginning to choke with emotion. "And I don't really know how to begin. I know you're going to be disappointed in me, but there is nothing I can do about what I'm about to tell you."

Anthony sat up in his chair.

"Well, what is it?" Ilene said, fear rising in her voice. "You look pale and you're leaning to one side, like you're in pain. A mother can always tell about her little boy. Something's wrong with you. We're your family, Vic, you can tell us anything."

Vic looked directly at Anthony, whose old country eyes flashed the way Vic's did, with a sparkle of kindness through the aloofness, so unsuspecting of the horrible news. The room was suddenly stuffy. Vic felt sick and dizzy sitting in his chair. Closing his eyes for balance, he gradually lifted his head and returned his gaze to his father's face, gulping down a wad of cotton in the process. He wanted to be a man in the hardest moment of his lifetime, and that thought alone allowed the words to come to him.

"Dad, I hurt my arm. I hurt it real bad," he said, trying to keep his eyes focused on Anthony without looking down to the floor. "Doctor Wilson and a specialist told me I won't ever pitch again. Doctor Whitman said the same thing. I tore a rotator cuff in my shoulder, and they say it won't heal well enough to pitch again."

A miserable stillness descended on the room.

"I know how much you were all counting on this, on me making it to the big leagues," Vic said, going on while he had the strength. "I know I let you down, all of you. You've been so good to me, such great parents to be blessed with, and I wasn't good enough for you. I want to pay you back for all you've done for me, those times you watched me pitch, feeding me, taking me to church with you, being the best family a guy could be from."

Vic put his hands up to his face. He couldn't look at his family. There was too much pain in seeing their faces. He stared instead at the floor, the floor smearing in his vision. "I'm sorry I couldn't be more for you," he said despondently. "I know I'm not much of a son now."

Noreen and Lorraine waited for their mother and father to speak to their brother. Neither girl moved, but both began to sniffle. Vic was their hero and he always had been, and now he was hurting and needed his family.

Vic placed the small plate of pie and glass of milk down softly on the floor. His head sank and stayed bowed for as long as it took to get some kind of response to the words that had destroyed the dream of that household. The others saw a slight heaving of his muscled shoulders as he sat direly in his chair.

Ilene waited for her husband to say something, imploring him with her eyes. Slowly, Anthony stood up, as tall as he had ever stood in his lifetime, not knowing what he felt inside or what he would say to his only son. Vic looked up at him, his eyes swollen and bleary, his muscular body suddenly boyish again. All eyes in the room were on Anthony. Vic leaned back on his chair and his sisters slid over to him, to support their brother in his time of need. Noreen put her head against Vic's knee and Lorraine held onto his other leg with her trembling hand. Ilene, ashen white, was terrified to find out how much Vic's baseball career had meant to her husband, and she was quivering and near tears herself. Leah sat petrified.

"You've been a good son," Anthony began slowly. "No trouble for any of us. You're going to have a family of your own soon, a family that is going to need you. It's a good thing to be needed. Do your wife and your child right by you, and life will take care of the rest. I'll call around for some good jobs. If you need to, you can stay with us. Your mother and sisters would like that."

The awful silence in the room returned. Anthony started toward his boy, but the wall between men came up like an impregnable fortress. He got halfway across the room before he veered off and walked slowly down the hall. He went into his bedroom and lightly closed the door behind him, the softest he had ever closed it in his life, and the others heard a muffled squeak as he fell onto the bed.

Ilene, her tears the tears of relief and comfort for her only son, went over to Vic, the apple redness returned to her cheeks, and with her two daughters wrapped her arms around her only boy and held him closely. "We love you, my son, we all do," Ilene said crying.

Vic opened up his arms and the women who loved him filled the space with love. Leah remained seated in her chair and she watched the women of Vic's family console her husband in his moment of anguish and shame. She thought they were a nice family to rally around him as they did. But she never went over to her husband in support of him. Inside, she was bitter about being denied her status as the wife of a baseball star. She had counted on the success that fame would bring. She had counted on that as one counts on air. Now she had worries of how they'd make it past his injury and pay their bills each month. They might even struggle for a time, or perhaps always struggle, like her own family had back in Tennessee. Never once had she imagined money would be a concern while married to a baseball star like Vic. It was, along with seeing California, the primary reason she had married him.

Leah felt herself turn to rock as she sat and watched another of life's bitter defeats hit her squarely in the face. Vic's injury was her injury. His wound was her misfortune. It didn't seem conceivable, but she changed irrevocably in the short time it took for her to sit there and watch a family come together in love. Acrimony heaped on acrimony as she remembered her lifetime. First a mama who discounted her, then Blake leaving for another, and then the sordid actions of the accusers. Now her own husband had let her down. As a larvae transmutes into a moth, Leah turned her attention to a defensive concern for self, alienated from her appreciative core, less the sweet child of youth and more the object of self-absorption and her own primacy. It hurt to look at her. It hurt to see the pain that made her withdraw. But there was no one who knew her well enough to see it. When Ilene and the girls returned to their places, Vic gulped down the huge piece of lemon chiffon pie in three large bites and poured himself a second glass of milk from the kitchen, and he smiled for the first time that entire day, while Leah sat longing for the man she thought he should have been.

Chapter 14

VIC EVENTUALLY SETTLED ON a sales job with American Paper Products and did very well at it. The pay was good and there was plenty of opportunity to move up in the organization. He dreamed of management someday. Seven months later Leah had a son. She named him David after her favorite character in the Bible, and recuperated at the apartment for six weeks past another change of the season. That first spring in California had been a beautiful one, the roses blooming in the gardens, the berry bushes lush with fruit, her own baby growing full inside of her. Then summer came in a massive heat wave that sent the temperatures climbing to over a hundred degrees for ten straight days, the fog staying away for weeks at a time. When she felt able, after the weather had cooled again and David had gained in strength, Leah set out to find a home to raise her baby in, a real home, someplace with a yard and a school nearby and friendly neighbors with children of their own, and she tried not to think of the disappointment of being denied her status as the wife of a budding baseball star.

Weekend searches led the couple to Fremont, a small town at the time, twenty miles south of Oakland along the last of the bay's flattest marshland, where the slow rolls of the East Bay hills adjoin the taller mountains of the Mount Hamilton range and the Evergreen Ridge. The home they finally settled on was new, small, and comfortable, the down payment a gift from Anthony instead of a wedding reception, but Leah had to forego her dream of living in the hills as the larger homes higher up were much too expensive for a young family starting out on a salesman's budget. She tried not to think of that, either, but some days she thought of it still and felt bitter.

Leah immediately set up a nursery in the bedroom closest to hers. Blue borders rimmed each wall, each inset with pointy gold stars and milky moons. Leah went to a drapery store in town and bought some navy blue curtains with a crisp white edging that matched the borders and hung the curtains by herself. They were cheap draperies and way too short for the windows, barely covering the sills, but Leah loved the color and she wouldn't replace them for the longest while. The church gave her a dark-wood crib stuffed full of baby blankets and a cushy foam pad, and Leah spent hours in the baby's room while her little David slept, placing a tiny night light low on the wall so she could watch her son sleep without flipping on the wall switch. She checked on him three or four times each night, and when he was awake dusted his bottom with baby powder until the room went airy white. To finish off the decoration, Leah purchased four bronze plaques from a trophy mart and had them custom engraved with scripture, hanging a different adage on each wall:

In the beginning...
This is my son, in whom I am well pleased.
I will fear no evil, for thou art with me.
Blessed are the children.

At night, Leah read passages from the Bible to her son laying on the floor next to the night light. She brought in blankets and pillows and read for hours at a time. She read mostly the books of David to her son, but she kept returning to the book of Genesis to begin each reading because it seemed most fitting to start with the greatest creation of them all. Leah was sure God was with her in those days. One night she swore she saw an aura around her baby. Leah often stood in the middle of the room, her hands on the gates of the crib, breathing in the smell of her son. Occasionally, she fell asleep in little David's room, leaning up against the wall or rolled over on her side on a floor pillow by the door, and Vic would have to come in the middle of the night and pick her up off the carpet and carry her back to bed.

One night, when Vic was away traveling, Leah tiptoed into David's room to check on him and stroked the thin tresses of his baby fine hair with her motherly fingers. His breaths were slow and peaceful, and he didn't fuss when his mama came near him, content to lay in the low light of his room and twist up in his fuzzy warm blanket. Leah inhaled the powdery smell of her baby and kissed him gently on his forehead.

To Leah, her baby looked like an angel. His preciousness made her say the truth to him, a truth she had never expressed even to herself but had always suspected.

"I love you, my sweet son," Leah whispered. "I'll always be here for you. You're my life now."

David continued to breathe in the rhythm of sleep, each teeny breath perfectly synchronized, and Leah listened for a minute to the wee air in his nostrils before she whispered again to him.

"There was a reason you were born," Leah said, as softly as she could. "Your father and I shouldn't be married to each other. We're not right together; I know that now. He's a good man in a lot of ways, he really is. You'll see that as you get older. He works hard, he works hard for us, and he means well, but it's not love between him and me. I don't love him like I should. I never have."

The baby turned on his side without waking up.

"God must have a purpose for you; the reason I married your father has to be you," Leah went on. "There's no other explanation. I've always loved another, but he didn't love me back. Nobody ever has, not like they should have. My life is to be with you, to be your mother. What I've done, the choices I've made, won't add up to much for myself, but yours can. When you're older, I'm sure you'll want to know why I did what I did, and you'll ask me what my motivations were in marrying a man I knew was wrong for me. I hope by then I'll have an answer for you, for I don't know why I've done what I've done. I've fought against myself for so long now it must be who I am; I must hate myself, I guess. I can't argue that anymore; it's too plain to deny. But I'll make sure you get the best of life, and I'll push your father to do all he can for you.

I made sure you'd be brought up in the grandest place of all, in California, away from the South, where the old ways would have ruined you. Nashville would have held you back, and I wouldn't stand for that."

David slept even deeper. Leah lifted the downy blanket off her baby's chest and folded it at his waist; he burbled once and rolled onto his other side, sleeping the deep sleep that babies do. Leah left the room on tiptoe and closed the door behind her, and when she made it to her own room she prayed a thankful prayer to God for the blessing of her son, and she prayed for the Lord to give her the strength to make it through a lifetime for him.

***

A short time later, Margaret called in the afternoon. It was dinnertime back in Nashville, but in California the sun was still high overhead. It was bright outside, but Leah sensed the grayness of tragedy and doom. Margaret's tone was subdued, her voice cracking, and Leah felt that had her mother been able, Margaret would have hugged her through the line.

"Hi, Leah, I've got some bad news, baby. I'm sorry to have to be the one to tell you what I'm about to tell you. You might want to sit down and get comfortable before I do."

Leah took a seat. "What is it, Mother?"

"Honey, I ran into Ronnie Wayfield from Sojourn Creek today at a Bible fair. I've known Ronnie since I was a child. Anyway, he said that Beth and her husband Tommy were killed in a car accident in Florida. I just thought you ought to know."

A horrible blackness descended upon Leah. The world went indifferently cold. "Oh, no, Mama, it can't be. It just can't be. Beth can't be dead. She's much too young to be dead. You're wrong Mama, you've got to be wrong about that."

"I'm so sorry, Sugar. I'm just so sorry to have to be the one to tell you."

Immediately, tears flowed from Leah's eyes and she felt her stomach wrench into an agonizing ball. Her sorrow was as heavy as a hunk of marble in a mausoleum.

Margaret heard her daughter crying through the phone. "I'm sorry, Sugar. I know how much you loved Beth. Ronnie said everyone at Sojourn is really tore up. I'm going to see Beth's mama and daddy tomorrow. Marian is coming with me. We're bringing a bouquet of flowers and some food for the family. They already had the funeral. Beth and Tommy were killed over a week ago."

Margaret heard more sobs coming through the line. "You okay?" she asked her daughter.

"I have to go, Mother. I'll call you later when I'm able."

Leah hung up the phone and ran outside. She shook so violently it seemed as though her body might disintegrate. Time stood surreally still. Waves of anguish overtook her. She cried, remembering the college friend who had lived her own way and who knew exactly what she wanted from this life, and Leah prayed with her heart full open, the tears streaming down her cheeks as she questioned why life has to sometimes be the way it is, standing mournfully in the California sun, her head lifted up to the sky, eyes red and blurry, so far from Florida and the turns of life. She saw Beth in her mind, the beautiful laughter, that sweet country face, the precious dimples and disappointed pout. She smelled the apple blossom lotion Beth used to wear and felt the happiness of her hug.

Through her sorrow, Leah put her trust in God.

"God, save my friend and her husband, Tommy," she wailed into the brightness of the sun. "I loved her, Lord, and her heart loved You. I know she did. When she read Your Bible, I could see it in her eyes. They were such pretty eyes, my God, such blue and pretty eyes."

A short time later Vic came home from work. Leah told him the news through her sobs. Vic changed clothes and went into the backyard and dug some holes for some pretty flower bushes. When he finished, after he had placed the bushes in the ground and patted the last of the sod around their pedicels, Leah watched her husband sitting quietly on the ground. He shook his head a number of times and then wiped his eyes with his hands. In a few minutes, he stood and walked over to the fence, his strongly built body leaning over the top of it, staring eastward toward the bluest of the sky. He stood at the fence for a long while, the sun low in the sky behind him, remembering his little buddy, the way he laughed and swung the bat, a hitch in his swing like a droopy slack in a line. The little guy never could hit the baseball much. Vic remembered Tommy's joy when he had first met and dated Beth, how it suddenly didn't matter that he couldn't hit a baseball very hard or even very well, that nothing mattered compared to what he felt for her. Vic might have stood forever looking eastward in the sky, but Leah called him in to dinner as the sun set into a glowing pinkness, and they ate their meal reliving the precious lives of their precious friends from their precious days together in Nashville.

That night, after watching him labor in the yard, Leah almost loved her husband, and she fell asleep in his arms instead of in little David's room, dreaming of Nashville and the countryside and of country girls who walk under the gentle care of the Master's springtime sun.

Chapter 15

TIME PASSED. THE 1960S arrived as a continuation of the stable fifties, of the pattern and ritual of suburban living that fed an undeclared angst in search of a name, and to most people not much seemed changed. Only the teeniest symptoms of malaise were noted by psychologists and social commentators, and if Leah and Vic weren't settled, settled in the way most married couples were settled in those ostensibly halcyon days, they were at least close to living the image. The bedroom never became a place for mutual pleasure, but Vic liked having someone at his side, someone to make his meals, wash his clothes and clean his house, and he liked having a companion to go places with on the weekends when he was home from traveling for work. Leah, for her part, liked having a husband who worked hard at his job and who built a life for her, and she tried not to think about what might have been had she married Blake or loved another in his stead. David grew into a toddler, full of boundless energy and a head of curly brown locks, running everywhere, never able to sit still for any length of time, and Leah kept herself trim just by chasing him around their home. There was a naturalness to Leah as a mother, her skin taking on a warm rose color and her eyes twinkling with pride, and whenever Vic hugged his wife around the house, Leah felt as soft to him as an old robe. Motherhood made Leah happy, and in those days her spirit was filled with a satisfied buoyancy and even delight, and seldom did she cry or complain.

Life went on in its usual way until the phone rang at three-thirty one morning. Leah knew something had to be wrong, especially since it was still dark outside and the phone rarely rang as it was. David was now five years old and his first tooth had just fallen out. That's how Leah remembered it, that horrible morning in 1963 with Margaret crying on the line through a crackling static and her own shakiness.

"Hi Honey, I've got some bad news," Margaret said, her voice cracking with emotion. "Your daddy is sick, very sick. The doctors think it's the worst he's ever had. His lungs are full, and he's struggling for air. They have no idea how long he'll last. Marian is here and so is William. I don't know about Kay. I sure hope you can come home, sweetheart."

Vic turned over to Leah, lifting his head off the pillow. He was groggy and irritable. "Who the heck is that?" he asked. "What time is it? It's dark outside, for crying out loud."

"It's my mother," Leah said in a hoarse voice, gathering herself. "Go on back to sleep."

"Honey, you there?" the voice on the end of the line asked.

"The line has some static in it, Mother," Leah mumbled. "What did you say again? Is Daddy sick?"

The line cleared up as Margaret spoke her next words. "It's bad, Sugar. Come home quickly. He may not last much longer than a day or so. Your daddy has been calling for you since yesterday evening, when he first fell ill."

Leah began to awaken to full consciousness, the horrible news sinking in and jolting her into a heightened state of awareness. She heard tears in the background. Dread swept through her body and instantly her heart ached in sadness. Suddenly, she was alert and decisive. "Oh my God, Mama. I'll be there tomorrow. I'll call you from the airport when I get there."

"Come today, darling," Margaret said, choking on the words. "Your daddy may not be here tomorrow."

Vic heard Margaret's last words through the receiver. He sat up in bed and rubbed Leah's back lovingly as Leah hung up the phone and sagged into his arms.

"My daddy's in trouble," Leah said quivering. "My daddy's in trouble."

"Walton," Vic seconded, looking away into the darkness and recalling the lanky old man in his mind. "My God, he's still so young."

Vic felt Leah's trembling, and he held her in his arms until she was steady enough to get up from the bed and shower. After a cup of instant coffee, Vic drove Leah to the airport before the sun came up, the sky over the eastern hills taking on the first lightening of day.

At the passenger terminal drop off, Leah spoke to Vic with a seriousness with which she had never before spoken to him. "I don't like leaving my baby," she said, pointing to a sleeping David lying in the back seat. Her face was horribly distressed, and she looked tired and frazzled in the breaking light of dawn. "He's never been without me."

Vic's eyes, tired of their own accord, tried to console her with a reassuring look. "We'll be fine," he said. "I'll take a few days off if I have to, and my mother can watch him while I work. I won't travel till you come back home. Think of your father. He needs you now."

The flight home to Nashville was long and dreary. There was high cloud cover and thunderstorms along the way that caused heavy turbulence and rattled nerves. Marian picked up Leah at the airport and filled her in on their ride over to Groveland Street with the details of their daddy's illness and the events of the last two days. His smoking had finally caught up to him. When they arrived, Walton was in bed, pallid and gaunt, his feeble breaths shallow and short, a fan whizzing in the corner by the window to provide a comforting flow of air. He had been calling out for Leah all day, holding on, waiting to say the words of love to his precious child, and he gasped when he saw her at the foot of the bed. With her there, he knew it was time to die.

The others had already said their farewells. Leah was the last; that was the way Walton preferred it, and he told his family as much. Nobody was hurt by his wishes; they all knew how much he had loved her through the years. Leah stepped over slowly to the side of the bed with her Bible in her hands, her heart heavy in her chest. Trembling, she sat down beside her daddy. Her eyes were sorrowful, and she brushed the curls back from her eyes so her daddy could see the full of her face.

The light of the room was subdued, and even with the fan swirling the air, the room was stuffy and hot from the stifling humidity that was Nashville's summer. Drapes hung in morbid stillness. The room smelled of medicine and inhalant and dirty linen. On the dresser nearest to Walton's bed were pictures of Walton and Margaret at their wedding, then as a young couple together building their life, and then the kids individually and in groups. A big picture of Leah at her high school graduation sat on the edge of the dresser facing the bed, closest to him.

Walton opened his sickly eyes. "Don't cry, my little Leah," he said, before another hoarse cough rattled the room. He choked for a spell, his face contorting and then easing, and he sucked in some air before speaking again. "I'm going to be fine. I've lived a long time."

Leah's face was dripping wet. She couldn't speak even if she'd have tried.

"It's fine now," Walton said to her in a whisper. "Don't you worry none about me." Walton inhaled all the stagnant air he could in order to speak again, and then he coughed and had to breathe in all over.

"You were *my* child," he said. "A daddy shouldn't have favorites, and I'd never admit it except for now, but I could tell you knew. And it's only because the others didn't need me as much. You never have to feel guilty about that. I loved them all they'd let me."

Leah bit her lip tightly to keep from crumbling.

"Your mother's been hard on you, because of Kay," Walton said. "She didn't want another child like her. None of us did. It was unfair to you, and I'm sorry for that."

Leah still couldn't say anything. Walton coughed again and closed his eyes, death tugging at his chest. It took some time before he could speak again.

"I know you loved that boy, that rich boy before your husband," Walton said. "I'm sorry you met him so young. Sometimes, the ones you love don't love you like you want them to."

Leah leaned in close to hear every word her daddy said. She smelled the familiarity of him. Walton was straining with everything he had left to summon the strength to speak the last words of his life, the words that had kept him alive the past two days.

"Life, my little Leah, don't always turn out the way you want it. But there's good in it anyway." Walton choked again. His hands were tinted blue, quivering whenever he moved them about, his face shaking in unison with his hands. After another delay he went on the best he could.

"There's your family, your children, work, and what you enjoy doing in your spare time. For me, it was hunting and catching fish. I always enjoyed being out in nature. Nature is life, it throws the good and bad at you, its beauty as well as its challenges. For you, it will be something else. Find it."

Leah composed herself so she could respond. "Daddy, for me it's being close to God, and close to the ones I love. I've looked for answers, Daddy; all my life I've looked for them. I want to know why I lived, what counts the most about living, and what the purpose of living is. It seems to all come back to love. I never loved anything more than you, my child, and my God. I saw, all those days, how much you didn't want to be here, what with Mama getting after you all the time, but you provided for us anyway and made sure we had enough. I knew you weren't happy, not as happy as folks should be. But you did your best for us."

Walton retched and the phlegm came up like glue, his eyes reddening from the coughing spell. Leah held his hand tightly as he gasped. His bones stuck through the sheets like javelins, and he sweat the clammy sweat of a high fever. Death was a vacuum sucking out the air of the room and Leah struggled herself to find a breath. After a minute or two, Walton patted her to let her know he could continue.

"It was no chore," he said, a faint smile on his purplish lips. "Watching you grow up made it all worthwhile. I used to check on you before I went to bed at night, trying not to wake you. Did you know I looked in on you? Oh, my sweet Leah, my baby girl, I love you so much. In the morning I never liked leaving for fishing without peeping in on you again."

Leah watched her daddy breathe with nothing coming in. She clung to his hand. Walton's skin was gray, his eyelids red and sticky, his face exhausted. He squeezed her hand desperately and then rested for a moment, his eyes clamped shut.

"Don't go, Daddy," Leah cried.

Memories of childhood filled her mind. She remembered the day when Walton took her fishing with him to Lake Montgomery, her line snarled on a branch, a hook stuck deep into her daddy's thumb, him bleeding on himself, wetting a fishing rag with lake water and pressing it firmly to his thumb. He just told her to yank a little softer next time and to *feel* the bite instead of jerking. He never complained or yelled at her, and she finally caught an ugly old catfish at the end of the day.

She recalled bringing her daddy to the open house at grammar school, him holding her hand, so nervous as he shuffled along, but also so proud of her. Schools made him feel uncomfortable, but he had taken her anyway because she had asked him to.

In the summers, Walton had made a hanging swing from an old innertube tied to the tallest backyard oak, and he pushed her from behind with his hands squarely on her back. She remembered his hands of love stopping her when she went too high. She saw the grease in the old work shed and the faded decals on the fishing boat and the mower lying next to the fence. Her mind filled with the smell of paint brushes in thinner buckets and wood rollers in pans, and she saw her daddy's gray whiskers on the weekends when he didn't shave. She thought of how shy a man he was and the patience it took to get that old motor boat to work, and the evenings spent 'round the fire.

Leah watched him open his eyes again. "I love you," Walton said, convulsing. "I'll take you with me."

Leah placed her head on her daddy's skinny shoulder, the bones sticking into the side of her face. Walton closed his eyes and his last breath was a faint moan.

Leah stretched her arms across him and reached back behind his neck, pulling his head toward her own chest. She cradled his head to her bosom, her river of love for her father overflowing its banks, past any boundaries she had ever known, and the pain in her heart was an endless drowning of sorrow and opportunity lost.

"I love you, Daddy," she whispered in anguish, rocking his balding head back and forth in her arms. "I love you so much."

The others burst into the room and huddled around Leah. "God took him," Leah cried out, her face a wash of disbelief and anguish. Her wail went out past the ceiling and into the void beyond. The room grew darker and the air much more still. It was as quiet as a tomb. A good man was gone.

"Dear God," Leah wailed. "Please take him. Please take my daddy home with You to heaven."

***

Leah stayed in Nashville for a few days after the funeral but she didn't drive through her old neighborhood or visit those familiar haunts of her youth, and she made sure to stay clear of Belle Meade and the Peabody district and anyplace else that smacked of Blake. With her daddy's death, Nashville had lost any appeal it had ever had. On the plane ride back to California Leah thought she'd probably never return to Tennessee, to any of the South for that matter, and when the landing gear shuddered into place on the final approach to SFO over the San Francisco Bay, Leah felt the feeling securely in her bones. Banks of fog hovered out over Highway 92, creeping their way in through gaps in the coastal range of mountains. As Leah deplaned she breathed in the chilly ocean air, a moist gust lifting her blond hair up and off her narrow shoulders, the last reddish torch of day highlighting the delicate contour of her oval face, so pretty in the sunset hour. Vic was standing on the tarmac, waiting for her with that same bright smile of his, a delighted David by his side.

"Hi, I've missed you," her husband said.

"It's good to be home," was all Leah could muster. She looked down at her son. "How's my baby?" she asked, hugging him to her leg. She lifted him up and into her arms. "I've missed you so much, my precious boy. I thought of you the whole time I was in Nashville. I truly did. I wish you could have been with me."

***

For the next interval of their lives, almost a year or so, Vic was remarkably attentive to his languishing wife, as he knew Leah was struggling with something grave within, a defeatism and bitterness she could never quite fully suppress. Leah had changed with Walton's death. Her lifelong frailty became more apparent, although it would be inaccurate to say she had lost completely her occasional robustness, for indeed there were still many moments when her face was warmed with health and her eyes flickered in delight. It was more that she felt victimized by life and also more alone. Inwardly, she began to doubt in herself. But she didn't want to talk about it, and when Vic brought it up one night over a late night coffee cake, Leah cried and said that nothing was wrong and could she please just be left alone. Vic didn't travel for six weeks after that evening, but when he finally went on the road again Leah sunk to another level and she never did fully regain her vigor.

It was tragic to watch her devolve and it hurt everyone who knew her, for it seemed so unlike her to lash out and sulk. It was as if the goodness of her nature was being slowly corrupted through nothing more than the mere act of living, as death and broken dreams so often mark the course of human life. She seemed in those days as an understudy to suffering. Her once considerate nature had been encroached upon by greed, and she borrowed from the till of life with no intent to repay. She began to take instead of give. Her valley of a smile had turned into a bitter gulch and dubious seemed her powers, even her connection to the Lord. Soon, she came to believe that perhaps she was ill-prepared for a life that required so much of her, and as is true for most who perceive their own inadequacies, Leah attacked others instead of first questioning her own foundations.

One night was typical, Vic returning home with good news on his lips after a long day of travel, when Leah launched at him for no apparent reason.

"You're an hour late," she said to him angrily. "Don't you have the decency to call or be here on time? If you don't care about me, you should at least care about your son."

Vic was tired. The drive from Reno had been a long one. He snapped for all the times when he had said nothing. "I can't care about my son," he growled. "I don't get to see him, even when I'm home. You keep him to yourself, away from me, smothering him, because you have nothing else in your life to live for."

Leah was shocked by the accuracy of his assessment. His words did more than stun or startle; they pierced her. How had Vic known she felt that way so much of the time? How had he known? His accuracy only made her madder and she lashed out at him again.

"What am I supposed to have?" she asked scathingly. "You? You're gone all the time. No father is gone that much. My daddy never was. Anthony either. I know because Ilene and I talked about it. So, you know what? You're the oddball here."

"I have to travel for work, so we can have things. Especially with all the shopping you do. Every single weekend, more junk for the house. The house looks like a clutter box."

"Shut up, just shut up," Leah screamed at him.

"Hey, what the heck is eating you?"

"You think your job is like playing ball," Leah raged on. "Going from town to town, tearing it up at night, while I sit home alone with a child, half the time scared to death. Some protector you turned out to be. Well, baseball is over. You didn't make it. You weren't good enough, okay? So it's time to be a real man now, to stay home with your family and be here for the both of us. It's time to grow up and be like the other dads on the block."

Vic thought of himself as a hardworking father and he resented being called otherwise. "The other dads have wives who love them," he yelled back, tearing his tie from his neck. "Wives who share their children, wives who love their husbands for who they are. Their wives don't sit around and wish they'd married somebody else."

"I don't wish I'd married somebody else," Leah said angrily, surprised again that Vic knew her so well. "I'm good for you. I keep a good house; I wash; I clean; I give it to you, too, when you want it, pretty good judging from the other night."

"Hey, c'mon. David's in the house."

"Well, then, get off my back. I'm a good wife for you."

The mention of David calmed them both down. There was a brief respite. "But you don't let me in," Vic said, pleading with his wife like a child for ice cream an hour before dinner. "If you did, we'd be together, not at each other's throats all the time. I'd trade all the sex for one night when you're really with me, not for obligation or duty, but because you love me."

Leah calmed herself down. Vic had sought a truce with those words. "I said that was coming and it will," she said, not even convincing herself. "Give it time. I'm just so busy with David."

"No, you're not busy with him, you love him," Vic said, his hands open and out in front of him, begging for Leah to understand. "And you never get tired of him, do you? You know why? Because love grows more every day when you love someone. We could be like that, if you'd let us. If he's fine to love, how come I'm not?"

"David needs me," Leah responded quickly. "You don't."

"Yes, I do. I love you," Vic said tenderly.

Leah looked off into the distance. She didn't want her eyes to give her away, for Vic to confirm what he had always suspected. It was much simpler to simply pretend. If she pretended long enough, maybe she could pretend forever.

The fight was over. Vic loosened his shirt and poured himself a cherry soda from the refrigerator into a large cup of ice and pulled a chair from under the table. He sat down and Leah sat at the other end of the table and waited for him to speak. "Well, instead of fighting maybe we should try and be happy," he said diplomatically. "Anyway, I've got some good news, if you want to hear it."

"What is it?" Leah asked sardonically.

"I'm going to be around more because I got promoted today to territory manager. Don told me when I called into the office."

Leah's rainy mood changed like the weather. Suddenly, she turned sunny and apologetic. "Promoted? Oh, my God, that's great, Honey. Why didn't you say so in the first place? Oh Vic, I'm so sorry about being upset when you first came in, I'm just so sorry for being irritable sometimes. It isn't your fault. Oh, Sweetheart, my God, this is great news, absolutely fantastic news."

"You sure?" Vic asked warily.

"Sure I'm sure. I don't know why I'm so bitchy sometimes. I don't mean to be. David's been some trouble today and, oh well, who cares about that anymore. This is wonderful news. Just wonderful news. Oh, baby, we did it."

Leah stepped over to her husband and gave him a kiss on the cheek. He felt the warmth of her face on his own and he saw in her eyes a joyous celebration.

"You got the big promotion, Honey," Leah said happily. "The company likes you, and Don likes you. You have to continue to impress him. He can take you far, take us far, and you know what, Honey, I'm proud of you. I'm so proud of you. Think of what this means for David."

Vic was thankful the fight had ended. He had his willing audience. "You know it's almost $10,000 more a year, with a better car," he said proudly. "I'll be more or less my own boss; Don will come in every couple of weeks for a day or two, the rest of the time I'm on my own. They gave me two choices: Sacramento or Modesto. They won't let me stay in the Bay Area, but the next move would be back here. You don't mind moving do you?"

"For $10,000 more a year?" Leah said incredulously. "Are you nuts? Of course, we're moving. But not to Sacramento. I don't like it up there. For some reason that town just never seemed right to me. Too flat and hot. What's the other place like?"

"We'll go see it this weekend," Vic said, rubbing his eyes. "You can get a mansion there for what this place costs. It's a small valley town, but it's growing. I played ball there one year. Summers are hot, winters about the same as here. It's a great place to raise a kid. The Little League programs are very strong."

Leah's mind was already busy at work. "I want a nice house," she said cogitating. "I know you can afford it now, Mr. Territory Manager, so it better be a beauty. Close to a good school, and with a big lot. I want a nice yard for David to play in, with a park nearby. I insist on friendly neighbors. Oh, and big wide streets with a line of trees like the ones where I grew up in Nashville."

"Anything else?"

"No, that'll do for now."

The rest of that night consisted of a good meal, congratulatory sex, and pillow talk of promotions and larger houses. For some families that's enough, or it has to be, and it was for Leah's.

Chapter 16

Back in the early 1960s, the drive to Modesto from Fremont took the better part of an hour and a half. Between the two towns lay a small group of sun-baked hills that gradually flattened into miles and miles of pasture and tillage. Canals carried fresh running snow water down from the Sierra Nevada Mountains to the valley floor below, liquid gold to the locals, allowing the farmers to grow their checkerboard pattern of green and gold squares, fields of corn and beets and alfalfa, for without the water the area would have been little more than a wasteland, most of the land rangy and raw. Brown-backed migrant workers toiled in the fields under broad straw hats, the women and children working the fields along with the men. A lone highway, Route 132, lead directly into town, traversing the San Joaquin river basin past the Old Fisherman's Club and the Sink Hole, the road typically clogged with farm machinery, slow moving tractors, and delivery trucks for the Gallo vineyards and distribution center that lay on the western edge of the town.

Downtown Modesto in those days was like a western movie filmed in Iowa: old stone buildings, whistlestops, tower granaries, colonnade courthouses, and swinging door saloons. The local newspaper, *The Modesto Bee,* fronted along main street next to a jewelry store fashioning a *Get a Ring Before She Gets Away* sign, and most every business was the proud sponsor of some charity or local Little League team. Modesto reminded Leah of the many farming towns outside Nashville, and when Vic pulled over for gas she had her proof that farming communities are pretty much the same all over the country.

An oily attendant, fresh from a lube job, came out to greet them. "You folks look lost," he said, wiping his hands on a red rag hanging from a blackened belt loop. "Not from Modesto, are you?"

"No, we're not, but I played ball here some years ago," Vic said proudly. "The Reds. I know my way around town from back then, but we're looking for a new area of town, in north Modesto, where I've heard they're building some nice new homes."

"Say, what's your name?" the attendant said grinning. "I follow the Reds. Have for years."

"Vic Boletti. I was a pitcher."

"Well I'll be," the attendant said, his eyes widening and his hand smacking his forehead. "I should have recognized you. You were good. Just here for a couple of seasons?"

"Actually, only one," Vic said. "I was sent back to the South to play Triple A, in Nashville. Then I hurt my arm and had to quit the game."

You'd have thought the attendant was in the presence of Mays or Mantle. "Too bad, because you sure threw smoke," the grease monkey said admiringly. "Man, you threw hard, I do remember that. Figured you and Wesley, the right fielder, husky guy that hit all those long home runs, well, I figured you'd both make the big leagues in no time flat. Hey, whatever happened to him?"

"He played with me for a year in Columbia," Vic said. "He hasn't made the majors yet. Last I heard he was still playing Triple A in New Orleans. He couldn't hit the curve ball, not the real big benders they throw up in the show. Say, could you fill her up?"

"Sure, and just take McHenry up about four miles and make a right at the last light," the attendant said. "You can't miss it. If you come to a stop sign, you went one street too far."

"Thanks," Vic said. The attendant began to move away, but Vic suddenly realized he had only been talking about himself and felt guilty about his self-absorption. He smiled at the attendant. "Say now, did you play any ball?" he asked him nicely.

"No sir, I wasn't much of a ballplayer, played a little high school ball here in town, hit two fifty my senior year, but I sure do love the game. Must have been something playing it in front of all those people, huh?"

"Yep, it sure was. But life goes on." A sadness fell over Vic's face. The attendant thought he might have offended him and he scooted off to help an old lady with a spraying radiator hose. When he came back he was wet with fizz, his shirt so filthy black the red lettering on his name patch was obscured and unreadable, and Vic never did manage to get the guy's name.

"That'll be five dollars," the attendant said. "It was closer to six, but I rounded down on account of meeting you."

"Why thank you," Leah chimed in from her seat. "That is right courteous of you."

The attendant dipped down for a peek into the passenger side to see the sweet southern voice that had spoken the kind words to him. "Your husband was the best pitcher I ever saw, Ma'am. Best that's come through Modesto, that's for sure. Good luck to you both."

***

Within an hour, Leah and Vic found a home they liked on a large spacious lot, not far from David's new elementary school. Six weeks later, Leah's new life in Modesto began, in a new home, with her territory manager husband and a good son by her side, and it was the smoothest time of her married life and also the happiest.

In less than three months, Vic doubled the business in his territory and he traveled much less than he had in his first years with the company, so his bosses left him alone. Summers in the valley are blazing hot, but the evenings cool down to excellent barbecuing weather, and that first year the neighbors came over for dinner more than they ate at their own homes. Leah taught the neighborhood kids *Red Light, Green Light* and *Mother, May I?* and played with them in the front yard at night like a schoolgirl, giggling as she ran by the lamppost, the summer moths zooming in and around the lighted post like pesky fighter squadrons.

Sure enough, it seemed that one big moth found her open mouth each night, to the howling delight of the children. She'd choke and cough and spit in exaggeration until the kids heaved over in laughter, but the swarming of the insects reminded Leah of the June Bugs she grew up with back home in Nashville, and her own playfulness on the warm summertime evenings brought out the best of the South and transported it to the great Central Valley of California. That was a good year that first year, 1965 in Modesto, and none of the neighborhood kids ever forgot about David's mom.

Modesto was a small town and small town meant conservative, and Leah liked that because conservative meant traditional churches steeped in the truth. One congregation, Northside, was recommended because the brethren were rock solid in the faith, with no deviation from the word as God intended it, humble and caring and especially devout, with a strong bus program for the underprivileged to ride and well-funded missionary work, dutiful in their care of the sick and the elderly, and they needed teachers for Bible School because they were expanding their membership and there weren't enough teachers to go around. After a month, the leaders of Northside recognized Leah's tremendous understanding of God's word and they gave her a choice of grades to teach, impressed with her knowledge of the Bible as well as her devotion to the truth.

One Sunday in late August, Leah was at her best, her heart purest in service to the Lord, her spirit one with the heaven she believed in. Leah had forever felt a special affinity for the less fortunate in life, their plight pricking her heart and bleeding her soul. It had been that way for her since her days on Groveland Street. The high school girls' class that Leah taught every Sunday morning at ten had soon grown from fifteen girls to thirty. Most were quiet and shy, but a few, Rebecca, Gina, Jane and Marlene, were talkative and inquisitive and together they formed the dominant group of girls at the church. All four were cute and intelligent, confident in their abilities and popular with the boys, honors seniors, and all close to leaving that fall for major universities or the best of the Christian schools. They asked most of the good questions in class and answered as many as they asked, and the other girls all admired and envied them.

It was rare when one of the others would say something, but that day one did.

Her name was Rachel. Rachel was a homely girl, without any friends or boyfriends, and being on the heavy side, probably fifty to sixty pounds overweight, she sweat as soon as any room warmed up past the freezing point. She didn't dress very well; her family couldn't afford nice things to wear; and most of the clothes she wore came from the thrift mart that lay on the outskirts of town or from the trade store for the poor run by a government agency.

Rachel did, however, have a good understanding of God's word and a deep love for Him. She read her Bible diligently and she came to every service without exception, even when she was too sick to sit up straight and pay a good heeding. One time, when she had a high fever from an ear infection, she brought a pillow from home so as to rest her head on the ledge of the pew just so she could make it through the full worship hour, so sick and so weak she nearly passed out from dehydration, and Leah had to take her home early before she fainted in church.

Rachel's life was hard: Her father was an alcoholic and her mother worked to pay the bills at a burger place in town. Some of the kids Rachel's age went to the burger joint and they saw Rachel's mother and made fun of her, her mother typically stooped over the frying bin or dragging a wet mop across the dirty floor while the younger, more attractive help served the customers at the order counter. Rachel hated that more than anything, her mother forced to flip burgers and bag food for a living while the kids around town laughed at her. Rachel did her part to help her family out by cleaning house for some rich families in town and by babysitting the brats nobody else would sit for, but the family barely made it by each month, and there was talk in town that the drunken father had sexually abused or beaten Rachel when she was still a little girl.

Leah often prayed to God to grant Rachel the strength to continue her worship, and she worried about her more than any of the other girls in her class. It seemed as though Rachel had been drifting lately and Leah noticed that her arms and legs were often bruised and that her eye was slightly swollen. That day, when Rachel's hand went up to speak, Leah called on her immediately, since it was the first time in a long while that Rachel had raised her hand in class.

"Mrs. Boletti," Rachel said, "you say that God loves everyone, but it doesn't seem like He is fair to all. If He's not fair to all, how can He be all about love?"

"What do you mean exactly?" Leah asked, her tone conciliatory and caring.

"In school, and sometimes in here, too, in seems like there's an in-crowd and then there's everyone else," Rachel said bitterly. "Some girls have what they want all the time, while others don't get it their way at all."

Leah had seen this coming. "Some are left out, is that it?" she asked Rachel tenderly. Leah folded her lesson and waited for Rachel's response. The quiet was hard to take, but Leah kept from saying anything until Rachel spoke again.

"Yes, Ma'am," Rachel finally said, sweaty droplets appearing on her forehead.

The best of Leah followed. The look in her eyes was so soft and tender that she seemed as a dove. "Rachel, do you feel left out, Honey?"

"Yes, Ma'am," Rachel said, embarrassed, staring down at the ground.

The other girls in class sat on the edge of their seats. Most had worried looks on their faces. Some clasped hands. "God hasn't left you out, not at all," Leah said, her eyes clear and purposeful. "The most beautiful person who ever lived was Jesus. He was shunned by most everyone he ever knew, betrayed by his own people, ridiculed on the cross and spat on, paraded through Jerusalem like a pariah, mocked and laughed at the entire time He was alive. He was beaten, beaten mind you, a social outcast by the world's standards, and He was finally killed for simply telling the truth. The son of God, crucified, while the world in which He walked and lived His days, just like you and I do, cared nothing for Him. But Jesus cared enough to die for all those people, even as they ridiculed Him without mercy."

"Yes, Ma'am." Rachel's head stayed bowed.

"Rachel, dear, look at me."

Rachel looked up. Leah saw the years of trying so hard to be so good on Rachel's face, the years when it would have been so easy to quit on God.

"God's only son cared enough to die for the same people who would kill Him," Leah said. "I think it's safe to say Jesus probably felt like He wasn't in the in-crowd. And I know when God looks down on you every day, like I know He does, when He sees His Rachel, who defends His truth and holds true to her faith even as she feels snubbed by the world around her, who comes here, when her own family says she's wasting her time, comes here every Sunday and worships God with that pure loving heart and in loving faith to her Heavenly Father, well, Rachel, He also sees your kindness and the beauty of your spirit, and there is no one in this world more special to Him."

"You mean that, Mrs. Boletti?"

"Yes, Rachel, I do," Leah said, struggling to keep from choking on the love she felt for God's beautiful child. "I've seen you study in this class, and I've seen you get closer to God, and I know how much you love Him. I know you come here on your own, you ride the church bus when others have their own cars, and your family can't afford a car for you. I know they don't support you in your faith, and I know it seems like maybe God hasn't spread the wealth around, that maybe you haven't gotten your fair share of what the world offers, but I haven't seen anyone in my time who is more deserving of God's love. The Lord says the most precious thing in life is the soul, and I have never seen a more beautiful and radiant soul than yours."

Leah put down her lesson and walked over to Rachel. She took her hand and Rachel stood up, and Leah hugged her in a loving embrace. When Rachel finally pulled away, her white face had reddened and streams of tears rolled down her freckled cheeks.

"It's been so hard, Mrs. Boletti," Rachel said, nearly breaking down, but trying hard not to. "I'm so alone. The only thing I enjoy is coming to church, especially your class. Thank you for teaching me so much about the Bible, and for giving me something to look forward to."

Leah hugged Rachel again. Rebecca, Gina, Jane, and Marlene all came over to Rachel and hugged her, too, each one in their turn, for a long time, all crying, not for show or for reputation or to please their teacher, but because they truly cared for her, promising to be Rachel's friends as well as her sisters in Christ, and to be there whenever she needed them.

***

The beauty of Leah in service to the Lord was most evident in those Modesto years. In fact, it was in those years, 1965–1969, that Leah strove most assiduously to serve her God, even more devoutly than she had been as a child, her faith growing not only from her strong foundation in the church, but also from a creeping sense of loneliness that naturally follows from a marriage without love. Church and the raising of her son filled the void of her life. What she valued became increasing delineated, and in reality David and her care for him had become Leah's only real purpose in the Modesto years other than teaching her high school girls on Sunday mornings. You might say it became more and more of her purpose in life. She cleaned the house and ran her errands, but her times with Vic became increasingly perfunctory and as more and more time passed by, she accepted that she would never be in love with him and that her married life was something akin to a chore.

Leah had never put it into those exact words before, the feeling more of a ruffling below the surface, until one day after school had started up again in the fall of 1968 and there was a sudden ringing of the front doorbell.

Rosalie, the mother of one of David's two best friends, Jon, was standing impatiently on the front porch with a plate full of sandwiches in her hands and a bag of chips and sodas at her feet.

"Hey there, what are the sandwiches for?" Leah asked her, as she opened the door.

"I thought you'd never answer. They're for us to eat," Rosalie said determinedly. "Our boys are in school, and I'm here for a talk, for a visit long overdue. Allen's grandmother from England flew back to London this morning after a week's stay with us, and I'm flat out sick of hearing about the Tories and what is to become of them. Like anybody cares about British

Republicans. I thought I'd go nuts if I heard another word about how the mother country has lost its way after the glory years of Churchill."

Rosalie was a neighborhood mom with four kids and a station wagon, and she was kind at heart, but also apt to run her mouth off for as long as anyone would let her. She had more pep in her than a cheerleader. Big into PTA, Rosalie held a seat on the local school board, was highly opinionated and intelligent, and she could be as direct as overland freight. Her husband, Allen, was a bureaucrat, high up in some government agricultural agency, commuting to Sacramento three days a week, but he was gone that particular day, testifying before some state legislative committee about a fruit pest and the preferred methods of eradication, and he was due back in a couple of hours. Rosalie had to be home by three or thereabouts to start dinner for him, but until then, she was Leah's.

Leah welcomed her neighbor inside her home.

"Leah, I made you a tunafish," Rosalie said, removing a plastic wrapper from the first sandwich. "You do like tunafish, don't you?"

"Sure do," Leah said. "How'd you know I was starving?"

"I could tell it was the day for us." Rosalie busily removed the chips and sodas from the bag and thrust one of each onto Leah's side of the kitchen table and spread her own food out before her.

After they gobbled down the first bite of sandwiches, Rosalie hustled to the point.

"You know, I've known you for some time now, but I don't know much about you. Our boys play together, but I don't *know* you, you know what I mean?"

Leah chuckled a yes.

"Let's hear what you're about, and see if I approve."

Leah broke out into a full laugh.

"No really, I want to know what makes you tick," Rosalie said intently.

"Well, I guess I'll have to tell you then, now won't I?" Leah said, patting her cheeks to stifle her laughter.

"I'm not leaving until you do."

Leah took a deep breath. She smiled at Rosalie. "Well, in my life," she began, "what matters most to me is God and my son. I like having friends, like you and Allen, and of course the Smiths and the Barclays are great people to chum with, I mean the barbecues we throw are a kick in the pants, good food and good friends and y'all are so friendly, and I talk to my family back home at least once a week, but my world is my God and my little son, David."

"What about your husband?" Rosalie asked provocatively.

"Oh, Vic is a great provider," Leah said candidly. "He works like a mule to support our family, the way a good man should work, and I couldn't ask for better when it comes to that."

"That sounds like an endorsement. I meant, do you love him?"

Leah was taken aback. "Sure, I guess so, but not like I love my child," she said forthrightly. "I think most mothers are like that, it's just in us to be that way. A man, any man, can never need us as much or be as full of love for us as your own baby can."

"Is that enough for you?"

Leah ruminated for a bite of tunafish. "Well, sort of. There has to be more, but that's where God comes in. Beyond your family, even beyond the love you feel for your child, there is the eternal need, the reason mothers and children exist in the first place."

"And what reason is that?" Rosalie asked, resting her sandwich on the kitchen table.

"To do God's will," Leah said quickly. "Being a good mother and loving your baby is doing God's will. If I bring David up to be a soldier for God, to be an example of what a good Christian should be, a human magnet to attract others to the Lord, then I will have done the best by God and also by my son."

Rosalie looked surprised. "I knew you went to church, but I didn't know God meant so much to you," she said. "And David, well, I sure hope he knows how special he is."

A faint contriteness grew on Leah's face. It seemed as though she was afraid to admit what followed. "I'll tell you something else, Rosalie. There's another difference as well. David is real, tangible, whereas God is not. It's the difference between the actual and the abstract. David is easier to love because he's in front of me every day, while God is a hope I have for the future. I *know* my son, but I don't *know* God. God is always a matter of faith, and even though I feel like I've felt God before, with faith there is always some doubt. Do you see the difference?"

"Why didn't you have more kids?" Rosalie asked, leaning forward.

Leah gulped down another bite of sandwich. "I couldn't. David was too difficult to deliver, there was severe damage to my uterus, and the doctors all recommended I didn't risk another child. Another pregnancy might have killed me."

"I'm so sorry."

"Don't be," Leah said misleadingly. "I love David so much I don't think I could have loved another child. He's everything I ever wanted in a son. He's my joy, what I value most other than my God."

"What about romance?" Rosalie asked skeptically. "And sex? Maybe I shouldn't ask, but do you enjoy sex?"

Talk of sex provided the break from the regret of not being able to have another child that Leah needed to return the conversation to a more carefree kind of talk. "Ah, so this is what this is about," she said coyly. "You want to hear about my sex life?"

"Yes, and why not?" Rosalie stated resolutely. She smoothed her dress and brushed crumbs from the table. "I want to know if you enjoy sex. You're married, aren't you? You didn't mention sex before, it most certainly wasn't at the top of your list, and I think you should have."

"Do you?"

"Are you kidding me?" Rosalie asked emphatically. "I've got four kids, and we practiced like a ball team to get them. I love what Allen does for me, to me, you understand, talking sexy with me on the phone or touching me nasty when the kids aren't looking, and sometimes if he doesn't hurry home I think I'll kill him."

Leah stared out the window. "No, I don't have anything like that," she said, with a hint of regret. "It's fine, it really is. Sex is sex." She tried to change the subject. "Do you love Allen like in the movies, you know, all for him?"

"I guess so," Rosalie said, her brow curling. "He's my husband. Is that what you're talking about?"

A discomforting silence followed as Leah's eyes drifted downward to the table. "No, it's not," she said, sorry that Rosalie didn't seem to fully understand her. She looked up at her neighbor friend again. "Keep this quiet for me, will you?"

"Sure, what?"

"Well, right before Vic, when I lived in Nashville, there was a guy I dated. I thought he was my boyfriend, but there was another girl his family wanted him to marry; his family was a high society family, always in the papers, and anyway, was he ever gorgeous. But that's not what I want to tell you about. There was more to it than that. He was so special, like a prince, a great mind, a grand future in the cards, you name it, but even that wasn't the reason I fell so hard for him. There was more still. Every day with him was like floating on the highest cloud in the heavens, with joy all around, and I couldn't wait to see him or talk to him on the phone. Oh, Rosalie, I was so dizzy in love I couldn't see straight. When I spent time with him, I was smiling so much my jaws hurt. I was happy, oh so happy, like a fairy tale come true, with a wonderful prince and a happily ever after, and my love for him would have never grown old. I know I was young, but it was real. I adored him, I would have gladly given him my all, and the only time I didn't adore him was when it seemed he didn't value us as much as I did or when I found out about the other girl."

"Did you have sex with him?" Rosalie asked, not fully understanding.

"No, but if I did, it wouldn't have been just sex," Leah said. "It would have been a physical continuation of what I already felt inside my heart, just another layer of love to be added on top of all the others. I loved him more than I knew was possible, I suppose. That's why it nearly killed me when he chose the other girl."

Rosalie sat in complete disbelief. "That's beautiful," she said mesmerized, caught up in the dreaminess. "You should write movie scripts."

"The relationship didn't last, though," Leah said, her face sagging. "I'm convinced it wasn't supposed to. But it was like a piece of heaven, and I think it was God's way of telling me what heaven would be like if I stay true to Him."

"Have you ever felt it again?"

"Almost," Leah said, holding her finger and thumb apart and pinching a small gap of air between them. "With David, there are times when I watch him eat or play or when he sits quietly and reads that I get so full I think I'll pop. He's my baby and he loves me back, without any conditions or terms, he just loves me for me and I'm accepted and I'm good enough for him, just like I am. It's a little bit different, though, than with romantic love. The romantic kind is not the same as what you feel for your child, unconditional like. They're close, but you're always aware of the difference."

"Here, I thought you couldn't wait for your handsome husband to get home," Rosalie said, shaking her head. "That's what all the wives on the block think. I'm surprised, but I won't say a word. You can count on me."

"You know the worst part of it, though?"

"No, what?"

"I would have been happy with Blake forever. Nothing mattered but us. There were moments with him when I felt so much love that I cried because there was nothing else for me to do but cry. It was like I was overwhelmed with love and crying was the only outlet left to me, or I would have exploded from the fullness I felt in my heart."

Rosalie took the last bite of her sandwich, the first one in minutes, and sat stone-faced like a statue. After a napkin wipe of her face she shook her head and then shook it again. "I've got some thinking to do," she said, as she scooped up the garbage from the table. "I'll talk to you later." Rosalie got up and walked out the front door and headed home. Leah looked out the front window and watched Rosalie cross the street. It was the first time she had seen her friend rendered nearly speechless.

***

Leah's love for her son grew stronger with each passing year. Sometimes, she felt so happy being his mother that the emptiness inside her became almost an afterthought.

The fullness of her motherhood crested in the summer of 1969.

About two hours due east of Modesto, high up in the Sierra Nevada, is a tiny alpine lake named Pinecrest, which sits surrounded by razor crags of charcoal rock that reflect the sun's rays like an array of polished mirrors. Further up, the mountains turn coarse and impenetrable, but at Pinecrest the mountains are friendly and lined with forested footpaths dense with the timberland sprawl of blood bark manzanita, scruffy trail brush, and long needled pine trees, and there is nowhere on Earth where the mountain air smells fresher. The water of the lake is crystalline clear, allowing huge sunken boulders to be seen hundreds of feet below the surface, as if the water were air. The road up the mountains is long and winding, meandering through a number of small towns that have stood still against the passage of time: Sonora, Jamestown, Miwuk Village, Twain Harte, and tiny Sugar Pine. Winter snows nestle between the trees, more than they blanket the land, and the wintertime is not as harsh as the more northerly of the Sierras. Legend has it that the indigenous peoples considered the lands a sacred meeting place of earth and sky that bestowed a natural peace on those fortunate enough to behold its wonders. .

In August of that year, Vic and Leah rented a log cabin hidden among the trees, homespun and cozy, with a stove fireplace and wooden timber beams. Leah made scrambled eggs and griddle pancakes each morning and then took long walks afterward in the cool mountain air while her men fished for rainbow trout on the sunny lake beneath her. With her Bible in her hands, she perched herself each morning on the same high granite boulder that overlooked the smoothest waters by the dam, sitting on a flat ledge of the giant rock, her hair glistening at the temples from her brisk hike up the hill. There, in front of the dam, the water was a stippled blue glass, thick and deep, and to the side of her a tributary tumbled into the lake in a ball of frothy whiteness. For some odd reason, Leah felt a sense of foreshadowing, as if being on a mountain rock before a spectacular lake was meant to happen again, the sensation tugging at her each time she positioned herself in the morning air.

In the evening, the family took night hikes on the trails that coursed the lake. The stars at night were beautiful in the sky, and Leah would pause on the trail and gaze in wonder.

"You see that one?" David asked, pointing to a star.

"Which one?" Leah asked.

"That one." He pointed it out for her. "That star is Deneb, it's in the constellation Cygnus, the Swan, and it's fifteen hundred light years away. The light we see tonight left that star fifteen hundred years ago. It also is one of the stars of the Northern Triangle."

"What's a light year?" Leah asked.

"It's the distance light travels in a year, going 186,000 miles per second," David answered. "About seven times around the Earth in one second. I thought I explained that to you already."

"Nothing travels that fast," Vic threw in.

"Light does, Dad."

"David, how do you know so much about the stars and such? I didn't even know light travels. My word, you're only ten years old," Leah said to her son.

"It's in that book Uncle William sent me for Christmas. The astronomy book. The one you said was too expensive for a boy my age. Remember? That reminds me: Dad, when are we going to get that telescope we saw?"

"When you cut enough lawns."

"Dad, you promised. You promised me that day. Mom, he promised."

"I didn't say the book was too expensive," Leah said, correcting her son. "I said it was more than your Uncle should have spent. There's a difference. I saw a similar book at Dougherty's, and it was over twenty-five dollars. And we'll get you a telescope for your birthday next year." Leah turned toward Vic. "Won't we, husband and father to this family?"

Vic nodded at his wife. David saw it and smiled.

"Well, the moon sure looks pretty on the water," Leah said. "And the stars have been beautiful since I was a child." Leah heard the slurp of a trout feeding on the surface. "What was that?" she asked.

"A trout," Vic said enthusiastically.

"We'll catch him tomorrow, won't we, Dad?"

"We'll sure give it a try. I'm thinking we should try worms behind golden flashers. We've fished enough on the bottom for one trip. Next year, we'll try flies."

Vic held Leah's hand as they walked together along the shore of the lake. The moon slid lower in the sky. David jumped in the middle of his parents, sometimes to make sure he was included, but often because he was scared to straggle too far behind, his dad telling him stories of roaming black bears and hungry grizzlies. Neither Vic nor Leah knew how happy it made their son to see his mom and dad hold hands and walk along the shoreline together. More than once, he jumped ahead just to be able to look back at them.

The grape of emptiness within Leah shrunk to a raisin on that trip from the closeness she felt toward her son. On the next to last day, Leah saw David from a long ways off come running up toward her, a stringer of rainbows flapping behind him in the dirt, and he stopped to show a couple of sunbathers his booty. Then he tore off again running up the gentle slope and toward his mother as the late afternoon's rays lit up his tanned cheeks. Leah made out a proud smile on his face. They had one more night to go at the lake, a night to read stories and eat s'mores as a family, to play card games and watch the fire pop and dance, and Leah was consumed with an immeasurable love for her son. She said a prayer of thanks, her heart as full as it had ever been, her love for her David consuming her.

"God, my loving and wonderful Father, thank You for giving me my baby. I never deserved such a reward, and only by Your grace do I have him at all."

When David made it over to her, Leah hugged him and David showed her each rainbow trout and what it had bit on to reach its demise. She hugged him again and he ran off to join his dad to clean up the fish for the fish fry that Leah had put off until the final evening at the lake. Fish dinners stank up the cabin. A trail of trout followed David in the dirt as he ran away and off to the cleaning table. He was a good son, and Leah would have been happy for all her days if only he had stayed a little boy who always needed his mother and her love.

Chapter 17

THE MODESTO YEARS CAME to an end in April of the following year, when Vic was promoted into management back in the Bay Area, his efforts finally acknowledged by the company. Leah choose the hills of Oakland in which to live, the glorious skyline neighborhood of The Crestmont, situated high above the bay in a copse of California Oaks and meandering poppy meadows.

The 1970s in California was perhaps the most 1970s of anywhere on Earth. It was a laid back time, casual and philosophical, hair worn long, the soul at search, and the fashions dreadful. The tumultuousness of the sixties was most willingly forgotten by all but society's most fringe and fanatical element, that odd assortment of radicals, hippies, and other hangers-on, and with the conclusion of the Vietnam War and the scandal of Watergate came an era of general peace if not economic prosperity. It was instead an era of *me.*

The backyard landscaping was completed a year after the family moved into the new Oakland house, a glass monster that espied five bridges, but for Leah new houses had somehow become a tiresome bore and the uniqueness of a new neighborhood and its fresh beginnings was instead transformed into stolidity and pessimism as reality finally caught up to her ambitions. After all, one can only pretend for so long, as the absence of love devours the soul and renders the heart unavailing. The demise that began with Walton's death, which had been largely deferred through the benignant Modesto years, accelerated in the fog-shrouded coastal hills of Leah's new home. Her strongest emotion was that she felt she *should* have been happy. Melancholy followed her around like a dreary shadow, dragging at her soul. Where once the fall of evening had been a cozy friend, now the night seemed like an epoch of despair. Only the glitter of the city lights below her windows at night seemed to inspire Leah to the former radiance of her childhood, connecting her to a time when her aspirations gave her hope for the future and a purpose to each day.

Often Leah chanted before the glowing host within her view as one might versify before the gates of a long-trekked Shangri-La, "How beautiful you are, how beautiful you are, my God, the lights, how beautiful you are."

Sometimes, David would hear his mother chanting and wander into the room, finding Leah sitting alone on the sofa, immersed in the bowl of shimmering brightness in her view. "What are you looking at, Mom? The lights again?"

"Yes, David, look at them. Look how many. They're so beautiful, aren't they? The lights remind me of stars in the sky, all twinkling together as one, so full of life and glory. I feel like I'm connected to them in some deep and universal way. I always have. See them, David. Look. Some gold, some silver, but all of them sparkling so brightly in the night. Lights are life. The world is dark, but life is light. Oh, do you see them? They're never the same lights twice."

Many nights, David would sit down beside his mother on the couch and lean on her. "They are beautiful, Mom. They're best on clear cold nights after a good rain, like the storm we had last week that cleared the smog from the air. The night Scott and Craig came over for dinner and you fixed that zucchini casserole. Remember? The lights are always brightest after a good, hard rain."

Then David would leave his mother sitting on the couch and go about his business, and Leah would stay in the glow of the lights for hours on end. Oftentimes, she fell asleep on the couch and woke up to a snowy white blanket of fog that had crept up the hillside during the night while she slumbered, and she smiled when she saw the clouds below the ridge laying cottony in the morning sun.

Leah never did miss Modesto or think of it much, but she missed Blake and loved him still these many years later, and that seemed odd even to her. She saw Blake's face in the glittering sea of city lights rising from the basin of the bay, and she longed for his touch as if it were that first summer of his graduation from college in Nashville back in 1956. She remembered their times strolling in the sun and laying her head on his shoulder during a summertime sprinkle of rain. That had felt so right, so perfect, his hand on her cheek, the soft kiss of his lips on hers. She remembered feeling full inside. Then she'd look around the emptiness of her living room. A feeling of hollowness would cause her to shudder, her throat would tighten, and she'd feel a sudden surge of panic in her chest. She'd have to rise from the sofa and walk around to keep from breaking apart or step outside for a breath of air. Some old songs from that summer still made her cry and she'd have to turn off her radio and lie in the darkness to hide her sorrow from her husband and the truth from her only son.

She tried to ignore her feelings, but one night they poured forth on an evening call from her sister, Marian. Vic was traveling for work and David was staying the night over at a friend's house. It seemed to Leah that her son spent more and more time away from his mother and preferred it that way. That hurt her. David was growing up. Someday, he'd be gone. Until the phone rang that evening, the house that night had seemed like a cavern, cold and lifeless, so devoid of any purpose, so silent in its dissonance. Leah answered the phone on the second ring, struggling to care.

"Hello."

"Hey, Lee," Marian said happily on the other end. "Just thought I'd give you a call to see how you're making out. It's cheaper if I call after eleven, my time. Charles watches every dime since we bought the new car and frankly his frugality is driving me nuts. He's why I haven't called in awhile. What have you been doing with yourself since I talked to you last?"

"I was watching the lights of the city until the fog came up and smothered them. I hate the fog. Seems like it comes earlier and thicker than it used to. It's as cold and gray as rain."

"You feeling okay? You sound kind of down."

"Yeah, I've been feeling a little low these past few days. I don't know what to do with myself. I'm bored to tears most of the time. Bored as a board, as Mama used to say. Worst is, I can't seem to shake my case of the blues."

"You staying busy?"

"As busy as I can. I've tried every hobby I can think of. Some of the Republican women here in town got me involved in local politics, to try and counteract these liberal lunatics in Berkeley, said it would be good for my mind, but I'm already bored with activism. I guess I should be more committed than I am. Somebody needs to defend the old ways."

"Good golly, those nuts still protesting out there? They need to cut their hair and get a job, that's what they need to do. Dumb idiots. Anyway, I could tell something hasn't been right with you. We haven't talked in well over a month. I've been worried sick."

Leah felt a shakiness in her body. "I've been worried about myself, too, to tell you the truth. Nothing seems to work anymore. I'm running around the house yelling like a madman half the time. Heck, I'm such a bitch sometimes, even to my baby, that it doesn't even seem like me standing there blowing my top at him."

"You?"

"Yeah, me. The other day David told me he thinks I divide the world into two kinds of people: those who can help me and those who can't. He said I'm a user. I didn't argue back because I think he might be right. I look in the mirror and can't believe it's me behaving that way. Remember how I used to tell you that I never wanted to make any mistakes in my life? Well, I think I've made some of the biggest mistakes you can make. I'll tell you, Marian, I feel more bitter and depressed about my life every day that goes by."

"How's Vic?"

"Vic has been a good husband through it all. He never raises his voice when I bitch at him, and then he buys me whatever I want when we go shopping. We're doing fine financially, and of course I love David more than I ever have. But as David gets older, my purpose in life is fading, and I don't know what to replace it with."

"Lee, do you love your husband?"

Leah didn't answer immediately. She was surprised her sister was on to her. "Sure, but I'm not in love with him," she said. "Not like I was with Blake. You knew that, right?"

"Yes, I could tell you still cared for Blake. You're my sister, remember? But heck, Lee, it's been so many years since you two split up, you just have to get past him."

"You ever hear of him anymore?"

"Sure do. He's married to that same old priss from Belle Meade he had back when. They have three kids now. Blake's in the papers as much as he ever was, but he lost the primary for senator after the news of his last extramarital affair, and he gave up politics after his daddy passed away. You ask me, his wife is nothing more than a muddy doormat. He's cheated on her for years, and she just takes it all to keep her big house and fancy car and her invitation every year to the Capitol Cotillion. His law firm, though, is real successful here in town, and I heard he may become the next president of Vanderbilt University. You'll never know how much I regret introducing him to you. Whenever we talked, you'd bring up his name." Marian hesitated for a second. "But, Lee, you sure ought to love your husband."

Leah moaned. "I guess my problem is feeling like this is all there is in life. You ever felt that way before? Here, I thought I'd know the purpose of my life by now, as old as I am, and I'm no closer now than I was as a little girl. Daddy used to tell me it'd be hard to find. Boy, was he ever right. I'm running out of time."

"We all get that feeling once in awhile, Lee. What about God? Mama says you've been going to church less, that she called one Sunday morning and you were home instead of at church."

"Mama should have been a spy. The church out here isn't very strong, too many liberals and reformers, half the congregations don't even follow God's word like they should, and that irritates the heck out of me. Shoot, they don't even read the Bible, some of these churches. They read books from scholars instead of God's word. Drives me crazy. Bunch of intellectuals is what they are, trying to outthink the Lord. Sinners is more like it. Old Calendar Jones in Nashville warned me about these reformists years ago. Smart old bird, that Calendar was. Plus, I was denied for a teaching position."

Marian was aghast. "You? Denied? Why did the church deny you? You've always known more about the Bible than anyone I ever knew."

"The only opening was the college girls class, and they want the teacher in that position to have completed college or done seminary work. I guess quitting college came back to bite me on the rear after all. My feelings are so hurt I may find another congregation to attend. Seems to be my way, doesn't it, to have to change churches? So I read my Bible at home and pray the Lord will forgive me."

"Don't quit on church, Lee. You know God is what counts most in the end."

Leah sighed a slow sigh of regret. "I know, I know. Don't worry, I'll get back to Him someday, close to Him like I was in Modesto."

"How old is David now, anyway?"

"Twelve. I'll blink, and he'll be off to college. Then what will I have?"

Marian shifted the conversation to something she knew would cheer her sister up. "Hey, Lee, you still got that great view of San Francisco and the airports by the bay, don't you? It can't be foggy all the time. We sat on your couch for hours on end, just watching the planes take off and land. All them lights. I never could get over that view."

"Yep, the lights are as pretty as they've ever been. Since you were out, Vic finished the backyard. Put in a sport court for David. They're best pals and play out there together and leave me alone with the lights at night. I love the lights, though. They seem to call to me to live among them. Oh, Marian, I'd love to be young and live free and be happy again. Remember when you used to tell me that as a kid my feet never touched the ground? These days, every step I take feels like I'm walking in quicksand. Why did I ever get married? I hate to say it, but I feel so trapped with Vic. Sometimes, I almost hate him for it."

"Lee, that's awful, Honey. You can't mean that?"

There was silence on the line, then Leah spoke in a feigned excitement to change the subject. She tried to summon giddiness, but it wasn't there.

"Oh, Marian, I almost forgot to tell you," Leah said. "I got a job as a secretary in a law office. I've been working my tail off. Two weeks now. It's kind of fun to be part of the labor force, but I'm already getting fed up with the hours and all the office politics. Seems it isn't how hard you work, but how much you play the game."

Leah heard a grin through the line. "I know how that goes," Marian said. "Oh, don't I know all about the games people play. Can't be as bad as the South, though. Church here is still pretty much the same way it was back at First Avenue when you told off Maude and her sidekicks. Politics, politics, politics. What a day that was, huh? I thought Mama was going to beat you to a pulp and me, too, for being nothing more than your sister. But there's good folks here, too, so I guess I shouldn't be as faultfinding as I am. But, hey, I'm sure glad you're working, Lee. It'll keep your mind busy." Marian paused on the line. She thought of something. "Hey, little sis, I need to go. I just remembered I've got a cake that needs frosting for a raffle at the school tomorrow, and I need to be up early to make a ham for Charles' work party. I really just called to say hi. I'll be thinking of you."

Leah felt a well-known pain. It hurt to say goodbye to her sister. She wanted to talk some more, but didn't want to appear selfish. "Pray for me, will you?" she asked Marian softly. "If God will listen to anybody, He'll listen to you. It sure was good to hear from you."

"I will, little Lee, I'll ask God to watch over you. I love you. Don't ever forget that I'll always love you."

"I love you, too. I miss you. Y'all be safe back there."

"'bye, little Lee."

When Leah hung up the phone and looked outside, the fog had clawed its way up the hill. The bowl of city lights had been replaced with an eerie blackness. It was as if the cities and the bay had ceased to exist. The biggest oak on the slope of the tallest hillside, bent and straggly, looked as if it were hanging over nothingness. Leah felt so alone looking at that old oak tree. She thought of death. Gray streaks of fog moved like a swarm of darting demons past her home and then further on up the hill. Soon she was surrounded by choking fog. Cold air whistled in through the windows and the house grew as cold as an ice box. The last of the neighbor's lights flickered off, and Leah's hillside redoubt was shrouded in total darkness. She locked the doors and fell asleep thinking of Marian and the happiest of times on Groveland Street.

Chapter 18

LEAH'S LIFE CONTINUED TO deteriorate. Five years passed with more pretense of the happy wife, David growing through his teenage years, and Leah dreading the day when he would move away. College beckoned him. Somehow, with a strength befitting all she had been through, Leah held herself together by working long hours and shopping the malls and specialty stores on the weekends. She accumulated possessions. Then, slowly, like the creeping crawl of a midnight snail across a spanning concrete concourse, Leah finally slid off the farthest edge and fell horribly to the ground. She cracked unmistakably. She developed the first of her night tremors, times when her arms went numb and her breathing became increasingly difficult, and she had trouble sweating as hot flashes consumed her body. She lost perspective. The walls closed in on her at night, and only the soft glow of the city lights provided any respite from the suffering of her world. She often went into rages for no good reason and she wouldn't talk to Vic for days on end. She threw fits and broke things around the house, and she'd stay out late just driving around without telling anyone where she was or what time she'd eventually come home.

Through it all, Vic was patient and understanding, and he worried more for Leah's frailty, her body becoming like tissue and her skin opaque and dry, more than he ever worried for himself and what would become of him. He noticed that Leah's motions were like a sparrows sitting on a branch too low, jumpy and without confidence, nervously anticipating springing horrors or sensing danger in each new gust of wind.

Another year passed of fraying nerves and living on eggshells. David turned eighteen. Where once her life had bubbled at the surface, now life seemed like an undersea trench, dark and shadowy and full of ghastly horrors. Leah sunk deeper into the depths. She started sleeping in the guest bedroom, falling asleep with the light on, the door closed and usually locked, a message for Vic to leave her alone, but she did so only after David went away to college. Rarely did she read her Bible or think of God. She drank wine to ease the pain instead of praying. She cared little for her soul. Vic never said a word about sleeping by himself to his son, and Mom and Dad slept together only when David was home for the occasional visit to keep up appearances. The pretense to the world went on like a boring play, drawn out and exhausted, the actors tired of their lines and the audience caring not for what happened next. Conversation in the home was at best perfunctory.

Sex and affection ceased to exist.

Leah worked twice as diligently in her job, but she derived no feeling of accomplishment for her labors; the money she made seeming unimportant and her time completely wasted. Her mind went sketchy and dull. As the rest of humanity walked past her on the missions of their lives, she finally prayed for a purpose to her living. Those prayers, little more than desperate pleas for help, said not in love for the Master or with good intentions or concern for others, but rather out of frustration for her predicament and imbued with cries of self-pity and bitterness, were the least sincere prayers said of Leah's lifetime. They were more like complaints than prayers. Leah's full hair of faith, those same curly and golden locks of her childhood years, had been reduced to a single strand of belief. The glory of the hills had turned to desolation and the seaside captivation of her first magnificent glimpse of the wondrous shores of Carmel seemed like it had occurred eons ago and in someone else's lifetime. California had in many ways become as uninspiring as Tennessee. The end of the line came when shopping and accumulating became a tiresome bore, and Leah knew her life had to change if she were to survive what had become her marital hell.

That change was Dan.

Dan was an esoteric man, graduated from Hastings Law School with innumerable honors, a few years younger than Leah, new to the firm, with a wife, two children, and a wandering eye. What could be said about Dan in which all agreed was that no one knew exactly what he was or what he stood for. He was a hard man to pin down. Tall and trim, his hair sandy brown and graying at the temples, his skin coarse and rugged and mountain windswept, more like a woodsman than a lawyer, Dan had steely blue eyes that were cunning like a wolf on the prowl. It was his eyes that drew her in. They were so powerfully blue, Leah thought, like speckled Prussian marble, piercing through to her hunger, and Leah felt his eyes on her body as he watched her move about the office. His watching excited her, and Leah's heart raced whenever he came near or spoke to her.

One day, the first day of winter that year of 1978, an especially cold and chilling day, the result of a cold front that had blown down from the gulf of Alaska threatening the bay with an unusual blanket of snow, Leah drove her car over to Dan's house to bring him a legal briefing for his review. Dan had called the office and asked specifically for Leah. He said it was imperative for her to come. The sky was already a smooth velvety black and there were no stars out that evening, the wind itchy and rasping. For some reason, Leah thought of her sister Kay. She hadn't much thought of her in years, but she did when she saw the blackness of the sky and the truancy of stars. Dan's wife and kids were off for a visit to her mother's place in Laguna Niguel, down south, a few days ahead of the Christmas holiday, Dan flying to join them the following day for a beachfront celebration.

Leah hesitated getting out of her car. Something grabbed her and held her to her seat. She thought of leaving the brief on the porch with a ring of the doorbell and a quick getaway, or she could call later and let Dan know of the brief's whereabouts on the doorstep. There were, in fact, options to what might happen if she went inside. She thought of adultery and the Ten Commandments, of the joining of husband and wife into one flesh in marriage, *what God has joined together let no man put asunder.* Her mind went to Luke's account of Jesus being tempted by Satan in the desert, how a starving Jesus could have so easily turned a stone to bread to quell his ravenous hunger, *but man does not live by bread alone*. Starvation is a much more pressing temptation than either sex or emotional emptiness, and yet Jesus had been so strong while she was being so weak. Her stomach wrenched over in shame. She saw Vic's face in her mind, her own husband from so long ago, working so hard to provide for his family, rising so early so often through the years, many times sick or not feeling well, and she saw her son David, her only son in this world. Together, they had formed her family, and as surely as night follows day there had been happy and joyous times through the years and plenty of laughter in the sun. It was undeniable as she thought about it, that both men had in fact been *her* men, and now it was equally as undeniable that she was forsaking them and leaving them for another.

Still, for all her misgivings, Leah climbed out of her car and into the evening blackness.

"Forgive me, God," she prayed hollowly into the darkness. "I'm so sorry about what I've become. I can't seem to stop myself."

When Leah arrived on the front porch Dan swung open the door and gestured her in. He looked at her and waited. Wolves are confident hunters. After a long stare into his cobalt hunger, Leah reached up and kissed him with her mouth wide open, staring into his eyes. She slowly unbuttoned his shirt as he unzipped the back of her dress, and soon they were both naked and lying in bed. Leah had sex again for the first time in many months, with only the second man of her lifetime, and afterward she felt no guilt about what she had done and she didn't cry or ask why.

The affair lasted for almost a month, when Dan ended it for another, more attractive and much younger woman, a college intern new to the firm. The girl was only nineteen years old and naïve as they come. But her face was flawlessly young. Leah noticed her own wrinkles like never before, and she bought expensive skin creams and wonder solutions and fretted two more wrinkles to the corners of her eyes. Primarily because she had nothing else to do with her time, Leah chased Dan for two months afterward, outside the office, stalking him in the yard of his home or from her car in the company parking garage, following him on the freeway and the grid of boulevards that fed the courthouse rotunda, at City Square in Oakland, where anyone could see her, bringing humiliation to herself as she struggled to find her pride against the shame of her desires. In less than two months' time, Leah had become an embarrassment to the world, as well as to herself, and she wondered if there was anyone in the world who could love such a disgraceful and miserable creature.

***

Vic was at home that Tuesday evening when it happened, hearing someone come in through the front door in what sounded like a floundering flurry. He heard a loud thumping noise against the wall, followed by another bump. The door slammed shut. Then he heard the familiarity of Leah's way of speaking, but there was another voice, that of a man, and Vic thought he recognized the deep fullness of the tone, although argumentatively harsher and much more laconic than the memory of that voice. Both voices were on edge. Then he heard shouting. He climbed out of his chair and walked out from the family room into the front entry area, where he saw Leah bent over and shaking. Then he saw Dan, whom he had met at some of Leah's work functions and parties, and he thought that something horrible must have happened to Leah at work that day.

"What's the matter?" Vic asked his wife. "Leah, are you hurt?"

"I'm fine," Leah said, holding her swollen cheek with her left hand. She looked contrite, as did Dan. "You better sit down, Vic. Here, sit in this chair."

Leah pointed to a chair in the living room before stumbling into the kitchen, wrapping a number of ice cubes up in a baggy, and holding it tightly to her face. She came back into the entryway and spoke directly to Vic, who was now sitting down in the chair, bewildered. It was obvious someone had hit his wife.

"Something needs to be said, by me, by Dan, by the both of us," Leah started. Her hands were trembling and her body was shivering from shock, but she was also strangely calm, the kind of tranquillity one gets when something dreadful is finally brought out into the open and the moment is upon one. "You need to hear what is about to be said. We can talk more after Dan leaves if you care to."

"If you hit my wife, you're a dead man," Vic said to Dan, rising from the chair. "If she made a mistake at work, if you or any other attorney hit her, I'll have your ass. There's never an excuse to hit a woman; I don't care what she did wrong or how much it cost you."

"Vic, it's not like that," Leah said interjecting, stepping between her husband and her lover. "Calm down. It's not like that at all."

Vic sat back down, confused as before but a trifle calmer. He thought maybe there had been an accident instead of a punch or possibly a courtroom brawl. "Vic, I don't know you very well," Dan said warily, "but you don't deserve what's happened here. It would have been better if you never knew, but Leah wouldn't let it drop. I don't love her, it was just a thing. Now she's gone crazy on me, on both of us when you think about it, and you have every right to be upset. I know you'll probably hate me. You probably should. Personally, I think you're way too good for her, but that's your business."

Vic's confusion turned to instant acuity. The full meaning of the situation hit him like a bucket of ice water. It was not insubordination or anything to do with his wife's performance at work, and it was no accident. There had been no courtroom brawl. It was cheating. Leah had cheated on him. Suddenly, his wife sleeping in the guest bedroom the past year or so and denying him sex came as a clarion call, and Vic realized he'd been made a fool for loving her all those years. Dan's words echoed in his mind over and over again, like a sinister voice in a torture chamber: *It was just a thing, it was just a thing.*

The silence at a moment like that has a voice all its own. It screamed at Vic: *Fool, Fool.* He tried not to listen to the silence, scraping his foot against the tile floor, rubbing his hand against the wall while looking away, anything to make some noise and drown out the awful sound, but the voice of insight wouldn't leave him alone. He felt so small standing there. The voice reverberated again and again without cessation, unmercifully, taunting him, laughing: *Fool, Fool.* It seemed as if the entire world had come to a end. The sanctity of his realm, the one beautiful regent he had always counted on, the mother of his son and the woman he had always loved, stood before him as the sexual conquest of another.

"Leah, do you love him?" Vic finally managed to ask.

Leah shook her head no. Her face showed an anguished sincerity. "Sometimes I feel like I do, but he doesn't care about me," Leah said, removing the bag of ice from her face. "He's a bastard, a playboy who cares only for himself. So no, I guess I don't love him. I don't know about love at all. He actually makes me sick, but it's better than what we have here. There's nothing in this place we live in; it's not even a home anymore. If there was anything here, Vic, I wouldn't have strayed."

A deplorable stillness filled the room, more than before, the betrayal of the human heart smearing the walls of the house in a disgraceful soundlessness. A look into that room that evening, a look exposing the evil that humans do to each other from nothing more than the sheer folly of their emotions, to say nothing of their insecurities and flaws, turned the stomach as does a stare into a death camp.

"You should go," Vic said, facing Dan. "Be thankful I'm not beating the crap out of you. The rest is between me and my wife."

"I'll go, but I came here for your help," Dan said warily. "I want her to quit following me after work. I don't want any more calls to the court or calls to my client's offices, and I don't want to see her car stalking my house again. I just want it all stopped. I've thought about changing firms to get away from her, but I'm not even sure that would do it. She has problems, Vic, she needs some help, and I can't be the one to help her. I thought the only way I could get her to quit bugging me is to let you know about the events of these past few weeks. Maybe the shame will do it."

"Oh, why don't you go rape another teenager, you sick pedophile," Leah screamed at Dan. "I have problems? You parade around the office like some high and mighty legal guru, and you're nothing more than a perverted child molester. I know who you're banging, and she's just a kid."

"What are you talking about?" Dan asked sheepishly.

"Oh, go trick somebody else, you sickening scum. Has the little pubescent even had a period yet? By the way, I'm telling your wife, so the party is over. Say goodbye to half your money. And wait till the firm finds out. You won't be able to get a job sweeping the hallways."

"I don't know what you're talking about," Dan said, dismissing her.

Vic had had enough. "This is your last warning," he said, threatening Dan. "And I mean it. Neither of us wants you here. I never liked you much, anyway, you arrogant weasel."

With that final warning, Dan made for the front door and headed out to his car to drive away into the frozen cold of the night. Leah stood pitifully in the entryway, ice bag held up to her face, her eyes beseeching for assistance on how best to endure the tragedy of her life. As a testament to how little she had left in that home, she almost followed Dan out to his car to beg him to see her again. But Dan walked on. He never turned around. It was the last Vic ever saw or heard of him.

***

The big house was even emptier than before, for even the illusion was gone this time. Leah limped up the stairs, dropping the ice pack once before picking it up in a hurry, and she retreated into the guest bedroom where she lay awake ruminating for hours. The silence that night was as deafening as it had been for her husband. But in the silence came a message for her: The facade of her marriage was now indisputably over, shattered like some fallen flower pot dropped from a high balcony onto a hardened concrete walkway, and now was the time to capitulate before more of her world was irrevocably broken.

Vic poured himself a gin and tonic and sat in his chair in front of the television, clicking at the remote control until he found a game to his liking. He drank all night that night, seven gin and tonics altogether, the last remnants of his trust violated, and as the sun rose in the early morn he wandered up the stairs and called softly to Leah through the guest bedroom door. He was plenty drunk and his head was spinning like a top on a freshly shined mirror.

"Leah, did you ever love me?"

Vic heard his wife roll over in bed. Leah cleared her throat before speaking. "Not like you wanted me to," she said weakly.

"I'm sorry, Vic, I just never felt it for you. Not, I think, in the way you loved me. I think you saw more in me than was ever there. I never really understood it, why you wanted me so desperately. You could have had so many other women, women who would have worshipped you, women for whom you would have been enough. I tried to love you, Vic, I swear I did. I stayed with you for David's sake. He loves you, you know."

"But I always loved you."

"I know you did."

Vic leaned his head against the door. He felt the knob with his hand. The door was locked as usual. He started to cry. "Why did you marry me?" he asked despairingly.

They were still talking through the door. For Leah, it was easier that way. Vic heard her sit up in bed. "I guess I wanted out of Nashville," Leah said regretfully. "There was so much pain in my home. It hurt to be the sister that my mother loved the least. And you know I always wanted to see California. I thought you were going to be a baseball star, and I'd be this famous wife of his and people would know my name and where I came from. I suppose you were my best hope to be somebody and get back at the world. I had to leave the South, Vic. Tennessee was killing me. I wanted my child raised where he'd have the best opportunities, and California provided that for him. I thank you for that."

"Was there anything I could have done any differently?"

There was a long pause. Vic heard the sheets ruffle. "Maybe," Leah said impassively, "if you had gone to church with me. I don't know. Maybe. Perhaps God would have worked some miracle for us. I finally quit trying to convert you when you rejected me so many times."

"You loved that guy before me, didn't you?"

Leah waited a bit to answer. "Yes, Vic, I did. I'm sorry."

Vic had a terrible headache and the world was spinning worse than before. He felt sick to his stomach. "I need to go to bed," he said. "We'll talk more about us later, when the alcohol wears off."

But Leah, her face swollen and bruised, her marriage in tatters, was through with talk. She thought not of her responsibility or role in the fiasco, her mind too concerned with survival and preoccupied with the image of what others would think of her adultery, especially the impressions of her only son. David's perception still mattered to her. It was about the only thing that did. Only with the tiniest of musing did her mind think of God and the sacrifice of His son Jesus for exactly moments like those. Instead, for a reason she could not ascertain, she thought of her home back in Nashville, the novels and Bibles laying on the end tables in the front room, next to the plum velvet sofa and her mother's favorite chair. It seemed like someone else's life she had lived since then. Her mind kept returning to the novels of Hawthorne lying on her mama's tables, to adultery and dark mysteries to be revealed. She fell back to sleep before she could pray, dreaming of scarlet letters and society's retribution for those who violate the most sacred of His covenants, and she dreamed in vivid red and of running away in a flood of crimson shame.

Upon awakening, Leah went to the courthouse in downtown Oakland and sued for divorce later that same morning, believing it was better to simply get on with her life, whatever that life might eventually bring. Solitude seemed fitting to her. She deemed her decision a great victory. The drive to the courthouse was easier than she had anticipated and she even smiled once before the smile hurt her jaw. Where at first she had felt numb to the world, that afternoon she suddenly felt carefree and happy. But the repose didn't last long. Her victory was Pyrrhic. When Vic came to talk to her later as promised, Leah simply closed the door in his face and laid down on her bed until he eventually went away. Seeing him, hearing him, brought her down, reminding her of a lifetime sacrificed in poor choices. The brief giddiness of the daylight had been only temporary, and that same night the pain came again and it was hard to breathe in her chest, as the freedom of the courthouse was lost in another night of blackened solitude and suffocating despair.

Chapter 19

FOR LEAH, THE NEXT few months were an especially empty time. The firm confronted her about the affair, the two senior partners acting as inquisitors general. Soon her work associates became much less like her colleagues and much more like a swarm of curious onlookers. Leah despised their condescending glances. She quit her job. She never did snitch out Dan to his wife, not knowing why exactly and caring little for an explanation as to the reason for her discretion. All she knew was that her vindictiveness had waned.

When Vic moved out and into a studio apartment two towns over, the house became as silent as a crypt. The fog crept in at night, but Leah was not afraid of the nighttime any longer, alone and lying in the dark. Many evenings, she didn't even bother to lock her doors, caring not about dying at the hands of an intruder while she fell asleep on her once prized couch or on the cold, insensitive floor. Death seemed a decent alternative to existence. The television sat silently in the corner, books went unread, and chores stacked up high as the skyline of Oakland within her view. Late at night, alone in the big house, she heard the far off roar of passenger jets, and she thought often of escape and of dying, and of how a life can stray so far from whence it came.

David never forgave his mother for her sexual indiscretion, refusing to talk to her or discuss the issue after his final remonstration, and Leah grew despondent with his rejection of her and missed him. Her son had always been headstrong and judgmental, but with this latest affront he had also turned unforgiving. Again and again she heard their final conversation in her mind, his words stinging like the poisonous bite of a viper: "You broke up our family for a lecherous scum, when Dad has loved you all along, a good man who gave you his all. Now you want my forgiveness? Well, I'm through with you. When you cheated on Dad, you cheated on all of us, even yourself."

"But I'm still your mother."

"No, from now on, you're on your own."

The pain Leah felt from those departing words was indescribable. Those words, those awful and horrible words, hurt Leah so severely that she finally quit trying to patch it up with her son. She quit calling him. He never called her. Leah knew her son well enough to know he wouldn't make an attempt to reconcile with her anytime soon. Her boy was headstrong and proud. No, David would wait a sufficient amount of time, perhaps even years, and then, and only with the requisite pleading of his father for him to be a good son, would he gradually make any overtures to his mother. Perhaps he'd never call again. So, with more pressing and immediate concerns, Leah turned her attention to an even uglier matter at hand.

Vic's attorney played rough in the divorce proceedings after convincing Vic it was in Vic's interest to do so. Leah fought with her own attorney over strategy, and as a result her settlement was less than she deserved. With the house sold, Leah moved into an apartment suite down near the water, underneath the windowed towers of Emeryville, with a spectacular view of the San Francisco Bay and the marina promenade. In her view lay three yacht harbors. Past the harborage, straight across the burnished waters of her vista, rose the majesty of the Golden Gate Bridge and the rising olive spire of Mount Tamalpais. It was a setting fit for a queen. Without employment, however, the place was far beyond her means, but at least most mornings Leah awoke to glints of sunlight and the smell of gourmet espresso wafting over from the village coffee house.

A bronze sheen rose daily from the estuary in the foreground, but further out the bay turned into a mixture of seaport blue and foamy green lime. Excursion sloops and sailboats bounced jauntily into harbor, one by one, their sails flapping loosely in the wind, their bows cutting steadily through the shiny copper chop, their sunburned captains ringing bells that dinged loudly of their passage. Handsome men walked along the promenade clad in heavy cableknit sweaters and drawstring pants, boat owners and yachtsmen and aspirants to same, and Leah thought often in those days of second chances and of marrying again.

But at the first glow of the moon, the coldness of the ocean rolled in like a thick oyster soup, enshrouding the bay waters in a dusky and clotting grayness. It turned misty and cold. The winds blew the clouds to the waistbands of the buildings and then swamped their rooftops as the fog swirled about. The moon tried to fight its way through the clouds, but the grayness swarmed the bay and then blackness descended upon the land. Nighttime in the apartment was a lonely time, even desolate, and in a building with hundreds of people Leah felt abandoned and forsaken. She no longer had any friends. Divorce had eliminated from her life almost everyone she ever knew. She thought of getting a dog, but the rental contract forbade it, and dogs were messy and required care. Leah, in those dour and woeful days, appeared as a lantern in a forested cabin, her flame expiring in the nightly drafts, the late evening hours taking the full measure of her energy and heaping upon her only more blackness and suffocating misery.

Another year of existence passed. The golden of the morning faded into dark despair and some days Leah didn't open her blinds to the world or step outside her realm. The air inside her suite grew stale and lifeless. She had tried living on her own, living without the companionship of others, by herself in a self-imposed solitude, but that wasn't working very well and waves of panic overtook her. The numbness of her spells at night turned into a series of painful fits, as daggers shot into her chest and cramped up her shoulders and neck in a series of throbbing spasms. She developed excruciatingly painful migraine headaches during which her vision blurred at the slightest intrusion of light. She began to slurp her food. Each day required more effort to leave her apartment than the previous one, and she watched television for hours on end and cried endlessly into her hands and wondered why.

One day, having overcome her inertia, and making it out onto the promenade, Leah wandered into a bookstore adjacent to The Transoceanic Courtyard at Viewpoint Square. The square was of new construction and Leah often went there for the scenic view of the bay and its bobbing sloops and cutting crews. A sense of new beginnings beckoned in the seaside breezes. Somewhere secretly inside of her, Leah had always believed she could recapture herself, or form a new and improved version of that little girl who had played so trustingly on Groveland Street, despite her shaking pain and sagging spirit. Maybe now was the time. It seemed to be. Pigeons fluttered on the cobblestone walkway as Leah entered the glass front door of the bookstore, bells tinkling softly on her entry. An older woman in spectacles smiled at her from behind the counter.

"Hi, can I help you?" the woman asked.

"Oh, I'm just looking," Leah answered. "Anything new and noteworthy?"

"Yes, there is a new book by Erhard Deppler entitled *Self Responsibility: The Hope of You*. He's a Harvard faculty psychologist and a very talented man." The woman pointed to a stand of books. "My last copy is over there on the top shelf. The book has been flying out of here faster than I can restock it. It's been getting rave reviews. Number two on the bestseller list and climbing."

"Thank you, I'll have a look."

Leah found the book and pondered picking it up for a good long minute. The book seemed to glare at her. Other self-help books loaded the shelves with advice on everything from how to lose weight to growing your wealth to selecting the proper mate for a successful marriage. There were books on science and philosophy and one on evolution and the inevitable progress of man. Leah thought back to her brother William and the conversation they had had regarding the primacy of evolution in science. She remembered him saying that she'd eventually reject Christianity's version of the origin of man. Maybe William had been prescient after all. But Leah kept returning to the first book, her eyes reading the many recommendations on the front cover jacket, endorsements from other academics and journalists, and even a glowing commendation from a Senator from Maine. There was no way, Leah thought, it was an accident for her to stumble into the bookstore that day. It seemed she was meant to read something in the store. Leah's hand went to lift the book from the shelf, the book the lady at the counter had recommended she read. At the last possible second, and only out of the corner of her eye, Leah made out a plain book of brown vinyl covering, and she stepped laterally toward it. On the cover, engraved in simple and understated gold lettering, were the words *The Bible.* Incomprehensibly, Leah picked up the Bible instead of the other book and began to read where the pages fell open in her hands:

> *The law of the Lord is perfect, refreshing the soul.*
> *The decree of the Lord is trustworthy, giving wisdom to*
> *the simple.*
> *The precepts of the Lord are right, rejoicing the heart.*
> *The command of the Lord is clear, enlightening the eye.*
> *The fear of the Lord is pure, enduring forever.*
> *The statutes of the Lord are true, and all of them just.*
> *Let the words of my mouth meet with your favor,*
> *keep the thoughts of my heart before you.*
> *Lord, my rock and my redeemer.*

Those were the first of God's words that Leah had read in many months, but it seemed so much longer to her than months. It seemed years. She cried at the familiarity of their religious cadence. Something in those words made Leah feel validated, and she linked finding a Bible on the shelf of a store that day to a confirmation of her old way of looking at the world, as if God had placed the Bible there for that very purpose, to reaffirm for her all that she had been before. And soon an idea came to her as an old friend in her time of need: Leah needed security, both emotionally and financially, for solitude was indeed a very lonely business, and her divorce settlement would never be enough to sustain her for very long. She walked out of the store without buying a thing, the bells tinkling softly behind her as she stepped lightly into the morning breeze of the bay.

Chapter 20

A FEW DAYS LATER, in what Leah attributed to the gracious hand of God, she met a man named Jay during an evening walk along the shoreline promenade. Jay was a sailing man, with flaxen hair made shiny from the sun, his face round like a jovial snowman, his nose bulbous but short, and he had a joyous disposition that beamed happily from his light-blue eyes. He was a carefree and adventurous sort, incapable of frowning, rarely angry or sullen, and he possessed an amazing ability to make others feel comfortable and liked. Norwegian by blood, Jay lived his days to sail the warmest points of the compass; in an earlier time he would have made a marvelous sea captain, traversing the globe in search of riches and land and indescribable treasures, returning only to the northern homeland for the deposit of booty before setting sail once again on the warm waters of the tropical seas. For Jay, the modern world was a bothersome bore, full of trouble and chaos and dissidence, but the sea was simple and sane, and above all else the sea was nature's purest form of clarity. His stories captivated Leah, bringing to her a sense of adventure she had lacked in her living, and in a matter of only weeks she wanted to live and sail the world with him.

Jay worked all the hours he could stand, saving his money for his excursions under sail, and when his stash was depleted, he'd find another port and take a job and save again for yet another junket. He had lived that seafaring lifestyle for over twenty years. His was an easy way to live, and, like Leah, Jay never thought much beyond tomorrow; what happened five or ten years down the line was of little consequence to him. Leah paid for nearly all their entertainment, but after a year of dating and saving his money, there was still no invitation from him to sail the world, and Leah began to think much about their future together and whether she had the right to ask Jay about what tomorrow may hold.

"Boy, it's a hot one tonight," Leah said, fanning herself, sitting on the wooden deck of *The Wanderlust.* Jay had named his sloop after the look his mother said she saw in his eyes that first time she had taken him sailing the waters of Newport, Rhode Island, where he had been raised.

"Scorcher, isn't it? I sure hope a breeze comes up," Jay said agreeably, tugging at his shirt to create some airflow over his sweaty stomach and chest. He surveyed the low sky past the edge of the bay, squinting. "Fogbank is out way past the gate, and the swell is unusually low. Not a whitecap in sight. Feels like the ports in the Middle East: desert rolls flush to the sea and bring the devil's breath with it, the sea as flat as a plate of glass. I've never liked calm, flat seas. Bad omen in a water like this. Come on, breeze, come on up and bring a swell."

Leah wet her lips with her tongue, a sign of nervousness with her. "Speaking of things coming up, when do you think you'll set sail again? Around the world, I mean?"

"Oh, probably in a few months," Jay replied, shifting in his seat before settling down in his chair again. "That's if everything goes as planned."

"And what is that plan, if you don't mind me asking? I've been curious about what you'll do."

Jay had been ducking this conversation for months. He winced and scratched his chin once before answering. "Oh, I guess my plan is to be in so good at my job that I can take a leave of absence, without pay of course, and know that when I come back, they'll still have a position for me if I want it."

"Is that realistic?" Leah asked skeptically. "Will the phone company do that for you? You said many people, younger, less expensive people, could do your job writing programs for the database center. Software is only going to get more competitive, isn't it? I mean, really, would they hold your job for you?"

Jay shrugged his shoulders. "Yeah, I think they would. I'm pretty good at what I do," he said confidently. "I've done a lot for the company when you think about it, made them oodles of money these past two quarters. The software program alone is worth its weight in gold. I'll tell ya, in my book they owe me big time for that writing. Brilliant piece of code, that *Fullsail*. Runs the whole network. Besides, their stock price is going through the roof. Don't you worry about me."

Leah took a swig of her wine and smacked her lips. "I'm not," she stated frankly. "I'm more worried about me. I'd like to know what's going to become of us. I have to look after me, don't I? If I don't, who will?"

"You got a point there," Jay said grimly. "In this world, you're on your own, baby. I learned that lesson early in life, and what a lesson it was. Like a tooth pulling. Took me a long time to get it straight. But I like my roguish independence these days, and I wouldn't have it any other way. That's why I love the sea. It's just me and her, and I can come and go as I please."

"What about love?" Leah said, getting directly to the point. "What about companionship? Do you care about love, or is that too threatening for you?"

Jay's jaw dropped. He nearly blurted out in laughter. "Now Leah, you're not pretending to be an expert on love, are you?" he teased her. He nudged his captain's hat upward and off his forehead for a better look at her. He remembered his charm and its importance to whatever successes he had had in life. He smiled a warm, empathetic smile at her, his face glowing in the sunset. "Hey, you know I care for you. But look at yourself: Would you ever love me? For crying out loud, you have walls so thick around you Third Army couldn't get through."

Leah leaned backward in her chair. She seemed acutely perturbed, the last of the pleasantry fading from her face, her eyes drawn suddenly into a hostile glare. "What walls? I don't have any walls. What are you talking about?"

In addition to his many other distinctive traits, Jay was also one of those men who didn't shirk from an argument, especially when he reasoned his input might actually help someone, and he thought Leah guilty of casuistry. "No walls?" he exclaimed. "C'mon, Leah, take a look at yourself. You're the only woman on Earth who won't say how she feels about a man. I think you're afraid of living, that's what I think."

"I don't see myself running out to sea to escape life."

Jay's hat fell off his head. He bent over the armrest to pick it up off the lacquered planks of the wooden deck. He looked at Leah with a purposeful stare, his face still calm and caring. "I'm not escaping. I *love* the ocean and the salt in the air. That's who I am. You want love, that much is obvious, but you're not willing to risk for it. I know you took a chance once, not with your husband, I know that, too, but long ago, when you told me about that glamour boy back in Tennessee who treated you poorly. It didn't work out for you, so you quit on love. But you haven't quit on the concept of love. You've got to love something, a voice inside your head tells you that most every day, but it isn't me you love. You're just looking for anything, anything to hold to, to give a name to what the voice cries out for."

"I could hold on to you."

Jay smiled at her again, but it was a smile laden with a saddened realism. He felt a twinge of guilt as he looked at her. "Sure you could," he said considerately. "But you wouldn't love me. Not enough for me to take you along for a long sail. We're not at that point in this relationship. And I'm not saying I'm at that point, either. Hell, I know I'm not. I'm honest with myself. Or at least I try to be. But even if I was in love with you, you wouldn't be in love with me, and you'd need to love me out on the ocean."

"Why, why would I need to love you?"

"Because out at sea, with nothing else but us, we'd have to love each other. Someday, I want never to port again, to sail the whims of the wild blue lady forever. I have dreams, you understand, dreams of the ocean."

"What dreams?"

"I told you about them."

Leah glanced away contritely. "I forgot. What were they again?"

Jay shook his head and spoke through a reluctant grin. "See what I mean? If you truly loved me, what I say would be more important to you."

Leah smiled her prettiest smile at him. Her eyes begged for a favor, the look the neighbor ladies used to talk about back in Nashville when Leah was still a child. "Tell me again. This time I'll remember, I promise," she cajoled.

"The heck you will."

"Oh, come on. Please?"

Jay sighed a fake sigh of frustration, uncorked the wine bottle, and refilled his wine glass to the brim. It was a good night for drinking wine, the truth in fashion, and the night young. He enjoyed sharing his dreams with anyone who'd listen to him, and Leah had given him another opportunity to pour out his soul. "Well, to begin with, I want to fish the leeward of Oahu for ono on a light tackle rod and reel, underneath the watchful eyes of the Pali; next, I'd like to photograph a sunset off the west shore of Zanzibar, then sail the Tahitians and the Philippine isles; after that, I'd walk the jungle temples of Malaysia and the rain forests of Indonesia; there's a bay near Jakarta where they say the water is so turquoise it actually hypnotizes; see the reef break one more time at Bali, feel the offshore breeze actually lift the wave higher, and then mainsail my fat behind straight into Singapore Bay."

"I'd like that, too, you know."

Leah looked so desperately sweet that Jay bit his lip to keep from laughing at her. "No Leah, you don't understand. When I'm on the ocean, I'm me all the way, and I'd have to have you be all the way, too. Not for me, but for the sea. The sea would have to be your first love, and you and I both know it's not. The woman for me has to love sailing the world as much as I do."

"So what happens to us next?"

Jay swallowed hard. "Well, I suppose, what happens to us next is that when I return, if you're still available, we'll do what we're doing now. I like you and I do care about you, but a good relationship needs total love. Without it, we're a hitched boat in a hurricane. You ever been in a hurricane?"

Leah didn't answer him. She had her answer. The sun fell below the horizon and it darkened quickly. When Jay went below for another bottle of wine, Leah stared out at the flat dark bay of San Francisco as the lights of North Beach and the towers of The Embarcadero rose brightly in the background.

A sliver moon cast a long white shadow on the near water before it widened out near the Marin headlands, covering the farthest darkness like a bottle of spilled milk. The wine played tricks on Leah's mind: Blake's face melting on the moonlight, then wavering on the water, back and forth, back and forth, obscured at times, then seen with the detailed clarity of a photograph. The moon drifted behind the first foggy cloudbank far out at sea, and Leah felt a cooling breeze pass through the Golden Gate and then come full into her hair. On the dark soup in front of her the powerless and empty gaze of a man broadened and then thinned into teary lines, the waves cruel in their antics, condemning her to a life without love, unable to help her even now, almost a lifetime later.

***

Jay left a month afterward and never returned. Within two weeks a new sloop occupied his slip in the yacht harbor and Leah quit coming by to check on the slip after the mooring of the new sailboat convinced her that Jay was undeniably gone. The new captain had a pretty lady with a German accent and long beautiful legs, much younger than Leah, hospitable and kind as well as a conscientious hostess, and the couple had a circle of hearty friends whose parties went long and happily into the night. Leah watched them many evenings from a nearby bench until her envy grew too great to bear, so on the last night she walked the lonely planks of the promenade back to her apartment in the chilling fog and vowed never again to return, the bay lapping against its onetime golden shore and the gulls screeching somewhere out over the water in the evening darkness.

Chapter 21

THE SAN FRANCISCO BAY AREA is full of all sorts of people. Leah met many different types as she wandered up and down the promenade on her nightly searches for a man, but she didn't make any lady friends that second summer on her own. Perhaps they could have helped her gain perspective, as life should be more than a quest for a husband. At night, Leah went drinking in the wharf's many saloons and ale house restaurants, laughing and carousing with a variety of men, but most used her for sex and for whatever else they could get from a desperate woman in such dire need. Eventually, Leah got wise and cut off those prospects unlikely to visit an altar, the men eventually moving on, in what seemed to her a virtual parade, one after another, giving excuses or simply walking off, and the rejection hurt Leah deeply and further diminished her already low self-esteem. She became increasingly shy. Meanwhile, her funds continued to dwindle. Leah self-imposed a deadline of two more weeks on the promenade, crying every night into her glasses of wine, and she was a couple of nights away from quitting her search altogether when one man smiled into her eyes after making love and stayed until the morning sun.

His name was Roberto.

Roberto was a stereotype: a Spaniard, born in Barcelona, lean and thinly muscled, with shiny straight black hair and tight olive skin that tanned to a gorgeous reddish brown. He wore cotton pants and emblem shirts, with deck shoes in a variety of lighter colors and a pastel string bangle on each wrist. He had worked in many countries through the years, speaking excellent English as well as Spanish, Greek, and French, and he spoke a fair amount of Italian as well, which he loved for its libretto. He had maintained his Spanish accent and mannerisms because he knew they were ingratiating to women, but he wasn't a phony man and he prided himself on his forthrightness. He had a petite nose, more like a woman's than a man's, and piercing blue-green eyes that reminded Leah of tropical coves.

Roberto was full of fire, his skin hot to the touch, and his spirit burned brighter than the shining sun. He bestowed flowers, danced to Spanish guitar, knew much about art, favoring El Greco and Diego Velasquez, played the drums and sang with passion, and loved any food made with cayenne pepper and plenty of salt and seasoning. He twirled Leah to almost any dance, spinning her around until she felt dizzy and exhausted, then roaring his approval like a lion over a carcass. He was five years younger than Leah, who was now in her mid-forties when she met him, but his trim waist and lean frame made him look much more youthful than his years, and people often guessed him to be in his late twenties or early thirties.

Leah enjoyed her time with Roberto and life passed quickly with him, as there was little time to recover from their nightly escapades. Roberto drank most evenings, never to any real excess, but he enjoyed wine with every meal and shots of fire gin or mixed drinks to inspire him afterward, and he was especially fond of a good cognac before he went to bed. He insisted that Leah drink along with him. After three months, Leah was exhausted from the festivity of their evenings and she slept in until noon most days, only to go out again at night drinking with Roberto, watching the sun rise again in the morning, the world spinning and Leah so tired from dancing that she thought she'd drop off her feet.

Roberto worked for a shipping company at the Port of Oakland and he exhausted his finances by the fifteenth day of each month. He had no savings to speak of. So Leah spent what she had on the both of them and neither thought much about tomorrow's bills. In that way Roberto was quite similar to Jay, as life was to be lived, enjoyed for the day that was, the time they had chosen to spend together as precious as a day's reprieve from jail. Nothing mattered to Roberto except the act of living, and he forbade any thoughts of what could go wrong in the passion of living for the moment.

One warm night, sitting together at an outdoor table on the Regatta section of the promenade, Leah's favorite place to people watch, the aroma of sourdough bread and boiling shrimp stirring their appetites to a slavering hunger, Roberto felt like having a talk. A gentle, dry wind came over the bay. The sunset that night was a blaze of reddish fire and yellowish flame. Roberto held Leah's hand as she looked out onto the water. The water sizzled. With so little breeze, the waterfront that evening was strangely silent, a lone sailboat drifting in with its sail bound to its mast and its motor cooing, the captain lifting his drink toward Roberto and Leah and Roberto tipping him back with a smile.

"Flattest sea I've ever seen," the captain yelled out.

"The bay, she's on fire," Roberto answered him.

The sailboat passed through the narrow water between two rock walls and slid into harbor.

Roberto turned to Leah. "We have fun, no?" he asked her.

Leah looked puzzled. "Why yes, of course we do. That's why I like you so much. About the only thing better than hanging out with you, would be some prawns and cocktail sauce right about now."

"Then why is there always trouble on your face, under your laugh, a look far off to someplace, someplace no one but you gets to go?"

"I don't know what you mean," Leah said defensively.

"Sure you do. Your mask, that look, that's who you try to be. You take time, lots of time, even when you don't know you take it, to make sure no one sees you. But I see because I know the look."

"I think you think too much," Leah said, trying for lightness. "I don't even know myself that well, so how are you going to know what I feel inside?"

Roberto chortled. "I'll tell you what I know," he said insistently. "You miss your son. Somewhere in your past, you lost someone, someone who made you feel safe inside your heart. But you don't look to replace this guy, whoever he is. You want nothing of love, not even from your son. You make rules, how you say in America, you know, a word like rules, what's the word? Help me out." Roberto smiled impatiently at her.

"Conditions?"

"Ah yes, that's it, conditions, conditions for people to love you. That way, when they don't follow your conditions, you can discard them, and never have to risk loving them without them first loving you."

Leah waited for more.

"I'll tell you something else, and these words you should hear," Roberto said professorially. Another smile creased his lips. "So listen close to me. Life has no guarantees. Everyone says that, I know the tales, but everyone is looking for them just the same, all the time while they live in this world. Leah, it's true, you more than the rest, because you refuse to play the game, unless the game is played with your rules. But life, my little guarded one, has its own rules and we must all play by them. The way to win is to enjoy playing the game, to take what you can, for tomorrow it can be taken away from us. One day, it will be gone forever, and you will have played the game without ever scoring a goal. If you are playing only to stop the other players, you no can score a goal. And if you no can score a goal, you cannot win."

"What's winning?" Leah asked wryly.

Roberto's eyes widened. Their turquoise beauty filled the promenade. "Winning is living with the dance. When you dance, you smile, you live to enjoy me, and the look into the distance, the empty one with all the sorrow in your eyes, is disappeared. When you dance with me, that is the only time you live without the need for guarantee. I see it as you laugh and breathe the air. Even when we make love, you want more to be there, some safe thing, to make you feel like you can let go and be free. But I cannot give you that safety, only you can give it to you. And safety comes from believing that life should be lived and that whatever the game throws at you, you can kick it away. The guarantee you seek comes from inside of you."

Leah could feel her muscles tighten, trying to shield herself from the truth, but Roberto wouldn't let the subject drop.

"Who did you lose, Leah? Why do you not have the safe feeling inside of you? What hurt you so much that you would protect yourself as a turtle in its shell? If you can answer these things, the game can still be won."

Roberto's blue eyes were like two seashores, so pristine and so beautiful that Leah had to answer him.

"There was a man once; we were both very young, but he didn't love me like I loved him, that is to say with all that I had in me. He was the only one that I ever felt that way for. Oh, Roberto, I loved him so much. When he left me, I lost my 'safe thing,' as you call it."

"Was there another, another one before him?" Roberto asked wisely.

"No."

"How about your father?" Roberto asked, pressing her, but still with a softness and sensitivity that graced his words. "What happened to him?"

"He died early in my marriage."

"Did you love him? Did he make you feel safe?"

Leah felt her throat tighten. It was hard for her to speak. "I loved my daddy with all my heart," she said, remembering Walton fondly. "As much as I could love anything. If you could have seen him, Roberto, how thin and yet how strong of a man he was, to work like he did to support our family, my mother bitching at him nonstop, ridiculing him, yet him there for me, for all of us, you would know why I loved him so."

Roberto waited for Leah to go on.

"My daddy," Leah said, "was the finest man that ever lived. He took so much trouble in his lifetime. But it never caused him to be bitter; he just loved me anyway. My mother was generally a monstrous bitch, but he stayed and fought for us, for me, and took it all in stride. My daddy was what every man ought to be in this world. Us women would be happy then."

Roberto waited for a sufficient time, so Leah would know he was truly listening to her. Then he spoke tenderly, with a heartfelt recognition of her past. "So one time a man no love you back, and the other time life took a man from you."

The cumulative weight of their conversation hit Leah at precisely that moment. Her bottom lip quivered and her eyes grew dreary and moist. "How am I supposed to win then?" she asked him acrimoniously. "Do you see why I quit on love?"

Roberto placed his hand on Leah's leg like a mother pampers a newborn. "Is there not one man who would never leave you? Someone who could give you the guarantee you seek?"

The answer came to Leah before she had time to think of it. It was as if the words came forth on their own. "Only one," she said instinctively. "He can never leave me if I love Him. He is bound by His word. He cannot break it. If He did, He wouldn't be who He is."

Roberto sprung backward. "Who is such a man?" he asked her incredulously. He seemed genuinely offended that there might be some kind of man that he hadn't figured on. "Such a man would not be a man, he would be more like a god," he concluded.

Leah smiled a respectful smile and placed her hand on Roberto's hand. "You *are* very smart, Roberto. God is the love of my life, or, should I say, He used to be, because He can't be taken from me if I love Him with all my heart. I live in high risk now because I am a sinner, and I know better than to sin. But God is the only one who loves me with a full guarantee. You could leave, all men could leave me; my own daddy left me, and all I ever did was love him. Even a son can leave, but God, He is forever."

Roberto looked at her disapprovingly. "You should think these things again," he stated bluntly. "God, I have no quarrel with Him; you should love Him beyond all the others. That I agree with. But perhaps God would allow you to love a man as well. I do not see why you cannot have both God and a man to call your own."

Leah looked at him tenderly. "Do you have someone in mind?"

Roberto's eyes found hers, equally tender in their gaze. "Yes, this man loves you, loves you for what we are. If you could love me now, with no guarantee, we could be together, perhaps for all our lives. Trust in life, Leah. You already have God to love you. Why not have a man as well?"

Leah glanced away. It was much safer then to change the subject than to look back at him. "I won't have God if I don't change my ways," she said mindfully. "I must find Him again or otherwise it could cost me my soul."

"Then find Him. But find me, too."

***

For days after their talk, Leah had no appetite. Her stomach fluttered like a turbulent airplane in a sudden storm. The hours seemed as eons and nothing made sense for any length of time. Leah went to the mountains of Bishop for a few days and then to Carmel and the rugged coastline of Big Sur. There, she sat on rocky points and watched as the waves surged foamy white against the shore, only to retreat again and meld into the blueness of the sea. She wondered, *Could life be beautiful for me again? Can I afford to take another chance on love?* Upon returning to her home, Leah stayed away from her phone and the promenade for two days afterward, and when Roberto called she let the answering machine record his voice without once answering it or calling him.

"Why you no take my call?" Roberto's voice would urge on the line. "Do you know how frustrating this is for me? All because I speak the truth. A man, this man, me, Roberto, is punished for telling you how I feel, honestly and from my heart, how is this life and how it can be for us. Do I lie? Well? You tell me. Do I? No, I do not lie, I have never lied, and soon I will break our rule to come over without calling you first. I love you. There, I have said it."

Leah considered his words. Her spells returned when she thought of being alone again with no man at her side, the tingling and shortness of breath stifling her good intentions for the day. Distress ended only when she recalled her wondrous times with the carefree and frolicking Spaniard: slow dancing to the picks of Spanish guitar at the Chez Bandera, the softness of Roberto's eyes as he lay sleepily on her pillow, an exhibitionist pose on the sands at Manressa, long embracing walks on the promenade after a good bottle of San Trevari and a cognac for a nightcap.

Leah, true to her nature, thought of the downsides. Roberto was flighty, that much was true, apt to go off on a whim, but he was likely to take her with him wherever he went, and he had professed under the moon that she made him happy. Leah thought of Jay in contrast. Jay had had a love, a love more important than her, a love for the sea, but Roberto's love was for life itself, for making the most of the days granted to him, and Leah was included in those moments in the sun. Inclusion felt delightful. Freedom lived where Roberto walked, and Leah yearned to be free. He loved her. He had said as much. They would struggle to pay their bills, and Leah would have to work again, and Roberto would never be a rich man or very successful in the eyes of the world, but somehow it didn't seem to matter to her anymore, and she missed him so much her chest hurt and her mind thought only of him.

Leah decided to take a chance on love.

Roberto hadn't called during the last two days and there was no answer at his apartment when Leah finally decided to leave him a message. The possible existence of another woman crossed Leah's mind; a waitress had been flirting with him only the other night in the bar at the Whaler, a spry young thing, pretty and buxom, serving them both cosmopolitans before their dinner, the little tramp touching his hand more than once while serving him his drink, but a calming voice in Leah's head said that no, it couldn't be so, that Roberto loved her, and that he wasn't capable of such an affront. He was much too honest for that, too caring and too sensitive, and he had no reason to lie to her.

On Friday morning the sky was already clouding over when Leah called the shipping company where Roberto worked, which she rarely did because Roberto didn't like to be disturbed while working. His job was especially hard labor, stacking and shifting large steel crates into huge wooden containers before hoisting them onto the hulls of the ships for securing; the job was noisy and frenetic and disruptions broke the pace of his work.

A woman answered on the first ring.

"Yes, is Roberto there, please?" Leah asked the receptionist politely.

The voice on the line hesitated. "Why, no Ma'am, he's not. Are you family?" the woman asked Leah. "This doesn't sound like a long distance phone call."

"No, I'm a friend of his, and I know he doesn't like to be paged while he's working. Could you see if he is walking around nearby?"

"Ma'am," the woman on the line said, "do you know his family, how we might be able to get hold of them?"

"No, I don't. Is everything okay? He's not in any trouble, is he?"

There was a long period of nothing on the other end of the line. Leah thought the call might have been disconnected, but she heard a faint drone of machinery in the background and the woman palming the receiver.

"Are you still there, operator?" Leah asked.

"Ma'am, are you a close friend of his?"

"Yes, I'm his girlfriend." Leah felt a burden lifted as her feelings poured freely from her heart. In her own way, with those words, she was admitting that she loved him. It felt wonderful to do so. "Actually, it's much more than that: I think he's what I've always been looking for. What's the matter, is he gone right now?"

"Ma'am, Roberto was killed two days ago," the woman said, so softly Leah barely heard her words. Leah gasped in horror. The woman waited patiently for some response, but none came. Thirty tortuous seconds passed. "A crane collapsed here," the woman finally uttered. "You must not have seen the reports on the news or read the newspapers. I'm very sorry, ma'am. Everyone here liked Roberto an awful lot. He was sure a nice man. If you want, I can have you talk to his boss."

Those were the last words Leah heard that day. She hung up the phone and wandered out to the promenade, walking for hours, in a fog thicker than any the bay could muster, aimless and lost. Although the sun was on the water as lustrous as any day the sun had ever shined, Leah never saw a single sparkle or felt the warmth of the sun on her face or saw its golden hue permeate the sky, as the waves continued to lap endlessly against the shore, meaninglessly and devoid of all their erstwhile beauty. She never recalled walking home after the moon rose over the estuary or waking that next morning to a cloudless sky, and all she knew was that she couldn't cry another tear for there were none left in her to cry.

Chapter 22

LEAH NEVER GOT PAST Roberto. Her tank had been nearing empty with little in reserve, and she couldn't summon the will to begin anew, her mind a prisoner to the notion of needing a man. Now, that too, was lost. To make matters worse, her money was dwindling fast. Since the divorce, Leah had sent Margaret money each and every month, without fail, a thousand dollars in a check or money order, some months a couple hundred dollars more, since Margaret had fallen in the backyard and couldn't work on account of a bad hip. Walton hadn't left Margaret much money when he died, and Leah figured helping out her mother was the least she could do for all her mother's trouble in the world. Leah had gotten little in return for her investments in Jay and Roberto, even less with the men who had used her solely for the pleasures of the night, and carousing the promenade had lost its glamour as well as its hopefulness. Life to her at that moment seemed utterly pointless.

After two more emotionally draining days inside her apartment, Leah finally walked the promenade again. Inconsolably, she watched as the bay's waves sloshed against the withering timber posts of a long pier that jutted out perpendicularly and away from the main concourse of the boardwalk. The pier hadn't been used in many years. Motor oil and gasoline slicked the surface of the waters. Way out in the deeper water the platform had collapsed and the last of the pier was a standing island of soggy timbers protruding from the bay like the ancient towers of a sunken city. A warning sign hung from a rusting wire fence at the entrance of the pier nearest to where Leah stood: *KEEP OFF, UNSAFE.* Barnacles clung to the waterlogged wood pillars supporting the promenade, the wharf creaking as the next tidal surge covered them in a wash of greenish soup, and as Leah stared out on the bay that day she felt as worthless as that old, discarded pier.

Leah stared at the pier posts for over an hour. She couldn't live like this. Not any longer. Her life was too empty, and she thought of herself as one of the barnacles, sticking to something for nothing, holding onto a life that wasn't worth clinging to, existing for the sake of existing, yet feeling the need to break away from the sorrow of the ocean all about her, away from the reminders of a life she had once lived fairly well.

As she walked beside the slurping tides of the bay, a man approached on the far side of the promenade. He seemed to be gawking at her, squinting at first, then wide-eyed, searching for a familiarity or a faint resemblance in her face. The man came over to her, uncertainty in his eyes. Leah stopped in her tracks and cocked her head. He seemed friendly enough. She didn't recognize him, though, as her memory scanned the years of living by the bay, the man sensing her unease.

"My God, I think you're one of Walton Caffrey's daughters, from Nashville," the man said in amazement. "I can't remember which one, but you used to come into my father's store on Walnut Street and buy bread and peanut butter for your father's lunchtime sandwiches."

Leah had no idea what the man was talking about. "My daddy was Walton Caffrey," Leah said, "but I don't recognize you. I'm sorry if I should. I truly am."

"Your daddy was the greatest fisherman in the world, Ma'am. He used to bring his catch by our store in the afternoon before going home that day. He'd show my father those stringers of crappie and black bass out back in the delivery zone where the trucks unloaded their boxes. Then he'd take his catch home and clean them up and bring some back for my father to fry that night for supper. My brothers and I loved eating those old fish. Crappie was our favorite. You and a dark-haired sister of yours came by the store for years. I recognize you from your curly blond hair and your pretty oval face. You have a face that is so incredibly symmetrical it's absolutely unforgettable."

"What was the name of your store?"

"Bob's. That was my father's name."

The corner store with the torn rug floor and the wobbly magazine rack suddenly came back to Leah. She saw the old cash register and the gum stand and the boxes of peppermints that lay scattered on the countertop. There was an old golden retriever that lay disinterestedly in the corner. She remembered the dog never moved.

"Oh, my, you're bringing me back now," Leah said. "I remember the store clearly. Walnut and Fourth. We lived on Groveland Street, around the corner, three blocks down from your daddy's store. You had a retriever dog. And a glass front door with a long crack in it. My word. Sure enough that door was cracked. And a gun rack on the wall behind the freezer. What the heck are you doing out here?"

"I'm traveling the country. I worked enough that I felt I deserved it. I sold my father's store in 1968 and joined the plumber's union and worked as a plumbing contractor until two years ago. I won't get my pension for another ten years, but I have enough money saved up and you wouldn't believe how easy and inexpensive it is to live on the road. I sleep outside in a tent from June through September and head down to Mexico and sleep outside on the beach in the winter. I don't even need a tent in Mexico. I had never seen San Francisco before, and I thought I'd check it out, but I can't wait to leave this glacier of a town. The fog here is colder than January back home."

"You've noticed."

The man laughed. "Yep, I can't take the fog. Goes right through you. You must live out here, I take it."

"Yes, I have since 1957. The road is that easy, you say?"

"Easy. And it feels like living."

"Well, I'll be. I never would have guessed it'd be so simple."

They talked for awhile. The man offered to buy Leah dinner, to reminisce about old times and how the world had changed and how nothing much good lasted, but Leah declined his cordial invitation and shook his hand goodbye. She made off without learning the man's name after giving him the excuse of having to meet an old friend in the city that night for an impromptu departure to Europe. She did not remember the man from the corner store in Nashville, he had been just a boy then, but the recalling of Tennessee gave her a pain in the pit of her stomach that lasted through the rest of the evening. As she walked home later that same night, Leah was possessed by a feeling of bitter vacuity. Now, it seemed, no place was home.

But the man's words of living on the road sunk in like a mattock into soft mud. Leah's usual conservatism was replaced with a newly found wantonness. That alone showed how desperate she'd become. She gave notice on her apartment the very next day without any regrets or second thoughts, and within a month she left the bay behind her, breathing easily and driving free.

Chapter 23

AMERICA IS A BIG LAND. That first summer on the road Leah drove to regions of the country she had wanted to see since she first flew over them on her way to Carmel for her honeymoon, reinforced on her last flight back to Nashville for her daddy's passing: the flaming southwestern deserts of Arizona and New Mexico, the tawny wheat fields of Nebraska, the rising majesty of Colorado and Wyoming, the desolate stretches of Utah's reddish tablelands. She saw the port cities of the eastern seaboard and the industrial heartland of the mighty Midwest, but she stayed clear of the South and particularly the sorrowful state of Tennessee. She preferred the West. She liked its spaciousness and its relative newness, as the West to her felt strong and enduringly essential. Prickling cactus, ground brush mesquite, and high mountain aspens soon became her roadside companions, and Leah learned much about the land, its many rolls and lulls, and what it means when a golden tan turns to roan and ebony engulfs a shadow. When survival is at hand one learns quickly. Cirrus clouds swirl in a creamy blue whirlpool hours before a storm, the birches and cottonwoods oppose their natural sway, and a gathering tornado silences the sky and stands nature at its most attentive.

For five years Leah drove the country, sleeping in the warmest climates she could find, burning her divorce settlement on hotels in the wintertime and the requisite gas and food. She drank to drown her sorrows, and she had largely given up on men. She quit trying with her son David, and she made up story after story for Margaret and Marian as to why she was never found in the same place twice. Alcohol reduced her immune system to a constant cough and she weathered like a prune. She was often sick. Her mother and sister kept her informed of the familial happenings back in Nashville: William had died from liver failure not long ago and left a wife alone. Rarely had he seen or spoken to Margaret or his sister. They never really knew why. No one had seen or heard from Kay in many years, and Leah spent most of her time after the conversations fearing that her own life was indeed as tragic and meaningless as that of her siblings.

That autumn, the autumn of 1988, Leah found herself approaching the twisting shores and rugged embankments of Lake Powell in the southernmost stretches of the state of Utah.

The land around Lake Powell was quite possibly the quietest place Leah had ever been; even the wind made no sound. There were no trees. Large rocks and chunky boulders in the shape of arrowheads lined the lonesome highway that traversed the lake like spear tips discarded by a journeying god. The land felt ponderous and permanent. A scan of the territory revealed little except a sense of prehistoric desolation. Late in the afternoon, when rain clouds gathered at the buttes, the land turned to a bloody crust and the sky changed from powder blue to a dripping metal silver. In the parched lands along the shores of the lake, chunky rocks and limestone buttes transformed her mind in unimaginable ways, providing a clarity for Leah like no other, as well as an indisputable sense of her own mortality.

Rain showers dripped on the windshield, but then the weather cleared and the rain passed further on to the south. Clear nights made the temperature drop, so Leah sought a cheap hotel with a warm bed and a shower and a toilet of her own. Sleeping in the car and on the ground for so many years had made her perpetually stiff and sore and her knee joints swelled at night to nearly the size of ripened grapefruits. She was tired and hungry and she needed food.

After another few miles of driving the highway by the shores of the lake, Leah came to a bend in the road that had been dug out from under two kissing buttes. In a flat area on the side of the road nestled beside a low mesa sat an old rancher motel, with ten rooms for its lodgers and a large gravel parking lot out front. Leah saw a lavender vacancy sign pulsing low in the manager's window and what looked like a reading lamp lit back behind the sign. She pulled into the gravel flat, stretching out of her car, and walked up slowly toward the front office door. It was so dark outside Leah couldn't see the contour of the ground, so she stepped carefully, like a soldier in a minefield, making her way to the door and yanking it open rather forcefully. The door made an awful squeaking sound on the suddenness of the pull, the handle clanking loosely in Leah's hand before nearly coming off, and from behind a counter rose a worn old woman with a cordial face, a lit cigarette dangling from her mouth.

"Got any rooms?" Leah asked the woman.

"Break my door, why don't you?" the woman said smiling. "Sure do, Honey. They're all fifteen dollars."

"I'll take one."

"Check out is at noon," the woman said, opening a reservation book with a list of rooms and names. "You're a good ways from the Canyon, I hope you know that. It's a lonely ride; you're smart to do it in the daytime. Sign here, will ya?"

When Leah came back from putting her belongings in her room and showering, she saw a small tavern adjacent to the office and wandered in. The room was dimly lit and reeked of cigarette smoke and burnt coffee. A wooden bar with a long beveled mirror and glass shelving flanked the far left wall, saloon style. There were no taps or spigots at the bar nor bottles on the shelves, and the curtains were all drawn closed and hung droopily and unevenly. Moose heads and deer antlers protruded from the walls and a number of wooden panels were rotted black.

"There's no bartender," a man shouted out from a corner table. The man was sitting off by himself, rangy and wrinkly, a patch of white stubble growing pointlessly on his chin, the veins in his arms extruding from his skin like a tangle of pressurized hoses.

"Oh, I'm looking for something to eat," Leah said casually.

The man smiled at her. "Something to eat, huh?"

"Something that's not too expensive," Leah said, coming over to him. "A burger or a sandwich would do just fine. Do you know a spot around here that provides a good meal for the money? Something edible?"

"You're in it," the man said abruptly. "Only food and gas until you get to Point Webb, five miles from the Canyon. Don't know if I'd call it edible, though. Emma can make you whatever you'd like, although I'd get the burger or the frankfurter and forget about the rest. Got stomach poisoning on the chicken salad once, and Emma flirted with a turkey mash about a week ago that the bird farmers sold her when she went over to Bullhead for some restocking. Poor Emma, mash was drier than the gravel out front. Same ugly brown color, too. Yep, get a burger or the dog. Get the chips to go with it; they're bagged."

"Do you have a name?" Leah asked the man. She suspected she liked him already.

"I'd get a beer while you're at it," the man went on, ignoring her. "Coke machine is busted, has been for weeks, and the water around here tastes like the ground. You'll see some of it in your glass, just floating around. What did you ask me again?"

"Your name."

"Oh yeah. I'm The Explorer. I don't have the kind of name you're referring to. I did once, but I forgot what it was. I'm not crazy and I'm not dangerous, so relax. I'm just me, and I like the name. I'd say you're originally from Tennessee. You aren't thick enough to still be from there. After that, I'd say somewhere west, most likely California. How'm I doing so far?"

"Very well," she said, quite impressed. "What exactly do you explore?"

The man unfolded his arms. "The Southwest right now, for over a year." He contemplated the ceiling and spoke rhetorically. "Man, has it been that long? Can it have been that long?" His eyes came back to Leah. "Guess it has been. Anyhow, before that I was in Argentina, Chile, Bolivia, and Mexico. Then Baja. Worked my way up. I'm originally from the East Coast. Farmington, Maine, to be exact. You must have hated Tennessee. People like you can't live in rigid systems. What ya running from?"

"I'm trying to learn," Leah said quickly. "And I've already learned that that drawl of yours, that country way of speaking, is something you've picked up because you think you'll fit in better around here talking that way." The man smiled at her again. "Anyway, I'm trying something new and different these last five years," Leah went on. "I didn't want to be where I was from anymore. This, this wandering through the states, it's my way of staying alive."

"Been mine for over forty years," The Explorer said, the grin widening on his face. Leah thought she saw a wink of his eye in the low light of the room. "Eventually, the whole country gets too small, and you'll have to go to another continent," he said, continuing on. "If I live long enough, the Earth itself will close in on me, and I'll need to go to Saturn or Mars just to be able to breathe. Thank God we don't live too long, huh?"

Emma, the woman at the office check-in, came out from behind the bar, over to the table where The Explorer sat with his arms folded in front of him. He kicked a chair out from underneath the table for Leah to sit on and relaxed his arms.

"You want a burger and chips?" Emma asked Leah nicely. "I heard The Wanderer talking to you about my menu. Got Bud and Coors to drink. Which one you prefer?"

"It's The Explorer," the man said to Emma, not the least bit offended. "You'd think you'd get it right one of these times."

"Whatever you say, Adventurer. Lady, you want a Bud or a Coors?"

"Coors will be fine," Leah said. "In a glass, if you don't mind. Oh, and how much is it?"

"Oh, your new friend here will get that," Emma said, chiding The Explorer to pony up. "Won't you now, Great Sage?"

"Sure I will," The Explorer said, eyeing Emma in mock disgust, stretching his lanky body out with a yawn and a cracking of his bony knuckles. He took a belt of gin and turned toward Leah, winking at her. "But I get an hour of your time. I get to hear the story of why you're so far away from California. Got to be a serious story there. Fair enough?"

"That's a bargain," Leah said. "My name is Leah, and I'll tell you my tale as soon as I get me that beer."

The beer came out in a flash, the foam oozing over the sides of a lukewarm mug and spilling over the lip forming a golden foamy circle at the bottom of the glass. When Leah tried to raise the mug there was a strong suction effect.

"Raise it from the side, like this," The Explorer said, showing her the style by holding an imaginary glass with his hand and sweeping it out wide before hoisting it to his mouth.

It worked. Leah upraised the mug and gulped down two mouthfuls of beer, her face scrunched up from the bitterness of the hops.

"You don't drink beer much, do you?" the Explorer smirked.

"No, I don't. I prefer white wine."

"Well, my dear, this hole is a long way from Napa. I was in Napa once, years ago, and I can tell you want to hear the story." He smiled at her, Leah smiling back at him. "Anyway, it was the day Saigon fell. April of '75. Yeah, the day Saigon fell. I remember that day now as clear as a whistle. Choppers tossed from our carriers into the South China Sea like so much garbage from a dump truck. Except you and I paid for that junk. What a waste. Whole miserable war was a joke. Still is how I describe the wine country. Still, and with nothing to do. There's a valley in Argentina, can't remember the name of it, spittin' image of Napa. Plaza in the center of town. Big bell tower in the plaza. Rio something. Or Esplanade. Name escapes me. Tell me you didn't like the wine country."

"No, I didn't care for it. They said it was enchanted, but I think they lied. It was worth seeing once and the wines were tasty and all, but you're right, it was kind of boring and the drive was winding and tediously slow. It was sure expensive to stay the night, I do remember that much."

A long silence followed. The preliminaries were done. The Explorer leaned in toward Leah, his eyes tightening into an investigative crumple. "Now then, what's your story?"

Leah sat up in her seat, somewhat startled. She took a deep breath. "It's a simple one, really. I married young to escape my mama and came to California where my husband was originally from, the land of opportunity and all. California seemed so grand at the time. So I had me a child of my own, a son, raised him, worked for a law firm as an office manager, did fairly well at it, the marriage fell apart when my boy grew up, and I didn't have much life left to stay for after that. When I was younger I needed companionship, but now it feels more natural to be alone. So I decided to go explore." Leah ceased her discourse. She looked The Explorer over and nodded to herself. "Say, is that how you got your name?"

The Explorer sat back in his chair, another knowing smile creased his face, and he patted the table a couple of times in confirmation. "Go on," he said encouragingly.

"That's it, that's all there is to me."

The Explorer knew better. "You ever clung to anything?" he asked her searchingly. "Something you've loved in your heart or valued your entire lifetime? A way of looking at the world, qualities you believe in, a philosophy perhaps? Southerners are big on philosophy."

Leah took her time and pondered his question. She could tell The Explorer was in no hurry to go anywhere, willing to sit patiently in the darkened quiet, and he would have waited until the end of time for her to answer him. He was a tenaciously punctilious man, much more than merely courteous or gentlemanly, genuinely interested in her reply because it added to his database of life experiences while simultaneously justifying his own existence. He *inquired* more than he asked, and the seriousness of his gaze demonstrated that he didn't want to be indulged or lied to.

Leah thought for another minute. She was thinking of subjects she had learned in school instead of what she truly believed. Then she came to it. "One thing," she said finally, impressed with her own resourcefulness. "Now that you ask, only one thing: God."

The Explorer leaned back in his chair and pondered Leah's response to his inquiry. "Well, that's as good as any," he said chuckling. "He might be all there is. You know what I mean?"

"I think I do. But I also think you'll tell me if I don't."

The Explorer yawned a comfortable yawn. "I will," he said easily. "But you still have about fifty-five minutes or so to do the talking, and I get what I pay for. After that, I'll tell you what I know, a rock heaved on the calm of your pond."

Leah proceeded to fill in the details of her life and The Explorer listened to her every word. At exactly an hour, he tipped back his last shot of gin and rose to his feet to fetch his coat from a nearby hanging rack. The bottle of gin sitting on the table was nearly empty, but in their hour of discussion he hadn't slurred a single word.

"Come with me," he said persuasively. "I've got something I want to show you. We'll have to drive. Get something warm, and I'll see you in the front parking lot in about five minutes. You'll be safe with me. I give you my word."

Emma came by to clean up the table. "Go on," she said to Leah. "He ain't no trouble. You're safer with him than being here alone." She turned to The Explorer. "How long you gonna be?"

"About an hour," The Explorer replied. "I'll have her back here in no time. She'll be much wiser by then. All my travels got to be for some good reason. This might be it. Heck, it might even save her."

Emma gave him a derisive grin as she walked away, taking a tray of messy dishes and glasses back with her to the kitchen.

***

Leah met The Explorer in the front parking lot and together they left the motel in his beat-up pickup truck. The truck was muddy from his off-road excursions, but the windows were sparkling clean as were the silver door handles and the metal floorboards. He had wiped them down for the ride. In the low light of a lamppost Leah made out decalcomania silhouetted on the back window, most for liberal causes, from saving gray whales to preserving rain forests in the Amazon, with one centrally placed sticker warning of the dangers of nuclear war. Low in the front windshield was another glittering sticker that imagined world peace.

They drove in the quiet of the night for a good ten minutes. The last mile or so The Explorer slowed down around every corner and crook in the road, peering out, eye marking something familiar in the darkness. Finally he came to it. A dirt path, big enough for a truck or a car, forked to the right; in the high beams of the truck lights Leah saw the passage had been cleared of rocks and debris, intentionally so, appearing safe for travel, the ground a combination of compressed gravel and hardened mud. They drove another fifty yards or so, neither one speaking to the other. Then Leah made out two large stones and an aggregation of jagged rocks resting against each other in a clustered semi-circle, like a miniature alignment of boulders in an ancient Druid rite, and the truck stopped cold in its tracks. No moon shone that night, but the stars were dense in the sky, so plenteous that the heavens seemed to glow as one collective band of platinum light.

"We're here," The Explorer said, opening his door and stepping into the darkness. Crushed rock ground beneath his feet as he walked forward a few paces. Leah climbed out of her side of the truck, trusting the stranger as thoroughly as if he were her own daddy, and she soon joined him in an open area between the truck and the semi-circle of rocks. The autumn desert air was cold at night, and Leah bundled up against it.

Easterly into the sky, Leah beheld a glittering tiara of stars: Sirius, Rigel, Betelguese, all magnificent in their brightness, the belt of Orion a perfect trey of amethysts on display, the empty space of sky beyond the stars as black as oiled velvet and twice as shiny, the glimmer of the galaxy alighting the two of them like a sprinkling of golden stardust. Echoes of David's young voice as he explained the stars to his mother ran through Leah's memory. She remembered the stars of autumn rising in the east when David had taken her into the yard during the Modesto years and told her their names and distances.

"My God, the sky is alive," Leah exclaimed.

"You feel that?" The Explorer seconded.

"I've never seen anything so amazing in my life."

The Explorer began his discourse without waiting for Leah's undivided attention. "Well, this place I call 'reciprocity,' the ultimate juxtaposition between *out there* and *in here*," he began softly. His manner of speaking was professorial and his speech assumed a sudden air of dignity. "The stars and planets as far out as the eye can see and the baseness of the earth directly below your feet, external and internal, maximized and minimized. The entire contrasted with the elemental. You with me on this?"

Leah was startled by the suddenness of his question, still stuck in the splendor of the nighttime sky. They stood shoulder to shoulder. "Yes, I suppose so, the sky is just so beautiful, I wasn't through taking it in yet."

"Well, go right ahead then. It is gorgeous, isn't it?"

Leah spied more of the spectacle. The sky was all encompassing that evening, past its usual confines of horizon and bordering blackness, its vastness revealed by the limitlessness of the night, and where the constraints of sight usually provide a manner of background for its edge, the universe that night flowed beyond itself and then back again. Leah felt its movements as if the sky were an ocean over her body.

"I'm sorry," Leah said. "You were saying?"

"When our people go *out there*, we're going to find more of what we have here," The Explorer said convincingly. "Planets revolving around stars, many of them with life on them, some with intelligent life, civilizations like our own, some more advanced than ours, every intelligent being in the universe trying to make sense of the unfathomable as it looks out into space. Frank Drake was right: the only variable we can't be sure of is whether we last long enough to confirm their existence. I know they're *out there*. I feel them. They're probably in some desert of their own as we speak, contemplating you and me. We're all looking for something different, something *out there*, but the answer is here in front of us every day. Was California really that different than Tennessee?"

"How do you mean?" Leah asked.

"The life issues. You know, why we're here, where the heck we're going? Have you answered any of those questions yet?"

Leah saddened. "No, I'm still searching. I thought I would have answered them by now."

Leah felt his grin in the nighttime wonder. "You know why you haven't?" The Explorer asked, setting himself up to serve the answer. "You've been looking *out there*. The answer isn't out there. It's in front of you. It's in you."

"You think it's here now, because of this place?" Leah asked him dubiously.

"No, it's been in you the whole time. 'Reciprocity' here, it just provides the proper setting. It's like that saying from antiquity, when Socrates went before the Oracle and asked the Oracle the meaning of life: *Know Thyself*. You gotta know yourself, baby, you gotta really know yourself. Take me for instance. When I graduated college, I knew something was missing in my life. You ever read Maugham's *The Razor's Edge*?" Leah shook her head no. "Well, no matter, but I was like this character Larry in the book, obsessed with finding myself, only I went ahead with a job and the daily grind of making a living anyway. It was the thing to do in those days. I suppose it still is. In the book Larry travels to India and gains perspective, embracing Hinduism and becoming a spiritual master of sorts, instead of going headlong into an unsatisfying career as did his friends. He shuns meaningless materialism to gain an inner peace, but at the cost of much ridicule from those absorbed in the material world. He loses his fiancée over it, because what woman wants to stake her future to a roaming malingerer who cares nothing for money? But unlike Larry, I worked, saved my coin, invested reasonably well, accumulated the usual trappings, lost them, slaved to get them back again, hit gold, lost it again, regained most of it, finally put enough away so I could see the world, but the feeling of emptiness never left me. I've tried it all: love, sex, group sex, booze, pot, acid, went through meditation and yoga, then spiritualism, founded my own political movement, joined causes, put my faith in technology, but nothing worked for more than a few months at a time. Always, the emptiness returned."

"What did you do?"

"I connected to my center, the essence of who I am. I asked myself one day, 'What does it for you? What makes you feel the most happy?' And I came up with being free. Just popped into my head." A look of resignation crossed his grizzled face. "Oh, the years I wasted doing what others wanted from me. All because I wasn't confident enough in myself to tell them to stick it where it don't shine. When I realized that, that I loved being free, the love, the sex, booze, all of it was good again and the melancholy went away."

"That's why you explore?"

"Yes. But I'm not exploring. I'm being me."

"Are you happy this way?"

"It's the only way I can be happy." The Explorer stopped himself before proceeding, pausing just long enough for a thought to come to him. Leah noticed his contrariety. He seemed suddenly unsure and anxious. He grunted to himself. "Only every so often, I get this strange feeling in the pit of my stomach that maybe I haven't thought of everything, kind of a personal regret without knowing exactly what I'm sorry for. Shakes me to the bone every time I feel it."

"I've often felt that same way, only for me it was a feeling of unraveling, of my coming apart as life went along rather oblivious to me. I hate the fact that life may prove indifferent to my struggles after all."

The Explorer made another guttural sound again in agreement. "Nothing worse than indifference. I despise apathy."

Leah beheld more of the shimmering sky above her head.

"So what's your center?" The Explorer asked her.

The briskness of the wintertime air, the stellar magnificence of the nighttime heavens, and the lightheadedness from a guzzled beer was more than Leah had bargained for. The importance of the moment slapped her into a sobering reality. Somehow, The Explorer had framed her dilemma in life absolutely perfectly.

"I'd have to say God," she answered him softly. "I've always wanted to spend my life with God. Until you referred to it as a center, though, I hadn't thought of myself as having a core. I've always felt I was two people living inside me, two people living in one body, each one aware of the other but neither one reconciled to sharing my soul. One of me wants to go home, and the other knows only to stay. All of my life I've struggled against myself. I've always wanted to know the meaning of life, but it feels like I keep myself from knowing it, like the flaws in me preclude me from understanding who I am. But I know I love God more than anything else in this world. It's just so hard to love Him here, so much of the bad in this life gets in the way of doing His will."

"Why God? Why not something else?"

The answer came to Leah as suddenly as a rush of wind. "God won't ever leave me," she said assuredly. "He'll love me if I do what He wants me to do, if I follow His commandments and hold to His truth. He promised me as much. If I can obey His word, I can have it all."

The Explorer took a step backward to gauge Leah's reaction to his next question. The light was much better when he did, her face so pleasant in the starlight, like a quotidian statue in a park, her countenance visible from afar but her beauty only truly discernible up close. A saintly glow came forth from her skin, her fine features seeming especially delicate in the rainbow of starshine that sifted down on her face. He saw why a man had once fallen in love with her.

"What's having it all?" he asked her sensitively.

"I suppose it's being loved forever," Leah said. She turned toward him and away from the sky. "But you think I'm wasting my time, don't you?"

The Explorer shook his head no. "I don't think so," he said, correcting her carefully. He wanted to ensure her continuation of honesty and her free flow of thoughts. "I'm sure somebody put all this here. But you're right, no one knows for certain how the universe was formed or for what purpose. That's why there's faith; that's why there's religions."

The Explorer, as he explained to Leah, had committed himself to challenging his beliefs, changing his own worldview many times in the course of his days, and he believed all people everywhere should do the same. He was one of those people in life who have much to say but no real audience to hear him. He cherished having Leah listen to him. In the splendor of the night, his gruffness was replaced with gentleness, and although it was true that he had begun their talk on a mission of instruction, his years of experience told him the conversation might be shifting to where he was in a position to learn something, possibly something profound.

His next question came without any further deliberation. When it flowed from his lips he wasn't even sure he had asked it. "Why do you believe so strongly in God?"

This time, The Explorer felt Leah's grin in the night. "Sometimes, I could *feel* God with me," Leah said nostalgically. "Once, on my street back home in Nashville, I thought I saw the sky changed from nothing more than a simple prayer. There was a peacefulness in the sky that I believe comes only from the company of God. Other times it seemed like He was with me in my room or when I read my Bible alone with my baby. God knows I've had my share of obstacles in my faith: my mother was a nightmare, my first boyfriend cheated on me, brethren from my church turned against me, my marriage was a sham, my daddy died, I divorced, so many men used me I lost count, another man I loved died tragically, the list goes on and on. I've been an adulteress and a fornicator, manipulating others for my benefit as well as my own selfish gain, and I've been a liar more often than I've told the truth. My son doesn't talk to me because of my adultery, and I can't begin to tell you how much that hurts me. Still, I felt God loved me through my problems, that He's always been there for me." She turned to The Explorer and whispered to him. "Have you ever felt God before?"

The Explorer was touched by her candor, and he recalled his own life in its totality before he answered her. "No, I can't say I have. Some might say the mind has a powerful potential, with different states of consciousness, able to conjure up what it needs for its own sustenance, to create its own reality."

"That's funny," Leah said, with a slight cock of her head. "The worst of me has suspected as much over the years. Like I said, I have another side, and I suppose you could say that my greatest fear is that God doesn't exist and that I've been a fool for believing in Him. Maybe I've believed in God because He was all I had. It hurts me to say that, because if it's true it means I was a failure, too afraid to make my own destiny, too afraid to stand on my own. My brother used to tell me science would eventually explain everything and that I was wasting my time believing in God. I'd sure hate for my brother to be right. But I've felt close to God many times, and I have faith He'll be there for me in the end."

The Explorer turned to her in the starlight and smiled an old grizzled smile. "Well, that's good enough for me. And I thank you for answering my question. And I must admit, I'm examining the situation in a different light. I have felt tonight like I was compelled to take you here, more than my usual need to pontificate to strangers, and now I think that it was for your story as well as your opinion. I sensed you had something important to tell me."

Leah chuckled, followed by a chest-filling breath. Her eyes penetrated deeper into the vastness of space. She saw beyond it, to what for her was the eternal home of God, to the ends of all that was. "God made all that, all that we see," she said in wonder. "I've always wanted to be with God. I don't want to die, but I don't have much to live for, either. I've done about everything I was meant to do here. The rest is existence. So I'd rather be out there."

The Explorer felt her desire to go to the stars as if it were his own. Inexplicably, the calling was in his heart as well.

"You afraid to die?" Leah asked him.

"Not till now."

"Why now?"

The old man gulped hard. "I don't know. It just seems like I don't want to face the power that made this universe without giving the creator His due." The Explorer took his eyes from the sky and pondered the ground at his feet. "Man, maybe I've been running all these years because I've been scared of dying; running gave me an escape where being in one place gave death a chance to find me. See, as long as I was on the road and running, death couldn't catch up to me. Wouldn't that be something after all? Here I thought I was living and all I was doing was running scared. I want to go on like everybody else, I guess; crap, I know I do, I can't deny that any longer, I'd be lying to myself. I want to dwell among the stars like you do and live forever. Man, I don't want to die."

The two of them stood in awe of the glimmering host, immersed in the imperceptible motion of the planets, the whirl of cosmic dust and gas, the incessant flickering of faraway suns, and the pervasive glow of the Milky Way. A clear, late autumn sky is dazzling in its stillness and suddenly a feeling of unmistakable immensity descended upon the two of them.

"You can almost hear the universe talking to us," Leah marveled. A feeling of universal connectivity surged through her being, infusing her with a sense of certainty that she couldn't quite claim. "And God made all that, all that we see."

The Explorer was too busy ruminating on his life and his life's purpose to comment. The feeling of enormity was all about him, overwhelming him, and for the first time the universe was not some mysterious conjecture of science, an impersonal aggregation of matter and energy, but rather something breathing and alive. He felt its awesome power. He wondered if in all of his travels he might have missed the true meaning of the night.

Leah sensed the moment, drawing nearer to him, like a mother approaches a sick child. His eyes were troubled and he seemed vulnerable and needy. "God loves you," she said softly to him. "He does, you know. You don't have to die forever. Nobody has ever sinned more than me, and I know God still watches over me. God knows how long you've been searching for an answer here."

The Explorer had to move, not from the physical closeness, but rather from Leah moving into his emotional space, because he was vulnerable and touched deeply in his heart. He walked a few feet in front of the truck and bent over, putting his hands on his upper thighs, before he returned to an upright position after a prolonged stretch of his tightening back. He had hurt his back carrying a girl on his shoulders years ago, on a peace march in Washington, against the war and against the establishment, against tradition and the ways of the world. Now he dabbed his eyes. It had been a long life, plenty hard at times, and he grasped the eternity of God as more than an abstract concept passed down through the tenets of religion. He thought of his own mortality and the eternity of a Supreme Being. If the universe is indeed timeless, he thought, then whatever power created it is also timeless as well. He suddenly wanted to be eternal like God. He wanted to live forever. That was a powerful thing for him to realize at that moment, and slowly, ever so slowly, The Explorer made his way back to his truck while Leah followed his lead, climbing into her seat and waiting for him to finish gazing into the heavens. The two of them drove back to the motel without saying a word to each other, and the good-byes were knowing smiles of friends who have shared something powerful and meaningful together.

The next morning Leah went into the lobby for a cup of coffee and a donut. Emma informed her The Explorer had left on his way to his next destination, but that he'd probably be back in a week or so. Seemed he always returned after being away for a time, Emma and the red desert lands being the closest thing he had to a family or a home, but Leah couldn't wait for that day and she set out south along the highway and sped off again toward the Grand Canyon. She never saw The Explorer again.

Chapter 24

LEAH LINGERED AROUND THE Grand Canyon for a couple of days. Where before the weather had been clear, now the sun settled on the land like patches on the ground, and listening to the air one could hear the wind whistle through the canyon and watch the river ripple in the shadows. A change was in the air.

Leah gave the turnabout no thought. She had considered driving straight through to Flagstaff after she left the barren and crusted ridges of Lake Powell far behind her, to the sanctuary of another motel, but she decided against it and slept another night in her car in the windswept loneliness of Monument Valley. The weather that night turned cold and nasty. Leah made the mistake of rolling down the window while it was still relatively pleasant outside and she fell asleep without bringing the window back up to its usual crack. Exhausted, she fell asleep with her hand on the window handle.

In the morning her throat was sizzling red and raw, a swarmy fever burning in her eyes, but sick and a day too late, she drove on to Flagstaff without stopping except for gas and a bottle of aspirin for her pain.

The last of the drive brought the high country. Pine trees and shoveled snow lined the sides of the highway and at first Leah thought she had fallen asleep while driving and was in the middle of some strange kind of dream; mountains in northern Arizona surprised her, but the mountains of Flagstaff were genuine mountains, alpine and stony and packed with firs, the skies a piercing blue and the air crystalline and cold. Leah found a motel on the edge of town, checked in for twenty-two bucks a night, unloaded her belongings, and fell into bed without undressing.

Leah slept for ten straight hours, but the last few hours were an uneasy sleep. She had nightmares of roadside sleeping and bitter cold, of incapacitating hunger and the nauseated exhaustion that comes from weeks of starvation, and of little money left at her disposal. When she awoke she was sweating and her chest had developed a soggy cough and a tickling wheeze on the slightest of inhales. Five years spent under the stars and the fitful sleeping on a hard ground bed had done much to set Leah back, and she grudgingly handed over another night's motel money and slept for another ten uninterrupted hours without so much as a stir.

It went on like that for that entire winter, Leah holed up in her car at night, blanket cradled up to her chin, the seat reclined to its final notch setting, she alternating between feeling ill and then hale again. Insidiously, pneumonia began to settle in her lungs and her once creamy skin began to sag and blemish from the paucity of daily cleansing and care. She looked dirty and haggard and so on the edge of life.

One night, a feeling crept sadly into her bones. With certainty, she knew that death had found her only husband in this world, a kindly ballplayer from Oakland who had lived to make the most of what this life had apportioned him and who had rarely complained through any of it. Although alone and in the dark, Leah's mind that night journeyed to thoughts of Vic in his lifetime, and she nearly wished him into her car thinking of him and their happiest of times together; perhaps it was a comparison she had fashioned, lying destitute and crooked in the discomfiture of her seat, so much the wiser for her freezing, between having a nice home and a warm bed to lie in and the life she had now living out of her car: *The world needs men like Vic.*

Indeed, Vic had died that winter. His passing was witnessed by few, certainly by far fewer than would have noticed had Vic fulfilled his childhood dream of becoming a major league baseball star. Instead, Vic had existed in relative anonymity, overcoming the inevitable reversals of this life by keeping his chin up against a sorrowful seeping of blood and the anguished look of his disappointed father. Far from being a star, he had lived among the people. Lying in her car, Leah reached to her side to feel the waviness of Vic's hair, and she thought she saw a new star appear lowly in the sky. That night, she dreamed of her husband, of stars that shine brightly, and of happier days gone by.

The road up the western side of Utah was as pretty as any road Leah had ever driven. Leah drove that road into the high mountains that summer, which came early that year, the snow melting sooner and the rivers flowing higher than they had in many years. When she reached the last roan butte of the basin before her mountainous ascent, Leah pulled her car over to the side of the road and gazed out on the desolation from the highest height of the land. She had spent years in the red clay lands below, years in the wilderness that had become her own, and Leah was from that barrenness now.

Summertime meant sleeping outside, in side-of-the-road sanctuaries or in the first growth of underbrush and firs, where she looked more like a backpacker or an adventurer than a woman without a home. In the fair weather Leah felt comfortable living as a nomad. As she ascended into the pristine towers of nature, the sorrel colored loam metamorphosing into a hardened quarry, her mind journeyed back to God and the ways of His word. She sought repentance wistfully, to be forgiven for the absurdity of her choices, and her heart ached to be close to the Lord once more.

Chapter 25

MOUNTAINS ARE LIKE NO other landscape on Earth. They are unique and they are boundless and they are to themselves. Rivers, streams, meadows, plains, deserts, and even the great seas are brought down by the earth itself, pulled toward its center, but the mountains stretch to the sky. Set against an overwhelming sense of timelessness, mountains feel somehow invigoratingly recent and even virginal to behold, for it takes much to scale a mountain and make it known. Mountains have a strength all their own and Leah felt that if she were to be strong again, strong in her faith and strong enough for the Lord to hear her pleas of forgiveness, she sought to be as one with a mountain.

After a week of drifting around the Grand Tetons and Jackson Hole Wyoming, Leah ventured northward to where the Yellowstone River flattens out into a broad valley at the western edge of the Absaroka. There, the blue of the river is as splendid as a cloudless summer sky, the many submerged stones and rounded pebbles flecking brilliantly through the sunlit water like golden trinkets tossed into a wishing pond. Aspens quake in the gentle breezes and the river gurgles as it passes underneath the watchful overlook of the highway.

A partially paved road, more ground flint and coarse grit than good traction asphalt, seemed to beckon to Leah, and she drove the hilly road up the steep mountainside for nearly a quarter of an hour. The road was bumpy and dry. Dried pine needles and humus littered the ground and roots clawed at the edge of the road. Finally, Leah came to a flatland cutaway with a view to a slender valley down below. A silvery lake sundanced at one end of the valley while a flaxen meadow undulated at the other, groves of chalky poplars filling in the rangelands in between. Across the expanse on the farthest side, shale gray peaks snagged passing cotton clouds before releasing them gently to the breezes. Flashing white tributaries cascaded into the silvery lake without making so much as a babble, their fine mists dissipating into the bluish reaches of the sky, not far above a shifting sun line dividing day and darkness on the ridge.

This was the place Leah had been seeking; it felt biblical.

In less than two days Leah acclimated to the location, soaking in the sun for hours at a time, laying on her blanket with only her undergarments on, drinking her water sparingly and munching chips and pretzels for her lunch, napping afterward in the relaxing shade of the needled firs, for the days were comfortably warm and the alpine nights cooled to an undisturbed pleasantness. Leah, in those almost halcyon of days, found it easy to sleep at night under the care of the stars and the rather nurturing eye of the moon.

On the third mountain morning it was time to pray. The idyllic valley lay beneath her, and Leah closed her eyes and breathed the fresh mountain air deeply into her lungs. The ledge on which she rested felt airborne, close to heaven and light and airy, and Leah set her Bible down on the coverlet underneath her body, lifted her face toward the sun, and let her thoughts go to God and to His love for those in need.

"God, my loving and wonderful Father, hear me now. My life, whatever it has been unto this day, has always been in Your hands. I have fallen short, my God, when You gave me so much, so much more than I deserved. Nothing can counter my sins, sins against family, against marriage, and against Your laws. I'm sorry, my God, for violating what You hold so dear, what You knew was best for me.

"When I think of Jesus, my Lord, Your son, who lived so righteously, with so much pain and loss, I am sorry again for failing His example in such a horrible way. Sweet Jesus, who begs for me, who tugs on Your heart and whispers in Your ear on my behalf. I love Jesus, my heavenly Father, who died for me, who hung in sacrifice, and loved me anyway. Thank you, loving God, for Jesus, so that I might have a hope of heaven with You one day.

"You are like this place, so timeless and so enduring, so true to who You are. My life is less than it should be, and it's been hard to find a reason to stay. I have lived here because You command me to, for I cannot lose my soul with my own pride. My soul is all I have left, my God, the will to start again, to try a new way, is lost forever. I have nothing left but You, nowhere to go, no one who cares only for me.

"It has been so trying, Lord, so humiliating and so hurtful, to live like I have these past five years. I must have looked the fool, so stupid to put myself in this predicament, so embarrassing for You. I am scared, Father, scared to die, and scared that I might fail You miserably again. But if salvation requires humility, to wallow in the nonsense of my life, then I thank You for it. I will suffer all You ask, lower myself as low as need be, to beg You for Your forgiveness. If my heart is right with You, Oh Lord, take me now, but if You need more, I will pay.

"What is left of my life, I do not know, I have no compass to guide me. Only You, in Your infinite wisdom, know what will become of me. I have no reason to live other than to fulfill Your will, and I am ready to go home. This place has been unkind to me, and I to it, but mine is the greater trespass. For I knew better than to err as I have, to betray the gifts You gave me. I could have been a beacon, an example for others to follow, to lead them onward to heaven. Instead, I choose my own way, the way of self, and others have suffered because of me.

"Cleanse my soul, my Lord. Make me whole again, white like the lamb, as pure as the snow. When the time is right, take me God, take me when You need another to love You. Take me, for I will love and cherish You for all of time. That is the only thing that can make me whole, with meaning and contentment.

"And if it be Your will, my Lord, I would like to understand my life, and why I was sent here to this place. Please, I beg of You, my Father, grant me this one final prayer and my only hope.

"Forgive me for my life.

"In Christ's name, I pray.

"Amen."

When Leah opened her eyes again, the breezes had quieted to a breathless stillness. Earth's own star didn't shine as much as it bestowed, its light a golden peace that bathed the mountains in soothing absolution, and Leah meditated in the mountain quiet, thinking of Jesus and the ways of redemption, remaining in her mountain lair for another two full days before returning to the highway to wander it again.

Chapter 26

FOR SIX WEEKS LEAH roamed the mountains above the tablelands, alone and lonesome, the power of the prayer dissipating in her mind, with only superficial human contact, her thoughts beginning to disorder, and when the disordering frightened her to the point of doubting her own continuance, she called Marian because she needed to hear a kindly voice and a connection to her past.

"Marian," she started. "Hi, Sis, it's me."

"Lee, is that you? Oh, my God, is that really you?"

"Yes, it's me, I'm sorry I haven't called you in a while, but I've been on the road again, seeing the sights and taking them to heart. Marian, you really ought to see the mountains of Montana."

There was a pause and Leah sensed her sister gathering herself. "Lee, sweet Lee, I have some terrible news," Marian said. She began to cry. Then another pause of silence before she spoke again. "I didn't know how to get hold of you. God help me, I tried. I called David and your last telephone number that I had, but David didn't know where you were, and the phone had been disconnected at your last number. Mama died three weeks ago. I was thinking of calling the police to look for you, but I didn't even know what state you were in. Mama loved you. She did you know."

Leah didn't cry at the news. Instead, she felt a stinging pain in the broad part of her stomach. The pain went so deep it frightened her, and so she offered but what she could. "I'm sorry, Marian. I know you loved Mama. I'm so glad you had your time with her through the years. Did Kay show up for the funeral?"

"No. It was a small service: me, Charles, the kids, Cleveland's children, Robert and Melissa, Aunt Rita, a few men from Morse Street, their wives. Fulton Hitcher from First Avenue and his family came by. The Barksdales. Oh, and Miss Childress. She's ninety-three. We all missed you, Lee."

"Golly, I'm sorry, Marian. I'm so sorry for not phoning sooner. But traveling like I have, well, I just plain forgot to check in with y'all. I'm so sorry."

Marian swallowed hard on her end of the line. What followed was very uncomfortable for her to say. "Lee, why don't you tell me the truth anymore?" she pleaded. "David said he hasn't talked to you in many years. You wander the country like a dad-blessed gypsy. God knows how you get by. Why don't you come and live with me? It's stupid not to, Lee, it really is. Charles don't mind, the kids are nearly grown now, and I'll always love you. You're all the family from our family I have left anymore. Tennessee, if you saw her now, why, she's as pretty as she ever was."

Leah was silent.

"Come live with me," Marian urged her kindly. She cried again and then regained herself. She was still shaken from Margaret's passing and talking with her sister brought it all back again. "All I ever wanted was for my family to be happy," she pleaded. "Why don't you just say you'll come live with me and be happy?"

"I can't, Marian. I'm not even me anymore. I don't know what happened to me, but you'd be so disappointed in what you'd see."

"No, I wouldn't. No matter what happened out there in California, I'll always love you. You'll always be my little baby sister chasing puppies down Groveland Street, with those puppies chasing you back home. So sweet, your Bible in your hands, Daddy pushing you in that swing out back, my little sister Lee, running everywhere." Marian cried again. "I've missed you so much through the years. My God, how much I've missed you, my sweetest baby Lee."

Tears came to Leah as well. She kissed the phone. "I have to go now," she struggled. "I love you, Marian, I always will."

"Don't go, Lee. I love—"

Those were the last words Leah heard. She hung up the phone before Marian could plead with her any further. She had to. The mountain air was turning colder and soon there'd be snow, and the prospect of the wintertime made her crave a home. Talking to Marian had made her heart ache. In her mind, she saw the two of them as kids, so happy as they rode their bikes together in the summertime rain. Leah's bike had been midnight blue with a white wicker basket and Marian's cherry red with flapping golden pennants. Her daddy repainted the bikes each and every spring. She smelled the chimney smoke of Groveland Street and her mama's pot roast kitchen and saw the neighbors standing in the yard. She missed her home and thought of Marian and her mama dead and cried again into her hands.

The cold of the air outside the phone booth snapped Leah back into the predicament that was her world. Finally, and only after considerable thought, she decided to head back to the coast, back to the seashore familiarity of California, to the hills and valleys that amble to the shore, as the Rockies readied themselves for the chilling blizzards of another winter storm season.

***

With little left to do now except visit the places that had been her home one final time, Leah drove the hilly route up to her old home in Crestmont Heights some thirty years after first coming to California on a whimsical dream of escape and a hope for a husband and a family of her own. She had left her home in Tennessee because of Margaret and Blake, the hurt of not being loved and of letting love go, and the backwardness of the South, embodied in the actions of the accusers, expecting to be the wife of a baseball star, to escape so unjust and unfriendly a land. Instead, she had run from something into nothing. Now, decades had passed.

The hills had aged. Even the sun seemed tired, having lost its luster as it settled listlessly on the bay. The trees had all grown taller now, the bushes rounder and much fuller looking, the rocks in the front yard much mossier than before, and not one sidewalk had avoided the inevitable cracking and splitting that comes with the unrelenting advance of time. She thought of David, his skateboard nailed to a large piece of plywood rumbling down the hilly court with the neighbor kids in tow on their toy trucks and wagons. The little amber pebble rocks Vic had spread to cover the ground were scattered about much too thinly now; patches of brown dirt shown through the pebble rocks, each one its own eyesore, embarrassingly visible from the court for all to see, and Vic would have hated that disheveled appearance after all his time spent toiling in the yard.

That night Leah stayed near her old home until the midnight hour to admire the glow of the flatland lights that hugged the timeless lapping of the bay. The lights shimmered as before, but now there were many more of them, especially toward San Jose and the sprawling cities of Silicon Valley, the ambling, undifferentiated towns that Leah had never cared for much in her years of living there. But there was still something magical about the way the lights twinkled to her. She felt the hunger in her soul. The planes that night flew in low on the horizon and ever so gracefully; Leah had loved watching the planes take off and land from the windows of her home. Now those days were gone forever. Somewhere down in all that gleaming was the promenade by the shore, the one on which she had walked so many times hand in hand with Roberto, dancing together to the rhythmic slurp of the tides, a sea breeze forcing a warm caress into his arms and a gaze into his loving eyes. She missed the promenade now. She missed Roberto. It all seemed so long ago, and an instant sadness fell over her as she stepped back into her car.

Leah slept in an empty parking lot at the base of the hill, not far from the headlands of her dreams, and she dreamed of oceans rushing to the shore and little boys who always love their mothers running in the sand.

Predictably, her car died the following morning in a drizzling fog and Leah sold it for a thousand dollars in cash, crying like a schoolgirl as she hauled the last of her belongings to a lonely stretch of highway that overlooked the wreckage of her ambitions. Although her own foolishness had led to her predicament, at that moment life to her seemed entirely unfair. That travel book of William's had lied to her, as surely as she had flipped its pages and sat marveling at their beauty; she saw that much now, and that was the moment when she felt most alone. California, it seemed, had also been a lie. She was as far away from Nashville as she had ever been and yet she had never felt quite as lost, and there are times when all that gets one through the day is the knowledge that there is nothing left to do except survive.

Chapter 27

HITCHHIKING. IT'S ALMOST AS good as having your own car, a bit more inconvenient perhaps, but also free, and hitchhiking could take Leah places she wanted to go. So she hauled the last of her possessions to the highway under a scattered sky that morning, the clouds leaden and cold, coughing her way past lonely bus stops and grotesque stares on the street from those who passed her by.

Hitchhiking is full of rejection. Thumb held close to her body in shame, Leah repositioned herself at the base of a freeway onramp near MacArthur Boulevard and gradually gained the confidence to stand noticeably on the curb. Cars passed by in the hundreds. Progressively, she stuck her arm further out into the roadway and wagged her thumb vigorously in an attempt to snag a ride. A short while later, a woman stopped her van and Leah threw her belongings onto the floorboard next to a bucket of cleansers with a hearty thank you and a quick glance out the window to avoid conversation or explanations why.

The woman was headed to San Francisco and she dropped Leah off where Howard intersects the most eastward curve of the Embarcadero, not far from One Hills Plaza and the Maritime Museum. Leah had walked the Museum with Vic not long after their honeymoon together in Carmel, and she had always loved the coffee shop that welcomed visitors to the Plaza. That day, from nothing more than a salute to a pleasurable memory of a bygone era, Leah bought herself a java and cream and tipped the man the same amount.

For the next two weeks Leah wandered through the city by the bay in a state of deepening apprehension, alternating between sleeping in parks or alleyways, as the streets were far too noisy for much sound slumber, but regardless of where she slept at night she found herself missing the quiet of her car. She lost track of days, and hours became as inconsequential as grains of sand in an endless desert. Weight fell off her like leaves from an autumn tree, and her fever became as predictable as an atomic clock, climbing at night, lessening during sleep, returning to normal by the first light of morning, then soaring as Leah moved about her day. She required frequent naps. Her face cracked like an old shingled rooftop and her lips were split and bleeding. She ate when she felt most able, but each meal cost more than the one before it, as she had only sixty dollars left to her name. Death stalked her on the hour.

Leah thought often of her prayer on the mountain and of traveling again, and she considered how best to find her way to a warm climate like Mexico or Hawaii for the remainder of the winter. But both destinations seemed so far away, so far from the world she had known and called her own. Memories played in her mind like a symphony. Subconsciously, she didn't want to leave the land where she had raised her son and spent her happiest years. For better or worse, the Bay Area still felt like home to her. Also, deep in that part of her mind that hated to admit the obvious, Leah knew how sick she was and that if she ventured too far away she might never be able to return. Debating whether to stay in the city or move on, Leah came to a section of the financial district near the towering Bank of America building, and she plopped down on the ground in a heap, resting her wearied body beneath an awning not far from the edge of the curb.

The sky that day was overcast and drizzling, but the wind was calm and the clearness of the air was more like a cold dry day than one wet with moisture. Sounds carried much further than normal, strangely even, with greater resonance and clarity, and Leah heard conversations from a distance as if the words were spoken directly in her ears. Two businessmen in fine Italian suits and shiny black Ferragamo shoes were standing on the edge of the curb waiting for a taxi ride. Each had a fine gold watch on his wrist. They were down a ways from where Leah had sprawled herself out on her sleeping bag, but the taxis passed the men without much notice and not a single taxi stopped for them. The first man, in his middle forties, was well-groomed, stylish and ingratiating, with a rugged face and an innate charisma that manifested itself as a confident smile, and he held himself the way an athlete does after a great performance. His eyes were a series of warm and friendly glances to whomever passed by. The other man was considerably younger, late twenties or early thirties, shorter, brusque looking, almost irascible, and at his worst he was impatient and obnoxious. He was fuming about not being able to grab a cab. He fumbled with his portable computer and cellular telephone, nearly dropping both before stuffing them into a leather carrying case embossed with his initials in shiny golden lettering. Both men, at the same time, followed a passing taxi with their eyes, their line of sight ending at the clump of Leah's belongings lying next to her on the sidewalk.

"How do they manage to sleep like that?" the first man asked the younger one, his gaze resting pityingly on Leah. "All the racket in this place: cars, those rumbling city buses, horns going off, cabbies shouting at each other. Whenever Adrienne and I stay here in town, I hear every sound people make. This place is as noisy as downtown Manhattan."

"You're not used to it," the younger one replied. His tone was condescending and arrogant. "Does your wife moving in your bed wake you up at night?"

"No."

"And do you know why? Because you're used to it."

A faint grin came to the older one's lips. "That makes sense. But there you go again, being practical on me. All you young guys are so practical. I've told you it's your best attribute in business. That's why Gladstone gave you that hike in pay last week. And the Weller deal doesn't happen if you're not as innately practical as you are."

The young one stared up at the older one without a hint of humor on his face. Another taxi whizzed by without stopping. He followed it with his eyes. "Stupid ingrate. Nobody in the lousy car and the immigrant idiot still doesn't stop for us. Weller happened because I'm smart, moron. And forget Gladstone. Took that imbecile six months longer than it should have for him to give me my money."

The businessman in his forties was a playful sort. "Mr. Practical, care to enlighten us any further?"

The younger one gestured to where Leah was slouched over on the sidewalk. "I know the city needs to clean this place up, you idiot. Year after year, more scum migrate here because of all the handouts you and your socialist bleeding hearts dole out to these losers. Liberals. The bane of civilization is the bleeding heart of liberals. The Kennedys, Johnson, Humphrey, and their ilk nearly destroyed this once fine country. The whole town smells like a sewer. A cadre of feminists and pussies have ruined this once gorgeous city, and I end up paying for it. The air here smells like piss. This is what my tax dollars get me?"

The older one cackled. "Do you think the money should be spent on shelters? Is that your point?"

The younger one shot him a dagger. "To hell with shelters," he said angrily. "That's for you and your protest generation, a bunch of pot smokers going to save the world from itself. Yeah, that worked. Here's a tip, you hippie era relic: Public solutions don't fix a thing. Repeat after me: the private sector. You can redistribute all the money you want and it won't help fix one, solitary thing. Not a thing. Ship these scum off to some desert area or to the polar regions and let them die there. Just get them the living puss out of here."

The older one laughed a hearty laugh. He put his hand on the shoulder of his associate. "I've always said, you're one of the most compassionate people I've ever known. The church may nominate you for sainthood."

The young man fought with determination to keep a smile off his face. He wasn't truly mad, more annoyed than genuinely angry, but he did feel passionately about the subject and to smile would have ruined his facade.

"Why the snot should I be compassionate?" he asked tauntingly. "You ever watch wildlife shows? The weak get eaten. Every species has some members that can't hack it. They should die. It's keeps the gene pool healthy. You have heard of Darwin, right?"

The older man grew more serious. "So what you're saying is that these people have no value. I just have to disagree with you. It bothers me to see a person end up this way. Maybe I don't do anything about it, but it still bothers me. Society is failing these people, when most of them, with a little help, could probably be productive citizens. My God, they're human beings."

"Barely."

"You can't mean that."

"Yes, I can. In the grand scheme of things, they're meaningless. And I shouldn't have to pay for them to piss all over my streets. Let the charities and the dumb idiot liberals take them into their own homes if they want to clean up the stinking town. I'm here to produce, to make something of my life. Capitalism is a biological system; you either hack it or you get eliminated. That's how it should be. It's altogether natural, all right?"

"Heartless," the older one joked. "And so calculating. Can I marry you? I've always wanted my kids to grow up to be insensitive tyrants."

A taxi full of businesswomen sped by. The younger one, increasingly annoyed, scowled at his associate. "You know it's true," he said. "Charities, religion, politicians, ideologies, nothing is going to save these people from themselves. And they should die because they're stupid." He glanced over at Leah. "The idiot over there has a Bible. A Bible? God is going to save her? Man, that's the definition of dumb."

"I'm falling more in love with you."

The younger man didn't respond to the drollery of the other. He glared over at Leah. "Imagine how this city would look cleaned up," he stated frankly. "Think about that, why don't you? Someday, this sewer of a city is going to drive businesses to Texas or Arizona where they don't put up with this kind of trash. What we need here in San Francisco is a new tax revolt and the stomach to let the weak die off."

At that moment, a taxi came around and stopped at the curb. Leah watched as the two men scooted into the back seat and continued on with their conversation, both glancing agitatedly at their watches, the taxi racing off up the street, nearly sideswiping another car as it sped through a yellow light at the first intersection before disappearing around the furthest corner and up a hill.

***

From that moment on, feeling so insulted and disgraced, Leah vowed to avoid heavily congested areas and chose instead to roam and sleep where she could best meld into the surroundings: in seedy neighborhoods and dilapidated warehouse districts, in condemned buildings and deserted backways, and in those places where the rubbish stacked up as high as the walls. She was from that land now, the land of the forgotten, one of those who had lost the struggle for existence as well as the wherewithal to begin anew, for whatever deficiencies they might possess, scattering themselves on the streets and awaiting the call of death.

Leah looked around. Everywhere she looked she saw the others like her, humanity's boils, laying pointlessly on the ground, their sallow faces the faces of those whom life had first defeated and then consigned to the trash heap of society, and Leah covered her face in shame. She couldn't bear to see what she had become, the cankers of the street a pointed reminder of the choices she had made.

But the charity of the human heart can run as deep as any ocean. Leah heard groans coming from afar, from a dark bundle curled lowly on the ground, and the wails of anguish caused her to lift her eyes up from her hands and forget about her own distress. She made her way over to a man lying sickly on the street. When she came near to him, she saw that his face was blotchy with sarcoma and his body frightfully thin.

She reached into her back pocket and pulled out one of her last twenty-dollar bills. She took his hand and clasped it.

"Here, I want you to have this," Leah said to him softly.

The man lifted his head and took the money feebly into his hand, immediately laying his head back down on the concrete ossuary, exhausted from the effort, as Leah pulled his blanket up closer to his chin for added protection against the cold.

"Thank you," he managed. His eyes were jaundiced and wobbly and he smelled of excrement. He closed his eyes again.

"I'll sit by you, if you don't mind," Leah said. "When you can, get some soup with the money and a loaf of bread. Bread lasts longer than anything else you might buy. Go to sleep now."

Leah sat close to the man and held his hand with her own, listening to him wheeze laboriously and praying that the man wouldn't die on her that afternoon. The darkening fog came as a reaper in the night. Leah felt the man's forehead. It was hotter than her hand. He shook hard against the wind, and Leah brought the blanket up tighter to his throat for comfort and held him with her arms.

"That's it, go to sleep," she whispered.

"So kind," the man mouthed to her. "Why so kind?"

Leah rubbed his feverish hands with her own. His hands were so bony and frail Leah thought she might break them if she held them too tightly. The man was so desperately sick. "Go to sleep. Go to sleep now. If there is any kindness in me, it comes from God. I'll stay and make sure you're warm enough."

Leah stayed by his side for three hours while the man shivered and slept.

Only later, when the fog had thoroughly blackened the street, did the man manage to stumble up and drift away and Leah wander further up the hill without him. After another dismal week roaming the city, growing sicker by the day and ever so despondent, Leah decided to escape to where her next ride took her in order to leave so horrible a place. San Francisco had lost its beauty forever and Leah wanted never to return. Scooping up her belongings, she wandered to the edge of the city and never once looked back, the skyscrapers of success rising behind her slender shoulders like villainous towers of cold-hearted glass, and Leah looked eastward past the silvery spans of the San Francisco Bay Bridge and saw an alpine mountain rising high into the clouds.

Chapter 28

IT IS FAIRLY UNCOMMON for truckers to pull over and give rides to roadside travelers because there are inherent dangers in doing so, and as a result many shipping companies have rules against the practice or otherwise discourage the activity, but Leah seemed especially harmless and a rigger soon stopped for her at a concrete mass of underpasses near the nexus of the Bay Bridge at Fremont and Folsom Streets. He was a muscular man of fifty, with a black bushy mustache and a dark clump of stubble on his chin, wearing a red pullover, tight fitting jeans, and heavy black work boots. He chewed chewing tobacco, his manner that of a hospitable rancher or a country clergyman, in overt juxtaposition to the airs of the city, and Leah could see from a picture hanging from his keychain that he often played pool and drank beer with his buddies.

"Thanks for stopping," Leah said gratefully.

"No problem. Where you headed?"

"Anywhere you're going."

"Well, then sit back and enjoy the ride because we got a long drive ahead of us. I'm headed to Portland, about fifteen hours' drive from here, without the rush hour, of course."

"You mind me sleeping on the way?"

"Not a bit."

"You sure?"

"Positive."

Leah slept until nearly Redding, a five-hour drive from San Francisco, when she was awakened by the slow grinding of the big rig as it made its way up gently rolling grades in the highway, slipping noisily between gears.

"Are you hungry, Miss?"

Leah stirred groggily. She smelled shoe polish and rubbing liniment in the cab of the truck. For some reason, both scents seem to rouse her appetite. "Yes, I could eat a bite. Can I buy you something for your trouble?" A pasty film had developed over Leah's eyes and it was an effort to see the trucker clearly, even as close to him as she was sitting.

"No. No thank you. I'll buy my own," the trucker replied politely. "Do you know how long you've been asleep?"

"No, was it long? I guess I'm not such good company."

"Off and on for about five hours." The trucker glanced over and winked at her. "Over five, come to think of it, because I stopped once for gas and you slept like a baby through that, too."

Leah smiled back at him.

The trucker ground another gear. "Say now, have you seen someone about that cough?" he asked worriedly. "It sounds terrible, and if you don't mind me saying so I think you have drifter cough. It's thick like a chowder. I've seen it in some other hitches I've given, and the cure is usually a shot of penicillin and months of bed rest. Tough bug to kill. Where you planning on ending up anyway?"

"Seattle, I guess. I was thinking on going south, but it doesn't much matter, I suppose."

The trucker looked at Leah in a combination of bewilderment and concern. "Well, I don't want to rain on your parade none, but Seattle ain't nowheres near Oregon and it's a medieval crusade from where we are now. It's clear up in Washington state. I can take you as far north as Portland, but then I'm back down to Lancaster for a haul of jet engine casings that I have to hustle over to Austin, Texas, by the third. Government contract with overtime pay. Why didn't you tell me you wanted to go to Seattle from the get go?"

Leah's throat hurt her so bad she could barely answer him. "I didn't want to trouble you for so far a ride."

"Well, I'd take you there myself, but I'm not going that far on this haul. Seattle gets cold this time of year, I do hope you know that. But rides are easy to catch on the Five, easiest at

Richmond Junction near Columbia Falls, two exits before the river. Loggers and lumber rigs mostly. One of our drivers will be through on Tuesday, a rover named Mack, good guy, he'll talk your head off about the NFL and why the league is going to pot, on his way to Vancouver for a pickup of computer chips from Japan. I had to sub the deal out to him when I took the Austin haul. Say something good about the Dolphins and he'll buy you dinner. I'll call him to make sure he's coming. He won't circle back though; none of us drivers do that. Days late are deducts. Remember, his name is Mack."

"Thank you. By the way, what's your name?" Leah asked the trucker.

"Kevin. But my friends call me The Big K. See it there on the dashboard?"

Slung over the dashboard was a custom leather covering with the name *The Big K* inscribed in bold cursive lettering. It was obvious the man was proud of the name.

A truck stop restaurant flashing a FRESH EGGS sign was coming up on the other side of the highway, its lights glowing warmly in the dusk stillness of the early evening, and after braking enough to prepare for a turn, The Big K swung the giant rig across the road and pulled into the parking lot, the hydraulics unleashing a hissing sound at full stop. Low mountains rose on either side of the highway, the detail of their foliage obscure in the fading ember sky, but to the north Leah made out the snow-capped pyramid of Mount Shasta rising high into the first of the evening's shadows.

Leah followed The Big K out of the cab and walked with him straight through the front door and to a booth without waiting to be seated. The restaurant was a typical truck stop restaurant, and as soon as soon as the Big K sat down, a group of flannel clad truckers waved hello to him from a nearby table.

"Eat here much?" Leah asked in a sickly mumble.

"A couple of times a month, when I do this run," the big man replied. "There's another place I prefer in Ashland, steak and potato broiler with a chocolate cream pie worth dying for, but I'm hungry earlier than usual today. You ever been to Ashland?" Leah shook her head no. "No matter. They have a Shakespeare festival there, if you're into that kind of thing. Hey, like the sign says, get the eggs. Protein will help you feel better, help you get over that cough of yours. They serve breakfast twenty-four, seven here. It's their specialty. One day they'll learn how to make a decent cup of coffee."

"How's the pancakes? Any good?"

"Very good. Get them with the eggs."

Leah ordered two scrambled eggs and a stack of buttermilk pancakes soaked with butter. The maple syrup was homemade. Obviously, the place was proud of their maple syrup as there weren't any other syrup flavors offered and no honey or molasses. The waitress brought over three tippers of syrup when one would have been enough. The Big K ordered steak and eggs and shared some of his beef with Leah.

"Like I said earlier, I pick up hitches ever' so often, except you don't fit the mold and it's troubling me because I can't figure you out. Most are drifters, can't hold a job or don't care to. When I was a kid we used to call them bums; today these fruitcakes probably refer to them as "culturally challenged" or some other such garbage, older guys typically, riding trains across country, working only when they have to, and I pat them down for guns and knives before I let 'em in my truck. Most are clean enough; the ones that aren't don't get a lift from me. I had to kick one guy's ass. Some are young, slackers I think they call them nowadays, broken homes and foster families, loafing about the country to avoid putting in an honest day's work. Runaways, too. I like runaways best because I get a chance to straighten them out, that is, if they'll listen to me. If they don't, I drop 'em off early. It's my truck, you understand."

"That's right nice of you," Leah managed to say.

The trucker nodded in self-congratulation, then waved it off. "Well, don't go thinking I condone their values any: irresponsibility, victimization, believing somebody owes you a living just for showing up. No sir, I learned early on in life that people make their own fate. There isn't anybody waiting to save you in this world, trust me on that."

"Well, I still think it's mighty big of you to stop for them."

Undeterred, The Big K went on. "You, though, I can't figure out. You're too old to be a runaway, too sweet to be a criminal, and too pretty to be a drifter. Your clothes are dirty, but not filthy, and they don't smell like the railroad bums smell.

You've been doing laundry now and again. If I'm prying too much, let me know."

"No, not at all," Leah said sheepishly. "I'm seeing as much of the country as I can, before ..., well, before I have to get back home. I never got to see much of America prior to this, having a child and marrying as young as I did, plus working a number of years for a bunch of demanding lawyers who never fully appreciated me. I don't have many friends, none that I feel comfortable enough to hitch with anyway, and I wouldn't want someone around me all the time, bugging me. I like my freedom. That's all there is to it. Really."

The Big K didn't buy a word of it. "You got drifter bug," he said disapprovingly. "You been roughing it for a few years. They all got that same cough. It gives you away. And you look sicker than most of them do. More than likely, it's because you're a woman."

Leah took a sip of ice water and took her time about it. "Hey, I didn't say how long I've been seeing the country, did I?" she said, trying to recover. "It's been so long I don't remember exactly how long it's been. But when I can't take it anymore, I'll go back home, and then I'll have seen all I'm going to see."

Leah sat there looking blankly at The Big K, hoping her explanation mollified him.

"Well, Missy, we got one boring drive ahead of us before we make Portland and I'm a good listener," the Big K said, foretelling his intentions. Twenty years of marriage had taught him not to push it too much when a woman wasn't interested in talking to him. He was a patient man, the long hours on the road fine-tuning that particularly commendable attribute of his, and it was indeed a long haul to Portland from the outskirts of Redding. There'd be plenty of time for a talk. The two of them ate their breakfast meal in relative pleasure, and Leah managed a good laugh on more than one occasion, the Big K paying for their dinners and then opening Leah's cab door for her as she stepped back cautiously into the truck.

The truck whirred on for hours. On and on it churned. The forests, long off in the distance, had crept steadily toward the road. Past Ashland, heading into the heart of Oregon, Leah woke up feeling much sicker than she had before her meal of egg and pancakes, the food settling into a greasy slick just below her clavicle, oleaginous and gurgling, burning painfully into her throat, her temples sweaty and ringing from a sudden pain in her shoulders. Weakly, she rested her head against the passenger door window and suppressed the urge to vomit.

"Pull over, will ya?" she finally pleaded.

The Big K had been watching her doze uncomfortably, tossing from side to side, in and out of consciousness. He had thought she might be nauseated. "Sure. You feeling sick?"

Leah groaned a yes.

"You were sleeping with your hands on your stomach and moaning like a dog that ate a bowl of poison. I was about to wake you since I'd rather you get sick outside the cab than in the truck with us. First chance I get, I'll pull over. Roll the window down if you need to."

The Big K maneuvered the rig over to the shoulder. Leah popped open the door as fast as she could, stumbling headlong into the night, where she eventually fell over and vomited.

"Here, take this," The Big K said, handing Leah a towel. He had come over to her side with such soft, soundless steps, so graceful and so reticent for so heavy a man, that Leah hadn't heard him step close to her, his presence an expression of support and kindness. He patted her back gently with his massive hand as she wiped her mouth clean with the rag. Gently, he helped her to her feet.

"You all right?" he asked her.

"Much better now, thank you. I know I'm a lot of trouble. Let me get my things, and I'll let you drive on without me."

The Big K propped her up and looked her squarely in the eyes. "Nonsense. We're going to Portland together, just like I promised you we would."

Leah grabbed his arm for support. "You sure you don't mind any?"

The Big K felt for Leah the way we feel for a motherless cub lost in the forest. The line of life is indeed precarious, and Leah's line that night was unraveling before his very eyes. He knew how desperately sick a drifter gets living on the road.

"Of course I'm sure. You're coming with me."

Back in the warmth of the truck, Leah felt like talking. It seemed to pass the time. The two of them prattled on about life and relationships and the merits of having a child until they reached a rest stop in Springfield, just shy of Eugene. Leah then slept through the rest of the darkness, a sick sleep, tossing and turning, having bad dreams, until just outside of Portland, the sun rising like a glowing violet pompon, the sky behind the sun gushing a grayish lavender absolution, dissolving the squeamishness of the night in the newness of another day. Leah felt better in the glow of the sun. The Big K never did get to hear the full story of this unusual woman from California; all he knew was that it didn't seem proper for her to roam about the countryside without a home, especially her being so sickly and so frail.

"I shouldn't care, but I suppose I do," he said unexpectedly. "What are you going to do after I drop you off in Portland?"

Leah shrunk in her seat. "See the city, I guess. I'll get a motel, rest up, and then see the sights of Portland. I've heard it's a lovely town."

"Ain't nobody searching for you, is there?" The Big K said, ignoring her. "Your face ain't on no milk carton? You might get so sick you can't find a hospital or a doctor, or you might get raped or killed by some lunatic. We talked a fair amount, and I like you. I don't want nothing bad to happen to you. There ain't a town in the world without its share of maniacs or perverts wandering around. Trust me, you don't want that kind of trouble."

Leah rolled her head away from the trucker as a sign she preferred not to discuss it any further. The Big K obliged her. In another few minutes, the big rig roared into the outskirts of Portland and a few miles later into the city itself, a stone's throw from the olden downtown. The morning traffic was a trail of red lights and wagging wipers. A steady rain pelted the windshield and grew heavier, fogging up the inside of the cab, the sky having lost the last of its lavender in the foreboding grayness of the rain.

"Let me off here, if you don't mind," Leah said.

"Why here?"

"It's as good as any. I can see the skyline from here, and we just passed a row of bargain motels. I'm experienced at this. This is my part of town."

The gigantic truck screeched to a halt at the end of the next freeway offramp.

With that, Leah grabbed her satchel and her sleeping bag, stepped out onto the wet pavement, and readied herself to close the door behind her, surveying the street. The rain felt heavy on her sweatshirt and the wind icy on her face. She turned round and faced the trucker again, the door half open on her side and the trucker gazing worriedly at her. The warm air of the cab floated out to her. It had been so cozy inside the cab, so nice to have a friendly face to talk to, so comforting even, but the unkindness of her world awaited her. She peered into the cab regretfully as the rain came down harder on her face.

"Thank you for all you've done for me, the dinner and the drive and how kind you've been," Leah said. "Please don't worry about me. I'll be fine. I appreciate it, really I do, but I made my decision a long time ago. It's my choice. I won't forget about you and your generosity. Good luck to you and your family."

Leah turned away from the truck and made her way over to a mangy motel on the other side of the street. A *$19 A NIGHT* sign in pink coiled lettering pulsed in the bottom right corner of the front office window and Leah had to snicker at the name: the *Dream Inn.* She took a room and sprawled herself out longways on the bed, sleeping straight through to the following morning, never hearing the big rig rumble its way back to the highway or The Big K yell out for her to take special care of herself and to watch the Five for Mack come Tuesday.

The next morning Leah felt desperately ill. She could barely breathe. She couldn't support her weight on her feet or feel any sensation in her toes, lurching her way into the bathroom half the distance on her knees, crawling as it were, bracing herself at the sink with both arms until she felt strong enough to stand herself up. The weakness she felt was indescribable. Her skin was a sickly oyster color and puss oozed from her eyes. Breathing felt like sucking air through a runny jelly, but somehow she gathered herself and checked out of the motel to wander her way about town in search of free places to lay her head.

She had only ten dollars left to her name.

For the next two days and nights Leah roamed Portland and slept off by herself, in city parks and behind old industrial buildings, spending one night in a breezeway behind a tractor factory and another in an alleyway close to a dumping yard. By chance, she found a supply shed hidden from view where she managed to pry some bricks loose with a stick and place what belongings she could no longer carry into the opening for safekeeping.

It hit her then. Leah had held up fairly well until that moment, at least emotionally, focusing on her physical suffering and attempting to pass the time, but then, against her best efforts to hold herself together, droopy tears formed in her eyes, and she had to cover her head with her blanket and cry from the realization she was too weak to carry her belongings any further. She patted her possessions softly: her hair brush, her large purse, an extra blanket, her makeup kit. They had been the closest things she had to friends those past few years and it hurt her to abandon them. She tossed her satchel and most of her tattered clothes into a nearby trash bin because they had grown too cumbersome for her to carry and she could no longer afford to wash them. She kept her Bible out with her and rolled the rest of her clothes into her sleeping bag and moved on into the freezing cold that was Portland in a storm.

That night she didn't know where she slept, collapsing on the hard concrete, too sick and too exhausted to care, with only enough strength left to unfurl her bag and toss it over her chest for the little comfort it provided. The last she remembered before closing her eyes was that she was clear of a roadway, hidden behind some type of walled structure next to a pile of scrap metal, and that she had wanted to call out for help but couldn't, shivering so uncontrollably that she scraped her head on the concrete and bled into her hand.

The next morning she awoke to a soft crunchiness on her bag, the rain of the previous day having been changed into a drizzling sleet by the windy frosting of the night, and as she attempted to turn over to shield herself from the icy wind she noticed that she could no longer feel her leg below the thigh. She rolled over and over on it, lifting and shifting it with her hands to stir the blood to flowing again, to get any sensation at all, but after several minutes there was only more numbness and Leah panicked thinking she might not be able to move about the town and find her way.

"Please God, don't take away my walking," Leah wailed into the dreary sky. Ice had frozen the exposed skin of her neck and hands that lay outside her bag, and her skin had gone purplish green and spotted white from a lack of circulation. "Give me that much. I got nothing else to live for."

Even then, at that moment so primed with an opportunity to vent the frustrations of her beliefs, lying so desperately on the frozen ground, so tragically and pathetically as it were, she nevertheless was certain of the benevolence of her God and there was nothing anyone could have done to convince her otherwise. The streets of the city hummed with the noise of civilization, the world spinning about its usual way, people living lives so much more gratifying than had been her own. But Leah didn't see it. She refused. Her Bible had stuck to the pavement in the freezing sleet of the night and she pried it loose with her hands, the old King James still with her after all those many years. Leah cradled her Bible to her chest to warm it and slowly, ever so slowly, like a flower bulb coming up through the ground, her leg began to tingle with the sensation of a thousand pricking pins, followed by a warm spurt of blood through her calf and thigh, and then came the familiarity of a leg that belongs to its body. Leah rose to her feet, lightheaded and trembling, but she was up and could move about. She walked as much that day as her leg could stand.

Her illness, however, was unaffected by matters of faith. By late afternoon, Leah's body was imploring her to quit wandering the town, the pneumonia gooey in her lungs, and she coughed up large amounts of mucous with the red of blood mixed in, her temperature shooting past a hundred and five, the accompanying sweats quivering her body into a succession of thunderous shakes and mournful wails of pain. The last few hours of that day Leah's condition degenerated by the moment, and the urgency of her travail led her to the little park by the narrow water. Somehow, with a presence of mind that was remarkable for her condition, she also sought a peace under the stars and a chance to understand her life in its totality, where all that remained for her to do was to lay in the quiet of the night and trust in her God to take her home.

Chapter 29

THE STARS ABOVE LEAH twinkled like diamonds. Around the stars, there was nothing but blackness: no moon, no planes, no searchlights, no glare from any buildings or street lamps, and all the clouds had waltzed to the east. Fate had granted her fair weather for her final thoughts, and Leah, after a day of wandering, after much prayer and woeful apprehension, had found the little park after all. Leah believed the Lord had been merciful to her, guiding her here to this place, to lay down and look up into the dome of life one final time.

That day was nothing more than the others and no less, only to Leah it felt like the last one, the final ride on a roller coaster ridden all day. Everyone was tired. It seemed like the time to go home, only there was no mother to grab your hand and make you leave, no park security to shoo everyone away. There was just Leah and the sky and her God somewhere behind it all.

The reliving of her life had been in her mind for an hour or more, and when she opened her eyes again they had already begun to stick together. The batter in her eyes was thick and pasty and ran down the bridge of her nose. Leah wiped her eyes with her sweatshirt, but there was dirt; it burned her eyes to a severe stinging, but the tears thinned the stickiness some and a few more blinks brought out the stars again.

Her breaths were shallow and fast. The time spent thinking had exhausted her and now there was nothing left to do but to lay and wait. She couldn't get up, even if she had tried, her leg fading away again, and her back was a dagger pressed to the bone every time she tried to move; in that much pain she couldn't roll over to start the pins in her legs to tingling again, so she grimaced and tried not to think about it.

Leah marveled at the power of her mind to fill itself with something. She lauded the will of her spirit for not quitting, not just yet anyway. A parade of those she had known soon followed. Her daddy was there first, then Blake, and then Margaret. David, Vic, Roberto, Beth, William, Marian, Kay, Dan, Jay, The Explorer, and The Big K all came to her next, not in any particular order, some coming back twice or more, but each one smiling and then gradually fading away. She saw them all, in snapshot poses and the living expressions that summed up who they were. Then they were gone like wafting vapors before a fan, and Leah wanted to call out to everyone she saw, but they left too quickly and her mind went blank again.

She couldn't leave just yet, but the call to go beyond this life was in her ears, so she reached inside and pulled at something, something she could tug at for a while longer, something to keep her alive. She found it hanging down from out of nowhere, a swaying rope that came dangling from the blackness up above. It was a life tether, and she wrapped both hands around it and hung on for her life.

She called the images back to her, in more detail this time, and the first one startled her.

She saw the accusers, every one of the pompous and bitter witches, but her heart turned suddenly and was filled with compassion. She had chosen God in a righteous fight against them and against their wickedness, with trusting faith and unyielding resolve, and the battle helped form who she was and where she had ultimately lived her days. She was right in doing so, to fight that fight, to uphold God's truth and to stop the treachery in His ranks, but any airs vanished with the thought of eternity and where souls should spend it. Instead, Leah felt only sorrow, and she prayed an instant prayer to God to save the accusers' souls. She wanted to see them again in heaven, with all forgiven, the hands of her Christian sisters joined with hers in a loving circle around their mutual God of forgiveness and his sweet son, Jesus.

The rope began to slip from Leah's hands, so she pulled on it tighter.

There was Vic, the top of his black hair waving in the breeze, his baseball cap off his head, with the lowest hairs near his ears pressed down at the hat line. They formed a perfect rim. The sound of bats cracking and gloves smacking were behind him, a boy living his boyhood dream, uninjured and full of promise. Leah and Vic looked at each other with a knowing smile. She prayed for her husband, and when she opened her eyes again Vic backpedaled one final time, his teeth gleaming as they so often did, for all those years Leah was married to him, and then he disappeared.

The rope slipped through her hands again, but she caught as much of it as she could. She wanted more time to see them all, but her breaths had fused into one and there was nearly nothing left to breathe out.

Blake's face came next. It was not the face that turned away that horrible day, but the face of an arrival. He was giddy and glad to see her and she reached up and put her palm on his cheek. His eyes softened for an apology, but Leah's hand of reassurance told him it wasn't necessary, and he thanked her and moved on and out of view.

Leah blinked and the paste thinned some. Roberto was suddenly in front of her, his hands held out in a welcoming gesture, an invitation to sing and to dance and to play in the night. Leah tried to rise, but she couldn't and Roberto motioned again for her to come and join the music. His sunburned face and flickering eyes were joyful and carefree and he summoned her one last time, persistently, coaxing and begging, until he finally understood that she couldn't come. He wanted her as much as before, and he bent down and kissed her with his warm lips as he gently stroked her cheek with the back of his loving fingers. Then, he, too, was gone, and the music stopped.

Leah gripped the rope even tighter. In front of her was her son, her David, her little boy grown up into a young man. Leah wanted to be stronger for him, to say what she had always felt, to show him after all these years how much she truly loved him. She tried to speak, but before she could, her son pulled her into his chest and wrapped his arms around his mother in a loving embrace. The baby she once held so tightly, with the smell of fresh baby powder patted on his tiny white bottom, sitting in the blue room of their first house together, now had broad shoulders and towered over her. He sweetly kissed the top of Leah's crumpled hair and stepped back for one last earthly look at her. In mutual respect, they beheld each other and David departed by pulling his mother's eyes skyward with his own where he knew he'd see her again one day.

Leah's arms, still clinging to the rope, were tired and her hands ached in great pain. The rope was being pulled upward and her fingers burned as the rope slipped. The last image of those she had known came to her just then.

Her daddy and mama were standing behind a dark wood dining room table covered with a white lace tablecloth that hung down past the sides and the ends. Marian, William, and Kay were seated in front of them, and Leah's nose was suddenly filled with the aroma of warm apple pies resting on the kitchen counter and the smell of chocolate-chip cookies baking in the oven. A fire popped and a light snow fell outside. There was a golden glow on the scene, a radiance of pure happiness, and Leah felt her family's fullest blessing. All had looks of soft-eyed love on their faces, but none of them said a thing. Then Margaret came forward. She was crying. She wanted to apologize and to say she was sorry for doing it all so wrong, but Leah stopped her before she took another step. "You don't have to say you're sorry, Mama," Leah said. "You gave me so much, and I've always loved you more than you ever knew." With those words, Margaret returned to the others and they embraced her and Leah watched them all drift away.

The rope slipped out of Leah's hands and uncurled into a straight line and was snatched up into the blackness above her. There was nothing left to see except the stars; Leah watched them gradually fade into the black nothingness behind them and she readied to shut her eyes one final time.

At that instant, the most horrible of thoughts entered the last of her mind.

"Oh, no," she cried out. "I don't have the answer yet. Not yet God, please not yet."

Leah's mind wail was all she had left in her. There was no strength to fight anymore, and the rope was gone. Above her, there was only the blackness everywhere, a life wasted or so it seemed.

Just as her eyelids began to close in death, the blackness above her parted in the middle and a strong white light, brighter than all the suns combined, came through a tiny seam. It expanded as it came forward, peeling the blackness away, finally eliminating it completely as it pushed and made its way in every direction. All around Leah, the air cracked with the force of the light, and everything in the front, to the side, and behind Leah shimmered with an intense white brilliance.

A sense of indisputable and overwhelming power swarmed everything around her, and there was no place to escape from it or turn her gaze. Leah didn't know if her eyes were open, but the light was everywhere, and it was all that she could see.

Somehow, and only with the help of the shimmering in front of her, Leah managed a deep breath, a breath she didn't have, a breath of awe for everything that was around her.

The force of the light was so strong it seemed to lift Leah off the ground, and she felt her eyes widen. Her eyes had been open after all. Suddenly, she was alert and the immediacy of leaving this Earth was postponed, for something wanted her to listen and to listen well.

Leah was in the presence of God.

A strong voice, equally powerful and soothing, came from the center of the light, directed downward and across in equal measure. The voice filled everything that was and the words were one with the light.

"Leah, the one who has suffered so much for me, my loving child and compelling witness to my greatness, I am with you now. I have always been with you, and you with me, my precious Leah."

Leah dare not move or think a thing.

"I have been with you for all of time, from before you were born into this place, and I have loved you for even longer. I am your God, and Jesus is my son. When you confessed before men that you believed in Him, and thus in me, I bestowed in you the holy spirit, to bring you to this day.

"I have loved you longer and more than you ever knew, and I have been with you always. I have loved you as a father loves his child, as one of his own, his own creation, for you have chosen me and proven your love for me many times.

"You have defended my truth, my words for man, when man would have made his own, and shown your love for me in doing so. You have honored me and made me proud, proud that I made you, proud that I never gave up on man. You have suffered so much for me, questioned when you must, but you never turned from me, never forsook me, when others have for so much less. I have kept you dear to me, in times when you weren't close at heart, because I love you so.

"Listen to your God, my sweet Leah, for I love you as God loves his people, as a father loves his child, as I have loved my son."

Leah couldn't recognize her own voice that followed or whether it was coming from her mind or her mouth, but the words came out as clear as any she had ever spoken.

"What would you have me to do, my Lord? I am yours. Just tell me so," Leah yelled into the light.

"Only listen, my child. For I will tell you the meaning of your life, for I have heard your prayer, and I will answer it."

The pain in Leah's body left her just then. She wasn't cured, not in any physical sense, but she was temporarily free of agony, free enough to relax without breathing and free of the panic that comes with the struggle for air. She was calm and attentive and anxiously waiting to hear what her Lord had to say to her.

The voice came again, the voice of God.

"Since you were young, you believed in your aloneness. There was separation from that which you loved, a chasm you sought to bridge, but you could not join the sides into one for all that you tried. It is that way for man, for all men, for no one can be whole when separated from me.

"The distance you felt from those you love is a natural distance, for man cannot become as one with me with other men, even with your own family, your flesh and your blood, for I willed it so. The separation was all around you, and it bothered you, for you wanted more. *But the more is me.* When I came to you in your room and softened the sky as you walked, in your time of need, you wanted not, and your troubles vanished in my consuming power. For that is how I intended it, for man to seek me, and when man seeks me in that way, in pure heart and bows before me, I am there for him. I love man, for it is natural to do so, to put right with right, to unite father and child into one. But man must bow. Man must ready himself to approach his God. The bowing is not for me, for I have it all anyway, and I do not need praise for praise's sake; the bowing is instead for you, to eliminate in your mind what might come before what is most right for the both of us.

"Man has done poorly at that, my sweet Leah. He has chosen false gods more than he has chosen me, his own creator, the one who gave him his all. I gave to man his existence, his awareness, and his meaning. Without me, man is lost. For without me, man is at the whim of the evil one, who would torture man endlessly for his own sport, to spite me for my creation and for my plan. But there are some, like you my precious child, who did not turn from me, who have clung to their love for me and pay with their very life. You lived for many years in the clutches of Satan, but your heart never turned from me. You stayed true to your Lord, in the only life you knew, and faced the blackness you saw tonight without the full knowledge of what lies beyond and trusted in your God.

"Man has free will, but is born into circumstance. You were born on the line, in an environment that both encouraged and discouraged service to me, and yours was more of your own choice than it is for most. For some, the circumstance is more conducive to service of me; for others, it is less. Only I know who is born into what and for what reason. It is my plan and not for man to understand. The evil one tempts man, but if a man's heart is right, the temptation is never more than he can bear. You chose me when it seemed like you wouldn't, and that is why I love you so. Special is your place with me, for you could have chosen another way. Instead, you valued me with your life, the only life you knew."

"But I sinned, my Father," Leah blurted out. "I sinned many times."

The light brightened. "That is why I sent my son because man sins. But man believes, too; he believes in my son, and therefore in my plan, and it is in that belief that man shows his best side. That's when you were at your best, my Leah, closest to me, and closest to my heaven."

Leah gazed into the light more intently than before, but said nothing.

"Man can be forgiven. The sirens of the world call to man, and he goes to them more often than not. The allure is great, but the righteous follow their heart home to me. The world is a grand place, with many fine attractions, but ultimately hollow, for it is impermanent. I will destroy it in time. You experienced these worldly pulls and even at your most sinful, your heart stayed true to me. I know when a heart turns away, and yours never did, not one time. When the evil one had you in his grip, your heart looked to heaven, so he could not take you from me.

"You lost love with a man, early in your life, and it scarred you, but even such a loss was never blamed on me. Your own mother choose to love another child more, and your father could not tell you all you wanted to hear. Your marriage failed, and your son choose his own way, a way you took as a rejection; in reality, it was he who needed to understand and love you more. Still, your heart wavered not. In your youth, you challenged two students, and the one who knew of me honored your words and remembered them always, becoming a missionary and leading thousands of souls toward the path of salvation. The other was touched also, and found me after my son pleaded for further intercession on his behalf. Later, you spoke of me to men who needed to hear of my existence, the man who wrote of sports and the wanderer of the desert lands. Both found me in their final days because of you and prayed for the forgiveness of their souls. Your own sisters in Christ erred in their faith and judged you in error, yet you prayed for their souls with one of your last breaths on this Earth. In doing so, you followed the example of my son, the ultimate expression of understanding and love for those who know not what they do and showed me again through your actions why I am proud to have made you."

The light above Leah brightened even more.

"I can forgive all your trespasses because your heart was with me."

"But sometimes," Leah exclaimed, "my thoughts weren't with you. I thought of the world first, and not of heaven."

"I expect that of man," the voice in the light answered. "All I can expect is that the heart stay true to me. A loving heart strives *not* to sin, but all men sin and fall short of my glory. It is the human way, and I realized I had to have a plan of redemption for man and through this plan to love him through the disappointment when he fails me. So I sent my son and you believed in Him. That is enough, my Leah, enough for me to forgive and to accept you into my kingdom."

"But what has my life meant, my Father? What was the purpose in my living?"

"For all men it is the same. Open your heart and seek the answer now. It will come to you. I promise you it will, and you will understand what your importance was here in this place."

Leah continued to look deeply into the light. For all of its brilliance, it didn't blind her. Instead, it simultaneously pulled her in and cleared her mind. There were no other thoughts of any kind, nor any concern for her body; Leah didn't know if she was breathing anymore and she couldn't connect to any sense other than her sight. She couldn't tell if she was dead or alive, but she knew she was something because she could think.

There was only the light ahead and also to the sides of her, and as she journeyed more deeply into it, the light soon went behind her. Now it was everywhere, even more than before, filling up all space and time. It didn't seem possible, but it was so. Thoughts came to her, and she spoke them without knowing whether they were in her mind or on her lips. They simply flowed like water from an infinite vase, continuous and clean, without any break, one effusion after another after another. There was no one to stop the flow of her thoughts, only her, and she would do so only when she had her answer.

"I was born here from a land of love, where all was the light, where all was my God," Leah started.

"Once born, I took on two natures, the body and the spirit, for before I had only known the essence, and my birth here brought to me a physical life.

"I was separated from the light by the body, but my mind knew of God from my beginning, before I was taught God's word and the ways of worship and of service to Him.

"When I started to know, to realize where I was, I knew of my separation from God, where once the light was my all, now it was only a part.

"Having basked in the glory of the light for so long, I missed the totality of heaven. I sought to connect in my new surroundings to the completeness of before, but I could not.

"Living in the world causes separation from the light and renders it inexorable. After a time, I knew I must survive here long enough to someday get back to the light through my eventual death.

"In my earliest years, I instinctually sought earthly love in an effort to overcome my body and the separation from the light; for love is the closest and most direct way to God, and I mistakenly pursued human love to find the totality again. I expected any and all human love to match that of heaven, but love on Earth cannot, for Earth is not heaven.

"I loved in error, wanting much more than people can give, and I put unnatural pressure on those that I should have loved correctly.

"For it is good to love your fellow man, to seek the love of a husband and a family, but it cannot be more. It can never be the light.

"The disappointment that comes from failing in human love in an effort to rejoin the light can cause great damage. It can turn your heart away from anything good, even God.

"Without the totality, I felt lost. I wanted to go home again, and only in the most tender of times did I feel close to being there. Those times were with my family and with my child, and, of course, with my God."

In a millisecond, Leah recognized what was happening. She was able to understand her life with an inner awareness that was never there before, as if a secret part of her had coexisted inside her mind for all those years. Death was causing her to transition from her humanness back to her essence, and the closer she came to departing this world, the more the secret part of her took over.

In a flash, she was back to the flow of her thoughts.

"My essence wanted to be fulfilled, to know itself once again, to go past the boundary of human love, out to that which can be completed and which lasts forever. That was the yearning in my soul and why nothing human could fulfill me.

"Only now do I see that I ought to have loved as much as I could on God's great Earth. It was my weakness for wanting it all here, in the wrong place at the wrong time and against God's plan, that caused me so much emptiness.

"My pride wanted heaven before it was time, when I should have known to wait steadfastly. As I read God's word, I should have learned patience, to do His work for all my years and then be saved by His grace, as the Lord has promised. But I was impatient, desirous of heaven on Earth, and thus deficient in my duties.

"My sin was to love the wrong way. Love, the way I sought it, could never match my expectation, and so I turned from it. With every perceived rejection, my heart grew colder. The years piled up and the love I sought never came. I doubted love and trusted it not, finally quitting on it altogether, so much so that I couldn't show my own child how much I truly cared for him.

"I never loved as a wife should love her husband, and I wasn't there for those who needed me. When I didn't get the full extent of the love I sought, I grew bitter and selfish. I became less and less like the light and more and more disillusioned. In the last years of my life, I became disconsolate and wretched.

"I had started my journey so happily and so optimistically. At every fork of love in the road, I chose the wrong path, and grew further and further away from my essence.

"I almost abandoned my hope for the light, believing that all love was impossible, but I couldn't stop my love for God. It was all that remained from my poor choices, and I needed something to stay alive. Now, I see it was my essence yearning to go home again, to reunite with my heavenly Father, that kept me believing in my God.

"I wish I could have loved the people in my life the right way and done more for each of them. I hurt so many when I could have healed them, for I knew what was correct in the Lord's eyes. My essence had great understanding, but my weakness put me further from my own inner knowing, usually at the time when I needed it most.

"But God understood my shortcomings and gave to me as I needed. He answered prayers in my room, He walked with me, and He heard me on the mountain. My Lord is with me now, granting me my final earthly wish, knowing all that I seek to know and leading me to the answer."

Leah was ready to right the vase, to stop the flow of her thoughts, to caress her answer to her chest and to let it fill her body and her mind. She had spent her whole life trying to find it and now the answer was upon her. All of the nights gazing up at the stars were behind her now and the loneliness that comes from being alone she would never feel again. The home that was and the home taken away were both just places in time. The bringing to life of a new life and the life that it would bring were only links in an eternal chain. The loss of love and the courage required to go on were so many ancient battles, anachronisms with no further relevance for where she now found herself. All that she had seen and all that she was, was for naught; there was only the light around her, the indisputable and ultimate presence of God, and one final truth to behold.

And then the answer came to her, the answer of her life, the answer God had promised her:

"Life is meaningless without everlasting love. I love my God, for He is everlasting and He is love, and He loves me. My purpose in life was to love Him, as I always have. I love you, God, my Lord and my Savior, and I always will."